Libby Purves

Libby Purves is a broadcaster and journalist, who has presented the talk programme *Midweek* on Radio 4 since 1984 and formerly presented *Today*. She is also a columnist on *The Times*

Her books *How not to be a Perfect Mother* and *How not to raise a Perfect Child* have been widely translated; *How not to be a Perfect Family* appeared last year to complete the trilogy. She also wrote *One Summer's Grace*, an account of a voyage around mainland Britain in a small sailing boat with her husband and two small children in 1988. She lives in Suffolk with her husband, the broadcaster and farmer Paul Heiney, and their two children.

Casting Off is her first novel.

'Bright, funny, and achingly perceptive, with the sort of ring of truth that comes extremely close to home'
Birmingham Post

'Often funny and, as one would expect, well written'
Sunday Telegraph

SCEPTRE

Also by Libby Purves

Non-Fiction

The Happy Unicorns (ed) (1971)
Adventures Under Sail, H.W. Tilman
(ed) (1982)
Britain at Play (1982)
All at Sea (ed) (1984)
Sailing Weekend Book (1985)
(with Paul Heiney)
How not to be a Perfect Mother (1986)
Where Did You Leave the Admiral? (1987)
How to Find the Perfect Boat (1987)
The English and Their Horses (1988)
(jointly with Paul Heiney)
One Summer's Grace (1989)
How not to raise a Perfect Child (1991)
Working Times (1993)
How not to be a Perfect Family (1994)

Children's books

The Hurricane Tree (1988)
The Farming Young Puffin Fact Book (1992)
Getting the Story (1993)

Casting Off

LIBBY PURVES

SCEPTRE

First published in 1995 by Hodder and Stoughton
First published in paperback in 1996 by Hodder and Stoughton
A division of Hodder Headline PLC
A Sceptre Paperback

20 19 18 17 16 15 14 13 12

A CIP catalogue record for this book is
available from the British Library

ISBN 0 340 63512 6

Printed and bound in Great Britain by
Mackays of Chatham PLC, Chatham, Kent

Hodder and Stoughton
A division of Hodder Headline PLC
338 Euston Road
London NW1 3BH

To Paul

AUTHOR'S NOTE

∫

All characters in this book are entirely imaginary and bear no relation to any living person. Apologies are due to the towns of Portsmouth, Torquay and Salcombe for various cavalier alterations to their harbour topography and tidal flow. The carpet tiles in the BBC Radio Drama corridor, however, appear as themselves.

Women can't throw overarm: every scornful cricketing school-boy knows that.

So Ray Brewer, in whose depths such a schoolboy still lingered, suffered a moment's irrelevant, open-mouthed surprise at the force with which a set of car keys hit his shoulder and bounced onto the quay with a sharp little jingle.

He had only just emerged into the cloudy late, August bright-ness from the tin-roofed boatyard shed in which he earned his living and was expecting no more diversion than the usual spectacle of the weekend yachtsmen fussing and huffing their way back to the car park from the boats which tinkled their masts aimlessly in his small marina. Then the keys hit him, impressively hard.

In order to do this, he calculated, they must have travelled fifteen feet upwards from the water below, and the same distance forwards. Not bad, to produce an impact like that at the end of it. Yet as he swung round, rubbing his shoulder, he saw that a woman had done the throwing. She was in the cockpit of a small boat passing the quay, and a pang of wistful admiration shot through him. Just his type, the dark woman on the blue-hulled yacht: big eyes, dark flying hair, not what you'd call fat, but nothing frail about her.

Ray Brewer had, in far younger days, seen land girls riding tractors past the school playground. He would be hanging over the gate, anxious for escape into the real world where men went to war or built boats, and women cooked their tea instead of nagging them to learn times tables. The girls on the tractors would come past and sometimes wave to him. The other lads had called the land girls names and laughed at their muscles and their canvas trousers; Ray had always secretly liked them. They were lithe, strong-faced, their curly hair all the more beguiling for its unselfconscious disarray. The war passed, Ray grew up, and conformed eventually with his peers by courting and marrying the blonde, giggling, home-making, sweetly dependent Mrs Brewer. He had, he would have said, no complaints. But once or twice, at dodgy moments in the boatbuilding trade, he had allowed himself to think that it might have been different if he had had a wife who – well, who maybe didn't set the tea as carefully or polish as much but who might have come down to the yard and done the job of the half-a-lad he could hardly afford. A woman who could hold the end of a deck beam while he joggled the other into place, who would have known which plane to pass up the ladder. A land girl of his own. One that got plenty of fresh air in her, not headaches from all that polish and Vim. For a moment, looking down at the woman on the blue-hulled yacht, his surprise turned to mellow appreciation.

She looked upset, though. Her arm was still half outflung towards him, her mouth a circle of shock. The flying hair, now he looked more closely, was very wild indeed; combined with the look on her face, it gave more an impression of Medusa or a Fury than the comfortingly steady land girl of his fantasies. Ray had not thought about Furies for years, not since the class teacher had a phase of reading *Tales From the Ancient World* at wet playtimes. Nor did he like the idea of them very much. Furies. Women running dog-mad. Not steady at all. Perhaps, he thought, if women did get too strong, they lost their steadiness. Mrs Brewer would, after all, do.

The dark woman's head went down, then up, and he could see her breathing hard. Crying, even. Tcha! Overwrought, thought the old boatman. Upset about something. Needs a sit-down and a cup of tea. Probably got hubby below decks having a sulk. She'll hit the quay in a minute if she doesn't concentrate.

But she looked forward again just in time, pushed the tiller across and let the boat slew round. Handy enough, Ray grudgingly admitted to himself. The boat shaved the end of the little pier, its exhaust coughing into the choppy grey water,

ever finishing a sentence, silently led the way to the office in the corner of his shed. Pushing aside half a mug of cold tea and a book of well-thumbed tide tables, he silently indicated the apparatus before retiring to open and shut a few drawers at random, well within earshot.

The man picked up the handset, listened a moment to make sure of silence on the calling channel, and began: '*Shearwater, Shearwater, Shearwater.* This is – um – Portsmouth new marina—'

'Brewmarine,' interjected its owner with a touch of asperity. Five years he had been here with his pontoons, a bit of private enterprise off a redundant naval pier. Five years of trading as a small marina and repair yard for weekend sailors, of keeping the toilet block clean, chasing up the shifty, newly-broke Lloyds' names and their suddenly penurious relatives for overdue mooring fees. Five years. A dozen cork tiles had already succumbed to gravity and fallen off the ceiling of his 'new' office. And still the yachties couldn't remember the proper trading name even if they did write their cheques out to it. '*Brewmarine,*' he said again, with bitterness.

'Thank you,' mouthed the man. '*Shearwater, Shearwater,* this is Brewmarine, over.'

The machine shashed and crackled, broadcasting silence. Urgently the man repeated, '*Shearwater, Shearwater, Shearwater.* This is Brewmarine. Keith speaking. Over. Over.'

More shashing, more silence.

'P'raps they're switched off,' offered Ray, hitching up his trousers.

'Well, one last time,' said his guest, trying unconvincingly for nonchalance. '*Shearwater, Shearwater.* Brewmarine. Over.'

Silence.

Then, leaning forward, the man suddenly almost hissed into the handset, 'Joanna. *You've made your point.* Over.'

More silence.

An incredulous smile spread over Ray Brewer's broad face. Made her point? Joanna? The wife, was it? Run off with the boat, had she, fenders dangling, chucking the keys at him, wooah! This'd be one to tell them! Fights he'd had on his pontoons, high shrill arguments, blows with boathooks, women storming

off to the car; even one man pushed into the marina by an irate wife after a particularly badly bodged attempt at mooring and two large chips off the gelcoat on the bow (£65.17, plus VAT, plus labour, he could see the invoice now). He'd never had one hijack the boat, though. With the boy friend, perhaps . . . Now that'd be a thing.

The thin-faced man suddenly became aware of the entertainment he was providing and, pulling his anxious, disjointed silhouette more nearly into the semblance of a man in control of his world, was visibly seen to resolve that he would provide no more. 'Thank you very much,' he said crisply. 'Nothing I can't handle.' And he strode out towards the car park where his irritated daughter still lounged, kicking stones at pedestrian seagulls with vicious accuracy. One of his elbows hit the peeling doorjamb of the hut as he went.

Ray whistled, strode over to the drawer and, after some scuffling, pulled out a record card.

Yes. SHEARWATER: auxiliary sailing yacht, sloop, 30 foot length overall, hull colour navy blue, 18 hp Yanmar diesel. Property of Mr and Mrs K. Gurney, Old Vicarage, Bonhurst. Berthing fees paid up to date. No recent maintenance invoices.

None of his business, really. He took down his keys from the wall and reached over to switch off the VHF. Then something made the old boatman hesitate and pick up the handset instead. He had, after all, spent half a lifetime at sea before setting up as a boatbuilder and nursemaid for weekend yachties. Perhaps there wasn't a boy friend. Perhaps the lady was out there on her own, with the dusk coming on and the cold north wind rising. 'Shearwater, Shearwater, this is Brewmarine, over.' He tried a few times more, then sighed, shrugged, and switched off for the night. None of his business.

Joanna Gurney, pitching southward with a faceful of tears, drove the boat forward through the slapping waves, towards the looming Napoleonic forts outside Portsmouth harbour. She heard none of the calls. The radio was off. It had been off since Keith had tidied the cabin, carried up the three bags, and padlocked the hatchway doors. The cabin, come to that, still was padlocked. To get at the charts or the galley, or to switch on the

radio or depth sounder, Joanna would have to turn the engine off for a few moments and remove the key in order to use its inseparable companion, the padlock key – unless she crouched down to fiddle the cabin key off its ring, which for the moment seemed unthinkable. Normally, one would unlock the cabin at the start of a trip, and that would be it. It wouldn't matter that the brass key of the cabin was dangling and vibrating the miles away on its ring attached to the ignition key.

Funny how one half-step away from normality could throw everything out of order. The winch handles for the sails were below too. *Shearwater* was really not ready for sea at all. Shouldn't be there. It should be just another modest fibreglass boat, lying idle alongside all the other weekend yachts as her owners drove, tired and glowing, up the motorway towards the Old Vicarage, the washing machine and the first drink.

And so it would have been, had it not been for a moment of particular and overwhelming emotional violence and a quirk of circumstance.

The violence arose from certain conversations, spread over two days – or perhaps ten years, she thought bitterly – with Keith. The circumstance was that when he went up to the car expecting her to lock up and follow, he took his own weekend clothes bag and sixteen-year-old Susan's. So Joanna was left aboard with her own bag, the cool box, the keys, and her anger. All she needed to do was to pick up the bags and follow him to the joint car and joint home, and on through another week of their lives, as she had a thousand times before.

But, shaken by a sudden violence, Joanna Gurney, aged thirty-seven and of hitherto sound mind, did something quite different. She stepped four paces forward on the pontoon and five back, throwing off the neat, plastic-sheathed mooring lines fore and aft; she started the engine, dragged the gearstick into reverse and steered the boat away from its berth (catching the bow a nasty thump as she did so). The defiant gesture did not buoy her up; she was already crying when she passed out of the marina and abreast of Ray Brewer's quay; already sorry, guilty, awash in hot, helpless, futile tears. Joanna was not, as a rule, a ready weeper. Certainly not since the children were born. It was, after all, a mother's duty to maintain a bright, optimistic, twinklingly brisk façade at all times. But there was nobody to see her now, no child to be worried, no husband to sigh. She had wept unhindered, seeing the harbour mouth far ahead through a fog of tears.

It was as she bent to dash her sleeve across her eyes that she suddenly saw the car keys lying on the cockpit seat. Had Keith, too, been rattled by the weekend's arguments? It was not like him to forget them. At the sight, she was instantly overcome by the restless maternal compulsion to avert family crises. The clouds of her own emotion fading, Joanna saw it all: Keith locked out of the car, Susan nagging about her train to London and having to meet Anneliese for the rock concert; Susan missing her train, snarling at Keith; he snarling back, having to find a garage on foot, not getting home until 1 a.m., with his Tuesday partners' conference to get ready for. She saw Susan flouncing off to hitchhike up the M3 and being picked up by a serial killer. While all the time the keys which could have prevented these crises would be lying on the cockpit seat on *Shearwater* under the weeping guilty eye of her mother.

Joanna could not bear it. On the quay she saw, through the mist of tears, Keith standing in his sweater, looking strangely old and fat. Sniffing, letting the boat sheer wildly about as she let go of the tiller, she accomplished the first and last classic overarm lob of her life, arousing Ray Brewer's land-girl memories and nearly crashing the boat into the quay.

And when the keys were safe ashore, the cloud of tears engulfed her again. Without thought or plan, Joanna turned the boat's head towards the sea.

2

'Mum's done *what*?' said the girl to her father.

'Taken the boat. Gone out of the harbour,' said Keith.

'What *for*?'

There was nothing but exasperation in Susan's voice. Sixteen she might be, a sophisticate, a frequenter of heavy metal concerts, a young adult prevented from driving, voting and staying out all night only by some laughable quirk of the law. But grown-ups were still as tiresome, unpredictable, unreasonable and weird in their ways as when she was four years old. These two had been sparring with one another all weekend, going on and on about the boat and the bills and Mum's loopy stuff about changing her life and selling the Bun. Hell!

'If Mum's not here, what about the Bun?' she began, then decided that this, too, was an adult problem. There was no way she could be forced to run the Bun herself. Not like she sometimes did in the holidays. With school officially starting tomorrow and the concert tonight, she was out of the Bun-running, and a good thing too. Susan hitched her shapely bottom off the bonnet of the car and decisively rattled the door.

'Look, I've got to get the train. I'm meeting Anneliese at Waterloo, OK? You said you'd drop me off.'

In times of utter bewilderment, any action is better than paralysis. There was something soothing to Keith in the action of unlocking the car, sitting down, adjusting his mirror, starting up, manoeuvring around the filthy, rusting Brewmarine travel hoist with its worn slings and flaky old chain, and driving through the Monday evening streets of Portsmouth towards the station. It was action. It put him back in control. For the moment, it would do.

Outside the dusty station, Susan jumped out smartly, banging her squashy bag against her tanned legs, and vanished with a dismissive 'Bye!' Then his paralysis descended again. Joanna, wife of Keith, mother of Susan and Lance, had gone to sea without them. Without warning or explanation she had vanished into a choppy, chilly, misty seascape. Alone. She had never even taken the boat out alone before. In their early sailing days she had been as keen to take command as he was; she had taken courses on navigation and seamanship and liferaft survival and two-cylinder diesel engines; she had talked of independence and the day when she would make a passage on her own. She had read the memoirs of the women singlehanders, Clare Francis and Nicolette Milnes-Walker and Naomi James, dreamed of a singlehanded Atlantic crossing and been grateful for Keith's mild encouragement.

But always there had been babies in baskets, crawling and staggering toddlers, children climbing onto the boom in lifejackets, teenagers wanting to learn to sail from Dad, who knew, not Mum, who cooked. There had been visiting friends of the children, too: saucer-eyed and nervous at the tipping and bounding of this strange weekend home, needing hot chocolate and benign reassurances. Somehow it had all drawn her eye away from the sailing of the boat across the sea, to the minutiae of the crew's warmth and wellbeing and cheerfulness. Keith noted, but never mentioned, that there had been less and less talk of her sailing one day alone. So she never had.

Perhaps she hadn't this time. Perhaps he dreamed it.

Slowly, he drove back to the marina and stopped by the gate to climb out and look down at the pontoons. *Shearwater* was definitely not there. Missing. Missing! Police, he thought. Missing person. Police. He drove off again, to look for some.

For the first time since the rage had struck her, Joanna Gurney had a decision to make. East or west? Battering straight ahead through grey waves, weeping, was all very well as a gesture, but the Solent is only a narrow sleeve of water between island and mainland. The Isle of Wight lay uncompromisingly in her way. East past Bembridge, or west toward's Egypt Point and Cowes Roads?

Or back the way she had come?

No, not back; not tonight. To turn against the sluicing tide, battle through the harbour mouth and into the marina, to tie *Shearwater* back with the same ropes and lamely telephone home – impossible. Until tomorrow. By then she would find, somehow, a form of words. Something beginning, 'Look, Keith, I'm sorry I gave you a shock, but you have to understand how serious I am . . .' Perhaps a bit of psychobabble would come in handy. Something about personal space, or assertive love, or family dynamics. Luckily, the Sunday papers were still lying below, full of useful phrases of this sort and exhortations to take up 'designer lesbianism', aromatherapy, colonic irrigation and a dozen other solutions to life's dilemmas. Hers, surely, would fit somewhere into the self-indulgent pattern. She didn't want much, after all. Couldn't he *see* that?

The boat snatched and bucked in the wake of a passing ferry, bringing her attention back to the present. Ahead lay the cramped anchorage of Fishbourne creek, in full sight of the mainland; round the point, at its eastern end, the intricate entrance to Bembridge harbour. *Shearwater* had visited both on innumerable picnic weekends. Even if the harbour charts were not stowed away behind the padlocked cabin door, Joanna did not want to revisit either harbour alone like this. She could not face the ghost of those happy picnics, that family contentment. But night was falling, the north wind still blustery, and she suddenly knew that she was bone-weary. She had to go somewhere and rest. Somewhere safe and hidden. 'Round the corner, out of sight,' she said aloud. 'Somewhere quiet. Quiet. Drop the anchor. I can do that. Quite capable. Done it before. Done the courses. No different being alone. Hundreds of singlehanded yachtsmen. Important thing is keep up your sleep. Anchor, sleep, then back to Portsmouth. Say sorry, sort it out. Sort – everything – out.'

With a jerk, she came upright again. Dropping off at the helm, under engine, crossing the Solent at six knots: it would not do, not at all. The shock of having fallen asleep – a second loss of self-control within an hour – woke her more thoroughly. She hauled the tiller towards her and slewed the boat's head south-eastward, to glide on the ebb tide round the island's green tip. Somewhere south of Bembridge Ledge, in Sandown Bay, there you could anchor. They had done it once years ago, waiting for a fair tide. There was a beach where small laughing Susan and serious nine-year-old Lance had made castles. Lance had measured out each side of his castle beforehand, and in the wet sand designed it in elevation and plan, like an architect. A wonderful child; all the more wonderful that he did not complain when Susan scuffed his design in one of her wild dances.

Sandown Bay. There were no rocks that she could remember, and a nice, obvious, easy approach. She could anchor far offshore and lie there unnoticed. That would do. She would be safe.

The forecast was for northerly winds, force 3 or at most 4: she had half heard it at ten to six while Keith packed his sailing bag and she wiped the galley and Susan sulked vaguely on deck in the poisoned atmosphere. Since they were not planning to go back to sea, she had missed the earlier synopsis with its deceptively casual talk of a low pressure area in the Western Channel moving rapidly across Europe and deepening 993. She had only by accident heard the forecast for area Wight during one of the silences. They were chilly, charged silences; for there still flowed, through their apparently practical conversation about who had turned off which seacock, an echo of the weekend's bitter marital argument about the Bun.

The Bun! Joanna was suddenly and horribly awake. The Bun in the Oven was Bonhurst's leading teashop. 'LOCAL WOMEN'S DREAM GREW TO AWARD-WINNING BUSINESS' the *Bonhurst Echo* had proudly reported, even though the award in question was only from the local Chamber of Commerce. 'JO AND MANDY'S SUCCESS STORY'. How was it going to open on Tuesday morning with its joint proprietress and weekday manager anchored sixty miles south of it, alone? Solicitude flooded through her. She could imagine shoppers standing puzzled outside the closed glass door, resenting the weight of their carrier bags, tapping and peering impatiently, wanting coffee and cakes. She could imagine the bakery order lying uncollected, going stale; the milk souring as the sun warmed the brick side wall where it waited in vain. She could imagine Zoë, the latest surly teenage waitress, arriving to find the place deserted.

True, Joanna had spent the entire weekend arguing with

Keith that she was sick of the Bun, had served her time with it, and wanted to sell up at any price, recession or no recession. She wanted to take another path through the second half of her life, as she had rather shyly put it. Keith had sighed, and clattered loudly with the washing-up; Susan had snorted. But a gradual, caringly managed divorce from the floury embrace of one's teashop was one thing; a heartless abandonment quite another. Mandy, of course, might step in. But then again, being Mandy, she might not bother. Perhaps Erika, if Keith asked her – which he might, of course, only he would have to explain, or make something up, and then it would be all round the town in ten minutes – Erika might . . .

Joanna bit her lip and shifted her feet uneasily as she stood, steering down the wind towards the tip of the island. Erika might step in. But the deal was that Erika handled weekends and holiday Mondays only, serving passion cake and scones to the tourists arriving to tick off Bonhurst Abbey (C14, notable clerestory) in their guidebooks; and tea to the homeward-bound Sunday travellers who knew enough to avoid the Fleet Service area and dive off instead down a B road for a decent brew. Erika did not work on weekdays. She had a husband to tend, and took her wifely duties seriously. Still, Erika might be willing to duck out of her Tuesday routines and come in, draggled blonde hair drawn back into her working bun, colourless and reliable. Keith could tell her some story.

Only Keith never told stories, did he? Keith was a model of righteousness. Perhaps he would tell everyone the truth, just like that. 'Joanna's run off with the boat, nobody knows where.' She giggled, the comedy of the situation striking her all of a sudden. 'Take life as a comedy, a romance, a melodrama if you like; not a tragedy,' Gabriel used to say to her in bed, years ago. 'You've got a choice, you know. It's in the eye of the beholder.'

Well, Gabriel was a bastard, turning other people's comedies into tragedies often enough and never staying for the last act. To hell with him. To hell with Keith, too, and his fussy desire to keep things what he called 'settled' and she called stagnant. Someone else would have to cope with the teashop for once and learn to take her defection as comedy, not tragedy. She had done Bun rotas for fifteen years. Sod the Bun.

She would, in any case, be home by lunchtime tomorrow. One night alone at anchor would give her time to think. Keith wouldn't worry. He would know she would be all right in this quiet weather on a familiar boat. She would call home on the VHF tonight, explain that it was an impulse and that she needed time alone.

As the light waned in the grey overcast western sky, Joanna patted *Shearwater's* side deck affectionately. Who would have thought it? The old boat, scene of so many years of family trips, turning out suddenly to be a refuge and a means of fleeing them. An irony; part of the comedy, the oddity, the funny-five-minutes she was, after long sensible years, at last having.

Joanna's tears were dry now; the engine puttered on faithfully, bearing her on the tide round Bembridge Ledge.

Keith, far from comical in mood, sat on a tatty plastic-upholstered bench reading for the fifth time a pamphlet exhorting him to say No to Drugs. His clients, particularly the legal aid ones, had often told him how unnerving they found police stations. Something about the atmosphere, they claimed, caused them to say things they didn't mean and confess things they hadn't done.

He, being left to untangle the mess which this weakness engendered, usually replied to this rambling line of self-explanation with a sigh (in bad cases, a snort) of exasperated disbelief. Only the other week he had been summoned to represent a woman of transparent respectability who had been pulled in for shoplifting without a shred of evidence. An over-zealous store detective had accosted her before she had even reached the till, let alone the door. But within two minutes of arrival at the police station, she had begun weeping and saying to an embarrassed young WPC that she was a wicked, wicked woman and deserved nothing better than prison. This, the store detective triumphantly claimed, constituted a confession. Keith had spent days trying to unravel this one and resented the extra trouble – and the smooth barrister the silly cow's husband had demanded, down from the bloody Temple, not that it was ever going to come near a court – quite a lot.

But now he began to see the woman's point. Guilt hung around him like a bad smell. He no longer felt like the confident, reassuring, streetwise solicitor who came into such places to straighten things out. He felt felonious, a suspect layman in his grubby Breton red sailing trousers and snagged sweater. He had waited five minutes for attention although nothing whatever appeared to be going on in the half-glimpsed hinterland behind the desk apart from a desultory conversation between a stout dark WPC and a policeman with a straggling blond moustache; but the very delay made Keith feel unworthy and even more ill-at-ease. By the time PC Littlejohn sauntered over to his side of the desk, the unworthiness had become a desperate, defiant chippiness. Keith, in fact, was turning moment by moment into one of his own more difficult clients, metamorphosed from a frightened civilian needing help into an ill-tempered desperado by sheer atmosphere and circumstance.

PC Littlejohn saw a yachtie, and stifled a yawn of irritation. Lost something probably. Left his little rubber dinghy tied to the steps with a granny knot and a hundred quid's worth of oars and lifejackets lying loose in it, then acting surprised when they got nicked. Sod 'em all. Give him a good stabbing incident any day. 'Help you, sir?' he said, raising his eyebrows.

'Yes – erm – I'd like to report a missing boat,' said Keith. 'And a person. The person is on the boat.'

'I see, sir. Could you give me your own details first?'

'Keith Gurney. Old Vicarage, Bonhurst. Solicitor.'

The policeman looked up, even less inclined to care what happened to this pathetic twat. He did not like solicitors at all. His three years in the force had taught him that they always took the shine off the most triumphant arrest and bad-mouthed you in court afterwards. Twelve hours on duty, drunks all over the seafront, and now a twat solicitor. Still, back to business. 'Perhaps you could give me a description of the boat. Sir.'

Haltingly, Keith did so.

'And who is the person?'

'My wife, Mrs Joanna Gurney. She's thirty-seven years old, dark, medium height—'

'On the boat, sir?' said PC Littlejohn. 'With, er, anybody?' Serve the twat right if his wife had run off.

'No. Alone. We'd just got back, after the weekend, and tied

the boat up, and when I got back from taking some luggage, she was motoring out of the harbour.'

'So you want,' said the policeman, labouring, 'to report the theft of the boat?'

'No, er, yes – not theft, she's actually a part owner, legally – half owner actually . . .' Keith was sweating now. 'Look, probably better if we just – perhaps if you just took the details – it isn't theft, and she's not been gone long – it's just I'm worried . . .'

PC Littlejohn laid down his pen and looked with distaste at the thin, brown-eyed man opposite. God almighty, what was he on about? 'Can I get this clear, sir. Your wife's gone sailing, in a boat she partly owns. Do you want to make a complaint?'

'No, but I'm concerned. I don't know where she is or why she did it . . .' Floundering, wrong-footed, Keith realized with a small shock that he was acting more ineptly than he had done for years, as ineptly as the stupidest client, running headlong into some trouble he could not quite put a name or shape to. 'She may be in danger, she's never been out alone before.'

The policeman, ever alert for an opportunity to tear up paperwork, saw his chance. 'Perhaps you should contact the coastguard direct, sir. They can keep an eye out, then perhaps you could go to your local police station in a couple of days if there isn't any news. When we talk about missing persons we generally mean more than an hour or two, sir. Otherwise we'd all be missing, most nights, down the pub, wouldn't we, sir?'

Keith was suddenly angry. 'Look, I'm telling you, she could be in danger. She's been a bit – depressed . . .'

'You have reason to think she might do something foolish? You should have told us that, sir. Sergeant!'

An older, kinder-faced man appeared, led him inside the station, took over. The wheels revolved, forms were filled, notes taken. Sitting on a hard police chair, blue uniforms and brass buttons opposite him, Keith went further than he meant to.

PC Littlejohn listened in the background for as long as he needed. Then, half an hour later, he went off duty, made his way in plain clothes to the Spread Eagle on the corner of Nelson Street, took a drink off a young friend with a local newspaper job and national newspaper ambitions, and told him the whole picaresque story of the thin lawyer in the oiled-wool sweater and the wife who had run away to sea. The young friend, very pleased indeed, bought him another and left him to drink it alone. This was a lovely one for the end of the Bank Holiday. Yes!

He headed back to his bedsitter, his computer modem, and seventy-five quid's worth of professional advancement. He wouldn't get a by-line, sadly, since the local paper might ask why he hadn't saved it for them. Bastards. Why should he? Tasty little story. Littlejohn had stopped short of giving him the name, but one call to an ex-girl friend in Bonhurst identified the only sailing solicitor in the place. A cross-check with Ray Brewer – in which the journalist prudently became Joanna's brother – confirmed it.

'Portsmouth police and coastguards,' he wrote, 'were called in last night when a 37-year-old housewife slipped her moorings and took her husband's boat to sea alone. Joanna Gurney, a brunette Bonhurst mother of two, more used to navigating a trolley round the local shops, gave hubby Keith the yo-heave-ho and bolted for the briny . . .'

The young man paused and squinted at his work. Very nice. Just the stuff for the agency. Anyway, the local paper would only have checked with the police and got Littlejohn into trouble. The dirty dailies wouldn't bother. Make a good filler, they'd probably all take it.

'Yo-ho Jo, her husband revealed, had never sailed alone and came within inches of hitting a stone pier on the way out of the harbour . . .' Better put in a bit about how she might have been suffering from depression. All bloody women suffered from depression, nobody was going to sue over that. And the bloke did say it to the policeman.

'Fears are growing,' he typed in, 'for the safety of the woman, whose mental state is said to be unstable after a period of depression . . .' Even the broadsheets might like that. The feminist columnists could have a chew on it. Woman runs away to sea. The Grand Gesture. Great!

Twenty miles to the north on the roaring Monday evening motorway, Keith drove in the slow lane, feeling rotten. Low and lonely, and faintly disgraced. He shouldn't have talked about

Joanna like that. She would be fine. She was fine. Anchored somewhere, getting over the temper. She'd probably be home before Susan got back from her jungle-music concert. Fuss about nothing, and he shouldn't have made it. Might be best to ring the police when he got in, to call off anything they might be thinking of doing.

In Sandown Bay, with a rattle and a splash Joanna let go the anchor in five metres' depth of calm water. Crouching, she held onto the chain and felt the tug when *Shearwater* pulled back and the swing of the boat as the anchor bit into the ground. She paid out ten metres more chain, hand over hand, and, shivering, went back to unlock the cabin and light the lamp against the encroaching dusk. Below, out of the wind, the cabin felt warm, with the musty, tarry, woody, comforting boat smell Joanna had always loved. She pulled a box of matches out of the rack above the stove, struck one, plucked the glass shade off the little swinging paraffin lamp and lit it. Big shadows of her hands danced on the bulkhead. Turning the wick down a little, she slipped the glass chimney back into place and adjusted the lamp again until it shone, clear and bright, on the varnish and the red cushions which glowed like a sanctuary lamp. Pumping the galley tap, she drew herself a mugful of cold water and drank deeply.

Home tomorrow. One quiet night at anchor, alone. Things would seem clearer in the morning. She pulled out the down sleeping bag from its weekday stowage under the bunk and loosened the strings on its two bags, one nylon and one waterproof.

The bag puffed out, comforting and engulfing in the small cabin, and suddenly a great weariness came over her. Without tea or food, without washing, cleaning her teeth, or doing more than pulling off her jeans and sweater, Joanna climbed into the bag in her T-shirt, reached up to blow out the barely settled wick of the light, and lay down in the dank gloom of the gently rocking cabin. Within seconds she was asleep, blown out like a lamp herself.

3

Sometimes, in the small hours, the wind rises for a while unforecast and threatening. It rattles windows along the shore, makes trees clatter disquiet into the peaceful sleep of householders, and blows fretful dreams into the minds of sailors at anchor. At three o'clock, Joanna woke to the grinding of the anchor chain on its iron fairlead. Her cheeks were wet with the tears already soaking into the cotton lining of the sleeping bag, and a slick of sweat covered her shoulders. The Gabriel dream was back.

The strange thing, even to her distressed mind, was that it had hardly faded after years of being half forgotten; years when it visited only occasionally, on nights of fever. Perhaps bad dreams of old disasters are discouraged by the reassuring banality of family life. Maybe in the face of the equable, competent atmosphere that surrounded Joanna and emanated from her, the dream had been forced into retreat. Sometimes, after one of its brief, partial night visits, she liked to imagine it abashed; no self-respecting existential nightmare, after all, would like it known that one of its regular haunts was the pillow of a Hampshire teashop proprietress, mother of two and member of the Law Society regional ball committee.

Certainly the Gabriel dream had not been back so complete or so vivid since the very first married nights. Then, once a month or so, she had been woken sobbing and shouting by a kind, anxious, infinitely reassuring Keith. No Keith now; alone in the little cabin, her canvas trousers and smock the only huddled occupants of the bunk opposite, Joanna writhed herself awake, trying to escape the dream's renewed and horrible force.

She had been on Port Meadow again, shut out and shamed and lost. But time had somersaulted, and Emily was not dead, but dying; dying because she, Joanna, had run away. And a moment came, in the darkness of the meadow, when she knew from the distant bells that death had struck. The bells said death was not a rest but a misery, an endless bad dream of rot and shame which had swallowed Emily, through Joanna's fault.

Joanna wanted to be dead too, if Emily was. She was walking towards death, across the slippery tussocks of wet grass, when Gabriel turned from the door – a door on a meadow? – but it had always been there in the dream, the door of his bedroom with the painted Chinese symbols on it. Gabriel said, 'Oh, come on, Jo, you aren't the dying type. You'd look silly dead.'

And he laughed, and shut the door, and she was out on Port Meadow alone, and woke to the sound of his receding laughter and a crushing awareness of failure and shame.

Although the Gabriel dream had not come back for years, she knew what to do. Wake up properly. Don't slide back into more of it. Drink a glass of water, sit up, and run through things in the right order. Most of the things, anyway. The historical truth was bad enough; but nothing could be as bad as the guilt of the dream. In the truth there was less guilt.

Hugging her knees, leaning her back against the hard wood of the bulkhead, Joanna told herself the story as baldly and unemotionally as she could. It was an old recitation, practised years ago to push the Gabriel dream aside without lying outright. Or telling Keith. She had never so much as said Gabriel's name to Keith. It was a private ritual, although never yet more eerily private than aboard the little boat, rolling and tugging at its anchor in Sandown Bay in the small hours of a chilly August morning.

Aged twenty, in her Finals year at Oxford, Joanna – then Joanna Telford, scholar of Somerville, white hope of her tutors, confidently expected to bring home a First of the better sort – had indeed been found wandering alone at 2 a.m. on Port Meadow. The nervous breakdown, of which her silence and apparent amnesia were considered evidence, led first to her incarceration in the Littlemore hospital and then to her return home to Hampshire and bewildered parents. Finally it led to her implacable decision to take a menial clerical job in a firm of Southampton solicitors, where sandy-haired, serious Keith saw and immediately loved her.

The 'nervous trouble', as her parents to Joanna's irritation termed it, made her refuse to return to Oxford for an additional year as the college urged; even when the Principal offered to extend her scholarship grant, she politely and adamantly turned it down. Young Jo Telford had simply decided, after the Port Meadow night, not to take her finals, ever. Never to have anything more to do with Somerville, with Oxford, and most especially with Leckford Road or Gabriel O'Riordan.

For he, tormentor of the dream, was real too. So was the room with the Chinese symbols in the rundown house on Leckford Road where amid the brushfire smell of pot Joanna, a year before her disaster, lost heart and virginity together to Gabriel's laughing, bear-hugging, embracing, warm shaggy energy. Even now, eighteen years a wife and mother, she had only to see a Chinese letter or pass a hippie craft shop smelling of joss sticks and she would feel a stab of treacherous desire. It had long been unfocused desire; direct longing for Gabriel it certainly was not. That had died with Emily.

But it was a bitter thing, thought Joanna in the whistling, gurgling, chafing, clanking cabin of *Shearwater*, that you could reject a man with horror, see right through him, and still have his scorn haunt your dreams half a lifetime later. If anyone should be scorned, it was Gabriel himself. Because of Emily.

Who was also real. At this point, Joanna's stern recital to herself of the events of 1977 faltered painfully. It was all right to have an affair with an older, fascinating, lawlessly hip poet-academic at nineteen; to be rejected by him on your twentieth birthday with an injunction to 'hang loose, stay cool'. That sort of thing was part of life's experience. Such experiences were not uncommon in the backwash of the liberated sixties, when a great stroke of luck befell the type of man who would in a simpler age have been recognized as cad, bounder, villainous seducer with twirling moustachios. Such men's luck lay in coming to their doubtful maturity in an age when free, no-strings, pharmaceutically sterilized love enjoyed an unprecedented vogue.

Casanovas then had a lot of scope. They could play you count-less songs about rolling-stone men leaving clinging women in order nobly to follow their destiny. They could model themselves on Bob Dylan singing, 'Go 'way from my window . . . I'm not the one you want, babe, I'm not the one you need.' They could screw you, win your flattering adoration, borrow all your spare money and never return it, spin you any halfwit philosophy they liked, and then get bored with you and chuck you out. And when you protested, they could make you feel like the fool. With one saintlike, patriarchal shrug they could convince you that you were a narrow-minded little middle-class girl. It was something, Jo often thought, to do with the beards; they made you feel as if you had been offered a glimpse of Moses' tablets, or a divine experience with Jove disguised as a swan, and had responded by starting to book wedding caterers.

Such men were not uncommon in university towns; and for a time nobody seemed to notice that they never did walk into the sunset to meet their vaunted Destiny on the open road. They stayed put, ushering a procession of adoring young girls in and out of their dens in a cloud of fragrant fuddling smoke until they saw the writing on the wall and allowed some particularly strong-minded girl to lead them up the aisle and into a nine-to-five job. Oh yes, Joanna had heard plenty of women laughing sheepishly in their settled, domestic thirties as they told stories of men who played the same tune as Gabriel: 'Someone to close his eyes for you, someone to close his heart? It ain't me, babe, no, no, no, it ain't me you're lookin' for, babe.' All this was just the embarrassing emotional juvenilia of anyone's life.

But an awkward quirk had prevented Joanna from telling her particular version of the standard seventies disaster story to any friend. She had never made a healing joke of it, because there was no healing to be had. Because of Emily. Because Emily – sunny, dippy, laughing Emily, cheeky, kind, unstable Emily – had died. Died of Gabriel, died of Joanna's failure to keep her alive. Emily had wound herself into half a lifetime's nightmares. The black, tolling, shameful nightmare of her death was real.

Eighteen years on, Joanna huddled into the sleeping bag. The brief night gale was easing, the chain clanking more idly and intermittently, the roll and slap of waves abating. She did not need to think too much about Emily. Not now. Emily's death had driven her out into the rain, onto Port Meadow, to hear the clocks and bells strike night hours across the northern wastes by the river. It had driven her from friends, ambitions, city and university into another kind of life: a kindly, domestic, community-minded, parent-teacher-association, teashop life. A safe, decent life. Her wretched adolescent ancestress had seen the futility of Gabriel, and run for cover.

She need not think too much of Emily's end, but perfunctorily forced herself to run through the coda: the other, minor guilty admission. The truth nobody knew was that she had not been at all amnesiac that night on Port Meadow, nor 'confused' at the mental hospital. She had only been tired and angry. Too much so to speak to the police, or college, or psychiatrist, or parents. She had faked the breakdown, as far as it went, and refused the degree out of nihilism and rage. She was perfectly sane all the time. But hell, she was young and it was a rough passage. These days they would have called her depressed and given her Prozac, and not condemned anything, even her pretending to be madder than she was. The expression 'right to silence' drifted across her mind from some item of legal news. Jo Telford had a right to silence. So did Joanna Gurney.

Silently now, she lay down, closed her eyes, hardly aware of the quietening boat, and slid into a blank, flat sleep.

In the Old Vicarage, Keith tossed and threw an arm across the empty half of the bed. He whimpered slightly, knowing in his sleep that his wife was not beside him.

In South London, silent sleepy men threw bundles of newspapers into vans. From somewhere west of Ushant, to the south-west of *Shearwater*'s anchorage, the depression began to move stealthily, heading for Belgium. A light rain fell, and the boat shifted its heading, doubtfully, then swung back. No change yet.

4

Keith woke at twenty to eight from a vague dream of discomfort. He had been reaching vainly for his missing wife and rolled too far until his arm hung over her side of the bed and grew pins and needles.

Cursing, he sat up, and switched on the radio which he and Jo kept tuned to Radio 4 and the measured rhythms of waking middle England. An urbane newsreader was concluding the review of the morning's press, with the familar note of faint, kindly superiority befitting the senior service of British media: '... *Daily Express*, however, sees the minister's tough new line differently. With the headline: HOW TO HANDLE A VANDAL ...'

Somehow, this morning, the tone jarred on Keith for the first time. What, he asked himself savagely, have they got to be so smug about? He jammed his arm into the sleeve of his wool dressing gown, catching his hand in the rolled-in cuff, then froze as the bulletin continued: 'Finally, several papers carry the story of the wife who, as the *Mail* puts it, staged a one-woman mutiny in Portsmouth harbour, slipping her moorings and heading out to sea while her husband's back was turned ...'

Stiff with horror, Keith felt a blush mount from his shoulders to his hairline; such a blush as he had not felt since he hit a flat note in a school oboe solo in 1965. The blasted, blasted police station! How many times had he warned clients not to prattle, not to spill details irrelevant to the matter in hand, not while ears were flapping?

'... some concern at her inexperience and mental state. The coastguard, however, report calm weather conditions and no cause for alarm unless, said a spokesman, the woman does anything silly. Or, as the *Globe* condescendingly adds, anything else silly. Still, it makes a novel solution, says the paper, to the stresses of family life. The *Sun* sums it up with the headline MUM AHOY!'

A chortle followed from the studio pair; the man said, 'It used to be the boys who ran off to sea, now it's their mums.' The woman gave a contralto, Radio 4 giggle and added, 'Can't say I blame her, this end of the school holidays!'

Keith walked into the bathroom and, unable to look Jo's shampoo and toothbrush in the face, shaved hurriedly with the electric razor he despised and kept for oversleeping days. He did not trust his shaking hand. Disaster. Disaster. If Jo was awake, switched on the boat's radio – also tuned permanently to the long-wave for the shipping forecasts – if Jo heard that, she'd think . . .

Oh, God. She'd think he'd raised the hue and cry on purpose because they had had a row about her wanting to sell out of the Bun. It might have been all right if they were the kind of couple who had explosive public rows all the time, tipped spaghetti over one another in Italian restaurants, locked each other out and shrieked 'Bastard!' through upper windows. Like many of his clients. But they were not. They had never, either of them, cried public shame on the other. The most snarling private argument, the most crabby drive to a dinner party had never made either of them snipe or score points in public. Not like Mandy and Alex who appeared to get some obscure thrill out of bickering at other people's tables.

Joanna, he knew without asking, did not indulge in those 'Oh, men!' conversations with other mothers; at least, not in any private detail. Equally, he did not dish the dirt with the boys. Only with the children, during that golden, pre-adolescent stage of mutual understanding between ten and thirteen, had they giggled openly over one another's shortcomings, untidinesses, inadequacies over spiders, snoring habits, and the rest.

And, curiously, even during their most poisonous teenage rants, neither Lance nor Susan had betrayed or belittled these admissions of marital abrasion. Their marriage might be ordinary, passionless, rather routine, but Keith had lately felt that with the children nearly grown, some of its bloom might return. It had good soil to grow in; the warm privacy of their eighteen years' sharing of intimate life was intact.

Had been intact. Keith looked round wildly at the familiar high-ceilinged bathroom, the cork tiles, the missing bits of coving. He walked through onto the faded pink bedroom carpet beyond, looked at the rumpled bed and the pine chest of drawers bearing the silvered twig Lance had made at school for Jo to hang her gold chains on. Everything seemed odd, shabby, exposed, as furniture does when it stands in the street waiting for a removal van. This was their nest, their warm stuffy refuge; but some giant force had taken the roof off, and giant eyes were peering in. The press. Oh God.

There was one hope: that the blasted policeman had kept their names out of it. He must get the tabloids, instantly. Must know.

Keith stumbled down the wide oak staircase they had once loved for its dignity and now found dusty and noisy, and paused to smooth his sandy, greying hair in the equally depressing (now he looked at it with these startled new eyes) Victorian hall mirror. Damn being middle-class, he thought irrelevantly. Damn buying too-big vicarages from a dreary period and feeling honour bound to fill them with furniture from the same dire era. Why couldn't they have a cheap, cheerful bamboo mirror from a Third World catalogue, like they used to on Egg Terrace when he was an articled clerk and they drank terrible wine and sailed a leaky Mirror dinghy?

His hand was on the doorknob when the telephone rang. Four times, so the answering machine in the study must be off. He was a solicitor. He had to answer, it was bred in his bones.

'Gurney,' he snapped.

'Keith, it's Man-dee,' said the telephone, flirtatiously. 'Keith? It is you?'

'Yes, Mandy, I can't stop now—'

'Yes, I know!' Mandy could stretch the word 'know' to three syllables at least. 'I just wanted to say how awful about Joanna. Is she OK? I mean, it's such nonsense they print, Alex is ever so cross, says he'd sue. What are you doing?'

The question was rhetorical. Mandy twittered on, 'Honestly,

when I saw that bit about her being depressed and on tablets, I mean, you'd think they'd check. What Erika says is, they never think solicitors will sue because of the publicity. Like that man they thought buried his wife in the garden. Anyway, Erika's rung already, she's popping in to open the Bun just in case Jo doesn't feel up to it or . . .'

'Mandy, I'm sorry,' said Keith, seizing the opportunity provided by Mandy's brief, hopeful pause. 'That's good about Erika, because Jo isn't here, she's taking a couple of days' break to, er, sort out the boat. And I haven't seen any newspaper nonsense. I did hear something on *Today*, but I don't suppose it's anything to do with us—'

'Oh!' squeaked the telephone. 'Ooh, p'raps I'll get Alex to fax them from his study, 'cos you ought to see what they say in case reporters come and do a thingy, you know, *doorstep* on you. Like Mary Archer. You could answer the door in a dressing gown, dead cool. Do,' she added artfully, 'get Jo to call me!'

Keith could see her, the minx, putting the phone down, admiring her nails, pushing back her silvery-blonde hair in its stupid Alice band and doing a little shrug and pout of glee at having got to him first with the bad news. He had liked Mandy once. In early years, when he used to come home to find her and Joanna sprawled laughing at the kitchen table, Lance tricycling round it and the babies Susan and Anneliese propped in their plastic chairs, she was a welcome sight. She was good company for Jo, someone to be pregnant with. They had always made an odd couple: Joanna dark and practical and intellectual, Mandy an ebullient presence with her cloud of hair like, Jo said, an explosion in a marmalade factory; with her leopard-print leggings and repertoire of shriekingly blue jokes. But the friendship, ill assorted as it was, dragged Joanna out of the nervy depression which had followed Lance's birth. That alone was worth endless gratitude. In return, their home, he felt magnanimously, gave Mandy a more solid base. A house with a man in it. A refuge to supplement her precarious existence as a single mother in a council flat.

He had been pleased when, still pregnant, the two women borrowed £10,000 from him to start the Bun in the Oven. And comically astonished, according to his wife, when they paid it back in profits two years later.

He had dutifully tried to be pleased when Mandy abruptly married his widowed partner, Alex. He had tried not to think of Alex's first wife, a concert pianist who had died slowly and heroically of cancer only three months before. He tried to understand that Alex – big, lazy, conventional Alex – needed Mandy's vulgar vitality to warm himself at.

But a decade on from that marriage, he could no longer see Mandy as anything but a bad dream or hear her affected 'Bye-ee!' without a deep churn of rage. He absolved himself, with difficulty, of mere self-interest in the matter, but the fact was that his rage had lately deepened and become more personal. Mandy, Man-dee, pushy, artful bitch, had persuaded Alex to pull himself and his capital out of the comfortable smalltown legal practice which suited him. Actually, Keith admitted to himself, it suited him almost too well. Alex had been declining into pipe-and-slippers contentment so fast that it alarmed even Keith. The man had had leather patches on his elbows at twenty-seven. But Mandy had swung him too far the other way, dressed him in sharp suits, reformed his stringy taste in ties, cut his hair, and engineered him into friendships with property developers and contacts with hard, dodgy, backslapping builders who wanted a tame lawyer as a respectable front. Alex was leaving the practice for more and, in Keith's view, grubbier money. Mandy had made him into something more modern but nastier. When Alex left Heron and Gurney at Christmas, Keith would be alone except for Gus Terson, the former clerk who had only passed his last law exams, at the third try, in spring. Unless another partner could be found. The very thought was exhausting and depressing. Damn Mandy.

Moreover, thought Keith savagely, padding into the study to set the answering machine, the woman had gone strawberry-blonde and taken to Alice bands and a clipped, mewing delivery learned at the gate of Anneliese's new private school. She had inflated ideas of herself and, worst of all, she had used Alex's money to turn herself artfully into a sleeping partner in the Bun in the Oven. She had distanced herself from the work surfaces, the drains, the menu writing, the wiping down and cashing up and the compulsory smiling at arrogant tourists and dithering old ladies. Mandy had persuaded Jo that it was somehow fair that if she paid a girl to work her share of the hours and merely dropped by occasionally to discuss policy, she could still be an equal partner in the profits.

It was a diabolically cheeky move. Even though Jo had to find and train the part-time girls, Mandy had come to seem like everyone's employer; even Jo, in low moments, admitted that when she was sweaty and harassed and Mandy came in looking immaculate, she felt as if she and Zoë were both staff, respectfully making way for Lady Muck.

All this, thought Keith, and Mandy wouldn't give Alex a child. Or so he, Keith, suspected. Alex used to say, 'Just never happened for us, old boy,' in a manly, dismissive way; but Keith had his suspicions. Mandy had managed to get pregnant at nineteen fast enough, by some passing Swedish gorilla off a Whitbread race yacht. Hence that tarty little Anneliese, a bad influence on Susan – who ought to be home and changing for school, right now, and had no doubt missed the early train after a night of shrieking and bopping in London.

He felt curiously better for his flurry of dislike for Mandy. Had he paused to analyse the improvement in his mood, he might have found that it was a relief to despise someone more than, on this wifeless, shaming morning, he despised himself. He jabbed the button which set the answering machine and went out for the papers.

It was not, after all, such a big splash. No pictures, for one thing, and it had come in late. But as a grace note to the Bank Holiday, the Portsmouth stringer's story did well. He could see why the review of the papers on Radio 4 had picked it up. 'COME IN, MUM-BER 7, YOUR TIME IS UP,' said the *Sun*. The *Mail* wrote elegantly around the story, muting its amusement with the line about Joanna's 'depression'. Nothing about 'being on tablets', though; Mandy's imagination had provided those. The *Globe*, latest of the new challengers born of the technical revolution in newspapers, made most of it, printing his name and Joanna's and slanting the story well in to the sex war. 'The last bastion of male supremacy, an Englishman's boat, is no longer proof against mutinous wives ... the solicitor left beached by his wife needed all his Dunkirk spirit . . .' Weak stuff, a fantasy spun round few facts and no quotes but, he had to admit, beguiling. Damn Jo. No, damn him, for being such a fool in the police station.

He read the papers in his study, before absently jabbing the replay button of the answerphone. It bleeped, hissed, and through a fuzz of VHF radio static, spoke in Joanna's voice. 'Keith. It's Jo.' He sat, frozen. The pause allowed him to hear the faint chattering breakthrough of other calls on the marine band VHF channels. Then Joanna spoke again from the grey plastic box.

'I want you to know that I heard the radio, and this is not funny. Sod you, Keith. I'll come back when I bloody well feel like it. I'm going for a sail. Tell Susan I'm fine. And good luck with her first day in the sixth.'

Keith played the message again, then sat silently as the tape ran into the next one, which began, 'Mr Gurney? My name's Kate Somerton, I'm a freelance journalist for the—'

He felt sick.

5

It was by sheer chance that Joanna discovered her new national fame. Waking stiff and tired at half past seven, she found her mind had formed a plan that was clear and plain and humble enough. She would call Keith on the VHF, making a link call through Niton Radio; then have a cup of tea, get the anchor up, and motor rapidly back to Portsmouth, home and duty.

Only, in the new wave of embarrassed gloom which now possessed her, she did not want any kind of conversation with Keith. He might sound avuncular, or headmasterly, or dry and legal, as he occasionally did these days. Better to be sure of the plan and its timing, briskly tell him, and ring off before he could gather his wits. But the timing of her return depended on whether there was enough diesel left in the tank; they had used the reserve five-gallon can on Saturday rather than face the Bank Holiday mêlée of boats round the fuel berth at Cowes. Last night, too wild and tearful to raise a sail, she had used a lot.

So, in yesterday's T-shirt and white cotton knickers, Joanna climbed on deck in the grey morning chill. Shivering a little at the damp northerly breeze, she pulled out the wooden dipstick notched in half-gallons, unscrewed the filler cap and slotted the stick into the tank.

It came out dry, except for its extreme tip. Less than half a gallon. An hour's running. Not enough for Portsmouth even without a headwind and foul tide. She might not ever have skippered the boat or been at sea alone, but fifteen years as a yachting wife made all these calculations automatic. She had known the wind was in the North the second she awoke and saw grey sea rather than green shore through the open hatchway. And now, the moment the dipstick emerged from the tank, she knew that motoring home was out of the question. With an exasperated 'Doh!' which sounded uncannily like one of the noises Keith made in such circumstances, she sat back on her cold haunches with one hand resting on the still-dewy canvas cover of the boom, considering.

She could sail back. A slant north-eastwards, a slow zigzag beat against the tide, maybe with the last bit of engine power, to get past Bembridge, then a tight fetch, just off the wind, to Portsmouth. It would be slow. She would have to tell Keith that. She wouldn't be home much before evening on the train. Unless he came to pick her up.

Suddenly, on the familiar boat, with Keith's old orange oilskins hanging in the wet-locker and his seaboots rammed under the step next to hers, Joanna wanted very much for him to pick her up and take her home. Which was perhaps why, returning dangerously damp-eyed to the little cabin, she switched on the radio before filling the kettle. A radio, as all the lonely know, is company. It had never, until this moment, been bad company.

'. . . how to handle a vandal. Finally, several papers carry the story of the wife who, as the *Mail* puts it, staged a one-woman mutiny in Portsmouth harbour . . .'

Stiffly, she listened to the end, to the last studio giggle, then made her cup of tea with a steady hand, as if the world had not just sharply tilted on its axis. The word 'alienated' floated into her mind, unbidden.

She was alienated now. An outsider. Her husband was not to be trusted. He had made the world laugh at her for a menopausal mutineer, laid her open to having coastguards calling her silly and impertinent whippersnappers speculating on her mental state in the *Daily* bloody *Mail*. Alienated. Beside the dismay, though, ran a light-headed sense of release. She owed nobody anything. The world had done badly by her. She was King Lear, noble in ruin, bayed by madmen, surrounded by ingratitude and betrayal.

These Shakespearian similes had always come easily to Joanna; she might not have a degree, but she had the cast of characters, all still there in her head, from Grendel's monstrous mother to J. Alfred Prufrock. All right then, Lear it would be. Off to the heath in rags and tatters, and to hell with the lot of them, most especially Keith.

As for Susan, she would be all right; she hardly spoke to her mother anyway these days without an exaggerated sigh of contempt. Somewhere in Joanna's mind this last year had tugged a set of memories: Susan small and loving, Susan eager at twelve, playing the clarinet in the school concert, dancing, hugging, laughing with her parents instead of sighing at them. But those dear vanished Susans seemed blurred and indistinct next to the awful clarity of the real, present, sixteen-year-old version. The only Susan she had now was the one who lay around on the bed with that slinky Anneliese, music blaring, cutting off in mid-giggle to stare up at an intruding mother with the cold, pretty impassivity of a pair of Siamese kittens. Susan had no need of her now. And Lance, clever kind Lance, who kept the family peace, was gone. He would be Inter-Railing round Europe thinking his great, straight-A thoughts for another two or three weeks at least. So she need not rush back. Keith could bloody well stew.

And Mandy – Joanna was surprised to find a harsh thought towards Mandy forming in her mind, because normally she banned such unsisterly thoughts, for ever defending her friend against Keith's visible dislike – well, Mandy could try running the Bun in the Oven herself for a change. To hell with them all. Howl, Howl, Howl, Howl, Howl, Howl, Howl, Howl! as Lear would put it.

The link call to Keith's answering machine took less than two minutes at that quiet morning hour.

When she rang off, Joanna went forward into the small heads compartment to clean her teeth, then frowned for a moment into the mirror. Normally she smiled into mirrors, but she rather liked the frown today. She tried a scowl. Not pretty, but striking. All those American feminists would be proud of her, running off on her own, scowling, like some woman in a bad-girl movie. Well, to hell with them too. There would be nobody but her on *Shearwater* today; no telephone, no customers, no welcome mat, no post, no newspapers. It would be, even if just for today, a boatful of Joanna Gurney, undiluted. Joanna Telford, even.

She finished her tea, pulled on the crumpled blue canvas trousers and smock, switched on the depth-sounder and electric log, and climbed out on deck. In a moment she had unlashed the tiller and freed the mainsheet rope, loosened the ties on the mainsail cover and sail, and pulled the blue canvas tube off the boom to stuff it tidily away. She ran forward to take the ties off the roller jib and, after fitting a brass handle to the winch on the mast, began to haul on the main halyard. The sail rose, fold by fold, its grubby white nylon gaining dignity as it took shape between mast and swinging boom. The boat rolled and tugged, feeling life coming back to it.

Finally she took two turns around the winch, tightened up the sail, pulled the kicking strap beneath the boom until it was taut, and went forward to fit the cold links of the anchor chain over the old-fashioned windlass and begin the long, to-and-fro pumping which would pull tight the chain which bound her to the sea bed. Then it would heave the anchor upright, trip its grip, and she would pull it on deck and be free.

The boat sheered around as she worked, its sail flapping. Her cold body warmed to the effort and blood began to flow more strongly in her. Years ago, when the boat was a new and shared adventure, she and Keith and the babies had always anchored, scorning marinas as no more than car parks on water. The tastes of growing children who needed to run along pontoons and fish for tiddlers and row rubber dinghies had changed their ways. Later, a kind of jaded lassitude and unthinking habit had made them haunt more and more marinas. It had been convenient but dull. She found herself enjoying the act of hauling in an anchor again.

When it appeared, dripping, at the stemhead she pulled it aboard and went quickly back to the helm, out of breath; kneed the tiller to her left and pulled in the sheet, bringing the sail under pressure from the wind. *Shearwater*, feeling the ancient stresses of sail, keel and rudder, swung obediently away from the shore and towards the gleaming green-and-grey of St Catherine's Point. West. She would go west.

Not crying this time, neither guilty nor shocked at herself, Joanna looked up at the sail, gave a strange little private smile, and bent down to release the rolled jib. The northerly wind, spun off the depression now tramping wetly over Brittany, caught the sail and heeled the boat onto a fast, graceful broad reach. Joanna reached below for a stale ginger biscuit from the night-watch bag and settled at the helm. 'Going for a little sail,' she murmured. 'Me and you. Bit of peace.'

6

'There's the Sussex child abuse thing,' said the Section 2 Features Editor, who was really the Women's editor, only smart tabloids no longer believed in such things.

'Sub judice,' said the star columnist of the *Globe*, a surly blonde in early middle age who wore rather too short a skirt and very much too tight a sweater. 'Besides, sod it.'

The Features Editor nodded, gloomily. Opinion pieces on child abuse were always a failure. Unless you were sure it was a fit-up by politically correct social workers, there was only one safe opinion to have: 'Shocking!' And this took up deplorably little space. So columnists always meandered off into half-baked, uninformed ideas about sentencing, therapy, pornography, and how it was all the fault of an insidious social rot dating from the 1960s. Or, alternatively, the legacy of the Thatcher government. The Features Editor turned a page of her notebook.

'OK, let's see: penis implants, Sharon Stone's bloke, the child prodigy – no, Dave's interviewing that. Bloody monster, its father wanted five K, I ask you.' She peered down the diary, pushing her enormous glasses up her nose. 'I know, what about the divorce figures? Up again.'

The star columnist winced. Her own second divorce, from the managing editor of the glossy magazine she also starred in, was reaching a noisy crescendo.

'I mean,' persisted the Features Editor, unwisely, 'you could do the personal pain, the guilt thing, the lonely moment when the decree absolute arrives in the post, the uncaring attitude of society and friends to what is basically a bereavement, OK?' She appealed to the rest of her staff, two thin pale young men and a bouncing blonde Sloane who was in charge of food and drink. 'Maeve did that terrific piece when the Princess of Wales—'

'That was about divorcing Ray,' cut in the star columnist (whose name was not really Maeve but who had decided in 1983 to become Irish as a career move). 'Divorcing Simon is not like a bereavement. More like having a haemorrhoid done. Anyway, if I write any buggery thing right now, his fat lawyer'll have me.'

'All the same,' said the Features editor, reasserting her authority with difficulty under the sooty terrorist glare of the ersatz Maeve. 'Marriage would be good this week. The Editor is very into marriage.' When the rude guffaws this remark engendered had died down, one of the pale young men stuttered into life.

'I mean – I thought – Jules and I thought – Maeve might be super on that Portsmouth woman, the one who ran off to sea in the husband's boat.'

'Yee-eess!' said the star columnist, the Voice of Wednesday. 'Dickie, that's it. Women's need for space.'

'Running away as therapy,' said the features editor.

'Why men deserve it!' said Dick. 'Bastards, we are. Jailers!'

'How every woman should do it!' said the food-and-drink writer.

'Except the Editor's nice new wife,' said Jules, and blew a lewd kiss at Dick.

Honour satisfied all round, the meeting proceeded. Maeve took the press cuttings from Dick and slipped off to her keyboard to begin pounding out her thousand pounds a week.

'Men on boats, as every sea wife knows, are tyrants. No, hold that. Men are tyrants anywhere, on land or sea. So it was refreshing . . .'

A mile away, in an older, more established newspaper office, the tail end of a similar meeting also focused on the Sailaway Wife story. Home news was scarce and political, foreign news depressing and monotone. The last two undeployed reporters, a chic bobbed blonde in leather trousers and a very young man with owl-like glasses, sat a little apart from their masters, wondering what their week held.

'She could be drowned,' said the news editor with relish. '*Tragic tiff that took a mother's life*. The agency's watching it, with the coastguard.'

'Nah,' said the Deputy Editor, who had a Moody on the Hamble. 'Calm as a millpond. She'll be OK. Turn up.'

'Then why hasn't she?'

'Engine failure, can't change a plug, drifts on the rocks?' said an Associate Editor.

'Sexist,' said another, of the opposite sex. 'There's a column in that.'

'Do we *want* a bloody think-piece?' said the news Editor. 'The *Globe*'ll have Maeve Mahoney on it, betcha. A woman's need to run away. Men are bastards. Every hubby is Cap'n Bligh at heart. No, tell you what,' he began suddenly to brighten, remembering that for once, thanks to an overenthusiastic training scheme, he actually had too many reporters – bloody spoilt graduate brats, they were – rather than too few. 'The *Globe*'ll run Maeve Mahoney's Wednesday woffle tomorrow. So we do nothing. Then on Thursday we do the interview. Scoop! Find the wife, exclusive pics on the boat, full story. Show up the *Globe* as the fluffy girly mag it is. We are a newspaper. We'll get the actual interview. Gordon, you go . . . No,' he cast around, 'Dinny, you go. Needs a girl.'

'*Where* do I go?' asked the sleekly groomed blonde reporter sulkily.

'Out,' said the News Editor. 'By the seaside. Go and see the coastguards. Show a bit of leg. Bung 'em a drink. Ring the boat parks.'

'*Marinas*,' hissed the Deputy editor.

'Find her, and get her story. If she turns out to be a silly cow, all the better, 'cos the *Globe*'ll be all over her with the feminist crap. If you don't get her by tomorrow, we'll run it on Friday. Go on, piss off. I pay you to be a reporter, so go and report something. Gordon,' his eye fell again on the youth, with disfavour – dear God, graduate trainees! 'You go to Bonhurst. Get the abandoned hubby and the rudderless teashop.' The News Editor smiled for the first time that day. He belonged to the old school, and hated to see reporters hanging around indoors rewriting news agency faxes. 'Go!'

Dinny, her pale bob flouncing, walked away down the long office, irritated. Gordon, younger and more excited, flipped through his Filofax to find Bonhurst on the railway map.

Out in the Channel, *Shearwater* left Shanklin and Ventnor behind and cleared St Catherine's Point to press past the island's less inhabited shore with the wind steady on the beam. Ahead, the clouds preceding the depression lay low and white, like a map or a mountain view of islands in a sky-blue sea. A sea-blue sky.

When she was a small girl, once, on holiday in an arid campsite in central France, Jo had seen cloud islands like these and imagined sailing a boat over the dull land horizon and up along the sky, round those white ragged headlands and into nebulous bays. These aerial Hebrides had stayed in her mind's eye ever since. When, on a school trip, she first saw the West of Scotland, she had recognized the dream landscape with a start and longed to sail the maze of blue between the cloudy islands. Later, on a summer trip to the Cyclades with Emily, they sweet-talked a fisherman into taking them for a day around the uninhabited islets. When Keith, hesitantly courting her in the solicitors' office at Southampton, diffidently told her that he sailed a dinghy and had dreams of a cruising boat, she had responded with such instant, eager joy that he had been charmed. Most girls talked of seasickness and men being tyrants on boats. Joanna, by contrast, immediately said, 'Could you sail to Scotland, or Ireland, really west, to all those islands, Aran and Inishvickillane? Or to Greece? You could, couldn't you, in a boat with a cabin?'

He had never thought of this; Channel crossings to Cherbourg or Dieppe were what the men at the Sailing Club talked of. But, in love, he said, 'Yes, one day. You could come too. We'll go on some courses together, get a bit of experience, then perhaps . . .'

Only once or twice since then had the dream seemed to near reality. For their honeymoon they had hired a little yacht and frightened themselves silly on a windy August tour of the inner Hebrides, nearly losing the boat (so they thought) in the whirlpools of the Dorus Mor while Joanna was doubled up with what turned out to be pregnancy sickness. Later, *Shearwater* had taken the family to Brittany. Between Houat and Hoedic islands, alone on deck with the children napping and Keith below decks, Joanna had entered the dream at last, alone, swinging between green blessed islands on a sea of ruffled, tender blue.

Then Lance woke, wanting to steer, and Susan needed changing, and Keith began fretting about whether they would get a berth at La Trinité. He put the engine on, sensibly, and it was over.

Now, hauling in the sails a little to fit the closer angle of the wind, Joanna saw headland after headland rolling before her towards the west. She had learned by heart once the lines from Frank Cowper's 1895 pilot book, and said them aloud now as the boat cut through the clean swell:

Promontory on promontory, peak on peak, the varied coastline wanders away to the golden West. Headlands of many shapes, tossing their summits to the sea like wild waves driven before the roaring blast, grow fainter and fainter in the mellow light, sinking gradually to the lowland where Melcombe and Weymouth shimmer under the westering sun. But again, away in the South West, far out like a giant wedge, the long ridge of Portland rises like some half-submerged monster from the western sea . . .

The sun was not westering, but the clean northerly air gave her a view all the way to the ancient wedge, the crocodile head of Portland Bill forty miles away. Forty miles, say eight hours in this fast breeze. Under Portland, tucked up the armpit of the great granite limb, lay Weymouth. Yes, she thought. Weymouth. The easiest harbour on the coast to find, easy to enter in an offshore wind, full of holidaymakers to take a rope from a lone woman sailor and help her tie alongside. A creditable distance away for a first solo cruise. Easy to phone home from.

She would ring home, of course. She ought to speak to Susan about school. The sixth form suit they had bought together from the second-hand school shop – with much wrinkling of Susan's nose, and mutters of 'Gross!' – was at the dry-cleaners and needed collecting before the official Wednesday start of school at Angela Merici. Today Susan would be able to wear her own clothes for the sixth-form induction day. A very sensible idea, Joanna had thought. Really, Susan's implacable opposition to doing A levels at school would surely crumble in the face of Mrs MacEvoy's pep talk about the privileges and responsibilities of the sixth. Susan would settle. But it would be a bad start if she had forgotten about her uniform suit.

So she would ring Susan. And if she was, calmly and collectedly, speaking to her daughter, it would be easier for Keith to break in and take the chance to explain his appalling treachery, his telling—

She pushed that train of thought aside and consigned it to the wind. Weymouth would do nicely. Fair stood the wind for Weymouth.

She fiddled briefly with the elastic cords on the tiller which made the boat steer itself – more or less – on an easy course like this, and swung herself below to forage for a breakfast of cereal and UHT milk. There were three nectarines left in the cool box ready to go ashore last night. She pulled two into segments and put them in the cereal bowl, took it up on deck and sat eating and watching the coast slip by. The chuckling sound of the water and the thrum of taut rigging were company enough. Quite what the King Lear part of her would do next, or say to Keith, she did not want to know. For now, the boat was everything: refuge and occupation, escape and homecoming. She slipped the elastic cords off the tiller and took it in her free hand again, steering for the sheer pleasure of steering, balancing the cereal bowl on her knee.

Up among the deed boxes in his crowded, dark-beamed first-floor office, Keith was on the telephone to Mrs Repton. Mrs Repton was not a favourite client. She was old and she was imperious, and seemed to have some memories of the way her own elderly female relations of seventy years ago used to boss their 'man of business'. Either that, or she watched too many satellite television repeats of *Upstairs Downstairs*. Certainly it was clear that she had seen a documentary about medical research the night before. Keith nursed the receiver on his collarbone as he listened, flicking his desk drawers and making desultory notes.

'. . . but *if* I leave my body to science, Mr Gurney,' Mrs Repton was saying, 'do I have any *guarantee* over the kind of uses it will be put to? I should make it *quite clear*, don't you think, that there is no question of – ah – ovaries. Or eyes. Or hair. My late husband *worshipped* my hair and eyes – unforgettable, he used to say . . .'

Keith played with his pencil, picturing the scene at the medical school on the arrival of an 87-year-old cadaver with a list of prohibited areas pinned to its bosom. 'Perhaps if you could put a note in writing,' he attempted. But Mrs Repton's flow was unabated.

'. . . my nephew Dr Plomley,' crackled the receiver, stridently. 'If I could be certain he would supervise everything personally – only it might distress him, do you think?'

Keith did think. Dr Plomley would, he felt, be unlikely to make the round trip from Edinburgh Royal Infirmary just to stand guard over his aunt's withered ovaries and unforgettable hair. Especially as she was leaving the house and most of the money to the Sunny Paddocks Horse Rescue Trust.

A tart rejoinder to that effect hovered on his lips and, as usual, died. Mrs Repton was a client; more, she was a human being who had once been young and hopeful and now was old and irritating. She was as much a child of God as he was, or Susan, or Lance, or Jo. In his private musings he liked the expression 'child of God', which was curious, since he had grave doubts about God. Perhaps it was just that when you are an orphan of nearly forty, and a solicitor, and going grey, and losing your grip and your hopefulness, a paternal white-bearded God starts to have a secret attraction again.

Gus Terson, a younger member of the cosmic family and the Heron and Gurney practice, burst in without knocking, upturning a rubber plant left on the floor by the partnership secretary Aimée who was God knows where. Round at Alex's, probably, thought Keith, so he could 'work from home'. Ha bloody ha. Dance attendance on Mandy's latest interior decorator, no doubt. The pot rolled in a parabolic curve across the carpet, scattering topsoil. Gus failed to notice it. He was one of those pink, bouncing, chubby young men whose very hair seems to spring with misdirected energy.

'Keith, can I have a word? Only it's the conveyance on the brewery cottages—'

The phone chattered on. '. . . Another thing, of course, is that I *don't believe* in all this money being spent on homosexual diseases . . .'

'– Mowbray says, is the search invalid if the local government reform thing happens? God, sorry, did I kick that over?'

'. . . spread by *unnatural* practices, so that would have to go in. No AIDS research to be done on my remains, do you understand? It has to be in *the will*. Mr Gurney? Mr Gurney?'

Gus had seen the plant and was scooping up potting compost with his fingers, making the mess worse than ever and still talking. 'This is definitely my first chance to say I made the earth move for Aimée, hyuk! Oh, you're on the phone. Shall I . . .'

Keith drew himself together. 'Mrs Repton, I have your instructions,' he said loudly. 'The line is very bad, so I must hang up now and speak most severely to the telephone service.' Cutting off Gus's guffaw with a glare, he continued in the magisterial style he knew Mrs Repton preferred in her man of law. 'Our young Mr Terson,' another glare, 'will send you a note of the proposed codicil. Good day.' He put the telephone on its rest and, as an afterthought, took it off again and laid it purring on the desk. He fiddled his filing drawer open and shut, open and shut. 'Gus, will you kindly not barge in, chattering. Alex is doing the Brewery cottages. Bloody well ring him.'

'I did,' chirped Gus, unabashed. 'He said he was tied up, but that it was a point you could surely clear up. Oh, hey, I forgot. He also said – he said Mandy said – that if Jo wanted her to pop round this morning—'

Keith slammed the desk drawer shut with unnecessary violence, made a noise approximating to 'Kchut!' and stood up. 'I have a call to make on . . . on old Mr Palmer. Back at twelve or so.'

'But the thing is,' protested Gus, who never liked being alone in the office (in case, as he often explained, some woman might turn up blubbing about a divorce) 'Mr Palmer is actually, you know, we heard last week, he's dead.' But Keith was gone. Gus was talking to an empty room and his principal was walking down Bonhurst High Street, rapidly, to nowhere in particular.

Had he looked up as he passed the welcoming glass-and-gingham frontage of the Bun in the Oven, he might have seen Erika, a becoming flush brightening her sallow complexion, serving coffee and a Tropical Danish (the kind with the bits of pineapple in it) to ever such a nice young man who said his name was Gordon.

7

The last of the ebbing tide carried *Shearwater* round St Catherine's Point, but by noon it had slowed and turned eastward, against her. The boat's speed past the distant coast of the mainland hardly slackened; after the gentle morning, the wind was fresher every minute, pushing her forward in powerful, rhythmic lunges across the lumpy sea. The tiller, with its flaking dark-gold varnish, felt alive. It thrummed and throbbed, dragging against Joanna's hand as the dial of the electric log rose to six, seven knots. Once or twice, the plastic dial surged to eight in the stronger gusts, and the boat's bows tried to round up towards the coast to the north. The westerly course grew harder to hold.

The sails were set too closely. Sliding down from her perch on the wooden coaming of the cockpit, stiff from three hours' entranced and exhilarated sailing, Joanna loosened first the heavy mainsheet then the jib. The sails lurched gratefully out on the port side of the boat, ballooning and pulling hard. Joanna could point the bow back towards Portland now, but the purposeful plunging turned into a wild downwind roll. Below, in the cabin, plates and cutlery clattered against their locker doors. The boathook, not properly secured, rolled irritatingly to and fro. The two dangling plastic fenders she had not noticed in her precipitate departure brought themselves sharply to her attention by banging on the side and bouncing almost onto the deck. She reached forward and untied one with her free hand, throwing it into the cabin. The other, nearer to the bow, bounced and mocked.

Each roll shook the wind out of the jib. When it filled again it was with intermittent, jarring jerks and sharp cracks of nylon sailcloth. Joanna winced, freed it off further to flog uselessly and, using the thin line leading to the roller on the bow, reduced the big foresail's size by a third and tamed it again. Her hand hurt from the burn of the control line but the boat felt better. The wind was well in the east now and far stronger than it had been when it was in the North. So it had – veered? Backed? She made a clock face with her finger, frowning, trying to remember evening classes in her old enthusiastic days. It had veered. 'Veering and increasing, backing and decreasing.' That was the rule. Something to do with the approach and departure of a depression.

This one was clearly approaching, and rather rapidly at that. The day was still sunny and clear but the seas were shorter and sharper as the tide piled water up in one direction, only to have it punched back by the wind. Wind over tide, the sailor's curse. Joanna leaned forward to adjust the mainsail, steering with the other arm twisted awkwardly behind her.

The boat's movement suddenly changed, warning her. Instinctively, Joanna leaned the tiller hard over towards the sail as the boom lifted dangerously, threatening to gybe violently onto the other side of the boat. 'Shit!' She hated sailing dead before the wind with this constant risk of gybing; once, on the Hebridean honeymoon trip, the boom of their modest little charter boat had slammed across with such violence that it detached itself from the mast. On *Shearwater*, it could easily break a wire stay and at worst bring the mast down.

'Shit!' She had come too far over; as she struggled to haul the helm back, a tall wave toppled the boat forward, snatching the rudder out of the water. A gust caught the mainsail and the boat's head pressed irresistibly round northwards in a terrifying, rolling broach. The rudder flailed for a moment helplessly in empty air and *Shearwater* leaned to port, gunwales under, water cascading into the cockpit and over Joanna's bare feet. Upright again, flapping, the boat hung as if suspended in time and space, waiting for orders.

'*Shit!*' With an effort, she pulled the boat's head round to point at Lulworth, further east than the distant root of Portland Bill but a safe course for the moment. The flogging sails quietened. Not easterly, that gust, more like south-east. Another veer. Things had changed quickly; but then, she had missed two shipping forecasts, midnight and dawn. Again, she made circles with her finger, plotting the way the winds blow anticlockwise round a depression. So it was – where? Moving across France?

With a sharp jab of self-knowledge, Joanna accepted that this academic theorizing was only a mechanism to stop her from telling herself the truth. This boat needed major attention, now. The mainsail, straining and dragging like a wild thing, threatening another broach every minute, would have to be reefed. Once wound down and reduced, the sail would be tamed, and no longer keep taking control. 'The time to reef,' Keith always quoted, 'is when you first think of it.' Joanna knew that Keith would have thought about it an hour ago. Now it would be harder than it would have been then; but it had to be done.

She would have to get some boots on, climb on the cabin top and reef. There was nobody else, and no choice. If she flew a whole mainsail much longer and the wind increased, the boat would become uncontrollable and something would get broken. 'Bugger!' she shouted, to give herself vigour. 'Bugger, bugger, bloody buggery wind!'

In Bonhurst, it blew Keith's jacket coldly open and lifted his thinning hair as he walked back from the Market Square towards the office. It was not an everyday summer wind. It felt nasty, a sharp little gale to mark the end of the warm days. It worried him, and wrapped him in his thoughts so that he did not see a dark young man with crumbs of Tropical Danish pastry on his jacket dart out from the ironmonger's doorway to accost him. 'Mr Gurney? If I could have a moment? Gordon Hawkings, I'm reporting the story of Mrs Gurney—'

'What?' Keith was on him, grabbing his arm. 'Has she been found? Is she OK?'

Gordon was wrongfooted. He took a moment to adjust from his vision of himself as one who sought news to Keith's conviction that he might be bringing it. 'Errm, not exactly. I was hoping we could have a quote, your point of view . . .'

Keith stared disbelievingly at Gordon. 'You're a reporter? Look, this is past a joke. My wife has gone for a sail, on her own boat, and you people fabricate some cock-and-bull—'

'With respect, Mr Gurney,' Gordon had got his composure back, 'you just asked me if she had been found and was OK. Presumably this means she is missing as far as you're concerned?'

'Certainly not. You jumped me, I had things on my mind. I'm a busy man. Good morning.' He turned away, up the step towards the Heron and Gurney brass plate and the sanctuary of his office.

Gordon felt his pocket for the reassuring whirr of the little tape and persisted, 'So you *are* able to contact Mrs Gurney? That's good, perhaps we could have a phone number, because my newspaper would like to offer—'

Keith swung round furiously. 'Look, do you know the first thing about boats? You can't bloody phone them! The whole point of going to sea is that pests like you can't ring up with a load of drivel. You don't break off in the middle of changing a sail or – or –' he looked at the racing clouds,' or shortening canvas in a gale just to answer the bloody phone!' He stepped into the front door of the office and slammed it shut.

Gordon, following the solicitor's glance, noticed the clouds and the wind whose significance he had up to that moment missed, and a beatific smile spread across his broad, handsome young face. For the first time it occurred to him that the annoying currents of air which were disarranging his hair, and the draughts he had suffered at the window table in the Bun in the Oven while pumping that blonde moron, were made of wind. Strong wind. That meant gales at sea. A tempest! Keith had escaped him, and appeared to have locked the door, but with only one more call he would have his story. All of it, all for him, unless that yellow-haired bitch had found the Gurney woman tucked up safe in some boat park and done a soupy girly interview. His brow furrowed, then cleared. Even if she was safe, not out in the gale thing, he had the worried husband, exclusive; plus the worried waitress and a couple of customers who said that Mrs Gurney was ever such a nice quiet lady. Now, with a bit of luck, he would get the best friend.

His back to the wind, Gordon flipped open his mobile phone – three weeks old, but it still felt pretty good, even if he had had to buy it himself – and punched in a number he had written on his wrist, courtesy of Erika.

'Mrs Heron? Amanda Heron? My name is Gordon Hawkings. I'm a journalist, passing through, and I'm terribly impressed by the Bun in the Oven, it's a really original, contemporary development of the traditional teashop idea. Is it right that you're the owner-manager?'

Possibly, he thought, he was laying it on a bit thick. But it seemed not. A series of ladylike squeals greeted his overture and acknowledged further compliments; finally the voice instructed him to come to an address in Market Street for a further audience and a bite of lunch. Gordon flipped open a small book he carried, dialled a number listed under 'PHOTO, agencies', and spoke briefly. Closing the telephone with a snap – it was, it really was, exactly like the *Star Trek* communicators of his boyhood TV idols – he headed up the road, more than pleased with his day so far.

Dinny Douglas, on the other hand, was having an appalling day. She had been frozen out by the police and grunted at by a noncommittal Ray Brewer who classified her instantly as a right little madam and would part with no information other than that the missing boat was blue. She had been laughed at gently by the coastguard service when she asked if any of their 'lookouts' had spotted the boat. There had been, they said, no lookouts in coastal huts since 1982. Had she been reading the *Famous Five* perhaps? She had met with outright derision from the eight marinas she had telephoned. It appeared that blue boats with sails were not scarce. Now, with her batteries running low, she had resorted to a malodorous telephone kiosk in Portsmouth in order to make a further appeal to the coastguard.

'Hi, Virginia Douglas here. I, er, rang earlier, about *Shearwater*.' She did not have much hope, but stiffened when she heard a small hesitation come into the voice which answered the enquiry. She had worked on that voice earlier with all the flattering, responsible sounding, woman-to-woman persuasiveness of her trade. It paid off.

'Oh – hold on – I spoke to you earlier, didn't I? We had a call ten minutes back. One moment.'

Holding her breath, Dinny traced circles with her neatly shod foot on the floor of the kiosk, holding the door open to dissipate the stifling smell of pee. The voice came back.

'Well, I maybe shouldn't tell you this, and it wasn't a distress call, I should emphasise that, but the old keeper went across to the Needles lighthouse this morning – it's automatic now, unmanned. But they had to take some photo or other for a magazine, and they went out with the magazine people in a fast motorboat. Anyway, they went out of the Needles Channel to do some pictures of the island from three or four miles south. And there *was* a blue yacht, out to the west. The old keeper rang in a few minutes ago, just to let us know, because they watched it for a bit and he wasn't sure it was all right. The sails were flogging, and there was quite a sea running, so they thought it might have problems. But the keeper says it could just have been having trouble reefing.'

The reporter wrote rapidly. 'Which way was it heading?'

'Well, they don't, do they? Boats, I mean. Not while they're doing things to the sails. They just sort of flap around. But they reckoned that when it settled down it was pointing towards Portland. West. Could be Poole, or Weymouth. Like I say, it's only a note we made. I'm not telling you this officially.'

Dinny stepped outside the box and considered, breathing deeply the clean air. Then she stepped back in to its smelly interior and rang a merchant bank in Leadenhall Street where a former boy friend worked.

'Jules? Dinny. Look, not much time,' she cut short his squawks of welcome. Annoying man he was, porky and self-important. 'Jules, sweetie, you go sailing, right? Tell me one thing. If you weren't very experienced and you were all by yourself and there was a lot of wind, would you go to Poole or Weymouth?'

Jules wanted to know where the wind was coming from. 'Oh, anywhere. You know, a gale sort of thing. But you're sailing west. Which would be the nicer harbour? For a woman, say, by herself.' She listened to the answer, wondered what a 'dodgy bar' might be in sailor speak and why a 'cross-tide' was a worry, but made her note accordingly. Then she adeptly brushed off his attempt to make a date and got back into her little car to find Weymouth on the map.

8

A hard wind behind you, pushing you along, disguises half its force. In a sailing boat, which seems to be borne up as well as along by the lift of the wind in the sails, it is easy to believe for a while in any rising wind that the force comes from the boat herself. She feels strong and proud and fast and commanding, as if she were flying like a bird and not, as is the truth, being blown along like a sheet of newspaper down a pavement.

The boat, of course, has more cunning than the newspaper. With the bite of her heavy keel and rudder and the aerodynamic trim of her sails, she exerts control. Her helmsman chooses her direction, down the wind or across it at a range of angles. But still, the boat or sailing ship is being blown. The wind is the prime mover. And the moment when the sailor best realizes this is when, to reef, he has to turn the boat's head into the wind and face its violence head on.

Joanna swung *Shearwater* round, hauling the mainsail in tight, lashing the tiller down and pulling the jib over to the other side so that the boat would heave to and cease its plunging forward motion. The full force of the east wind struck her like a blow. Her hair streamed back, her eyes closed involuntarily against it, and she gasped as her throat filled with blown spume. Opening her eyes again she saw several things that she knew she should have seen earlier: the whitecaps on the waves and the high, confused sea. Ten minutes ago she had been blithely riding it, not allowing herself to worry.

With sails secured, the boat lay relatively quiet, hove-to, prevented from sailing forward. It pitched up and down with a bearable seesaw motion and heeled away from the wind.

Bracing herself against the motion, Joanna pulled the hatch open and climbed into the cabin. She found boots, a harness, the winch handle for the lines which pulled the sail down onto the boom, and an oilskin jacket. Keith's. Her own hung next to it, but after a moment's hesitation she took his. Sticking the handle in her pocket, she clambered back out. She rolled up the jib until there was only a small triangle of steadying sail to hold the boat's head as near the wind as possible, then freed the wet clammy rope of the mainsheet from its jammer and gave it a few feet of slack to let the wind out of the big sail. This was always the worst moment, reefing; when everything first began to flog and shake and rattle uncontrolledly. Usually either she or Keith would hold the boat steady on the helm, sailing with the jib tight and the mainsail loose while the other clambered and hauled and fastened the big sail into its new, small shape. Their teamwork was automatic and unquestioning now; sometimes in the early years they had shouted at one another angrily, out of fright, but now such manoeuvres as this happened smoothly and without recrimination. Like an old-established double act of circus acrobats, they hardly noticed how good they were at co-operating and anticipating one another's moves on the deck.

Neither of them had ever had to reef *Shearwater* alone. The method Joanna was trying now was her best guess at the way to do it. She clipped the harness to the wire along the deck and began to creep forward, avoiding the murderous flogging of the boom. The noise, of rattling blocks and howling wind and whistling rigging, failed to drown her soft, deliberate, swearing.

Fifty miles NNE of Joanna, Keith was answering the telephone.

'Mr Gurney? Jane MacEvoy here, at St Angela's, sixth form centre. Susan has not arrived today, and has left no message. I hope there hasn't been any confusion. We do expect sixth-formers to register on induction day, you know.'

'I'm sorry,' said Keith who was at home, in the kitchen, padding around in yellow socks making himself a sandwich. The pub, with pink bouncing Gus, had proved an unbearable thought, and besides, Joanna might ring. He went back to the Old Vicarage because he had hopes of the answering machine, and wilder ones of Joanna being there in person, smiling sheepishly, arms outstretched to him.

Neither had materialized. Now he shifted, irritably, at the piercing authority of Mrs MacEvoy's tone. 'I thought Susan had gone in. She might be a bit late. She went to a rock concert in London last night, end of the holidays, celebration, sort of thing . . .'

'If she's missing, Mr Gurney, we ought to think of taking action.'

'No,' said Keith hastily, wincing at the associations this suggestion called up. 'She definitely came home.' He looked around at an African craftwork striped bag, a traffic cone with half a dozen signed messages on it in felt pen, a puffy pink jacket, and a pair of what appeared to be workmen's boots. These items were variously disposed around the kitchen floor; in the sink were two crescents of gnawed pizza crust, an apple core and a Diet Coke can. You always knew when Susan was home. 'I think she might be – I'll phone you back in a moment, if I may.' He put down the telephone and the piece of cheese he was clutching and crossed to the doorway, treading, as he did so, on a half-dead wasp. A stab of pain took his breath and it was hoarsely that he shouted 'Susan!' up the stairs. Through the hall window he could see branches moving, thrashing and bending in the wind. 'Su-san!'

Nobody answered. Keith climbed up the stairs, crossed the landing, and flung open the door of his daughter's room. Usually he knocked, according to the best modern principles of giving young adults respect, privacy and personal space. Now, on his painful foot, he limped right in. 'Susan, what the hell—'

Two heads rose from the tangle of bedclothes on his child's vast double bed. One bore the familiar striped, shaggy crop, blonde streaks on Joanna's black. The other, he noted with disfavour, was Anneliese's, with the all too familiar pixie features and sleek white-gold Nordic waterfall of hair. Susan yawned.

'S'all right, Dad, we've not gone lesbian. Stayed over with Annie's cousin near Waterloo. Jus' got in at nine, had a sleep. Where's Mum?'

'You are supposed to be at school. Mrs MacEvoy has been on the phone. This is the induction day for your sixth-form courses, and you are supposed to take it seriously. Anneliese, I'm surprised you haven't got anything better to do.'

'Annie isn't going back to Angela Merici. At all. She's going to the FE college. It doesn't start till Monday. If you'd let me go there, I'd be fine. School is lucky to have me.'

'Mrs MacEvoy—'

'Mrs Mac can wait. I'll be in tomorrow, won't I?'

The staccato truculence of his daughter was something, Keith felt, that he would never get used to. Lance had been argumentative and self-willed but had never thrown off such sharp, hot sparks of pure aggression. He was like his father and preferred not to fight. Susan seemed to thrive on it.

'Anyway, I asked you. Where's Mum? I need my sixth-form suit if I'm going to school.' She yawned again.

Keith had slept badly, made a fool of himself with the reporter, been needled by Mandy Heron, and trodden on a wasp. It was too much to expect him to notice that within his daughter's surly question could be heard, just, a perilous little wobble. *Where's Mum?* Or to reflect that she too might have hoped, on creeping into the silent house this morning, to find Joanna back. He erupted in fury.

'Mum has taken the boat to sea. The weather is not good; I have got a forecast and it is not one I would want to be out in. She may be in considerable danger. And you lie around in bed, dodging your responsibilities. Get up, get to school, and apologize to Mrs MacEvoy. Anneliese, you'd better go home. Your mother will be wondering where you are.'

He left the room where the two girls looked at one another, silent for a moment. Then, 'C'n I borrow your blue leggings, Suze?' asked Anneliese.

'Sure,' said her friend, and huddled back under the duvet. 'I'm not getting up yet.'

As Anneliese dressed, Susan curled gradually smaller under the covers and her thumb stole to her mouth. Anneliese paused by the door. 'D'you want to come round later? Have supper with us? Mum'll be cooking the fattened calf.'

'*Fatted*,' said a voice from under the duvet, whence only a tuft of blonde-and-black striped hair now showed. 'Yup, thanks. I don't want to be here.'

'We could work out,' said Anneliese, 'how you're going to tell your mum and dad about the big plan.'

'Yeah,' said Susan. 'Thanks, Annie. I'll be round.'

Anneliese slipped out, down the stairs, past the kitchen. Her father's partner, once 'Uncle Keef' to her when he did the playschool run, was eating a piece of cheese and staring out of the window. The first splatters of rain on the glass distorted the trees which swayed and thrashed in the chilly garden. She had been fond of Uncle Keef, even though he now seemed a creature from another era, probably Jurassic. Even worse than her stepfather, who at least wore jeans. She hesitated.

'Shall I ask Pops – Alex – to come round?' she said with rare diffidence.

'You could ask him,' said Keith without turning round, 'to go in to the office. I shan't be in this afternoon.'

'Okeydoke,' said Anneliese.

Standing by the mast, Joanna clung on with one hand against the bucking, rolling, senseless motion of the boat. She bent, undid the topping lift which would support the boom during the operation, and tightened it. Then she undid the main halyard and began to drag the sail downwards. The task was harder than she had ever known it. Gusts filled the sail and slapped it around, folds of harsh sailcloth skinned her knuckles and tore at her nails, and the boom, swinging out of control, crashed into her knees. Once, clawing for the sail with both hands, she slipped and struck her cheek hard against the cold metal curve of a winch. On her knees, she sobbed with the sudden pain and with fear. She could hit her head and die out here, alone on this bucking boat on the grey water, and nobody would know. But all the time she sobbed, she went on clawing and dragging until a good bight of sail was down and she could find the second big eyelet on the forward edge of the sail and manoeuvre it onto its hook to form a new, low tack at the corner of the sail.

Two hands again, one to hold out the hook, the other for the frantically kicking sail. Who said 'One hand for yourself and one for the ship'? What sort of ship had that many one-handed jobs? She balanced, one foot out behind, her knee bent, like a fencer.

At last the tack was down, the halyard tightened again. Stage one complete. Now all she had to do was select the return end of the deep-reefing line from the two which ran along the boom and out through blocks on its end, and use the small winch whose handle she had in her pocket to haul it in, bringing a bundle of redundant sail neatly onto the boom. Then make fast, tidy down the sail with its small cord reef-points, and get sailing again.

Fishing for the small brass reefing handle in her – Keith's – oilskin coat pocket, she inserted it into its hole and pulled at the reefing line. Her hand, she noticed detachedly, was shaking. The last time she had seen it shaking like that, like some object on a spring that did not properly belong to her, had been in the morgue, when Emily—

The boat, caught by a violent gust, staggered suddenly. A wave slapped hard against its leaning side, sending a thin, drenching salty shower ten feet above the deck. Behind her, a violent thump; as Joanna turned, startled, to see the forgotten white rubber fender dancing on the side deck, her foot slipped on the wet cabin top and she clutched the ropes along the boom for support. They gave, and she slithered down painfully onto the side deck, still clutching a festoon of rope. The small winch handle spun off, bounced on the side deck and somersaulted into the sea. Glancing towards the stern, Joanna saw the bitter ends of the reefing lines in the act of pulling through the blocks on the end of the boom, to flap uselessly over the stern.

Keith finished his piece of cheese, rang Mrs MacEvoy, and went slowly upstairs to Susan's room.

'Suze? You all right?' He no longer felt equal to the role of stern father.

'Yep,' said the duvet.

'Mum'll be all right, you know. Probably back for supper.'

'Yep.'

'I rang the MacEvoy, told her you'd had train problems and you'd be in tomorrow.'

'Yeah, OK. Thanks.'

He patted the foot of the bed in a small futile gesture its

occupant could not have felt, and went downstairs to where the silent telephone was.

Joanna, her dark hair flying in sticky salt strands around her eyes, was back in the cockpit. The loose reefing lines – or one of them – had to be threaded back through the block on the end of the boom, else the sail would not set. There was the alternative of taking it down completely and carrying on under jib, but without the full control which two sails gave, *Shearwater* would not go to windward. Suppose the wind veered further and drove her towards the shallows of Christchurch or Poole Bay? She had to be able to sail the boat efficiently. Besides, if she was in charge, alone, she wanted to be properly in charge. The bloody boat could learn who was boss. A new spirit crept into her. This was a fight, and fights could be won.

Sniffing, shivering slightly, she pegged the boom in tight, fixed the webbing line of her safety harness to the eye in the cockpit, picked up the dangling ropes and stood cautiously upright on the stern. The rolling was worse here, her hand shakier. After five minutes fiddling and threading, she crouched back, deathly sick, on the cockpit floor. The job was done. She dragged herself back, under the shaking boom, to kneel by the mast and haul the line tight. Without the winch-handle it took every ounce of her strength and made her palms raw.

When it was over, she came back to the cockpit, sat down, eased a little more jib out on its roller, and unlashed the tiller. The boat's head, pointing out to sea, was hauled round towards the dark snout of Portland again, the mainsheet eased, order restored, quietness and purpose recovered. Once again, although with half the frenzied energy of the morning, *Shearwater* tramped obediently westward.

9

Mandy Heron, Gordon decided, was pretty amazing for a teashop lady. Her ash-blonde bob and flat black pumps, the perfectly fitting white drill Bermudas, the pearl choker on her white neck, and the crisply upstanding shirt collar peeking from the expensive cotton sweater knitted with rosebuds – all these were the uniform of the provincial, upper-middle-class young matron. The look was familiar enough to him from his time on a local paper; plenty of women dressed like this had told him, in high, commanding, good-natured voices which always reminded him of Donald Duck, what to write about their charity do, or public school dance, or dinky interior design business called something like 'Suki's Stencils'.

But they were never sexy. They had an aseptic look, as if they washed too often, briskly, with a loofah. A chap never fantasised about leaving his fingerprints across their clean little tailored rumps or sliding a hand under their teddybear-patterned sweaters. They were bright and cheerful and self-assured and sexless. Whereas this one was seriously disturbing. He would be hard put to it to fault her Princess Di disguise, but disguise it clearly was. This woman was not, definitely not, what she dressed as. If the others were school prefects this was the school Bad Girl: grubby, wicked, and desirable. Not that she was grubby but . . . the way her breasts pushed out that sweater, the tilt of her hips as she led him into the house, the extra notch she had tightened her Gucci belt, the rounded babyish curve of her cheek and the Marilyn Monroe pout caused Gordon, who was still very young, to have some trouble with his breathing. He was glad that it was the draggled Erika, not Mandy Heron, who had served him his Tropical Danish earlier in the morning. He could not have choked it down otherwise.

As for Mandy Heron owning a teashop, that was another facer. He had visualized some cosy stout scone of a woman, bun-faced and greying at the temples. And Erika had told him she was married to a solicitor. That was equally improbable. This bimbo was never married to a lawyer unless – his thoughts were growing wilder – solicitors round here went in for black leather jeans and biker chains. She'd never let you out of bed, this one—

His thoughts were mercifully cut off by their arrival in a long, pale-gold, immaculately tidy living room. Anneliese was not allowed to spread teenage mess all over the house as Susan Gurney did. Her mother's domestic roots lay not in book-strewn intellectual Bohemia but in the cramped, fiercely guarded gentility of council estates. Nor did Mandy have the slightest wet-liberal compunction about slapping, threatening or shouting at children. Her house, therefore, was always tidy. There were two pale leather sofas in the room; on one, a handsome and prematurely grey-haired man of around forty was lying and dictating to a mousy secretary.

'. . . let me say again what a pleasure it has been comma over the years comma—'

'Alex,' said Mandy, 'leave that now. We've got a visitor. He's from the *Chronicle*, to write about the Bun in the Oven, isn't that fun?'

The silver-haired man sat up, feeling for his shoes with stockinged feet. His face, Gordon saw, was still young, creased with the lines of easy laughter, blue-eyed, relaxed and lazy. The flickering worry in those eyes now did not suit him. He did not have the look of a man who ever worried.

'Mandy, you are –' he said. 'Can I have a word? In private. Aimée, thanks, petal. You can get into the office now, Keith might need you.'

The secretary gathered up her things and left, with a curious glance at Gordon. The couple went through the end door, leaving the reporter to a lightning appraisal of the room. Money in evidence, fresh paint, over-ruched curtains – ritzy tastes but not a bottomless pit of money. Those leather sofas were not all they pretended to be. He moved cautiously towards the door they had gone through and was rewarded by a snatch of argument.

'. . . *obviously* about Joanna. Mandy, show him the door, it's not fair on Keith—'

'Alex, I shan't give anything away, and it's super publicity for the Bun, Jo will be thrilled, she's bound to be, it's good for business—'

Gordon leapt back hastily from the door as Mandy's voice grew nearer.

'– so anyway, Alex, I've said he can stay for lunch. OK?' Without waiting for an answer, Mandy reappeared alone, favouring Gordon with a naughty smile. 'Now. Drinkies? Kitchen's cosier.'

Alex met Anneliese in the hall as he was looking for his jacket. 'Annie, hello. Good concert?'

'Hi, Popsy,' said his stepdaughter, dumping a backpack. 'Yeah, triffic. We crashed out at Suzy's all morning. Her mum's vanished in the boat apparently.'

Alex, one arm trapped in the torn lining of his tweed jacket, stopped and looked at her.

'Annie, how much do you know? For sure? Joanna might just have gone sailing with someone down at that yacht club they go to. You can't believe the papers.'

'Well,' said Anneliese judicially, 'Uncle Keef came in, really wound up, and yelled at Sooze for not being in school, which she doesn't want to do anyway, she wants to come and do design with me at the college. Not my course, not fashion design, but magazine design. So anyway—'

She drew a breath and Alex, accustomed to having to prompt his womenfolk back to the point, patiently asked, 'What did Keith say?'

'He said,' Anneliese screwed up her pretty face, remembering, 'he said Joanna was in bad weather and considerable danger. So. That's what he said. And he said could you come into the office, because he wasn't going back.'

'Annie', said Alex seriously, 'I don't know what's going on, but your mother has got a bloody reporter for lunch, who pretends to be interested in the damn teashop. Will you do one thing? Just don't tell him what you just told me. Nothing about danger or Keith being worried. Please? Either Joanna really is in trouble and the press will make it worse for everyone, or she isn't and she'll be bloody livid. So *stumm*, OK? And if you could head your mother off saying anything, that would be—'

'Oh-oh-oh-oh no!' said Anneliese, shaking her blonde curtains of hair violently. *'Moi?* Come between Mum and newspaper stardom? With photo, *Hello Magazine* style, in Gracious Drawing Room? I would rather wrestle steaks off a man-eating tiger.'

'What photo? What d'you mean?'

'There's a smudger hanging around in a car out there, all the kit, big leather cases hanging off him, face like a baboon.'

Alex put on his jacket, tucked the ripped flap of lining up his left sleeve – Mandy was not a seamstress – grunted, and left the house. As he passed the open kitchen window he heard his wife's clear voice saying, '. . . absolutely my best friend. We started the business together when we were expecting. . .'

Joanna's teeth were chattering, but from cold rather than fright. *Shearwater* had settled now on her westerly course, and each rising sea behind her only lifted the stern, slid diagonally under it with a foaming hiss, and dropped her back harmlessly into the trough. The sailing was fast, but dry and controlled. The elastic cords on the tiller could hold the boat's head steady, for the moment. Thank God for a long old-fashioned keel and a balanced rig. Joanna watched the boat hold the course for five minutes before she decided it was safe to go below for a moment.

In the cabin, the motion seemed worse. She braced herself with her feet and rapidly pulled out from a locker a T-shirt, thick sweater, knitted hat, and dry towelling scarf. She stripped off to the waist, discarding a damp, salty bra without bothering to find another, and pulled on the dry clothes. Dry trousers could wait. She glanced up at the telltale compass set into the cabin roof: the course was still fine. She had looked after the boat; now she must look after herself.

She filled the kettle, lit the gas on the wildly swinging stove and clamped the kettle over it; put powdered soup into a mug and wedged that in the sink. No bread on board – they had thrown their last slice to the seagulls on the balmy sail home yesterday, which now seemed a month ago. There was a whole malt loaf, so she stuffed that in her oilskin pocket, together with the last nectarine.

A glance at the compass: still fine. The kettle whistled, and Jo poured the water onto the powder and noodles in the mug. A sickly, monosodium glutamate smell filled the cabin and seemed suddenly to be exactly what she had always dreamed of eating. With care she reached up to put the scalding liquid on the cockpit floor, praying no freak wave would make it slide and spill before she could climb out. Lastly, she took the portable long-wave radio, wrapping it in a rubbish sack against spray. A politician spoke, slightly muffled, through the grey plastic, promising a full inquiry about something or other.

Back on deck, all was the same. She almost did not hear the howling of the gale now, so familiar had it become. Seated by the tiller, only occasionally nudging it to correct the course, Joanna drank her soup, ate the whole malt loaf, and sucked at the squashy nectarine. She watched the seas rise and fall and hiss between her and the misty black shape of Portland Bill.

Normally, lunch would be a cup of the excellent filter coffee they sold at the Bun and a wholemeal ham salad bap from its menu. She would eat it in the small kitchen, listening for the 'ting!' of the door that announced a customer. Who was in that kitchen today? Erika would have been drafted in, no doubt, if that strict husband of hers agreed. She could hold the fort until the latest of Mandy's girls turned up to work the two-till-six shift. Joanna, biting consideringly into her malt loaf, hoped Erika would stay on to supervise young Zoë. She, Jo, had been doing just that for three months, since the comparatively reliable Donna had left. Zoë was not reliable. You could tell her what to do a dozen times – kindly, of course – and still she would not do it. So Joanna either stayed in the teashop or came back three times during the afternoon to check that all was well.

It never was. Once, Zoë had served a bowl of sea salt instead of sugar to a tired family off the motorway. Once, she locked herself out of the till. Once, she served cheese scones from the box which held yesterday's throw-outs, en route to a nearby piggery.

Sometimes, Jo wondered why she could not bring herself to

blame Mandy for these lamentable inroads into her free time. Mandy was meant to be in charge of the afternoons, not just to hire any passing moron and then turn her elegant back on the problem. She, Joanna, was unloading bakery orders at eight every morning; afternoons (and a share of lunch at busy seasons) were, immemorially, Mandy's responsibility. But all Mandy actually did now was to pay Zoë, or whichever girl was her current replacement. She did not even train them; indeed, so long was it since Mandy had served a customer herself that she probably would not know how to. No normal business partnership, and few normal friendships, would tolerate such an arrangement for two minutes, Jo knew. It was as if Keith or Alex were to stop solicitoring and put some halfwit articled clerk behind his desk and claim that this gave him the same rights as the remaining partner. It was nonsense.

Yet she had never complained. She was not remotely afraid of Mandy, nor of a quarrel – Mandy forgave quarrels in seconds. But somehow, whenever her friend had been selfish or otherwise appalling in their seventeen years' acquaintance, Jo had found herself oddly unmoved to protest. When Mandy dumped baby Anneliese on her for an hour and stayed out all night, she had coped, even breastfeeding Annie with her own Susan-milk. She had not even remonstrated, in the morning, when a hungover Mandy with marmalade hair in disarray had turned up demanding black coffee. When Mandy used to borrow her sweaters and give them back stretched and pizza-stained after shrieky nights out with the latest gang of lads, Jo merely washed them, without comment, and listened to the outrageous stories of how they got that way. When Mandy married Alex, the 'something blue' she wore was also something borrowed, Joanna's Janet Reger eggshell-blue silk teddy. It had not come back yet. Mandy got away with murder. She treated Joanna, Keith often thought, more as an indulgent mother than a friend.

Joanna did not see herself as a mother to Mandy. It was just, she reflected now, as if a voice always murmured at moments of exasperation, 'That's her, that's Mandy, that's the deal.' Mandy was a selfish, robust survivor. Someone who never needed to be worried about because she looked after herself. Mandy was

a sunflower who always turned her face to the bright lights and
the fun.

Joanna could never remember Mandy depressed or sheepish,
self-doubting or apologetic. When her Swedish sailor left her
pregnant, she called him every sort of bastard in the book but
greeted baby Anneliese with gleeful pride. She took earnest
young Joanna's proffered company and support as no less
than her due, although in the small-town society of Bonhurst
the friendship was widely seen as 'odd'. When the Social
Security caught on to some undeclared earnings, Mandy only
laughed and somehow came up with the £750 she owed in
record time.

Jo never liked to think of that 'somehow'. 'Oh, I sold some
stuff,' Mandy had said airily. But what, in her meagre flat,
could have been worth £750? Nor, Jo reflected, did anyone but
she know that the mysterious sale involved three nights away
in Portsmouth while Jo babysat. Keith *certainly* didn't know.
Nor Alex, God forbid. But Mandy, the debt paid, had laughed,
winked, and turned towards the sun again. She was good to
have around. If you were low, she goaded you until you, too,
looked towards the light.

That must be it, thought Jo. Mandy cheers me up. By rights I
should have spent those childrearing, school-gate years keeping
company and talking babycare with nice middle-class girls like
me, wives of teachers and solicitors and Waterloo commuters.
My friends should have been women who regarded themselves
as too grown-up to flirt, whose conversation was all of self-
improvement and their children's education, who went to
toddler groups and organized PTA coffee mornings and had
hushed discussions about Prozac. But none of them ever made
me laugh the way Mandy did.

Not since Emily. And Em had gone, into the darkness. With
Mandy, you knew she was not going anywhere – not unless there
was champagne on tap and plenty of admiring men with money.
Em was a jewel, but the nettles grew on her grave. Mandy was a
selfish tramp, with all the finer feelings of a rhino, but she was
still here. Still laughing, and making her friend laugh. Even if, as
years went by, the laughter Mandy provided seemed hollower,
and thinner, and less nourishing to the spirit.

Out in the grey, foam-flecked Channel, Jo pushed her drying hair back and looked at the horizon, feeling suddenly very alone. She glanced at the clock, and switched on the radio. Nearly five to two. Shipping forecast.

'Thames, Dover. East or south-east, 5 to 7, increasing gale force 8, possibly 9, later. Rain later, good. Wight, Portland, Plymouth. South-easterly gale 8, increasing 9, later decreasing southerly 4. Rain showers, Good.'

Behind *Shearwater*, the seas still rose, and hissed, and slid forward, throwing her into a rollercoaster motion. The sails, well reefed, pulled obediently towards the west. Joanna listened to the reports from coastal stations, noting that Portland was already reporting force 8. She looked around the glistening wet deck and up the mast. All was secure and in order, the boat running freely and not overstressed. All was as it should be, tight and seamanlike.

Except that she was alone, quite incompetent to face such weather, unfit for command, pathetic. Once, years before when she had just passed her driving test and bought an old car with the profits from the Bun, she had driven to London to the theatre with an old Oxford friend. On the way back, she stopped for petrol and the car would not start again, or even turn over. It was as if the independence and competence she had been enjoying all evening had been a thin veneer that had cracked apart to reveal her as the fibreboard sham she was. A skinny youth in a tattered vest, stopping by on his motorbike, had whipped up her bonnet and condescendingly screwed the terminal back onto her battery, and she had driven home chastened and humbled.

She was only twenty-two then; and since that time the protective cocoon of early marriage had maybe kept her soft, and glad to be soft. She had recognized something about herself that evening on the garage forecourt while the hard young man was rescuing her. She saw that whereas in her little business, or in her kitchen with baby Lance, or hand in hand with Keith, she was competent and even tough, there might be a world outside where she would not seem so. Joanna was prone to these sudden self-doubts; there was actually a kind of stoicism in the fact that nobody else knew about them. Mandy, who suffered no self-doubt whatsoever, would probably have howled in public anguish and broken down utterly if she felt as bad about herself as Joanna quite often, quite routinely, did.

Joanna, alone in the cockpit of her small boat in the gale, felt humiliation well up in her now. *Mum ahoy . . . runaway wife . . . unless she does anything else silly . . .* Keith had been right to report her like a runaway child. Abashed, disgraced, a silly woman out of place, she felt the slow sad tears of self-abasement trickling down her face.

But she continued, mechanically, to steer safely down the wind towards the blackness of Portland Bill. Her cold arm on the tiller would not give up. 'Emily gave up,' said a small voice out of the howling grey waters. 'Emily let go.' Joanna did not. Under her hand the boat moved on, serious and steady, through the unforgiving waves.

10

Keith heard the forecast at home, in the vicarage kitchen. Susan had slammed out, muttering about 'going round Annie's', a turn of phrase he normally deplored but this time did not notice. He sat, head in hands, coffee cooling in front of him, thinking.

The coastguard had a description of *Shearwater*, knew that she was short-handed, and roughly where she could be. There was nothing more to be done in that direction. It needed a red distress flare, a drifting boat, wreckage or a radio call for them to act. That, or a firm report that the boat was in the charge of a dangerously irresponsible or ill person. He forced himself to work out what could be happening.

If the telephone call had been from the Solent, Joanna could well be in shelter by now, after sailing off her bad temper. But if she had gone further west, carried on the tide and the pleasant northerly wind of the morning, this gale would have caught her in Poole Bay and be pushing her towards the shore. She might, in that case, have the sense to head back through the Needles Channel on a narrow reach – only she would have to reef the mainsail heavily to do that, and do it alone, without a steadying hand on the helm. Neither of them had ever done that. People did, of course, all the time; singlehanders crossed oceans. But they were exceptional, tough people.

Maybe she would be sheltering in Yarmouth – an easy entrance – or up the Lymington River. But she would have rung. Wouldn't she?

So – Keith frowned, and drank a mouthful of coffee – suppose she was further west, heading, say, for Weymouth or the naval harbour at Portland? She would still have to reef to be safe;

and would need to make a decision about her landfall. Another two hours of this gale would pile big seas up in that corner of coastline, to bounce back with confused violence in toppling glassy mountains. It would be dangerous for anyone without a powerful engine and precise local knowledge to close the coast. One mistake and a boat could be swept ashore. Even with a fair wind like this, a sailing yacht could lose control in a very rough, confused sea, the power stolen from its sails by the wind-shadow of the waves themselves. An approach to Weymouth would be dangerous, even with the engine's help; and the engine was very low on fuel. It must be, the way she had been gunning it out of Portsmouth harbour last night.

But Joanna knew all that, didn't she? His wife had always been full of sense at sea. More than once a brief cabin door or chart-table conference with her – even when she had an armful of babies, in the early days – had saved him from doing something silly.

'Mmm,' she would say. 'How many hours of tide did you reckon we had? Then won't it be against us on the bar?' Or 'If we change course now, we could be in Cherbourg in three hours, and we can still get to Alderney tomorrow if it's a false alarm about the fog.'

She used her head, all right, but the boat decisions had always been, in the end, his. Sometimes he thought it might have been different if Lance had not come so quickly. She would have taken over more, maybe sailed alone with her own friends on weekends when he had to work. He would not have opposed it; welcomed it, rather. He had never understood his men friends and clients who clung stubbornly to power within their marriages and only ceded responsibility to wives or grown children after a fight. Boats, he felt, and families too, were safer for having more than one confident, competent person in them.

No, she was capable. There was not one job aboard *Shearwater* that Joanna could not do as well as he did. She could steer, navigate, and handle the sails. She had sense. She might make the right decisions today.

Only, in this kind of case, with no easy shelter to hand, the most sensible and seamanlike decision is to stay at sea, overnight if necessary, running before the gale in open water. That would be safer than risking the lethal conflict of land and sea near the coast. All the yachting advice magazines, all the Royal Yachting Association instructors would tell you that. The only trouble was that not one ordinary yachtsman in ten would follow such advice. Every time the wind blew hard in the Channel, people risked almost anything to run for harbour. They pleaded weak crews, seasickness, children, even work deadlines. Sometimes they made it; sometimes they were rescued by the lifeboat; some even sent up distress flares from yachts which, with a bit of resolution, could well have stayed at sea and ridden out the gale.

Keith sat, turning an almost empty coffee cup in his hands. There was no need to think of lifeboats. Please God, no. Jo had sense. He wished they had not quarrelled. It was a stupid quarrel anyway. She could give up the Bun in the Oven tomorrow and they would manage. Sixteen years was, he saw now, a long time to be shackled to a teashop. Maybe it was a long time to be shackled to a provincial law practice – the memory of Mrs Repton's telephone call made him shudder, and then grimace and, briefly, laugh. Perhaps he could get out too. Do something else. School fees? Susan hated Angela Merici and Mrs MacEvoy's brisk rule. She didn't want to do A levels. Wanted to do one of the new vocational courses, Media and Publishing Design, at an FE college with poxy Anneliese doing her fashion diploma. Wanted to live in a bedsit near college and come home at weekends.

And why not? He, who had opposed all Susan's plans and lectured her on the importance of a sound academic base, suddenly wondered: why not? At least she had a plan. And it was stupid to compare her with Lance who had never had a report below A or A+ all his schooldays, had had three universities fighting over him, and finally accepted a major scholarship to Cambridge. Why shouldn't Suzie choose? He remembered the tuft of black-and-gold striped hair sticking out from under the duvet and a tug of tenderness made him draw in his breath, deeper than he had breathed since the moment on Ray Brewer's jetty.

Why not, why not? Why not let Jo sell up the Bun and shake the icing-sugar out of her life? Why not take his capital out of the partnership, sell the Old Vicarage, get rid of the damn furniture, pool the money and go sailing for a couple of years? Perhaps, his lawyerly caution prompted him, buying a cottage first so they had a base to come home to. Somewhere like Egg Terrace, their first home: three up, two down, kitchen out the back. Back to basics. Do a bit of freelance legal work, just enough to feed the two of them. Read books, go for walks, never, *ever* go to Rotarian functions in the chilly corn Exchange. They could let the children have what extra they needed to survive on the attenuated state grant; otherwise tell them to get holiday jobs. *Why not?* If only Jo came back safe . . .

Adrift on a sea of new possibilities, his sails shaking, his hand for once off the tiller, Keith sat at the kitchen table and slowly, deliberately, emptied his coffee dregs onto the scrubbed wood. Just to see what shape the puddle came out.

At the other end of the small town Mandy Heron and Gordon were getting along famously, halfway down a bottle of Australian Chardonnay and going well. He had his notebook out and, admiring remarks about her kitchen completed, was down to business. She sipped, and smiled roguishly, and basked in the young reporter's attention.

'Joanna – like I said, she's absolutely my best friend. We started the Bun in the Oven together, while we were still expecting. So of course I know her better than *anyone*.'

Mandy paused, and leaned forward, carefully keeping her shoulders back so that her sweatered breasts would fuddle the boy even further. She loved to fuddle young men. And old ones. She was entitled to her fun with this one, anyway. Mandy was no fool, and had known all along that Gordon was not remotely interested in giving his readers a thrilling insight into the marketing of two-cup pots of tea and the freshness of Eccles cakes. She read the *Chronicle* and its rival the *Globe* with great enjoyment every morning, sipping her black coffee in her streamlined kitchen, shivering with happy *schadenfreude* at the misfortunes of the famous. It was obvious to her from the start that Gordon's need was for 'colour' details about Joanna, the Sailaway Wife.

'Jo's more involved in the cafe now, of course. I'm more

executive these days, planning, policy sort of thing.' His pen, which had hovered hopefully at the mention of Jo, fell limp. Mandy sipped and smiled. The boy was really desperate for his story, bless him.

Her need, on the other hand, was for company and diversion in the dull middle part of the day. Mandy, if truth be told, was bored to screaming point. When asked – usually by Keith – why she no longer personally worked her afternoon shift in the Bun in the Oven, she generally talked about being busy and entertaining Alex's new business contacts and 'charity commitments' – at which Keith audibly snorted. Sometimes she even said, rather piously, that she 'liked to give young girls a chance of a job'. This enraged Keith even further by its suggestion that Joanna, by struggling with cake boxes early every morning, fixing the plug on the hot-water boiler and making egg sandwiches for bossy old ladies, not to mention propping up dopey Zoë all afternoon, was somehow inconsiderately depriving the new generation of work.

The truth was that Mandy hated the Bun in the Oven. It had been fun at first, a kind of dare. When Joanna had suggested it, over a cup of vile bottled coffee and a stale hot cross bun on the oilcloth of the High Street's only daytime restaurant, it had fired Mandy's imagination. She could see Jo now, hugely pregnant, as she was too; and hear her saying, 'Mandy, this is foul.'

'It is. It's like mud.'

'And we come here twice a week to drink it, and I'll be down even more when Lance is at playschool. And there'll be clinics and stuff when the new babies come. Why do we pay these people money to feed us this disgusting liquid mud?'

'Because,' Mandy had said, 'it's here or the WonderBurger, and that's worse coffee. And you can't get a pushchair in.'

That was when Joanna had put forward the big idea.

'Why don't we have a café? Let's rent the old charity shop. We'll rake it in. All the women like us will come. Keith'll lend us the money from his dad's legacy. Do him good to have a flutter. Oh, come on, Mandy. Remember Julius Caesar: "There is a tide in the affairs of men, which, taken at the flood, leads on to fortune."'

It was one of the nice things about Jo, thought Mandy fondly now, that she never adjusted her conversation or her quotations just because Mandy left school at sixteen – well, fifteen actually, what with the three months' suspension. All the other mothers in their primary school-gate circle did. They said things like 'Opera – a sort of play with music', or 'Washington – in America, you know', which drove Mandy mad. Joanna just chatted on as if she was with one of her old student friends, and if Mandy didn't understand a reference, she would say so. And Jo would explain or lend her a book. She had read *Anna Karenina* that way, and been to the Shakespeare Festival. Once, Mandy had thought of doing Open University, but that was before Alex appeared. Marrying Alex was a much more straightforward project for self-improvement.

Anyway, Mandy and Jo and the Bun had taken the tide and made a fortune. By their unexacting standards, anyway. Everyone came to the Bun: shoppers, mothers, chaps on their lunch hour who wanted to avoid the pub, people off the M3. They never did hot food except Welsh rarebit or toast, but the baps were well stuffed, the cakes varied, everything fresh; there was leaf tea and fresh ground coffee from the beginning.

'It's a good café,' Mandy said now, to Gordon, 'because even when we were broke, just starting out, we did really classy things.'

'You ran the café together, at first? I mean, you worked with Joanna?' asked Gordon, steeringly.

'Yes. That's right,' said Mandy. 'It was good fun.'

At first it had been fun. Like a rolling party, only with money coming in. Jo laughed at Mandy for her fierce delight in cashing up every night, seeing all that earned money in the till. She would run it through her fingers, gloating. 'Well, you don't understand. In our street, money was stuff that comes from the Social. From the Giro.' Mandy's mother had left her when she was five, shouting at her father that he could have the little bitch since he was the one who spoiled her. Her father had taken it hard, and alcoholically.

The Bun opened from eleven till four at first; the women would wheel the two babies down while Lance toddled furiously alongside on reins. Susan and Anneliese were both champion sleepers, and Lance reliably happy with a small red plastic table and chair in the roughly screened kitchen area, pouring sugar and glue and poster paint on brown paper and muttering stories to himself. The café developed a homely, kitchen atmosphere, and early mistakes were forgiven by a charmed clientèle. The Environmental Health Officer was benevolent (she had a family of her own) and gave notice of her rare inspections. The Bun in the Oven flourished as the children grew.

'Do you, er, own or rent the building?' asked Gordon, deciding to approach the subject of Joanna obliquely, despite a nagging sense of deadline.

'We own it now. Since ten years ago.' That had been the first big change, in 1985. The owners, a charitable trust falling into disrepute and dispersal, refused to renew the lease because they had to sell. There was no other High Street site available in those boom years – Christ, thought Mandy, today we could take our pick – and the asking price was exorbitant. Mandy would have been happy to get out – by that time marriage to Alex was starting to look like a real prospect – but Jo was stubborn. She approached the bank, got a loan agreed for half the asking price on the freehold, and went back to the trustees of the ailing charity with a deadpan, take-it-or-leave-it cash offer, insisting on a decision within twenty-four hours. The charity's trustees were desperate to realize their few assets and the gamble paid off. They got the Bun for a song.

It gave Mandy, in particular, a malicious pleasure to have scored such a victory over the Mary Magdalen Reforming Foundation for the Rehabilitation of Unmarried Mothers. But it was the last pleasure the Bun was to give her. With a loan to pay off they had to abandon the pleasing amateurishness of their short hours, hire schoolgirl help on busy Saturdays, and keep professional accounts. They still flourished, and Jo appeared to enjoy it. To Mandy it was a bore, and gradually, after her wedding to Alex, she withdrew her interest until she devised the scheme of replacing herself with waitresses. She knew it was unfair, but if Jo put up with it, more fool her.

Gordon, watching her, saw a quite incongruous flicker of guilt on Mrs Heron's lovely face. He pressed home the advantage.

'What sort of person is your partner, Mrs Gurney? I'm terribly disappointed to have missed her, but I gather she's on holiday.

I'd have liked to get your different, sort of complementary, perspectives on running the teashop so successfully. But perhaps you could give me an idea of what she's like?' He took a gulp of wine and waited with deceptive casualness.

Mandy leaned forward and put a warm, delicately manicured hand over Gordon's, causing him to choke momentarily on his drink and whang the top of his ballpoint with his suddenly tensed thumb. It rolled, a little red cylinder like a doll's house bomb, across the vinyl floor. They both watched it for a moment. Then, 'Sweetie, you are such a bullshitter. I do know why you're here, you know. You're only interested in Joanna because of the story about her running away to sea. Give me one good reason why I should help you.'

It was said with such affectionate, flirtatious mockery that Gordon could not immediately absorb the challenge. 'No – I – er – honestly, it isn't that—'

'Bollocks. Course it is.'

'Well, all right. I'm only doing my job. I do want to know about Mrs Gurney. But the teashop is part of the story, isn't it? Good for business. That restaurant which Janey Paterson ran is coining it in.' He had hardly finished saying it before he bit his tongue, horrified.

Mandy looked at him, consideringly. 'Janey Paterson was murdered and cut up and put in the left luggage at Reading bus station,' she said. 'Nice one, Gordon. That's just the way to interview the worried friend of the missing woman. Did you get it out of a book on how to be a reporter?'

Gordon rose, stiffly, gathering his newspaperman's dignity around him. 'I'm sorry to have troubled you. Thank you for your help.'

'Any time,' said Mandy. Deftly, she scooped up his notebook with Erika's quotes in it and slid it into the front pocket of her Bermudas. There was barely room; Gordon could not have got it out without committing a prima facie sexual assault, and he had noticed a slinky teenage daughter crossing the hall a few minutes back. Moreover, this damned woman was married to a solicitor. He was helpless. The headline 'REPORTER ON ASSAULT CHARGE – HE WAS LIKE AN ANIMAL, SAYS WOMAN' danced before his eyes. Mandy offered him a pussycat smile. 'Hang on a tick and I'll make you a sandwich to take with you.'

And she did. Gordon, who hated cheese sandwiches, waited obediently for it in the hope of getting his book back, but only the foil packet was pressed into his hand at the end of the humiliating minutes. Mandy reached across, slipped an apple into his pocket, straightened his tie, and patted him on the shoulder. 'Don't you worry about Joanna,' she said. 'She'll be back. She knows her way around. We're almost old enough to be your Mum.'

When he had gone, Anneliese sauntered into the kitchen. 'Who's the guy throwing packed lunches into the hedge?' she enquired.

'A *nice* boy,' said Mandy. 'Friend of mine from Fleet Street.' She liked the feeling of the boy's notebook, fresh from his inside jacket pocket, nestling on her thigh. A girl was entitled to take her fun where she could find it.

11

It was ten miles off Portland that Joanna made her decision. The humiliating panic of the shipping forecast had passed and she had steered on westward for close on two hours with the tears drying on her face, hardly thinking. *Shearwater* rolled, and strained, and groaned, sometimes dipping the end of her outstretched boom into the water in the wilder racing waters off St Alban's Head. The boat leaned towards the land with a force that made Joanna instinctively keep her course offshore, pointing almost at the tip of Portland Bill as they passed the lesser headland. The south-easterly wind was sending a train of waves along, north and west of the boat's track, pushing her inwards. In less than two hours, surfing along these waves, she could be tied up in Weymouth, phoning home, eating fish and chips – the sickness past, Joanna was ravenous now – and cadging a shower off one of the bed and breakfast landladies. By nightfall, she could be home. And dry.

'Fairytale,' said Joanna aloud. Then, to the wave train, 'Bugger you.' It was strange; if Keith had been aboard, the decision to give up the idea of Weymouth would have been discussed, and mildly dramatized. The unpleasantness of the inevitable conclusion would have been cushioned by conversation and the simple consolations of human agreement.

Keith: Jo – could we have a word?

Joanna (appearing through hatch): Yup?

* * *

Keith: I've been thinking – this sea's getting up a bit. It won't be very nice outside Weymouth.

Jo (thoughtfully): No. Bit like threading a needle at speed. That narrow entrance. I bet south-easterly gales throw waves right over that pier where the anglers sit.

Keith: I'm afraid I don't fancy it.

Jo: Could we go back to the Solent? I suppose not, with so much east in the wind, it'd take half the night. What about Portland?

Keith: They've closed it to pleasure boats, remember? Since the bomb. Anyway, you'd still have appalling seas bouncing off the breakwater.

Jo: Oh, shit. We could stand on round Portland Bill.

Keith: Jo, I think the sensible thing is to stand on.

Jo: Then what?

Keith: Well – it sort of means we have to keep going. If this blows through we could turn back. Or try and get into Bridport or somewhere. Otherwise, Torbay. It's a short gale anyway, they reckon. Probably be right down by morning.

Jo: Well, that's a night sail, then. I knew we should have got up for the early forecast.

Keith: I should have woken up.

Jo: No, I should have. Never mind. I'll get some food made. (Vanishes below).

None of this could happen. She was alone. Nor did the conversation need to unroll at all: it would have been mere comfort-talk, the habitual exchange of old sailing companions. It had been obvious to Joanna for at least an hour that Weymouth would be far too dangerous an approach in these seas. Especially for an undermanned, virtually engineless small yacht with an inexperienced skipper and with even stronger wind forecast as the afternoon went on. She and Keith would have played the game of discussing it, but neither of them would have been doing more than getting their own judgement reinforced. Unless one of them argued for the rash, tempting course of running in regardless.

Once, pregnant with Susan and with a tiny, seasick Lance, Jo had done just that on a difficult sail up-Channel from Plymouth. Keith had caved in to her earnest requests, and to save two hours plugging against the tide up to Dartmouth they had run in across the Salcombe bar, notoriously deadly in strong onshore winds. They got in safely, with a cockpit full of water, but the look they gave each other when they had silently moored the boat was a look full of death. Their deaths, Lance's unbearable, pathetic small death; the unborn child's unconscious death.

They were subdued all evening. There was activity to seaward, lights and engines and ragged ends of shouts, while they cooked their risotto and settled the baby. That night on the radio news they heard a solemn report of the loss of two racing yachtsmen, swept overboard when their harness buckles snapped – on Salcombe bar, half an hour after them. Joanna had crept across to Keith's bunk and lain there with him, cramped and warm and silent. Neither apologized aloud, but Joanna knew she should not have asked, and Keith that he should not have given in. She thought of that night now, after sixteen years of survival and family life, and said aloud, just for the comfort of it, 'OK, Keith. On we go. Take no risks.'

Her head turned towards the seaward end of Portland, ten degrees closer to the wind, *Shearwater* sailed better. Joanna fixed the elastic cord, watched it for a while, then, satisfied, swung herself down through the hatch. She lit the flame under the kettle to make some more powdered soup, then lit the little swinging oven and grovelled under the bunks for a packet of part-baked, vacuum-packed rolls she had remembered earlier during her moment's reverie about the Bun in the Oven and how faithful Erika would be coping. Yes! Under the tinned peas and the spare kettle. *Two* packets. And a tin of Spam. A night's provisions. She stabbed open the sealed packs and put all six rolls in the oven, setting the little timer to ring in eight minutes. The timer reminded her of Susan who had bought it to time her hair dye, grown too expert to need it, and left it in the kitchen fruit bowl for weeks. Jo had annexed it for the boat.

A glance up through the hatch showed the boat steady on course, and no other vessels in sight. Joanna went forward to the cramped heads compartment, used the lavatory, and while she sat there rummaged briefly in the first aid box, steadying herself against the boat's pounding. Caffeine tablets. She had taken them at Oxford to help her sit up until four with essays; she had bought these on impulse in a chemist's four years ago while she was renewing the boat's emergency kit. Keith disapproved. 'For night watches? We hardly ever sail long nights now. And when we do, we need to be able to sleep off watch.' Joanna had bought them all the same. She supposed that they were still in date: caffeine, surely, could not lose its potency? The yellow phial went into her oilskin pocket, together with the glucose tablets.

On the way back to the main hatch, she stopped by the chart table and pulled out Stanford's *English Channel, Western Section*. The great curve of Lyme Bay was familiar, its eastern edge bounded by the sweep of Chesil beach and the rising snout of Portland Bill, skirted with wavy little symbols marking the dangerous offshore tide race where two streams fight southward for ten hours in every twelve. She must keep a distance from the Portland Race: five miles to be safe.

North and west of the Bill, Chesil beach itself streamed away, eerily straight, without shelter, graveyard of ships throughout history. Small harbours were marked: Bridport, Lyme Regis, Exmouth, Teignmouth, none of them of the remotest use in an onshore gale. She knew that without checking: the curve of this bay, all sixty miles' width of it, would fill with roaring water tonight. The proper, sensible place to be was out on the diameter of its semicircle, up to twenty miles from land, heading south-west towards Start Point.

Assuming she rounded Portland at six or seven o'clock and steered for Start, and assuming the forecast was right about the gale's abating, she could then come up the bay a little and make it into Torbay at dawn.

Torbay bulged out, a pimple of sea on the smooth buttock of

Lyme Bay, a bite of blue taken out of the white land to the west. If the wind went south as forecast – 'Wight, Portland, Plymouth. South-easterly gale 8, increasing 9, later decreasing southerly 4. Rain showers, good' – Torbay would be fine shelter by then. Torquay lay to the north of the bay, Brixham to the south. It would be dawn by then. Easy to go in, look round for masts, find a marina. Or anchor again while she gathered her wits for a solo approach. If the forecast changed at six o'clock, or midnight, and the wind blew on from the south-east, she could run round Start Point and anchor in Bigbury Bay. Or, by noon tomorrow, make the infallible, all-weather, ultimate shelter of Plymouth.

Joanna stabbed each harbour on the chart, noted down some compass courses on the back of her hand with Biro, and climbed back on deck. Whereon the wind hit her like a hammer blow and made the whole plan seem preposterous. Sail to *Devon*? Alone? In a gale? All night?

Yes. Either that or give up. Either head for Devon, under control, or send up flares here and now and hope to heaven that someone would see them. The watcher on the shore would alert the coastguard, radio for a lifeboat. Soon she would feel strong male hands reaching out to her, wrapping her in blankets, comforting her. She would be in an ambulance, then fetched from hospital by Keith, taken back to Bonhurst, put to bed with a hot-water bottle . . . the possibilities danced for a moment in the cold spray from the bow.

But *Shearwater*, all around her, seemed to shudder in distaste. Old voices from her learning days came back to her, from the days when she had no babies and dreamed of lone voyages. They were the voices of bluff old explorer-sailors in their understatedly British memoirs, of maverick singlehanders like Blondie Hasler saying, 'Every herring should hang by its own tail', and refusing to carry a radio. There was the voice of a sailing instructor telling the boatload of scared trainees not to worry about the yacht riding big seas, but to feed themselves and work on their own strength because 'we're the amateurs, the boat's a professional'. They were the bar-wise voices of dismayed yacht club members after the Fastnet Race disaster, when crews took to liferafts and some of them died even though their yachts were found days later, still afloat.

No. You stuck with your boat. Propped in the hatchway, watching *Shearwater* steer herself through the seas, Joanna decided. No surrender, no silliness. She would try to get this decent little boat decently to harbour, and risk nothing. If she called a lifeboat it would be *in extremis*.

The alarm on the timer went off and she slid below again, cut off the master gas tap, poured her soup into a mug and took two hot rolls from the oven. Provisioned, she settled back into the cockpit, took off the elastic cords, glanced at the scribbles on her hand and set a course of 255 degrees compass, 250 degrees true. *Shearwater* leaned a little more and tore along, hurling up spray, crashing into the sides of waves, aiming well south of the smoky bulk of Portland.

By mid-afternoon, the Bun in the Oven was winding down for the day. Erika and Zoë were serving their last customers, a couple of middle-aged women with a weakness for Mississippi Mud Pie. They were strangers in town who chatted to Erika after she had sternly banished Zoë to the kitchen to clear up her latest disaster with the sugar bag and the milk.

'Yes,' Erika was saying. 'I try to keep it homely. It's my own business, you see. It's more like a child than a job, really. You have to love it, else there's no soul in a place, is there?'

It was a game she often played, undetected, on her weekends and Bank Holidays in charge. Except in emergencies like this, she could only work on those days. On weekdays her husband, Ted Merriam the ironmonger, required his lunch and tea cooked and on the table by 1.00 and 6.00 p.m., respectively, not a minute later. He also required that the house should be clean, laundry done, and shopping put away. He could not abide a woman fussing about with housework when a man came in to sit down of an evening. It wasn't right. A man's home, Ted often said, was his home. It came of being fifty, thought Erika. She was barely thirty, but the ironmonger's wooing had been too much for his newest, shyest girl assistant to resist, so there she was, married in the old obedient style of his generation and not hers.

However, on weekends and Bank holidays, rain or shine,

Ted Merriam and three invariable companions took a packed lunch and went fishing. The four men had been doing the same thing since they were twelve. And strangely, on these days he seemed to become younger. He did not mind a late supper, or a scratch supper, or a tumbled house, and was – to Erika – quite good enough company to console her for the rather outdated (prehistoric, she privately thought) household standards he demanded most of the time. On fishing evenings, she had even got away with calling him, to his face, the name she had long given him in secret: Fred Flintstone.

On such days Erika was happy. She alone ran the Bun, with its pleasure-seeking proprietresses nowhere in sight. Wiping down cake trays, straightening tables, presenting thirsty customers with perfect trays of tea and toast gave Erika Merriam a joy so deep and serious and vocational that sometimes, as now, the only outlet was in fluent, harmless, wishful lies.

'I do use girls from the town as waitresses, but it's not easy training them to do things right. I'm thinking of reorganizing the kitchen a little, perhaps involving Zoë more – she's not a stupid girl, I just think she needs proper training – and I'm hoping to start doing hot lunches. But you have to think of all the contingencies, don't you, when you're running your own business?'

The two ladies (crop-haired artistic types, on a buying tour for their own small craft shop in County Cork) agreed enthusiastically. It was as well, really, that Erika had not played her fantasy game on Gordon that morning. That really would have muddled his line of research.

On the train to Waterloo, Gordon was fuming with lonely rage. Bitch! *Bitch!* Bloody woman! Stringing him along, wasting his time, nicking his notebook and putting it in her – aah, *bitch!* The scent of Mandy, the bouncy curves of Mandy, the tanned cleavage of her, the warm hand on his arm, the outline of his notebook against her thigh were all too vividly with him. He was glad he had thrown away her cheese sandwich or he would be, he knew, sniffing and biting into it even now, for reasons unconnected with his stomach. Well, not too closely connected, anyway; four inches to the south of it was where he angrily ached just now.

Hateful bitch! Women were in any case the bane of Gordon's life. Pushy little cows like that Dinny Douglas, sleeping with the managing editor (so he wrongly assumed) to get straight onto Fleet Street without the humiliations of local council reporting. Power bitches setting up women's networks to stop men rising – as they always had and obviously should – to their properly dominant position in newspapers! Women columnists, like Maeve Mahoney, earning a hundred thousand a year for scoring cheap points off men, making generalizations no man would ever get past the most Neanderthal Fleet Street editor.

And now, a suburban bloody vamp who stole your notebook and dared you to get it back. In the pub, he had sometimes listened respectfully to the big boys, back in their safari jackets from El Salvador or Bosnia, telling how news films or tapes had been taken from them by murderous thugs. 'I didn't argue,' they would say. 'He had a Kalashnikov, and I'm a devout coward!' And they would laugh, and bask in their peers' admiration.

But how could he ever admit to having his ring-backed notebook confiscated by a blonde in an Alice band who subsequently straightened his tie and packed him off with a sandwich? 'I didn't argue, she had a tight sweater on and I'm a devout wimp.' He stared out moodily at the bending trees and thrashing branches of Surrey in the gale.

Never mind. The office would never know what happened. Nobody would. He had a bit of Keith on tape anyway – handy that, him being a lawyer. At least he couldn't complain about the actual quotes, and any spin that got put on them was up to Gordon. He remembered plenty from the Erika bint in the teashop. As for Mandy-bitch-Heron, she of the hips – Christ, the hips! – and the mocking pout, she would be quoted all right. And described. Oh yes! She would get a surprise package from Gordon in the morning. So would her poxy friend Joanna, and Maeve Mahoney and the housewives' choice rag *Globe*. And Dinny Douglas, rot her. Unless, of course, Dinny had found the woman. Hell!

He would have felt better if he had known that Dinny was even now standing disconsolately on the end of Weymouth pier, looking at a rough grey sea and wondering whether to go into yet another reeking telephone box and plead to be recalled to the office. He would have felt even better if he could have seen his editor listening to the PM headlines on Radio 4 about two lifeboat searches and one yacht fatality in the Western Channel and saying, above the chattering of the faxes and keyboards, 'God, that's it. "FOR THOSE IN PERIL – Gales Strike Unwary Sailors as summer goes out like a lion." Run it under the Chancellor on the front page. Then human stuff on page three – do an RNLI appeal box, stuff on hero lifeboatmen, but big pics of the dead guy. And hang on, there's another page in it. Alan! We can do "Fears For Those Still Missing at Sea". Where the fuck has Gordon got to with the missing housewife?'

12

Night fell. The low pressure deepened and ran towards Belgium, its fronts shrieking the last of their short fury over southern England. Alone in the Old Vicarage, Keith watched the nine o'clock news which led on the yacht death in the Channel. A small boat in mid-Channel had been knocked down, dismasted and holed by its own falling mast. The helicopter had picked up two of her three crew from the liferaft, but a man of twenty-seven had not been seen since the dismasting. Terse rescuers in survival suits gave the bones of the story; the survivors appeared briefly, teeth chattering, talking about the suddenness of the gale and the hugeness of the seas. Reading between the lines, Keith deduced inexperience and that they had been carrying full sail at the time of the knockdown. Poor sods. Jo would have reefed early. Wouldn't she? She was always in favour of it in their discussions. Cautious.

The news went on, talking of lifeboat services fully stretched and cars flooded by waves on the seaside promenades of the south coast.

It was dark outside. Keith shivered, turned off the television, and went to his desk, looking for some work, any work, in which to lose himself.

Alex and Mandy sprawled on their leather sofa, watching their huge television. Mandy, thinking of young Gordon's furious, unwilling submission to her whim of the afternoon, giggled delightedly as she edged up to Alex on the smooth cushion, letting her kimono fall open to show more lightly tanned flesh.

'Mmmm?' she enquired, planting a kiss on his ear. 'Mmmm, Panda?'

'Hang on, I'm watching this. Look, it's obviously nasty out at sea. Hope Jo Gurney's all right.'

'She will be. She's not stupid.' Mandy had never anticipated a calamity in her life. Not her mother's defection, not her father's drunken death, not her Swede's vanishing back to sea, not her own pregnancy. Her way was to expect everything to work out all right. Generally, it did. When it didn't, Mandy found a way to wriggle out of the worst results. Alex's theory was that this was because she had not used up all her energy worrying. He had always thought, watching the Middle East hostage wives on TV, that if he were in a cell in Beirut Mandy wouldn't worry. She would expect him back any day. It made him, strangely, more fond of her than ever. She was nuzzling him now.

'Mmmm? Panda? Cuddleup?'

'Baby. You never worry about anyone, do you?'

'She'll be all right. Mmmmm.'

'Would you worry about me if I was in a boat tonight? Out at sea, in a gale?'

'Nope.'

'What would you do?'

'Come and get you, in my lifeboatman's gear, if I happened to want you. For anything. Mmmmm. You'd fancy me in yellow oilskins, wouldn't you?'

'Mmmmm . . .'

'With nothing underneath . . . look . . .'

Alex gave up on the news and his vague plan to finish the office letters, in favour of an early bed. Much later, ungluing herself from his sleeping form, Mandy rolled lazily onto her front and felt, under the mattress, the shape of Gordon's notebook. Hazy memories of Bible study came to her, something about committing adultery in your mind being just as bad as doing it really. Just as *good*, she always thought. Mrs Amanda Heron dropped off, smilingly, to sleep.

In the windowless newsroom of the *Chronicle*, Gordon read his story in page proof. Magic. His name, black and solidly satisfying. The picture of the Gurney woman with her teashop award, fished from the local paper's archives by a diligent picture desk. She looked tragic, big-eyed, hopeless. Brilliant! He had pulled every heartstring, stuck in every knife, made the most of every quote. At this rate, he'd get a staff writer job on the paper, or better himself, go to the *Daily Mail*, before the year was out. And Dinny Douglas was still stuck in Weymouth, bleating to be brought home. Magic, magic, magic.

He walked up and down the long room, holding the page proof casually, his name outermost. The back bench subs, who had seen it all and knew that it would be chip wrappings by tomorrow, failed even to lift their heads.

In Tedneric, the neat villa where Ted Merriam returned grumpily on each work night and cheerfully on fishing days, Erika was recovering from an evening of damage limitation.

'Potato and corn fritters,' she had said brightly when he got in, breathing deeply. 'And gammon and peas. Oh, Ted, you do look tired. I thought it would be nice if you sat on the patio with a drink first, unwind a bit. It said in my magazine you ought to relax before you eat, or you get an ulcer.'

'What you mean is,' said Ted flatly, 'you haven't *made* the tea. You been working in that caff.' But he had sat, and had a beer, and stared out moodily across the playing fields to the river. What profited a man if he had the best run ironmongery in south Hampshire, but had to wait for his tea? Erika, sweaty from rushing home, had flung the fritters (stored in the freezer for just such moments) in the deep-fryer, put the gammon under the grill, and tipped a kettleful of water onto the peas. Now, laying the table, she chatted brightly through the patio doors.

'See, Ted, won't be a minute. I think it's nice, us both working on the High Street. You could've popped in for your dinner – I know we don't do it for customers, but if I took in a pan I could do you a fry-up easy. That pub's ever so crowded, and those pies have got BSE in—'

'She back tomorrow, then? Mrs Gurney?' Ted stumped in and sat heavily on the chair.

'Well, I don't think so. Ted . . .' Erika hesitated, pitching her appeal as best she could. 'Ted, I oughter help. I wouldn't care if it was just Mrs Heron, snotty cow, but Mr Gurney was ever so polite. He came out from his office to see I was all right.'

The big ironmonger ate in silence for a while. He respected Keith Gurney, and that wife of his seemed a decent girl.

'You could get home earlier,' he said at last. 'You could get that waitress of theirs to lock up.'

Erika thought hard. Yes. Not worth pushing further. Zoë could lock up. She could always ask Mrs Heron to go in and help her, last thing. Wouldn't chip her nail varnish just to check round. And it *was* her business.

'Course I could, lovey. Got you a lovely pudding today, anyway. It's called Mississippi Mud Pie. I think that's a disgusting name, isn't it? Funny, how people give nice puddings these horrible names. Like blommonge.'

She chattered on, soothing, and Ted Merriam relaxed and ate bland sweetness and thought calm, peaceable, fluent thoughts of reeds and rods and fish instead of spiky, hard, awkward, jangling thoughts of ironmongery. Erika smiled secretly, and thought of crisp paper napkins, eager customers, a jingling till and the warm smell of floury baps and soup. Wrapped in their separate paradises, the Merriams settled for the night.

Anneliese and Susan were stretched out on Annie's black duvet, full length, relaxed as young cats. Anneliese, with all her mother's happy insouciance, had made Susan turn to the sunlight again and feel silly about her dark forebodings. Susan knew that as soon as she was alone again, the dark bits would come back, curling up the edges of her thoughts like tattered, rotten bits of old carpet. She needed Anneliese to keep her mood smooth and flat and bright.

Dad never understood that. He just thought Annie was a frivolous little tart, you could tell. Mum understood. Well, she always calmed Dad down about it. Susan, fleetingly, found herself wondering whether Mum felt like that about Mandy. At sixteen, her mother's feelings were a dangerous, taboo area to Susan. Sometime, she knew, she would have to face up to thinking of her mother as a person, another woman. Not yet. For the moment she could remain a grotesque. Another mad old wrinkly, put there to thwart teenagers. She put her mother aside, to concentrate on talking to Annie.

Right now, they were talking about sex. Anneliese, Susan knew, had Done It. She, Susan, had not. Love did not, for the moment, come into it; they had both had bruised hearts the year before, and agreed to give up love for the moment. Annie's episodes of Doing It, anyway, had not been with the loved one. It had been with Andy Carson. And, Susan suspected, one or two of his mates. Details were never discussed between them but general principles were, endlessly.

'Mum says,' began Anneliese after a pause, twisting her bright hair, 'Mum says sex is no fun at our age. She says it's only fun when you grow up a bit.'

'She prob'ly says that to stop you doing it and getting AIDS.'

'Nope. She says I can have the pill, and condom money, and just be careful. But she says it won't be any fun because boys aren't much fun compared to men.'

'Why not?'

'Well, 's obvious, innit? All the books say the woman's got to have her, you know, satisfaction, and that takes longer. And boys are ever so quick. So you don't get the, you know. Orgasm.'

'It said in *my* book, and in sex education,' the two doubled up in embarrassed merriment at the memory of Mrs MacEvoy's sex education talks, 'that the man ought to make the woman have a, you know, satisfy her, even if it was after he'd finished.'

'Yeah,' said Anneliese. 'But the thing is,' here she took on an air of authority, as the pair tacitly admitted that they spoke not as equals but across the gulf of Susan's inexperience, 'by the time they're finished, you sort of might not feel like any more fiddling about. I mean, you know, wet rubber things, and him all red and his eyes screwed up.'

'You mean your mum might be right? It's no fun at our age?'

'Unless we find an older bloke, I suppose.'

'Puh-leeze! Yuk! Some old wrinkly, like in that Melvyn Bragg thing on telly, or Lolita, some bank manager—'

'And he'd get bossy—'

'Sort of like your dad, all heavy, serious—'

'Then they get old, and you'd still be keen, and they're past it.'

'Judy Hopgood had it with a bloke who was *forty*.'

'Where did he park his Zimmer frame?'

The pair shrieked with laughter and their conversation passed on to less absurd ideas.

Along the corridor from his scornful stepdaughter, Alex – forty-three and counting – slept with his arm round the wonderful flesh of Anneliese's mother.

And further along the little town, Keith Gurney thought of going upstairs but stayed at his desk instead, because he could not bear the bed's emptiness.

13

The light was slower to fade at sea. Reflections of the day seemed to be held in the heaving, white-streaked surfaces around the boat, beaten to pewter in the troubled evening light. Gleams of sun shone onto dark grey cloud, sometimes illuminating the mast and sails like a spotlit prop on a dark stage. The whole effect, Joanna thought, was stagey: the wind too self-consciously howling, the light too artificial. Even the occasional spatters of rain were too wet and too brief to be real – some stagehand must have thrown a bucketful of water from offstage. A panicking stagehand, late on cue.

Joanna laughed aloud. There had been a nasty, twisting hour in the fringes of the Portland Race, when the helm seemed to fight her and the sails heaved great despairing flaps in the troughs of the waves, but that was over. The fading light found her clear of the Race, well out into the great bay and sensing something else which strangely raised her spirits.

The swell grows longer west of Portland. The English Channel, from being a mean and pinched waterway funnelling from seventy miles wide to twenty-one at Dover, suddenly becomes a hundred miles wide, and its sea bed swoops deeper towards the Western Approaches. Almost free from its constricting corset of land, the sea begins to breathe again with the rhythm of the deep Atlantic rollers. The squabbling, sandy abrasive meanness of the eastern Channel chop gives way to the clean, long rhythms of the west.

Joanna had felt this change before, sailing with the family; but never had the peace, the pleasure and freedom of the deep sea entered her spirit as it did now, alone.

Darkness came. Hours of night lay ahead, forty miles to landfall and an uncertain destination. But she was happy. The boat was under control, the seas manageable. Portland Bill lighthouse flashed astern on a bearing – she picked up the small compass to check it – of 065 degrees magnetic. That was as it should be. *Alles in Ordnung*, as her old German teacher used to say.

She tied the helm and slid below to light the masthead lamp: one switch to light one bulb, showing green to starboard, red to port, white astern. To save power, she also lit the small paraffin lamp over the chart table. Its low shielded glow would not disturb her night vision and would do to check distances and lighthouses without using the brighter neon light. Oh, this boat, this familiar boat! She felt a surge of love for it, for its compact practicality, its orderly shippiness, its dutiful precision, its homely solid shelter against the storm.

She sat a moment in the moving pool of golden light, sharpening a pencil and marking *Shearwater*'s position line off Portland Bill. She estimated the distance by a glance at the log, and put the log reading – 19073.5 – with a neat naval triangle alongside her confident X on the chart. Thirty-two miles to Torbay, forty-five to Start Point and Salcombe, over sixty to Plymouth.

If Keith, or Mandy, or Alex could have seen her they would have been startled. There was a fit, calm decisiveness about the way she sat, one foot braced against the motion, hair pushed behind one ear, concentrating. Her air had nothing of the emollient, diffident or motherly in it. The way she looked now was at once very new and very old: Joanna had last looked like this when she was a student. Before Gabriel, and shattering ecstatic love; before Emily, and disaster.

A glance on deck: all well, flying westwards. She turned back, her dark form in the companionway suddenly irresolute, hesitant, anxious and feminine again, blurred by twenty years of compromises. The VHF radio telephone above the chart table was nagging her. Fair was fair.

Keith had been pig-headed and patriarchal, and failed to understand her cry of despair and her need to give up being a provincial teashop proprietress and be – something else, for God's sake. A student again; good God, she'd work part-time in someone else's teashop to finance it if necessary. Anything, anything to unbind her identity from that of fruit scones. He had not understood. He had reported her to the police and exposed her to being called silly on Radio 4.

But Keith did not deserve to be left wondering whether she was drowned. She, too, had heard the news about the dead yachtsman and the busy lifeboats, filtering out through the plastic bag wrapped round the cockpit radio. She ought to tell Keith where she was. And Susan ought to know. Funny, how little she had thought of her younger child today. It was as though Susan's course had veered away from hers months ago, off into a distant teenage land, so that they had to shout and signal to one another across a void. And today she could not be bothered to shout.

The link call was quick to get through. Twisting her hair nervously in her hand, moving her shoulders uneasily, Jo sat in the soft, lurching lamplight. Three rings, cosy sounds from another planet. Then the answering machine, saying that Keith and Joanna were unable to come to the telephone. A beep. Hesitantly, she spoke.

'It's Jo. Just to say I'm OK. Reefed the boat this morning. We had – I had to stand on round Portland for safety. I'll probably get in to Torquay or somewhere in the morning. The boat's fine. I think the wind's actually down a bit—' she glanced around, startled. The wind was indeed down a bit, but she had not realized that she knew this until she heard herself saying the words. It was odd, being alone. Perhaps nobody ever really knew anything consciously until they had the need to put it into words. 'So, should be fine. 'Bye. Talk to you tomorrow.' And flatly, uncertain again of everything, she climbed back on deck and stared ahead, into the darkness.

At his desk in the Old Vicarage, Keith slept on, his head pillowed on Underhill's *Law of Trust and Trustees*. He never heard the ringing telephone, nor the message, nor the beep. But something – 'I'm OK', or 'should be fine', or just the tone of his wife's voice – got into his dreams and quietened them. He slept on rather better until he woke with a start at one thirty, saw the winking light on the telephone, played back the message and went stiffly, gratefully, to bed.

By then, the presses had rolled and thundered under London and Manchester, spinning out long stretched skeins of paper bearing Gordon's half-truths and Maeve Mahoney's rantings. Vans in the livery of *Mail* and *Mirror*, *Globe* and *Chronicle* were screeching to a halt in wet empty streets, throwing out early bundles and speeding on.

Shearwater moved fast, too. At midnight, Joanna unrolled three inches more jib to keep the boat's speed up as the wind eased. At one o'clock, she clambered on deck in her harness, undid the deep reef with cold, stiff hands and hauled more sail up. The increase in power held the boat steady and fast through the darkness, across the rhythmic, twisting waves. To keep herself awake, she steered by hand, watching the compass. Two-seven-oh – two-six-oh – two-six-five. Mustn't sleep. Mustn't. *Nessun dorma*, none shall sleep. From *Turandot*, long before it was the 1990 World Cup song. That was better: something to think about.

Alice, almost the only friend from Oxford days Joanna still saw, had summoned her to London the year before for a night at the opera. Alice worked for the Royal Opera House and got occasional pairs of tickets; her husband Andy had decided dislikes, one of which, unaccountably to both women, was Puccini. 'You'd think,' said Alice, picking up Jo in her battered blue 2 CV at Waterloo, 'that a man who could sit through *Salome* could bring himself to come and see *Turandot*. But no. Says the Chinese references in the music are patronizing and tacky. Says Puccini is naff and speaks to the deep naffery of the British public, and should not be encouraged by taxpayers' money. But it's an ill wind—' Alice braked sharply and raised an unladylike finger at a taxi driver. '– It lets me have someone new to sit next to. I thought of our nights in the gods at the New Theatre in Oxford, weeping hot salt tears over Desdemona, not to mention yummy Welsh conductors with 1960s hairdos. Only you would do. I can't sit next to most people at the opera; they're either too clever or too stupid, or flap around with the sodding score. It's lovely to see you. And those who get to peep at rehearsals tell me this *Turandot* is *lush*.'

Jo was always absurdly shy and flattered when Alice remembered her. Alice had got her First, Alice had struck out across

Europe alone, come home and married the gloomily fascinating Andy, a junior don at Hertford College and later London University. Alice moved in chic intellectual circles, wore huge black glasses with panache, and drove her terrible car across London like a demon. Jo, beside her, felt the full inferiority of her provincialism, her teashop life and her scuffed heels. Only the subject of Lance's stupendous GCSEs – five As, three starred, three sciences and two languages – gave Jo any confidence. Alice, however, was unconscious of Jo's sense of inferiority and of her admiration, and rattled on all the way up to the Covent Garden balcony with the enthusiastic irreverence for grand opera which had made her a good companion years ago.

'Catharsis, that's why I can't resist it. Hardly costs more than primal scream therapy, and you don't get the sore throats 'cos Gwyneth Jones does the screaming for you. I love Turandot anyway, she's a sort of primitive Chinese-Italian Andrea Dworkin. All men are rapists, you know? That aria about how she'll never submit to one of the bastards, since her ancestress got ravished and murdered – that's probably why Andy won't come. And the set, they say you won't believe it – old Peking; severed heads everywhere, fab.'

On the boat, alone, Jo closed her eyes. She could see the *Turandot* set: Chinese balconies filling the stage, intricately latticed shutters so that patterns of light shone out from behind the central pagoda. The great cloudy moon rising, serenaded by the chorus; the pagoda where Calaf, the lover, sang *'Nessun dorma'* and the hackneyed World Cup song was made suddenly fresh again. She had sat rapt, shaken more deeply than the absurd and terrible fairytale deserved, thinking of the ruthless princess and her riddles. None shall sleep . . . 'within my heart my secret lies, and what my name is none shall know . . . a l'alba vincero!' Jo sang it, under her breath. 'At dawn I shall conquer!' The opera had stirred her as one sip of brandy stirs a teetotaller, dangerously. The death of Liu the slave girl, killing herself for love, made Jo shake; the closing chorus, echoing the *'Nessun dorma'*, made her weep.

To Alice, Jo's silent pallor at the end of each act was a source of not unkind amusement. 'Got you, hasn't it? How's Keith gonna keep you down on the farm now that you've seen Paree?' It was a game to her, a joke, Jo realized. Alice had never left Oxford, not really; she had gone on reading, seeing, responding to books and art and music with undergraduate passion and freshness. She and Andy, for ever broke, were for ever buying pictures with the poll-tax money and having to sell others; they thought nothing of piling their clever children on a sleeper to Venice or driving to Glasgow in their rattling car to check out the newly built Burrell gallery.

Alice had no idea of how estranged you could become from that world and those responses. She could not conceive of how commonsensical life was in Bonhurst, how prone you got to deadening everything with cups of tea and saving your empathetic tears for satellite TV reruns of *Random Harvest*.

Shaken, she even said to Alice as they left, 'I don't know, it was just that Liu reminded me of Emily.'

A shadow of puzzlement crossed Alice's face. 'Emily – oh. Yes. You were pretty close. Awful business.'

'It was why I never took finals,' Jo had said, amazed at her own broaching of the long taboo subject.

'Didn't you? God, I forgot. Amazing how little a degree matters, after all these years.' Alice breathed an exaggerated sigh. 'I don't know when anyone last asked me if I had one.'

Amazing how *much* it matters when you haven't got one, thought Joanna sourly, and suddenly the gloss and splendour was off the evening. She had thanked Alice, refused her pressing offer of a camp bed in their living room, gone home, slipped in with the sleeping Keith and lain awake – *Nessun dorma* – until it was daybreak, with no chance of conquering anything, or doing anything but chase Susan to school and open up the Bun in the Oven. And there was no mystery about her name. Mrs Gurney, that was who she was. Nice Mrs Gurney at the teashop. The solicitor's wife. With that clever son and that, er, interesting daughter.

The splendour was back now, though. The clearing sky showed stars, bright patches behind the scudding black cloud shapes, pinpoints of light like the lanterns behind the lattices of old Peking. She sang, odd words linked by humming: '*Nessun dorma ... O principessa ... a l'alba vincero! Vincero!*' At dawn I shall conquer. Calaf loomed, magnificent, but behind him Princess

Turandot even more magnificent and unmerciful. Poor Liu faded in the shadows, eternal victim of her own loving weakness. Icy strength like Turandot or doomed sweetness like Emily; no third choice for women, was there?

Did Alice say that? What cynicism. Of course there was a third choice. You could run a sodding teashop in sodding Bonhurst, and be a good mother . . .

Her own sleepy giggle woke her; that, and the flap of the unguided mainsail. Her hand had fallen off the tiller. The lights of old Peking resolved themselves into the cold, impersonal flashes of the Berry Head and Start Point lighthouses, both suddenly visible. Joanna stood up in the swaying cockpit, stretched, and reached for the caffeine tablets and her flask of tea. At dawn she would conquer Torquay.

14

The travelling depression which had brought the gales slid away with the night, to lose itself in Eastern Europe. Behind its bright sharp winds and splatters of rain came a universal grey mugginess. There was no dawn to speak of on that Wednesday, only a gradual lightening of the sky from charcoal to a dreary slate. The clammy air found its way inside Joanna's clothes and made her shiver crossly. At ten past six, looking up at the great wedding cake of the Imperial Hotel, Torquay, she rolled the jib and made a hasty, untidy stow of the mainsail.

Her feet slithered on the wet plastic of the deck. She was tired now, almost mindless as she did these familiar jobs. On the way back to the cockpit she hung out two fenders either side and fixed a mooring line to the centre cleat on each side, in case. The red and green lights on the ends of the Princess and Haldon piers were still alight at six thirty when, the pilot book open on the damp cockpit seats beside her, she steered the last few hundred yards towards Torquay harbour.

Above the harbour hung damp trees and the sleeping town, teetering on its rocky outcrops and peering round wooded crags. She saw the bridge, the crinkly red church tower, and the absurd pavilion flanked by green domes. The distant whine of a milk float and the sputtering of *Shearwater*'s engine were the only sounds to break the indifferent silence. The piers had fishing boats alongside and no crews stirring; the marina looked fairly well filled, mainly with vast powerboats registered in Jersey or Guernsey but a few masts of sailing boats tinkled metallically in the remains of the breeze. She smelt that weedy, fishy smell which land visitors think of as the smell of the sea but which to sailors is, unmistakably, the welcome smell of the shore. Gulls whirled overhead.

Tie up, tie up; she must moor the boat, somehow, anyhow, and lie down. On the outermost pontoon lay a towering, solid motor yacht, a classic gin palace, its davits and hanging dinghy arrogantly blocking her way through to the only visible vacant berth. Joanna steered slowly towards it, the port-side mooring line in her hand. As *Shearwater* came alongside, gliding in neutral, she left the helm, dashed forward, and with a clumsy lunge got her line round a solid cleat on the big white boat's stern. Stepping aboard its pristine deck, she moved forwards to brace her boat against the larger one by taking the line forward, round a gleaming chrome samson post, then back aboard the little yacht.

At rest, tied up. God knows who to. She killed the engine and, with a deep, shuddering breath, stood upright, pushed back her hair, and began the familiar task of putting proper lines out. Bow and stern, springs and shorelines, one by one they came out of the stern locker, neatly coiled in some other harbour. She worked mechanically and mindlessly, capable only of the obvious, unable to think more than a step ahead. Long ago she had fed and changed babies at dawn in just this state, her mind wiped clear by weariness.

As the distant church clock struck seven, *Shearwater* lay secure and quiet. There was still no movement aboard the flashy motor yacht; something about its bland curtained windows convinced Joanna that it was untenanted. Relieved, she swung below and kicked off her boots. Ignoring the frowsy chaos of the cabin, she blew the lamp out, drank the cold dregs of her dawn cocoa, and paid a brief visit to the heads to wipe the salt out of her skin with a cold damp flannel. There were not enough words for weary, she thought, slithering into the sleeping bag. Tired, fagged, knackered, done up; exhausted, prostrate, dead beat, swinked, whacked, jaded; dog-tired, bone-weary . . . no, never enough. Drawing her knees up, yawning helplessly, Joanna Gurney slid into oceans of unconsciousness.

Erika was the first to see the paper. Ted liked a cooked breakfast and needed to leave the house at eight. He took the *Globe*, for the fishing column and the investment pages. Her small luxury was to have the *Chronicle* delivered and to read it while she made the breakfast. Eyes widening with alarm, she read Gordon's prose with all the gratifyingly close attention he could have desired.

Startled back into reality by the acrid smell of burning bacon, Erika leapt distractedly to her feet and used a most uncharacteristic string of expletives. Ted Merriam, emerging with senatorial dignity and slicked-back hair from his morning ablutions, was shocked to find her standing there, blackened pan in hand, wisps of blonde hair over her face, cursing like a fishwife with the newspaper scattered all around her on the floor. It was not the way, he thought resentfully, that a man ought to have to start a working day. Grunting, he sat down at the table and picked up his pristine copy of the *Globe*.

Mandy came down half an hour later, leaving Alex singing 'Ol' Man River' in the shower. Anneliese was deep in the *Chronicle*, reading the fashion pages first as she always had since babyhood, and barely looked up. Mandy took the *Globe* and a glass of orange juice into her corner near the Aga, and turned, as several million other women did on Wednesdays, to Maeve Mahoney for a dose of amused exasperation.

RUM, MATRIMONY AND THE LASH: Men on boats, as every sea wife knows, are tyrants. No, hold that. Men are tyrants everywhere. So it was refreshing to hear of Mrs Joanna Gurney, the Portsmouth woman . . .

'Ooh, they might have checked!' Erika was saying to Ted at that moment, peering annoyingly over his shoulder. 'I thought they had to. She doesn't live in Portsmouth.'

. . . who finally cracked, and sailed off into the wide blue yonder with the family boat – but without her bossy lawyer husband Keith. I hope she finds the Yo-heave-ho more to her taste on the other side of the briny, and enjoys her break from living with Cap'n Bligh. Most of us just have to hack it, Ma'am – but we're behind you all the way. Why should the men get to wear the peaked hat and the parrot through life, while we girls swab the decks and – once they're sick of us –

get made to walk the plank when he fancies a second mate – or a third, or a fourth?

Mandy whistled, half delighted, half afraid, visualizing Keith's embarrassment and Alex's loyal rage. Still, Alex couldn't blame her for this one – different paper. But thank God she hadn't told that boy from the *Chronicle* anything he could make anything out of. She read on. Three hundred words of laboured nauticalia later, Maeve concluded, *'One thing is for certain – Mrs Gurney won't be wanting a husband in every port!'*

At this, reading over Ted's shoulder, Erika giggled. It was a brief, high, nervous giggle – she was still unhinged by the *Chronicle* report – but it had offended Ted who rose, gave her a reproachful look and stalked off majestically to work.

Mandy did not giggle but shook her head, then sipped her juice and let the newspaper lie for a moment unheeded.

Blinking feminists, always got it wrong. Keith wouldn't say boo to a goose. Just like Alex. These middle-class men were a doddle, in Mandy's expert view. Very biddable and quiet compared to the ones down her street when she was a kid, all pigeon racing and rough sex and cutting back your house-keeping. Middle-class men were easy. Alex was a saint around the house compared to the kind of lad she would have married if she hadn't luckily been up the duff and out of the running at nineteen. Keith was a woolly lamb compared to someone like Ted Merriam, who was practically Hitler as far as Erika was concerned. If Jo ran off on an impulse, it wasn't because Keith bullied her. Silly cow that Mavis what's-er-name must be.

For the first time, Mandy gave a moment to wondering quite seriously why Jo *had* done it. Mandy was not given to considering motives; people did what they did, and you dealt with it. Half the time she didn't know why she did things herself. That business with having the reporter round and teasing him, for instance. She had no idea what possessed her. Bit of fun, really. She supposed she must have just thought Jo ran off for a bit of fun. To shake things up a bit. She had used the 'depression' and the 'tablets' to tease Keith with, without thinking, but would she have even known if Jo was low? She hadn't seen so much of her lately.

Mandy twisted uneasily in her chair. Jo was a good mate. She had been the only one who ever bothered with her in the old days, before Mandy married Alex, sent Annie to Angela Merici, and was more or less accepted as a middle-class Bonhurst wife. Jo was like, well, a sister. A big sister. The sort that's more sensible than you but not always telling you off all the time. In the years after her mother had gone, small Mandy often used to imagine a big sister, someone to look out for her on the dodgy walk home from school, when the boys called names. She had never found one. Not until Jo.

So, was Joanna upset now about some stupid thing? She used to get low and worry too much about the kids, specially Susan. Mandy used to know automatically when Jo was feeling down because she let her hair go straggly. That was the cue for a coffee and – before they both gave up – a fag. And for a bit of inspirational stuff from Mandy concerning the next holiday or some gossip about the assumed sex lives of their neighbours or the latest hilarity about how Ted Merriam got waited on hand and foot by poor old Erika.

But there hadn't been much coffee and chat lately. The kids were grown up now, nothing to worry about. Susan was sixteen, for God's sake, like Anneliese, virtually another adult in Mandy's tough view of the world. Even if the Gurneys were planning to make her stay at school, in a uniform, Susan was of an age to look out for herself.

But if Joanna was in trouble then she, Mandy, ought to do something about it. She would do something about it. A brief flicker of guilt crossed her mind concerning the Bun, but Joanna seemed to like the old Bun. Enjoyed running it. Surely . . .

Mandy paused in her train of thought, looking down at the insolent tousled picture of Maeve Mahoney. *Did* Joanna like the Bun? Did she like her life? Did anyone know if anyone else really liked their life? The thought would not have tormented Mandy for long – thoughts rarely did – but its short duration was cut even shorter by a squeal from Anneliese who still had the *Chronicle*.

'Bloody hell, Mum, look at this!'

Together, they looked. All over the town, people were looking. Gordon had got his audience at last, hanging on his words. The big picture was of Joanna, cut from the award photo taken when the Chamber of Commerce had honoured the Bun in the Oven with a Councillor Tranter Memorial Plaque for Community Business. The plaque, however, was artfully cut from this picture and the word MISSING, in stencilled red capitals, was angled across the bottom. Joanna's eyes looked haunted, her smile uncertain, but then that was how you tended to look after listening to a speech from the chairman of the Bonhurst Chamber of Commerce.

Lesser pictures were dotted around in boxes and over it all was the headline 'THE MOTHER WHO RAN AWAY INTO THE STORM', and the deep-black, really quite gratifyingly thick lettering which said 'BY GORDON HAWKINGS'. Transfixed, Mandy and Anneliese read on.

> As death-dealing gales lashed the South Coast yesterday, one small town held its breath. In the dainty tea-shops of quaint old Bonhurst, there was only one topic of conversation. Was Joanna Gurney alive, or had the sea taken her? And what possessed a quiet, well-liked housewife who worked part-time in a teashop ('Oh, Gawd!' said Mandy) to leave her bewildered, innocent children ('Innocent? Lance? Hah!' said Anneliese, who had almost managed to seduce him at her fifteenth birthday party) and grieving husband, and deliberately to sail out into the Channel, alone and inexperienced, with a severe gale warning?
>
> What made her so desperate, so uncaring of her little children's pain? ('How old exactly does this plonker think they are?' said Anneliese.) What went wrong in this woman's marriage? people were asking. Why, in cosy middle England, was she so friendless? Were neighbourly doors closed to her agony? Why could she not care any more about her home, her husband, her little job?

'That's a bit dodgy, legally,' said the envious woman's editor of the *Globe*.

'No, it isn't,' said her deputy. 'He's only saying people were asking it. He never says it's a reasonable question, does he?'

'Mmmph. Still wouldn't fancy his chances at the Press Complaints Commission.'

> I walked the stricken streets of Bonhurst yesterday to find what

undercurrents in an ordinary decent English market town can lead a gentle, conventional solicitor's wife to take such a desperate flight into danger.

'Oh, Jesus!' said Mandy. 'Do you think she is all right?'

'She will be till she reads the rest,' said her daughter uncompassionately. 'Your bit, Mum.'

Mandy noticed her own picture for the first time, taken as she was opening the door to Gordon. The bastard photographer must have been behind the Leylandii hedge. She looked OK. A bit Bardot, with the wind blowing her hair forward.

'Mum, read it,' said Anneliese. 'Apart from anything else, Susan'll be down in a minute. Get your story sorted out. Or get packed and go to Katmandu. Or something.'

Mandy read on.

Perhaps the best clues to Joanna Gurney's torment come from Mandy Heron, proprietress of the chintzy, old-fashioned Bun in the Oven café which employed her. In her luxury home behind a screen of trees at the better end of town, Mrs Heron sighed and admitted that she was not surprised the struggling older woman had cut and run. 'We all get depressed,' she said. 'Life can seem meaningless at our age. It is very hard for a woman to accept ageing, and the menopause. She was once absolutely my best friend, but as the years go by . . .'

'How old,' asked Anneliese again, 'do they think you two actually are? And if they think that, how do they work out the bit about the innocent little children?' But Mandy was not listening. Stricken, she was reading, seeing herself in a distorting mirror.

Mrs Heron blames herself for not seeing how disturbed life had become for her former friend and waitress. 'I'm more executive these days,' she explained ruefully. 'Jo . . . well . . .' It is not hard to fill in the gaps. Mandy Heron, attractive and ruthless, the quintessential 1980s Essex Girl made good, flying high with her business interests; Joanna Gurney depressive and mousy, always in her friend's shadow, with her arms in the washing up, feeling at a dead end down at the dingy café they used to run together long ago.

* * *

It had been the 'dingy cafe' which had caused Erika to burn the bacon as she stood horrified at her kitchen counter. Mandy, whiter than her daughter had ever seen her, went on reading.

Erika Merriam, a neighbour who is running the café during Joanna's crisis, showed me the pathetic evidence of dead-end despair the lonely woman felt, dealing out scones to an uncaring clientele as she planned her last flight into the storm. 'A lot could be done with this place,' said Erika. 'But Mrs Gurney isn't very go-ahead. She won't have a microwave, though we could make a fortune doing baked potatoes, and she won't use teabags.' It was as if the missing woman had turned her back on the twentieth century, turned her face to the wall.

Outside in the street, solicitor Keith Gurney (another snatched picture, of Keith looking windswept and burdened with the carrier bags in which he transported his law books home since his briefcase was appropriated by Susan) *struggled home with food for his two anxious children, and scanned the sky. Pathetically, he grabbed my arm as I appeared, a professional man caught up in the nightmare for which none of us are prepared, the nightmare of a quiet wife's aberrant behaviour. 'Has she been found? Is she OK?' Sadly, I had no answer. A few moments later, his composure restored, the stricken husband explained more quietly that he knew what his desperate wife must be going through at sea, alone. 'Changing a sail, shortening canvas in a gale . . . you haven't time to think.'*

But for the watchers on the shore, time hung all too heavily yesterday as hour after hour, the news from the Channel grew grimmer.

Mandy put down the paper and stood up. Tears were running down her face, smudging the sooty mascara she always put on as soon as she got up. She pulled her sleeve across her eyes, making things worse. 'Alex,' she said. 'Get Alex. I never said a word of it. We've got to sue.'

Alex, summoned, read it rapidly and shook his head. 'Never get anywhere,' he said. 'Two, three years, endless time and money, all to prove you never said something that doesn't damage you anyway. Hopeless. Jo could sue for being called a dead-end waitress, but I bet she won't. The only one I'd take a flier on is Keith. He could have a case over the Captain Bligh piece.'

'But Jo's gonna think – oh God, Alex, help me, I'm really upset. I never thought – I mean I never said *anything* to the boy.'

'You had him in the house. Without witnesses, and with his notebook.'

'But – hey, I even took his notebook off him, that's how much I wasn't helping.'

'You did *what*?'

'I took it off him. He was fishing for stuff about Jo, pretending he was interested in the café, so I whipped it into my pocket. Confiscated it. Like at school.'

'And?'

'Well, I straightened his tie and made him a sandwich. Sort of like a little boy. He stood there, you could see he felt caught out. It was a bit of fun.' She clasped her fists to her brow and wailed, wordlessly.

'I suppose,' said Alex, frowning, 'he could make a case against you for assault and theft.' He looked at his wife with affectionate exasperation. 'Knowing your idea of a bit of fun, probably sexual harassment by innuendo as well. Drop it, Mandy. It's chip wrappings. It's up to Jo and Keith whether they go to the Press Complaints Commission.'

'And that's the other thing,' cried Mandy, now really upset, pretty face distorted, tears in her usually untroubled baby-blue eyes, pacing the kitchen more out of control than Alex had ever seen her. 'With the picture and all that suicide stuff and the wind – where *is* Joanna? Is she all right? She could be bloody drowning, and we all sit here—'

Alex's warning gesture came just too late. Behind her, framed in the doorway, was Susan. Mandy turned, aghast and tearstained. The girl looked at her, expressionless.

'Can I see the papers?' she asked. 'Please?'

15

Port Meadow spread around her. Underfoot it was spongy between the hard tussocks, the sleek grass wet from the summer rains. It was dark, and the death bells were ringing. Dully, she looked towards the door with the Chinese symbols, waiting for Gabriel.

But when the door swung open, there was nobody there except Lance, making too much noise with his big boy's feet as usual, and she said, 'Ssh! Lance! You'll wake Emily. She's been sailing all night, she needs her rest.' There was comfort in that: of course Emily was only asleep. She was tired. But Lance kept clumping – on the roof now – and tapping, so that it seemed Emily might wake and something terrible happen. He was shouting, too. 'Er, ahoy! I say! Anyone there?' Perhaps he was looking for Gabriel who was in the fuel can all the time, complaining about the smell of diesel. What else could you expect in a fuel can?

The tapping became more insistent, dragging Joanna up long inclines of sleep. It was real tapping now, on the main hatch. Through the cabin windows she could see deck shoes and nubbly expensive socks. Sitting up, sweaty and creased in her T-shirt, she hopped awkwardly towards the hatch like a contestant in a sack race, with her sleeping bag clutched round her waist. Holding it up with one hand, she pushed the hatch open with another and peered through a curtain of sticky, salty dark hair at an immaculate young man dressed as if for Henley Regatta in white duck trousers, a monogrammed blazer, white open shirt and butter-coloured hair cut in public-school style with short back and sides and a long forelock which curled over his eyes as he bent to peer into the gloom of the cabin.

'I say, I'm terribly sorry, my skipper asked me to check who was here.'

'I came in very early. What's the time now?'

'Ten to eleven. Gosh, it was windy out there last night. Did you come far?'

'From Portsmouth.'

'Gosh, rough, I should think. The thing is, he doesn't usually like people mooring alongside.'

'Well,' said Joanna, feeling her scattered sleepy wits gathering fiercely around her again. 'He shouldn't moor up bang in the fairway so that his davits stop other people getting through to the other visitors' berths.'

'Gosh, well, that was me actually. Skipper went off in a hurry on Monday night, big business deal, we were late because of the wind. Only he can't drive, so I had to moor up and drive him, and it was dark. I thought the marina bods would sort it out, actually. Thing is, I can't move the boat now because he's got a satellite conference call, and he might lose the signal, so—'

'You want me to move? You're going out now?'

'Well, if it's no trouble. We're not going out until tomorrow, bit of a do in the town tonight, speeches to local businessmen, then we're off to Plymouth in the morning, but he really doesn't like—'

'All the other big boats on the outside visitors' pontoons have boats rafted outside them. It's what everyone does when harbours are full. I bet if I ask the marina they'll tell me to stay here.'

'Yes, but—'

'I haven't got any diesel left anyway. And you're still blocking the way to the only empty berth. And you say you can't move because your boss is working on board. I've got shorelines out, I'm doing no harm to anyone, I've slept precisely three and a half hours, and I want a shower. I'll be gone before you are anyway. So, no. Sorry. Maybe later.' Joanna smiled to soften her refusal.

The young man, whose name was Guy Pastern-Hopkins, shifted uneasily. This personal secretary job had sounded so attractive, perfect for a new, third-class graduate: learning about big business, yachting every weekend, meeting models . . . Increasingly, though, the diplomatic demands of the role were wearing him down. His father, a bluff Cambridge veterinarian who thought the whole thing hilarious, said that he supposed Guy had been hired to be the acceptable face of Eddie McArthur but that, if so, it was as big a waste of money as putting a pink ribbon on a warthog. Sometimes, miserably, Guy thought that was not a bad description. He could have got a job as an MP's personal assistant, as several of his college friends had done. At least MPs had to *pretend* to be nice. His employer didn't.

'I don't normally say,' he attempted now, 'but my boss is actually Eddie McArthur'.

'Who?' Joanna was bluffing now. Even an intermittent, casual, provincial follower of the news knew who Eddie McArthur was. From frozen food to teenage fashion, from privatized railways to cable TV, he had interests in everything. He owned one newspaper outright – the *Chronicle* – and was rumoured to be surreptitiously collecting shares in two far more august titles. When Robert Maxwell died, Eddie McArthur bought great swathes of his empire (and, eerily, put on two stone in two months). He was reluctantly accepted by the establishment, and alternately bullied and flattered politicians. Sometimes he would fly them halfway round the world in his private jets only to insult them roundly on arrival. He gave parties of unspeakable lavishness and made only ten-minute appearances at them himself. He never gave interviews, but tales of his thin, nervy, cowed wife and sullen daughters filtered out into gossip columns from behind the electronic security gates of his mansion in Northamptonshire. Every financial journalist dreamed of finding the weak point in McArthur's armour, every young Fraud Squad officer of being the one to prove him a crook. But nobody had. He continued to kick his way through the establishment, to hire green graduate secretaries and drive them to nervous breakdowns, and to sate the sexual appetites thrown off by his intense, spinning egomaniacal energy.

Joanna was impressed. In the morning she had only focused on the mooring points of the big boat alongside, treating it as a wharf and seeing the rest as a vague irrelevant haze. Now she saw it whole: a great muscular wedge of a powerboat, forty feet long and almost as high with its flying bridge and forest of antennae. The name *Privateer* was gilded onto its stern, and she vaguely remembered reading that McArthur favoured a relatively small motor yacht so that he could come and go in yachting harbours without special arrangements. He had a number of coastal businesses. So this, she supposed, was the nearest any unconnected member of the public could get to the legendary tycoon: they lay only millimetres of fibreglass apart. She, in her battered family boat, was closer now than if they were neighbours in Egg Terrace.

An odd business, yachting. Some friends from Southampton had once found themselves anchored in a Scottish loch next to Princess Anne and Commander Tim Lawrence, and they had entangled their anchor buoy ropes and enjoyed an affable chat from their respective dinghies. On any weekend you might find yourself, an ordinary family boat, sandwiched between an evangelical prayer cruise full of chanting Dutchmen, a battered old fishing boat full of waterborne New Age travellers, a tycoon or two, and a TV personality having a weekend with someone else's wife. It was a very mixed society, boating. The thought had often cheered her up. But Eddie McArthur was something else again.

Guy was watching her. 'So, um, you see, there's the security aspect – there isn't anyone in the marina office, otherwise I'd—'

'Bollocks,' said Joanna. 'I'm not an assassin.' She felt a little light-headed, very hungry, and enjoyably stroppy. 'It's Mr McArthur's fault for being in the way. If he wants me to move he can come and ask me. And get out of the way to that empty berth. If he's a gentleman he might help me get some diesel.' She smiled at Guy, a smile which made him for a moment wistfully wish he was on her side, and blotted him out by firmly pushing the hatch shut.

Below decks, she dressed quickly in the same fetid clothes as yesterday, pulled out a clean cotton sweater and jeans from her bag, put them in a red canvas holdall and added a washbag, shampoo and towel and a pocketful of change for breakfast and the telephone. She hurried. If she was off the boat, they would hardly dare tow it away. Anyway, she doubted they had the manpower; she had read in some magazine – with much sexual innuendo – that in his summer tours McArthur whizzed around the coast with only a male secretary and the current mistress, finding his relaxation in driving his boat himself and summoning cleaners, caterers and the maintenance engineer to whatever harbour he was in by mobile telephone. If there had been crew, she reasoned, they would have been sent instead of the ineffective Guy. And they would have moored the boat properly in the first place. So battered blue *Shearwater* could lie alongside in peace for an hour or two. It would be a good story to tell Mandy. Mandy loved the idea of raunchy tycoons on big yachts. On the one occasion when the Gurneys had unsuccessfully taken her sailing, she had spent all her time at sea shivering in distaste in one corner of the cockpit, and in harbour had stared longingly at the biggest, most vulgar speedboats in sight. Mandy. The thought brought back home, Bonhurst High Street, Keith, the Bun in the Oven, Zoë, the milk to collect . . .

Joanna clambered out, putting it all from her mind like a puzzle too hard to solve. She locked the hatch and climbed across the extreme bow of *Privateer*, as politeness dictated, away from any accidental view into the cabins. Landing on the pontoon with a light bounce, she walked quickly up towards the office and the showers, her sea legs making her sway a little on the unmoving surface. Before anything, she must shower away the salt, the sweat, and the weariness. Then face the day. Ring Keith. Decide what to do. Somewhere, the reasonable and responsible part of her knew exactly what to do. Go home. But that part was shrinking and weakening. Other things in her were jostling for attention, and the sensation was odd, uncomfortable, but strangely exhilarating.

Keith, surrounded by newspapers, was in the office with Alex and a hovering, fascinated Gus. When traduced by newspapers, most lay people get over the shock by ringing their lawyers to say 'Sue the bastards!' The lawyer then bears the brunt of the hysterical complaining, and generally – if he or she is a calm, responsible, middling sort of lawyer – talks the traduced one out of it. Keith and Alex had no such outlet, being lawyers themselves. Made helpless by their own knowledge and caution, they raged.

In Alex's half of the cosy, untidy, dark-beamed office the two men sat together on chairs from which they had swept a muddle of documents. Alex, his customary languor kindled into animation, his greying hair ruffled above his square, handsome face, held the *Globe* in his fist as though he was planning to swat flies with it. Keith, his shirt untucked at the back, his tie lying at his feet like a discarded snakeskin, was resting his feet on the *Law of Tort* and staring at his wife's 'MISSING' picture in the *Chronicle*. The two men were communing more closely than they had at any time since Alex's announcement that he was leaving the practice to work for the Badstream Delauney property consortium.

Gus, who was pretending to tidy a shelf near the open door, thought that for the first time he could see how these two men had come to be partners in the first place. They had been at law school together, he knew, and gone straight into partnership – just like he and his fiancée Tiny meant to, one day – but for the past two years, since Alex started planning to sell out and work for Badstream, Gus had hardly ever seen them have a conversation that was not about work. They had gone all polite and formal. Now they were sitting together like friends. Keith looked ten years younger, far less stiff. Aimée, who had been equally agog in the doorway of her neat cubicle between the main offices, was unwillingly absent, having been despatched to the Bun for coffee and Danish pastries when Alex divined that Keith had not eaten since the failed cheese sandwich of Tuesday morning.

'It isn't the Captain Bligh stuff, I can take a joke,' Keith was saying.

'It's appalling,' said Alex warmly. 'Unfounded, mischievous extrapolation, no attempt made to speak to you, the whole thing based on a very skimpy agency report. At least a case for the Press Complaints Commission. You're *named*. And named as a solicitor.'

'No, it isn't that,' protested Keith, although in truth he felt warm towards his partner for caring. It took the burden of personal outrage off him and enabled him to concentrate on Gordon's contribution to public misinformation.

'It's Jo. She's being made out as a suicidal dead-end meno-pausal bad mother . . . Oh Jesus, Alex, what's she going to do? I started all this. Now the whole town's out there reading it.'

'She'll understand, I'm sure . . .'

'And Susan. Alex, I'm sorry you're landed with Susan. She rang up, you know. She says she won't come home, and she won't go to school. Said we'd made a mess of everything.'

'I know. Don't worry,' said Alex, who had heard Susan say a great deal more besides. 'She can stay with us. Give Mandy something to think about. I'm really sorry about Mandy. I saw the reporter, I should have thrown him out. But she swears she never said any of that. It didn't sound like her anyway.'

A silence followed. 'Yeah,' said Keith, only because it was growing into an awkward one. 'No, I'm sure she didn't.' He swivelled his chair a few degrees away from Alex and fiddled with a box of paperclips. There had been something a little too formal in his tone. Alex leaned forward and shaded his eyes with a hand, not looking at Keith either.

'Keith,' he said. 'I think she was crying. All these years, I've never seen Mandy cry.'

Still Keith said nothing.

Alex went on, 'I know you're not always so keen on Mandy, but she really, really is upset. She's genuinely very fond of Joanna. Keith . . .'

Gus, who had stood very still near the door, sidled out. With rare tact, he intercepted Aimée on the stairs and diverted her and the coffee into Keith's empty office. As he looked back, he saw the two men, both sitting as still as statues, not looking into one another's eyes.

The shower was hot and powerful, the relief of having clean hair and skin almost intoxicating. Joanna walked out into the quiet grey morning and smiled: at the spiky palms, the seagulls perched on the traffic lights, the pavilion and the seafront theatre. The moment was good. Moreover, in the marina office, the holiday-relief boy who took her berthing fee was not particularly interested in which boat she lay alongside. Displaying a smooth economy with the truth that rather surprised herself, Joanna had merely said that she was tied up to a motor yacht which was definitely not going out until morning; she had a hunch that if she said *Privateer* she would be forced to move immediately. Even the dumbest, most bored student temp would be afraid that annoying Eddie McArthur could lead to trouble. He might buy your boss's business and close it down out of sheer pique.

But she had got away with it. That, and the shower, and the deep inexpressible pleasure of landfall which still hung around her like incense made Joanna enter the telephone box in her clean warm clothes almost purring with contentment. All she wanted was breakfast and a quiet mindless browse through some undemanding newspaper; and that she would have, once she had let Keith know she was safe. That she must do. All these years of motherhood had taught her that the prime duty of the absent is to signal their safety, like satellites bleeping dutifully once per orbit.

Her heart, however, started to hammer as she dialled. She put the telephone down again, and rested her head against the cold glass. Hunger and apprehension suddenly made her dizzy and dispelled the cloud of euphoria. Since Monday's row, she had only spoken to the answering machine, twice. All she knew for certain was that Keith had somehow reported her defection to the authorities, in terms which made the review of the papers on Radio 4 speak of 'concern at her inexperience'. She had no idea in what spirit Keith had made his report. Concerned, or revengeful? Piqued and spiteful, or just untrusting of her 'inexperience'? One way meant he didn't think much of her behaviour, the other that he doubted her competence. Or sanity.

She knew Keith, had lived seventeen years beside him, borne his children. But now she could not call up his face or voice or anything about him other than his wronged husbandly status and the fact that he had gone to the police. Must have done. Unlike Mandy, who adored it, Joanna had always hated the word 'husband'. It stifled her. Keith himself was not stifling, far from it; but the word, the concept, was. Her mother had always said 'I must ask My Husband' in a voice of awful doom. Was she ringing an angry husband, a worried one, an uncomprehending one who thought she was going off her head? Would he, could he, somehow set in motion forces to capture her and counsel her, to wrap her in therapy and medicines and sit her in a room with a hissing gas fire as the college psychiatrist once did, years ago after the Port Meadow night? Well, if so, she wouldn't speak. That was her defence. Silence. Just like before. Say nothing, because nobody would understand.

Joanna's hand was damp on the receiver now. She wiped her hand on her cotton sweater and adjured herself to get a grip. She was not a troubled twenty-year old but a mother and business-woman pushing forty. Nobody could make her go to any doctor.

Maybe Keith would accept her flight as an aberration, hardly speak of it, and expect her to come home as if nothing had happened. Maybe they would sit down to supper tonight comfortably, go to bed after *News at Ten* and get up at seven thirty – checking the post hopefully for Lance's cryptic postcards – and make ready for another day. A day in the Bun, shopping on the way home; an evening's desultory chat in front of the television and a couple of small battles with Susan (must keep a united front, keep her nose down to work, get those A levels). And so to bed again, each reading on their own side, exchanging a friendly kiss before sleep.

Then there would be the Friday rush to get the café accounts done and Saturday orders ready for Erika; and down to the boat for a weekend pottering around the Solent creeks. Or a yacht club rally, with drinks on the biggest boat and a lot of chat about school fees and loose covers and how clever Edward and Hermione were to think of using a chicken brick in the boat oven, saves all that *mess*.

Maybe Keith expected, quite reasonably, that she would come back to all that with nothing changed at all. A settled, pushing-forty, middle-class, routine family life. The sort of life that if you were terminally ill, or unemployed and homeless, or bereaved, or a Middle East hostage would seem like a dream of comfort and freedom.

The kind of life that, from inside, could make you feel as if you *were* a hostage.

Only you couldn't complain or petition for release because you knew that in a dangerous and unfair world you were one of the lucky ones. So you worked your socks off collecting jumble and holding bazaars for Somalia and Bosnia, for Save the Children and cystic fibrosis research. And you still felt guilty. And even guiltier if, suddenly, seeing in the corner of some news film the spiky mountains of northern Iraq or the icy inlets of the Falklands, you forgot the sombre story you were meant to be concentrating on and longed to be on those distant mountains or frosty strands. Anywhere, as long as you could see the sun rise over new horizons and walk under a burden no heavier than the day's needs.

Then you would be overcome by shame and common sense, and blush from the neck of your warm Husky jacket to the roots of your discreetly streaked hair. Or, if you were really daring, you thought, 'Well, goodness, we do need a change, I wonder whether the holiday budget would stretch to a little adventure this year instead of dear old Benodet?' And then you qualified it: 'But of course the children do adore Brittany, and it's so good for their French, and the ferries are very reasonable, and the men love their golf . . .'

And you never changed a thing, in the end, but stayed on your rails. Mostly your husband carried on beside you; sometimes he didn't. Men seemed to have a lower tolerance of these decorous, dull provincial lives than women. They broke out regularly, even if they did rather lack imagination in the escape route they took, via the yellow brick road to bimboland. But with or without them, you the woman were always there: a rock, a pillar of the community.

Unless you suddenly blew a gasket, started shoplifting like Meriel Saunders, took to drink, got involved in a cult, or mutinously ran away to sea.

And then what became of you?

Not really wanting to know, Joanna at the third attempt managed with shaking fingers to dial Keith's office number, and put a pound in the box. Gus was in Keith's office, keeping out of the way, when the telephone rang. Motioning Aimée to her own desk, he picked it up. 'Oh, yes, great, Mrs G. I'll get him.' He put down the receiver carefully, as though it was made of glass, and walked past Aimée's hutch to the door of the office opposite. 'It's Mrs Gurney. For you,' he said. And Keith, without a word, stood up and walked stiffly through to his own office, closing the door behind him.

Joanna heard Keith's footsteps, moving across the boards of

the lobby outside Aimée's cubicle; the door closing; the footsteps soften and slow as he reached the carpet by the desk, and at last his breath.

'Jo? Joanna? Are you all right?'

'Yes, of course. I'm in Torquay. The marina. The wind's right down. Keith, I—'

'No, Jo, listen. Before anything else, I'm sorry. I wasn't sure what to do. I went to the police station. I should have gone to the coastguard, or just waited. Some little bastard of a reporter got told somehow. It just caught their eye, that's all. I'm sorry.'

Suffused with relief, hearing the old, boyish friend and confidant Keith instead of the looming problematical Husband of her fears, Joanna laughed and leaned back against the glass wall of the kiosk, grinning with relief. It was only Keith.

'Oh, Keith, don't worry. It's only a one-day wonder. I lost my rag, that's all. All we have to do is tell people the newspaper stuff was made up and that I was always supposed to take the boat to Torquay to get – I dunno, sea miles for the Yachtmaster certificate or something. They'll have forgotten it by now – it's only one day.'

There was a silence. Joanna looked out at the famous Torquay palm trees, gloomy against the grey sky. At last Keith spoke.

'You haven't seen the *Chronicle* and the *Globe*? Today's?'

'No. I just woke up, I'm only just about to have breakfast. Why?'

Keith's voice changed. 'Jo, I'm on my way. See you in Torquay. Two, three hours. OK?'

'I don't understand. The *Chronicle*?'

'No, no, I shouldn't have said anything. Stay put, I'm coming. Don't read them. I'll explain everything. I've talked it out with Alex.'

'Alex? What's Alex got to do with it?'

'Susan's staying with Anneliese. I've said she needn't go to school until the fuss has died down a bit.'

'Until what has? Keith, she was due back on Tuesday and you know how Mrs MacEvoy is.' The line bleeped.

'Yes, but – oh, Jo, look, we can't talk about this on the telephone. See you early afternoon. I'm leaving now, straightaway. And I do—'

She had not been watching the money tick away. Her pound ran out, and the line fuzzed and died. He had said, 'I do . . .' Do what? Do love you, miss you? Do wish you hadn't done it? Do need to be back tonight in time for the Law Society regional meeting? Do worry about asking Erika to hold the fort?

Slowly, Joanna walked out of the telephone box into the moist air and crossed the road to the newsagent next to the café on which she had set her sights. Within a minute she and her newspapers were safely installed in the window of the café, with a fried breakfast ordered.

Within three minutes she had moved to the very back of the café and a table invisible from the street, and was gazing disbelievingly at her own monochrome, haunted, 'MISSING' face. It was testimony to her hunger that, automatically and without tasting it, she ate her way through bacon, two fried eggs, a sausage, a round of black pudding and three triangles of leathery toast while she read. After the third time through the *Chronicle*'s account of her life and eagerly anticipated death at sea, she stood up, paid the waitress at the counter. She kept her head down and her hair hastily scraped back behind her ears to look as different from the photograph as possible. Burning with angry shame, she stepped out into the watery sunlight of noon and walked back down the pontoons to where, behind the absurd, towering bridge of *Privateer*, her *Shearwater*'s mast gleamed and rattled its halyards in the breeze.

16

Edward Warren McArthur was not in a good mood. His swoops around the coast were most satisfying when they were uninterrupted. Athough most of his time was spent in the usual ruck of haggling meetings with business-school suits and tiresome regulators, these maritime excursions enabled him to play the role he preferred, of old-fashioned merchant prince or Hollywood mogul. He loved to anchor in a bay, speed ashore in the launch, descend unexpectedly on one of his coastal companies, terrify the managers with his legendary black brows and vanish off to sea in a vapour trail of white foam.

To be penned by the gale into a public marina and then spend a scheduled, place-carded evening in the Imperial Hotel addressing West Country businessmen and councillors was a vexatious interruption to these pleasures. Since the West Country was his next target area, however, he needed to press a few hands extra hard in advance of some planning applications. His own staff would do the detail, but only a charismatic, almost archangelic descent by himself would have the necessary impact. He could already almost hear his own voice, booming out inane courtesies, insulting nobody for once, using his power to flirt instead of terrify. It bored him in advance.

Moreover, his latest mistress Thérèse, a sleek Parisienne, had refused to come back to Torquay late last night after a furious row over his insistence on sleeping aboard after his meeting in Exeter. 'Eddie, *je t'adore*,' she had said. 'But not zis boating. *C'est affreux*. And zese marinas are very *petit-bourgeois*, it is a horror. The rough water make me sick when you go slow, and bump when you go fast. I will stay wiz you in a hotel. Or you come and visit me. *Au revoir*.' He had kissed her hand with all the ironic gallantry at his command, but inwardly seethed with irritation.

Eddie liked women. Needed at least one in the bed every night. His liking was strictly limited: he didn't like them when they argued or cried, hated having to meet them in a business setting, couldn't abide the grating conversation of his squeaky wife and daughters. He just liked popsies. Even as he kissed Thérèse's white hand, he decided to return to the commercial sector. He would hire a girl for this trip. No, two girls. It was a long time since he had that sort of expert attention. To hell with style and class. Thérèse had those, and they only led to trouble.

The escort agency had been, as ever, complaisant when telephoned by Guy at 11 p.m., but even they could not get girls from London to Torquay instantaneously. So he had slept alone and badly. The energy Thérèse should have dissipated was still crackling and fizzing through his dreams until dawn; then he woke to find some scruffy blue sailing boat tied to the gleaming flanks of *Privateer*.

He had told the elegant but unsatisfactory Guy to get the thing moved, but the moron had come back saying that he couldn't unless he could move *Privateer* forward along the pontoon to make space for it to get by. 'Later,' snapped McArthur. 'I've got calls to make. If you can't moor up properly in the first place, I'm not having you fannying about while I'm busy.' Guy did not dare point out that he had had to make the big boat fast in the dark and the gale while being shouted at, and then drive his employer and the sulky Thérèse to Exeter through the driving rain. Nobody ever pointed out things like this to Eddie McArthur. Instead they merely rose, as he liked to put it, to his high standards, and learned from the experience. He was doing them a great favour by bullying them.

And what gratitude did he get? Emerging now onto his flying bridge after an hour's curt telephoning, he saw to his fury that the shabby blue boat was still there, with a chic, poised blonde girl sitting on its roof as if she was waiting for somebody. 'Hoy!' he bawled. 'You have to move that boat! Can't you read?' The girl was, indeed, only inches from the large red sign 'NO MOORING

ALONGSIDE' which Guy had rather belatedly remembered to put up.

'It's not my boat, I'm afraid,' said the girl, looking up at the squat figure in sunglasses and peaked hat without recognition. 'I'm waiting for the owner.' She looked past him. 'I think she's coming now.'

Eddie turned. There were three women coming down the pontoon: two girls side by side, who by their immaculate big-haired, tight-legginged presentation could only be deliveries from the escort agency. Ahead of them was an older woman, dark and striking in careless cotton clothes, who walked rapidly with her head down. She had just overtaken the sweating Guy, who was staggering under the combined weight of two mock-Gucci holdalls in one hand and a five-gallon can of diesel in the other. Brief satisfaction flickered across Eddie's face. Guy could stow the tarts below, then move the blue boat, then go away while he looked over the girls. Raising a hand and cocking a thick black eyebrow in a practised satanic smile, he called down to them, 'Ah! Good afternoon!'

They giggled and waved. The dark woman was now, to his fresh irritation, climbing across the bow of *Privateer* as if it was some ordinary yacht in the middle of a Bank Holiday trot of family boats. She was carrying the marina's coil of hose, so her progress was impeded as she unrolled it, the end squirting water across his deck. At last she stepped onto her own boat whose mast jerked and swayed as her weight came on the side deck. Still carrying the spurting hose, she stopped dead, staring at the blonde in the cockpit.

They made a striking contrast in female types. The dark woman was wild-haired, flushed, strong-looking, dressed in canvas and cotton; the blonde immaculately bobbed and disdainfully dainty, the concave curl of her hair at the sides artfully arranged to show her earrings. She was made-up, red-taloned, chic in leather trousers and a loose but elegant green jacket. The dishevelled woman did not seem pleased to see the other one. From his high bridge Eddie could hear only snatches of their conversation, but something made him stay.

'. . . Virginia Douglas, Dinny Douglas . . . the *Chronicle* . . . very interested in your story ... opportunity to put your side ... authorized to offer ...'

Eddie eased himself down the companionway steps as rapidly as his bulk would allow and slid open the window on the main wheelhouse deck below. This brought the conversation much closer. It was not every day that a proprietor got to eavesdrop on one of his own reporters at work. With a chequebook, too, by the sound of it. He was not very pleased with the *Chronicle* right now: too many libel payouts, slipping circulation, a general sense of demoralized freewheeling. The editor was a thug, which ordinarily would not have bothered Eddie in the slightest. He employed many thugs, although for his immediate entourage he preferred something a bit more Oxbridge, like Guy. The trouble was that he suspected this editor of being an incompetent thug. Why was this girl offering money to some tiresome yachtswoman, not even a pretty one?

The dark woman didn't seem co-operative. He craned to listen.

'... how you have the nerve ... pack of lies ... wouldn't talk to you lot for a million quid. Get off my boat. Go. Now! I mean it.'

'Mrs Gurney,' said Dinny, 'I do think you should reconsider. This is your chance to tell your story. If some errors have been printed, what better—'

'Go away.'

'It could help a lot of other women—'

Something moved, fast and shining, and there was a scream. Investigative chequebook journalism really works much better, thought Eddie with a chuckle of glee, if you first make sure your subject is not holding a running hose. The dark woman really did have an excellent aim and knew just where to put her finger over the nozzle to transform the tap's trickle into a thin, powerful stream. He watched as his distant employee first tried to fend off the water, then turned and ran, slipping, to the foredeck and swung herself across to *Privateer*. Careless of his territorial rights, the dark woman kept the water coming. Once or twice the blonde stopped, turned, and opened her mouth as if to remonstrate, but the cold water was playing on her face and she spluttered uselessly.

Eddie McArthur, thrice divorced, permanently angry, bored with toadies and intolerant of anyone who did not toady, had very few real pleasures any more. Sex was merely a need, business no more than an itch; the only times he really laughed were at private moments in his private cinema, watching slapstick. Chaplin, Laurel and Hardy, the Keystone Cops – these touched a depth in him that nothing else could reach. This furious woman with her hose, routing the chic spluttering journalist, made him laugh like that now, alone in his gleaming wheelhouse. He sat back on his pastel leather bench and his laughter rose high, cackling, whooping, choking.

Dinny Douglas heard it from the pontoon where she knelt doubled up, gasping and dripping and seeing for the first time with horror the name *Privateer* with its connotations of – oh God, oh God, oh proprietor, earthly god. Suppose he was on board? Gathering her soaking jacket around her, she fled up the pontoon.

Joanna, shocked at herself, reached mechanically to unscrew the top of her water tank and put the hose to its proper purpose. She heard the laughter as if from a long way off. Her hand was shaking. Perhaps she was mad, after all. Perhaps it was her own maniacal laughter she could hear.

Guy and the escort agency girls heard it from the cabin.

'Here,' said the younger of them nervously. 'He's not a loonie, is he?'

'No, no,' said Guy, hating his job even more than usual. The girl was very pretty, couldn't be older than his little sister, seventeen or eighteen, nothing like a tart. 'I'll mix you ladies a drink, and then we'll see about lunch.' He left them in the main saloon and went forward to the galley, his broad oarsman's shoulders in the blue blazer momentarily filling the narrow doorway.

'Nice, he is,' said the younger girl approvingly. 'I bags him, you can have the loonie.'

Her colleague, Marie, who had been on *Privateer* before, clucked in irritation at this naivety.

'He's the *staff*,' she said condescendingly. 'He doesn't get a sniff. No chance. You and me, Della, we are here to keep his Lordship happy. Both of us.'

Della stared at her, appalled. 'What, one after the other?'

'*No*,' said Marie, wishing the agency would not send out these new girls on special jobs. She normally went out on doubles, business doubles, with Inge, who knew her stuff. 'Together. You know. We do an act, fake it. He watches, takes pictures, joins in, or whatever he wants.'

'What, undressed? Wiv another woman? That's disgusting! I never done that!'

Guy came back with two brandy and gingers. Della appealed to him.

'She's having me on, in't she? She says we're both here for the boss, the bloke, Eddie? Three up? That's not right, is it?'

Guy squirmed, helpless. 'Well, he's very hospitable, and of course looking forward very much to seeing you both. I'm sure you'll have a super time.'

'Can I go on deck?' asked Della balefully. 'Think this one over?'

'I'll show you. This way,' said Guy. 'Got a small job to do myself.' He led her up the steps through the double door to the wide stern deck with its white leather chairs and awning. His diesel can stood incongruously on the floor.

'Just a sec.' He hefted it – nice muscly arms, thought Della, and ever so polite – and climbed over the rail to ease it down into Joanna's humbler cockpit. 'I say, *Shearwater* – I don't know your name – I brought you some diesel. Can I take that hose back for you, if you're finished? Then if you want a hand moving . . .'

Joanna, still numb but grateful for practical diversion, accepted his help with the hose, knelt to fill the diesel tank, and gave him back the empty jerrycan. 'Thanks. I will move. I may go out later anyway.'

'Are you all alone on that big boat?' asked Della. 'That's amazing. On holiday?'

'No,' said Joanna. 'I'm just – taking it somewhere.'

'I used to do yacht deliveries,' said Guy. 'That's how I met Mr McArthur, in the vac. He offered me a job as his secretary. I thought it'd be a terrific way to learn about business.'

'And is it?' asked Joanna politely.

'Funny business, more like,' said Della, less politely. 'Gets sent out to collect two of us girls at once, don't you, Guy, mate?'

'Delighted to meet you, Mrs Gurney,' said Eddie McArthur, reappearing on the stern deck with a folded-back copy of the *Chronicle* in his hand. He had fetched it from the pile Guy had dutifully put on board at dawn, because he was curious to know what the soaked reporter had been chasing. Since women had been running out on him with more or less violence and eccentricity ever since he was fourteen, sometimes cutting up his trousers, once setting fire to his car, he could not see much interest in one who merely sailed away. The story seemed to him feeble, gutless and overdramatized – all the things he most disliked about his newspaper. The thug would really have to go.

Meanwhile, there was this woman. He could bait her a little. Get her story. Phone the newsdesk, scoop his own staff, underline their incompetence, sack the thug. Eddie McArthur – who had actually, when he was up on the bridge laughing till the tears came, looked quite appealing, had anyone been there to see such a rare sight – now pasted on what he mistakenly thought to be an attractive smile and aimed it at her. 'A windy night you sailed through. Gave our readers quite a scare. Perhaps you would join us for lunch?'

Joanna felt the day running out of control. These things did not happen to her. She sailed decorously, with Keith and sometimes the children, had family evenings playing poker in the cabin and long bracing walks on cliffs. She was the kind of sea wife who met other nice couples on nice boats, and drank from wine boxes with them. The sea itself was the only adventure; otherwise, their sort of cruising was a homely pursuit. Why should it be that the mere absence of Keith plunged her into a chaotic world of storm survival, tabloid chases and hose attacks? Why was she suddenly involved with a Jilly Cooper cast of sultry call girls, demon-king tycoons and twits in blazers? Was there some magical quality in husbands that kept these things from happening to you?

Or was it just Torquay? Keith had always said that Torquay was too full of the ghosts of Edwardian swells and chorus girls for his liking, and give him Brixham any day, which at least smelt healthily of fishing nets. She should have gone to Brixham. She *would* go to Brixham. Right now.

'I'm sorry, I have to leave,' she said firmly. 'If you could throw me my shorelines, er, Guy?'

'Dear lady,' said Eddie, fiddling with his little black moustache and unconsciously strengthening her conviction that she had stumbled into a poor melodrama, 'you must at least do me the honour . . .'

Joanna could think of many things to say. She could have pointed out that this suddenly pressing host had been trying to get rid of her all morning, and none too politely; or that she did not feel equal to lunching with two overdressed girls, a caricature of an upper-class twit and a press baron, not in her diesel-stained canvas trousers. Or just that she had a need to go out to sea, alone, to think over certain problems related to the fact that his pet newspaper had just knocked askew her relationship with husband, best friend, teashop, neighbours, and self.

Instead, she said, 'No, I'm awfully sorry. I have to sail to – er – Brixham,' and took a shoreline from the obedient Guy. The other one could be slipped easily from the bow. She did that, then came back to the cockpit, started the engine, and began gathering in the other lines with the concentration of a child learning cat's cradle. She did not look up at the row of watchers: Marie interested, Eddie McArthur growing red in the face, Guy composing his face nervously into an expression which would neither breach his code of manners towards a lady nor enrage his employer; and next to him Della, with an unfathomable look on her face and a fierce grip on the rail.

'So, er, thanks. 'Bye, then,' said Joanna, bending to the gearstick and still not looking up. *Shearwater* edged forward, her fenders bumping against the big boat.

'Have a nice trip,' said Della, provokingly. 'Wish I was on *your* boat.'

Grateful for a direction in which to exercise unquestioned authority, McArthur turned on her. 'What do you mean, you stupid little whore?' he demanded. Della, quick as lightning, slapped his face, picked up her mock-Gucci holdall and threw a leg over the rail, her neat little foot groping for a moment then finding *Shearwater*'s moving deck. Joanna, preoccupied with turning the boat's bow outward, realized too late what was happening. As the stern of the smaller boat began to swing, just clearing the motor yacht, Della looked across the lifelines, full into Guy's astonished face. She ignored his open-mouthed, outraged employer and spoke to him directly.

'Pity,' she said. 'You could be such a nice boy.'

And Guy jumped.

Joanna, impeded by flailing flannelled legs and reaching hands, and rattled by the roar of fury from the master of *Privateer*, could see nothing for it but to kick the motor into full ahead and aim for the harbour mouth. Della thought she heard her say, under her breath, 'Things like this don't *happen*.'

17

Shearwater's engine was not accustomed to have sudden, strenuous demands made on it. Jo's action in kicking the lever to full ahead was met first with a sort of startled obedience, then with outraged sputters of rebellion as the elderly machine gasped for air. Joanna, her whole being focused on not getting stuck in the middle of Torquay harbour, drifting helplessly while a black-browed captain of industry shouted abuse at her, bent to ease back the throttle. She hit Della's pretty ankle rather hard as she did so, and not entirely by accident.

'Owww!' cried Della, lurching sideways onto Guy's strong arm. Finding that she liked it, she kept a tight hold of that limb. 'Oww, watch out!'

'Steady,' said Guy chivalrously. And to Joanna, 'The poor girl's had a bit of a shock.'

Joanna could think of so many cutting ripostes to this pair of preposterous cuckoos that she found herself unable to say anything except, 'Well, at least sit down out of my way. I take it you don't want to be dropped off on the pier?'

The question was hardly more than rhetorical. Aboard *Privateer*, Marie was now screaming like a steam whistle and Eddie McArthur could be seen waving something which looked startlingly like a gun. Marie, in fact, was rather enjoying her scream. Years of police raids had convinced her that if a girl can't get away, her best recourse in a crisis is to be noisily distraught while keeping an eye on the route to the fire exit. The screaming threw men – generally, after all, the source of danger or embarrassment – off their balance. Seeing Eddie (who she remembered as an unnervingly cold and peremptory client even by her standards) thrown so very far off his balance was exhilarating. Besides, it was perfectly obvious it wasn't a real gun. Marie screamed on, happily.

Eddie discharged the pistol into the air with a violent report. High overhead, a ball of red fire described a parabola through the air, and then another, and another. Aboard the churning, scrabbling *Shearwater*, Guy reassured the two women. 'Verey pistol. He keeps it instead of distress flares. I had to renew the licence last week. He's only trying to scare us.'

'He's not doing badly,' muttered Joanna. Looking back, she could see a marina official running down the pontoon towards the disturbance. Elderly boat owners were walking down from the Royal Torbay Yacht Club and looking curiously at the big motorboat, some with dawning recognition. 'D'you know, I think it's that chap, McArthur, the multi-million newspaper feller.' On balance, Torquay looked a pretty poor habitat for Guy and Della right now.

'Er, if you don't mind,' said Guy, 'we'll sail with you until we get, er, clear.'

Della nodded, shining-eyed. Having made her own bravura, world-changing gesture she was content for the moment to be led. This was adventure: a man on her arm, young and so devastatingly handsome and kind; an unknown destination, an angry pursuer. A year ago she had left a dull house in a dull road on the edges of Leicester, hoping for adventure. Without a GCSE to her name, without so much as the word-processing course her mother had wanted her to go on, London in recession had not proved to be paved with gold. Or adventures. So there had been men, and escort work – because she really did know how to behave and how to look, and whatever her mum said, it was a real talent, that. And escort work had turned into something that the red-taloned ladies in charge called 'Realistic, dear. Giving them value. It's a service.'

But it had not been adventure. Once, coming out of a West End club with a hick American weighing all of twenty stone and bragging ceaselessly about his big Thing, dirty bugger, Della had been sure she saw Prince Andrew. But so far, until now, that was it. This adventure was therefore overdue, even if it did seem a pity to have this rather cross lady to thank for it. She rubbed her ankle.

Joanna steered past the piers and felt the boat rise again to the swell outside, a deep unsettled movement of the waters left over from the easterly gale. The wind now was a steady northerly breeze, so she bent to unroll the jib. It unfurled with the usual crack and flap, its full spread making the boat jerk and heel slightly.

'Oooh! said Della. 'We sinking, or what?'

'No, little one,' said Guy soppily. 'You're quite safe,' and added, 'I'll look after you.'

Joanna killed the engine's clatter with a sharp tug on the wire and turned the key with a click. Heading south slowly, with just her jib, *Shearwater* lost her bustling mechanical nervousness and became again a sane, balanced, graceful thing, an environment in which to think clearly. The relief of being clear of the land was intense. Ahead, the sea was grey-green, the shape of Berry Head reaching out and diving to the sea, the sweep of Torbay's white beaches falling into picture-postcard loveliness as the buildings receded and melted into the landscape. It was a calm but living place, that boat moving across that water; a place for reflection, for lovers to talk quietly or troubled hearts to be alone.

'So, all right,' said Joanna after the three of them had had a moment to contemplate the peace of the bay and the engineless silence. 'What – where do you – where shall I drop you?'

Guy had not worked six miserable months for Eddie McArthur without becoming adept at diplomacy and the soft answer that turneth away wrath. Sitting in the corner of the cockpit, his hand on Della's thin white arm, he framed one now.

'Umm, the first thing is that I really – we both really – must apologize for imposing ourselves on you and intruding on your holiday—'

'It's not a holiday!' said Joanna, violently pushing back her flying hair which was, in its new clean softness, being blown all around her face by the following wind. 'If you really want to know, I'm the mutinous runaway wife in the newspapers.' The hair whipped her eyes and gave her a desperate look, witchy, slit-eyed, ragged black.

'I thought you was her,' said Della. 'Me and Marie read the

paper with that really sad picture they took. You're ever so much prettier, though. Would you like a bobble for that hair?' She fished in the pocket of her holdall and proffered, with candid seriousness, a short piece of Lurex elastic with plastic crystalline bobbles at each end.

Joanna, touched in spite of herself by the simple feminine observation of her need, accepted it and, holding the tiller between her knees, swept back her hair into a ponytail. Now only a few wisps blew forward, giving her the air of a schoolgirl fresh in from hockey. She smiled at Della who, seeing the witch face softened and transformed, smiled back. Guy ploughed on.

'We really don't have any right to impose on you but the thing is I've worked for Mr McArthur for nearly six months now, and I know what he can be like – terrifically talented, of course, I really sort of admire him – only I don't think that Della ought to go back. Not now she's hit him. He's quite short-tempered and very keen to get even with people.'

'He's a fat pervert,' said Della. 'You're not catching me back there. And I'm not going in any bed with Marie. She's a cow.'

'I should think not!' said Guy warmly. 'He has no right to ask—'

'It was you that booked us,' said Della, turning suddenly on him like a kitten in a fluffy rage. 'You must'a known.'

Guy took this like a professional. 'I wasn't expecting anyone like you,' he said, bending his head towards her in a way which made Joanna, fifteen years older, suddenly and sentimentally wish those years away.

'What d'you mean, like me?' fluttered Della.

'Young. Pretty. Nice. A girl like you – how did you get tangled up with an escort agency? When I saw you at Paignton station I knew it must be a mistake.'

'It's a long story. I'm not what you'd call full-time. I've got modelling offers and that.'

'I'm not surprised,' said Guy warmly, gazing into her wide blue eyes. 'You'd be a stunning model.'

'Oh, I dunno. But I'm def'nitely not doing any more escort work. I only been there a couple of months, filling in.'

Joanna, on the helm, looked at her uninvited passengers with helpless incredulity. She should be irritated by them, she thought, and probably would have been if she had been going anywhere with a firm plan in mind. But numbed by a long night, a short sleep and a rude awakening, she had been existing, ever since breakfast with those terrible newspapers, in an emotional void. Whole areas of normal reaction seemed to have closed down in her. All she could do was the next thing, the obvious thing. It had been obvious that the water tank needed filling, as they always filled it in marinas. A brief focusing of her rage had made it equally obvious that the newspaper girl – Binny? Ginny? – must be hosed from the deck. Once that was over she had gone back to filling the tank up blankly. The invitation from the black-browed demon king and the little melodrama on the motor yacht's deck had been only a pantomime in which she really, really did not want to go on stage with the other children. And as she escaped it, it had taken a few moments to realize that she had acquired two of the cast in the form of this young couple.

For a couple they were indeed becoming, before her very eyes. The pantomime had switched from Beauty and the Beast to Cinderella, with this handsome young rowing-blue clearly willing to play Prince Charming to a slightly shop-soiled Cinderella. And, bereft of normal responses, she could only look at them with a kind of bemused acceptance and wonder if she had to play the fairy godmother. On the whole she thought not. They couldn't be more than two or three years older than Lance and Susan, they were sitting in her cockpit like Lance and Susan, and yet she was not responsible for them.

There was something comforting about that. She had been responsible for the young for so long, so long; ever since she was young herself. There were babies who woke and fretted, toddling children who might drown or be snatched, who had fevers and tantrums. There had been schoolchildren with sadnesses and worries and toothache and lost games socks; then teenagers in revolt against everything that nurtured them. Oh, teenagers! Full of the life force they had drained out of you over the years, but using that force to scorn and batter you for your emptiness. Irrelevantly, she remembered Susan ranting at her about not wanting to go into the sixth form. No weapon had been too dirty for her daughter to use against her.

'What's the point? You got A levels, you went to university, and you end up serving scones to old bags in Bonhurst High street. I'm not going to end up like that!' It would have been easy to give in, to shrug – as Mandy did over Anneliese's woeful GCSE results – and say, 'Let them make their own way.' Joanna could not. Susan's future was her responsibility, like so much else. Have a baby, and the responsibility never left you; not at midnight in the throes of your own rare bouts of marital passion, not when you slept exhausted with 'flu and woke ill and unrefreshed with a day's work ahead. Always, always, you watched over them. And if you deserted them, as she was now deserting Susan (oh God, Keith on the A303, heading for Torquay!) you felt alien from your own self, ill and afraid.

But she was not responsible for these two. They could go to hell their own way. Listening to them was almost a balm.

'Mr McArthur isn't my career. It's been my first job, after Cambridge,' Guy was explaining to Della. 'Bit of a false start. I always meant to go into something to do with sport really.'

'You are clever, going to university,' said Della. 'Me, I couldn't even get GCSE.'

'You don't have to be so clever,' said Guy. 'You go to the right kind of school, they practically force you in. I got a pretty bad third. I mainly played rugger and rowed and played tennis.'

'I like a man to be fit,' said Della. 'Sporty. I love Wimbledon, that Agassi.'

'I bet you'd play a terrific game of tennis,' said Guy warmly.

'I never played,' said Della, and looked up at him, full face, sweet as a flower. Joanna had seen Anneliese do that to boys; Susan had never quite learnt it. She ducked her striped head and stammered, surly from caring too much. Poor Susan. Anneliese's way, Della's way, worked every time. Guy came in on cue, his broad, handsome face alight.

'Tell you what, when we're back in London I could teach you to play tennis.'

'That'd be really nice.'

'You could come to my club. It's in Maida Vale, and we could go for a Thai meal.'

No, thought Joanna, this is not even Cinderella. Babes in the

Wood, more like. She would be hopping around scattering leaves on them any minute.

Steering on across the bay, she realized that they were already a mile out and felt her situation painfully coming back into focus. You really could not meander off to sea with no destination. Not two days running, anyway.

'Where exactly,' she asked, 'were you thinking of going? Now, this afternoon.'

'Well, er, what would suit?' asked Guy politely. 'As I say, we are very aware that this is putting you to a lot of trouble. We'll just go along with your plans. Tide's running south for a bit – nice wind. I presume you're going this way.'

'Yes, I think so,' said Joanna. 'Certainly no point going up to Teignmouth, and I'm not ready to go back round Portland yet either. Not tonight.'

'Well, south then. Drop us off at – I mean you're spoilt for choice round here. Up the Dart, Salcombe, Brixham—'

'Not Brixham,' said Della beadily. They turned to her in astonishment. What did this urban sparrow, this painted, dainty little blonde geisha, know about West Country harbours? Guy and Joanna suddenly saw themselves in contrast to her: big-boned, healthy, middle-class, yachting hearties.

''Cos we *said* Brixham, in front of him,' she explained. 'Your loony boss. So he'll come and find us.'

Joanna privately doubted whether McArthur would do any such thing, but the idea seemed to throw both her passengers into a frenzy of insecurity. She had noticed this before in people who worked for tyrants: they became nervous and diminished and looked over their shoulders to the point of paranoia. Like the year before Alice got her Royal Opera House job, when she had worked for a television executive, a terrible black-bearded prima donna with a taste for humiliating his staff. Alice used to stay odd weekends with them and baby Lance at Egg Terrace. Joanna remembered how she was seemed always to be half expecting her boss to burst in and shout at her, even at breakfast. Alice jumped out of her skin once when his voice came on the *Today* programme defending the BBC against the government. Guy and Della had the same hunted look; they were both clearly convinced that Brixham spelt disaster.

'Well, gosh, you never know,' said Guy. 'He can run that boat himself. I was there for the donkey work but he's actually quite a seaman, I'll give him that. And it's very fast.'

Della, unfamiliar with such ready use of the old word seaman, looked momentarily startled.

Guy went on, 'But of course the main thing is we've really got to fit in with your plans. This is your boat and we weren't exactly invited.'

'I have no plans,' said Joanna again, heavily. 'I was going to go home. I think. My husband is – oh, God, he's actually on the way to Torquay. What's he going to do?' The vision of Keith arriving in Torquay to find her flown was too much. She began to falter. 'I was going to go home, probably, but I read the paper and . . .' Tears treacherously welled up in her eyes. 'I can't . . . decide. Oh, shit!'

She was really crying now, jolted out of the surreal mood which had kept her going since breakfast. She sobbed on, adrift on the embarrassment and absurdity of it all. *Shearwater* ceased to be any comfort; she was oblivious to the boat's glad purposeful progress over the swell, to the gleams of sun on the grey-green sweep of the coast and the lazy circling of gulls. Bowing her head, steering without thinking, she wept.

Guy was not good at many things apart from sport, but weeping women were his speciality. His younger sister had been prone to weep over everything from sick kittens to Bette Davis films, and he had long ago grasped the vital point that understanding why women weep is not necessary to comforting them. Unhesitatingly, he stood up and put an arm round Joanna, and took the tiller from her.

'Here, sit down. I think you were jolly brave, sailing in on a night like that, all on your own. You can't have had much sleep because I went and woke you up, and I bet those papers printed a pack of lies. It's – it's – a damn shame.'

Joanna, curled up sobbing in the corner of the cockpit with one cotton jumper sleeve across her eyes and nose, said something she was later to think extraordinary and significant. She could not have told her own mother, or husband, or doctor such a thing but to this strange young man and this absurd little bimbo she said, muffled, 'It's not the lies. Lies are just lies. They don't matter. It was the true bit. About having no friends, and being desperate.'

She genuinely had not known this until she said it, but realized instantly that it was so. Being described as a dead-end waitress or an abandoner of small children did not matter. It was froth and nonsense, part of the gaudy fiction of daily journalism. What had struck to the heart, even as her busy, justifying brain had fulminated against Gordon's inaccuracies, was his entirely accidental flare of truth. Her own truth, the secret emptiness.

She was a respected, happily married, competent, prosperous, responsible businesswoman, wife and mother with a circle of friends. But she was also alone and desperate and meaningless. Gabriel had known that when he threw her out. Must have. He had laughed at her in the dream for thinking she could die like Emily. Emily must have known it too and gone away into death without talking to her because she could not have helped. Now Gordon, who was a stranger, a cubbish reporter of no great gifts, and who had never even met her, had by some chance guessed right.

Partly right. He was wrong to hint at suicidal intentions. Joanna had not sailed suicidally into the storm. A long instinct born of sailing, a moral sense born of fundraising for the lifeboats would have prevented such a use of the sea or the boat. But the flight from Mr Brewer's quay, she knew now, had been an impulse from the same bitter root.

'I wasn't running away,' she said now. 'I was *throwing* myself away.'

'But you didn't,' said Guy. 'Because here you are, and jolly good luck for me and Della, and this is a really nice boat. And the sun's coming out. Would it be all right if I made us a cup of tea?'

Joanna looked up and saw the bay, and the curve of the jib, and Guy steering, and Della offering her a heavily scented and slightly grubby lace handkerchief.

'Yes,' she said. 'Yes, do. There's longlife milk. Then we'll work out what to do.'

18

By the side of the A303, north of Yeovil, Keith Gurney bent struggling over the Peugeot's rear offside wheel. Cars buzzed like angry hornets and lorries thundered past him: taking bananas from Southampton to Somerset for ripening, car parts on a roundabout route via Wales for inscrutable Japanese quality-control reasons, and deliveries of Taiwanese table decorations to corporate functions in Minehead and Exeter. Each one brought its own gust of diabolical wind, making his sandy hair stream out sideways, sharpening his face to gawky youthfulness as he crouched over the stiff wheel nuts. 'Hell, hell, hell!' he murmured.

Back in the picturesque premises of Heron and Gurney, Solicitors, Aimée and Gus were sharing Keith's uneaten Danish pastry and discussing the morning's epic developments. Not since Mrs Cothill's shoplifting charge had there been such stirring doings afoot in the middle-class sector of the small town. Women did, of course, go missing, fleeing back to their mothers or off with men. Husbands absconded from family and community life as often here as anywhere else. But a particular lustre was cast over the present crisis by the involvement of the national press, the swashbuckling manner of Mrs Gurney's going and her comfortable familiarity to customers of the Bun in the Oven.

Gus and Aimée knew that if they were to walk through the small, red-gabled, proudly dull little town they would hear the matter discussed everywhere. In the wool-shop queue where fussy pensioners tormented the assistant with demands for taupe-and-amber double-knitting fleck; in the fish shop; amid the trendy kitchen gewgaws and fretwork chicken friezes of

Cuisine It All; in Ted Merriam's ironmongery which stood
opposite the latter and glared at it from behind a fringe of no-
nonsense aluminium saucepans. And most especially it would
be discussed in the post office and the building society, where
resigned queues built up nine or ten deep behind the imperious
county ladies who drove their four-wheel-drive monsters in
from the outlying farmhouses for the Wednesday afternoon
bridge club meeting. The affair would be less avidly talked over,
perhaps, in the big outlying Pricedeal supermarket at the edge
of the council estate; but in the pretty town centre, there really
was no other topic. So Gus, and more especially Aimée, felt a
slight glow of pleasure in knowing that they knew more.

'Torquay, Mr Gurney said he was going to,' said Aimée after a
long analysis of just how worried Mr Gurney had looked when
he came off the phone. 'My mum had her honeymoon there.
Palm trees, she reckoned. Ever so romantic. D'you think he'll
bring her back tonight?'

'I suppose,' said Gus, 'they might want to sail the boat back.
That'd take a day or two.'

'Do you think she's, er, actually coming back?' asked Aimée.
'I mean, are they all right, those two?'

Gus suddenly felt his position as qualified lawyer and incipient
partner.

'Sure they are. Here, you take lunch now and I'll get a
sandwich later when Alex gets back.'

Aimée departed, wondering whether to do the wool shop or
the post office queue first with the news about Torquay.

Gus stood up, threw the rest of his pastry into the waste-paper
basket, and swivelled round on Aimée's office chair, fiddling
restlessly with her old Amstrad computer. He ought not to
gossip with the secretary. It was a terrible habit in a man of
law, as his father the Judge would no doubt tell him. Only
there was nobody else to gossip with, and it could be a lonely
life for a young man, underpaid in a provincial backwater run by
bossy old tabbies and pompous Rotarian duffers. Mrs Gurney was
different: younger in manner and outlook than any of the other
senior wives of the town, who were in his opinion a poisonous
pack of ex-head girls who went on and on about dog training and
sank alarmingly into middle age at thirty-five. You could have a

joke with Mrs Gurney. He had thoroughly enjoyed lodging at the Old Vicarage when he first came, before he got his own flat up the High Street. He had fond memories of evenings when he had not been able to bear another minute with Snell's *Equity* and had sneaked downstairs to watch *Bonanza* on satellite TV with Susan; or played Scrabble with Mrs Gurney and Lance (no chance of beating Lance) while Keith worked at his desk.

Mrs Gurney was really clever. Shouldn't be in that boring tearoom. He had hinted as much once while they washed up after a dinner party a year ago. He was meant to be guest of honour, having just announced his engagement to Tiny, but his old, lodgerly habits came back at times like these and he could not be kept out of the kitchen. Passing him a dripping meat dish, Joanna had surprisingly agreed with him about the Bun.

'Only, you see, when Lance and Suzy and Mandy's Anneliese were babies, the teashop was something Mandy and I could do as well as look after them, because we've always kept it dead easy, no hot food. It was our bit of adventure and independence. My own money. Something to be in charge of.' She had passed him a plate with the sudden flashing smile which transformed her rather stern, regular features. 'I always knew it was a rut. I was going to stop when Susan was at secondary school and do an Open University degree. Then it started making more money, when they put up the "HISTORIC MARKET TOWN ALL SERVICES" sign on the motorway. And Susan hated the High School, so we switched to paying fees, and I kept on. I was so much in the habit, and I'm not qualified to do anything else. And I do like to help out, financially. With Keith working so hard, and things being tough in the practice since the house market collapsed . . . you know.'

Gus knew. All around, in London as well as Bonhurst, he saw just such fossilized lives. The unemployed were not the only casualties of recession. People in work grew timid too, afraid to change and develop, abhorring risk, never making way for the next generation, standing stock-still for fear of slipping backwards. He had been extremely lucky to be taken on as clerk in 1992, considering that every law practice in southern England was reeling under the impact of the housing slump. At first, Keith used to joke about swings and roundabouts, saying,

'What we lose in conveyancing we pick up in divorce.' But as the recession bit deeper, it seemed that people around Bonhurst could hardly afford even divorces any more. The office telephone rang less often, except with the sad cases for whom kind Keith did not log a quarter of the hours he worked. The third partner, Ned Bandon, retired and was not replaced. Alex moved down into Ned's office, leaving Gus the sloping attic. Now Alex was going, and Gus guessed that if he took up his father's proffered capital to buy the vacant partnership, there would not even be a new clerk. The partnership income simply would not stand it. He and Keith would be alone with Aimée.

Still, it was one step nearer his real ambition: a husband-and-wife partnership: Terson and Terson. Him and Tiny. He glowed at the thought of Tiny. Prettiest, funniest law student of their batch, best beloved of Gus for five faithful years but currently languishing in a huge London firm. Tiny only wanted to marry him, move to some Hampshire farmhouse and commute to undemanding small-town work in between raising babies, dogs and chickens. That was the long-term masterplan.

The marrying bit was easy, and scheduled for December. Tiny, who was Hong Kong Chinese, was planning to look adorable in a white fur parka cloak. Her people had the capital to buy a partnership and would give it as a wedding present. If only Keith wanted two new partners instead of one, they could both move in at Christmas when Alex left. Tiny would be brilliant with the local clientele: a five-foot glossy Chinese doll might initially be a change from suave greying Mr Heron and trustworthy Mr Gurney. But, as Tiny had said, expertly demolishing a bowl of fried rice on his last visit to London, if the characters in *The Archers* could get used to an Asian woman solicitor called Usha, Bonhurst could get used to having their wills drafted by Li Pan Terson. And she would wow the Hampshire magistrates, all of whom she suspected of fantasizing about Suzy Wong (pause for Tiny's impression of an Oriental temptress striding into court with a whip and thigh boots). And if any clients did jib at her, Gus could compensate by being very male and very English indeed to provide protective colouring, couldn't he? (Pause for Gus to do his very brilliant impersonation of a fusty old judge failing to recognize an egg spring roll presented to him in evidence.)

Oh yes, Tiny and he would be a great team. Perry Mason and Tonto, Rumpole and Man Friday. With children and chickens. Lost in his daydream, Gus forgot about the disappearance of Joanna Gurney for a moment. They would have a dog, a really big red setter which could sleep in its basket in the office corridor. Clients who didn't like dogs could bog off. He was really, despite his proud new qualifications, still very young.

The telephone rang. 'Terson and – I mean Heron and Gurney,' said Gus. 'No. I'm sorry, Mr Heron's in court this morning.'

This was a euphemism born of habit. Alex was not in court. He had, at the fleeing Keith's behest, rung the coastguard to report Joanna's safety and cancel any watch for her, then driven home where he found Mandy alone in the kitchen rereading Gordon's report with those alarming rare tears running down her cheeks. He had taken her into his arms, limp and sad, but got no sense out of her beyond, 'Jo will think I said those things. I can't go out. I can't go to the caff, honestly. I'm a letdown, aren't I? Oh, Alex. I dunno what to do. I never felt like this before. I've done all sorts of naughty things, you know that, but never like this. I didn't even do it, but I feel worse than if I did. Alex, I wish I was dead. I really am a no-hope slag.'

He had reluctantly left her, instructing Anneliese to stay in the house and administer tea. As he passed the dining-room door, he half noticed Susan Gurney, that surly stripe-haired child, looking extremely busy filling in some sort of printed form.

Now he was downtown again, standing in the back kitchen of the Bun in the Oven with Erika Merriam. This, at least, was something he could do. Summoning up all his urbane smoothness, Alex set about charming this straggle-haired, beaky woman into solving at least one of the problems thrown up by Joanna Gurney's escapade.

'Mrs Merriam, first of all I'd like to say how grateful my wife is for the way you've taken over. She's not well herself—'

Erika sniffed. Alex took no notice. A lot of women in the town seemed to sniff at the mention of his wife; if she didn't mind, he supposed he must not mind either.

'– and you see Mrs Gurney's had to go away for – it might be another few days. I think you normally just do weekends and holidays for her, don't you?'

'That's right,' said Erika. 'My husband likes me at home.'

'Ah yes, Ted,' said Alex. 'Anyway, we do see how awkward it is for you, filling in—'

'Excuse me. A customer,' said Erika.

She left him leaning on a shelf of white-and-gold saucers, marvelling at the sudden crispness that could come over shy women when they had something to manage. She returned a moment later to catch him pulling a curl of chocolate from the side of a waiting gateau, and so cold was her stare then that he slammed the plastic visor down over it and smirked apologetically.

Erika began to assemble a tea tray for two with deft hands. 'You really shouldn't—' she said, and stopped.

'I know, I know,' said Alex. 'Sorry.'

'It's just that we're not supposed to let outsiders in the kitchen. Hygiene regs. Like you aren't wearing an overall.'

She herself was neat in pink gingham. Joanna's faded blue apron hung in the corner, and with it a smaller, grubbier one. On the back of the door hung a small pink gingham housecoat like Erika's, unworn by the look of it.

'I'll go. I'm very sorry. You're very good at this job, aren't you? All I wanted to ask—'

'You want me to come in, I'll come in. Till Mrs Gurney gets back. Ted can put up with it. Only I'm leaving Zoë on her own after the dinnertime rush, so it does need someone to lock up at five. Zoë's not fit to have a key, she'd lose it at some disco. If Mrs Heron could come in at four . . .'

'Either she will or I will,' promised Alex. 'She's not well.'

'There's cashing up, too,' said Erika, with the air of one who did not believe in any illness of Mandy's, and never would. 'And putting the takings in the night safe.'

'I can do that,' said Alex. 'I used to work in an ice-cream shop in the vacation. Keith and I ran the best ice-cream stand on Brighton beach.'

She looked disbelievingly at him, and put two scones, a bowl of blackcurrant jam and a jug of milk onto her tray alongside the teapot and cups. 'Yes. And there's checking to be done. Plugs out, work surfaces clean, floor swept, rubbish out the back, *sealed*.'

'I can do that. Or Mandy will. Mrs Merriam, we really are most grateful. I think Mrs Heron and Mrs Gurney would want me to say that this extra responsibility deserves extra, er, salary.'

Erika looked at him coolly as she turned towards the door with the fragrant, immaculate tray. 'It's not a problem. I don't think Zoë will be trouble. I'm going to stay on an hour today and get her into some routines.'

Alex watched her go, then heaved himself off the shelf and followed her through the door, into the prim tearoom. 'Thanks. Again.'

As he left, a thin dreadlocked child in a miniskirt, tube top, and cloud of sullen attitude came in through the door.

'Zoë. You're late,' he heard Erika say. 'There's a new clean overall for you behind the door, and a ribbon to tie your hair back. It's better if you look the part. Get a step on, now.' Alex escaped, marvelling.

In the dining room at the Herons' house, Susan Gurney finished her form, folded it, and put it in a heavy, expensive long lawyer's manila envelope brought to her by Anneliese from her father's desk drawer.

'I think you're really brave,' said Anneliese. 'There'll be a row.'

'Don't care.' Susan licked the flap and banged her fist down hard on the envelope. 'Mum's bogged off, Dad's chasing her round Torquay, Lance is poncing around on his personal Starship *Enterprise*, it's my bloody life.'

'What do you mean, Starship *Enterprise*?'

'Got a postcard the other day. From some crumbling observatory, Prague or somewhere. All it said was "Nothing matters except the laws of nature and the power of Love". Weird.'

'Weird.' Anneliese proffered a stamp, then changed her mind and put out a hand for the envelope instead. 'I'll take it in tomorrow. Mum's driving me to Southampton. I'll be going into the Purser's, no, whatsit, Bursar's office. I'll drop it in.'

'The bedsit all signed up?'

'Yup.'

'D'you think we'll be all right, sharing? Not have rows, all that?'

'Yup.' Anneliese shook her white-gold mane, with the lop-sided, wicked grin that lifted Susan's heart. With Annie, you couldn't always approve, but you did feel better for being around her.

'Will your mum mind you sharing?'

'Thrr-illed.' Anneliese rolled the word out with relish. 'I told her it was a schoolfriend I was sharing a flat with. She said thank God, I thought it was a Hell's Angel chapter. Anyway, we'll be back every Friday night. It's only to save getting on the early bus. And there's room for two drawing boards. We can even work.'

'I do want to work, Annie. It's not a skive. I'm gonna be an art editor. I'd do it the other way, do Art A level, only not with MacEvoy's Fusiliers. Besides, the college course gets me further in, and I need a head start. Publishing's really competitive. And I can't stay at school. I can't.'

'No way. Gross. It's your fault for getting so many GCSEs. I saw it coming. More than six and you're doomed to A levels. Scrape five Cs, like me, and all you have to do is bring home a few leaflets about trendy new GNVQs and even Alex caves in. Glad to keep me off the streets— ssh!'

Mandy was in the doorway, pale and quenched. With dexterity born of practice, Annie slid the envelope under the table, but her mother noticed nothing.

'I've a headache. I'm going to bed. Sue, if your mother rings . . . tell her I'd love to talk to her . . .'

Neither girl had ever seen Mandy so hesitant, but concern evaporated in the heat of their own needs.

'Mum, you are taking me to Southampton tomorrow? To college, for the signing-on thing?'

Mandy looked blank. 'Oh – yes. Of course.'

'Can Sooze come for the ride?' Anneliese held her breath. Would it occur to her mother that Susan was supposed to be a lower sixth student at Angela Merici in a bottle-green suit, not free like Annie to schlepp around a further education college twenty miles away? Mandy, as she had suspected, was too distracted by the morning's events for such ratiocination.

'Yes, yes. Fine.' Mandy turned away rapidly. Susan looked too like Joanna. The straight little features, the big eyes and full mouth were smiling at her, delighted at the prospect of delivering her own envelope. But Mandy saw only the ghost of Joanna's features; of her friend, the only friend who had always stuck by her, who might now be dead, who if alive would be disgusted with her. She saw those features distorted by disappointment and reproach. Without a word, she left, leaving the girls to face one another and, simultaneously, jauntily, put their thumbs up.

On the A303, Keith straightened up, wiped his hands, threw the jack and spanner back in the boot with the flat tyre, and climbed into the driving seat to wait for a gap in the relentless stream of lorries. He would be in Torquay by four. In time for a cup of tea, with Jo.

19

The cup of tea that Guy made did Joanna good. Her outburst of grief passed quickly and, strangely, seemed to leave no awkwardness behind it. Everything was too surreal for embarrassment: the boat composedly rocking southward across a glittering afternoon sea, the willowy elegance of Guy in his college blazer, the incongruous figure of the girl with her red talons and carefully made-up baby face. Della, who had begun to look queasy as the waves grew longer south of Berry Head, refused her tea and now sat silent in the corner of the cockpit, with an old Arran jumper of Keith's wrapped round her shoulders in their flimsy blouse. Guy patted her fake-tanned, goosepimpled knee occasionally. She seemed not discontented.

Joanna and Guy sipped their tea on either side of the helm as the north wind pushed *Shearwater* steadily down the coast towards the Mewstone Rock.

'He'll look for us in Dartmouth, for sure,' said Guy. 'Better not go there.'

'He probably won't look for us *at all*,' said Joanna, for the fourth or fifth time.

'You don't *know* him,' said the young man with a shudder. 'He's probably never been slapped and walked out on before.'

'Bet he has,' said Della, rousing briefly from her sick torpor. '*Bet* he has.'

'Well, not by a personal secretary. I'm his employee, the lawyers made me sign twenty sorts of contract stopping me from *breathing* unless he says so. If Della had come away alone, things might have been all right. But me coming has probably made things worse for all of us. He'll be angry.'

'He can't do anything if he does catch us,' said Joanna dampeningly. 'This isn't a James Bond film. If he does anything, it'll be to ring his lawyers, stop your money, all that stuff. Even Robert Maxwell didn't actually go around drowning people.'

But nothing would convince her companions that they were not fleeing for their lives. After a few minutes' contemplation of this thought, Guy even anounced, in a tone straight out of Hornblower, that they should 'cram on all sail'. With Joanna's amused permission, he raised the mainsail and dragged out the boat's worn and grubby spinnaker from its bag to hoist that as well.

It was an atrocious sail, orange and green and hideous, made twenty years ago for another boat and so ill cut that at the slightest provocation it twisted inextricably round the wire forestay. Joanna hated it. Keith and Lance had bought it in a boat jumble sale when Lance was fourteen and razor-keen on racing. The two of them used to rig it enthusiastically while Jo and Susan jeered from the cockpit. Once it had fallen off its halyard and dragged under the keel, just in the entrace to Poole harbour, causing the boat to veer out of control and almost hit the chain ferry. Watching Guy haul it up and steady it on its pole, Joanna could almost see Lance, her boy, her cheerful genius, on the foredeck again. Guy adjusted things to his satisfaction and swung back into the cockpit. Glancing at the log, Joanna observed that this rig gave *Shearwater* an extra three knots, raising their speed to seven nautical miles per hour.

'What top speed does *Privateer* do?' she asked unkindly as Guy admired his rig.

'Thirty knots.' Guy ducked his head a little sheepishly. 'I know. But he might not get out very quickly, and if we could just get round the corner . . .'

'What corner, exactly?'

'Look,' said Guy. 'Six miles beyond Start Point, just past where you'd turn up the channel into Salcombe, there's a little hole called Starhole Bay.'

'I know it. You stop there when the tide round Start Point is against you, going up-Channel. Steep cliffs all around. There's nothing there.'

'Right. Well, we could anchor there – if you agree – tonight.

Nobody would notice or expect us there. We could disguise the boat a bit. Then in the morning, very early, we could sneak just inside Salcombe harbour, Della and I could get a taxi, and you'd be clear of us.'

As a plan for foiling an imaginary pursuer, thought Joanna, it was not bad. There were enough bits and pieces of food, emergency tins under bunks and the like, for the three of them. There were three sleeping bags including Susan's. Della could have that. She would – she shamefacedly caught herself thinking – wash it before Susan had it again. Della was rather more extravagantly scented than was usual on board the boat.

'OK,' she said. 'Only I have to get on the VHF and leave a message for my husband. He thinks I'm in Torquay. He might even be there already.'

Guy took the helm, and once again Joanna sat below at the chart table, in a far calmer ship this time, and went through the rituals of a link call to the Old Vicarage. Just as she got through, an anxious face appeared in the companionway.

'Keith,' she began. 'I've had to leave Torquay. I'll be in—'

'No!' hissed Guy. 'It's a public airwave. He might be listening in. The Boss!' Joanna flashed him an irritated look and went on.

'I'll be in, er, on, er – safe harbour anyway. Don't worry. Tomorrow I'll go in to—'

'No, not even that!' said Guy, anguished. 'It's not safe!'

'Don't give us away!' squeaked Della. 'He's a pervert!' And threw up over the side, noisily. Guy turned to her, full of concern, and momentarily ignored the helm. The spinnaker seized its chance, collapsed with a rustle and a flap, and wound itself round the stay with an expertise born of long practice. The trapped jib cracked and shook.

'Shit!' yelled Guy.

'Owww . . . are we sinking?' said Della, raising a grey face, eerily streaked with blusher.

'It's going to rip!'

'Anyway,' persevered Joanna, shutting out the racket with her left hand on her ear. 'No, shut up, you two, it's too bad – Keith, I will ring – from Salcombe. 'Bye.'

Furious, she stamped back up the steps to the cockpit. 'No, *really*,' she said. 'What's he going to think?'

'You said the harbour!' wailed Della. Guy switched on his diplomatic heat-lamp again, full beam, and calmed her down with platitudinous soothings, most of them shouted from the foredeck as – skilfully, she had to admit – he freed the great orange and green sail.

'More tea?' he said at last, returning to a quieter cockpit.

'If,' said Joanna, 'you take that bloody spinnaker down first. Now.'

In the offices of the *Chronicle*, Gordon sat with a polystyrene cup of coffee, basking in the quiet glow of achievement. A shadow fell across his desk. Looking up, he saw the News Editor, massive in his grey ribbed cardigan, with a piece of scrawled paper in his huge hand. 'The Editor,' he said sourly, 'has had a call from the Proprietor. Were we aware, he says, that our pisspoor Page Three story omitted the most newsworthy aspect of the whole affair of the sailaway teashop lady?'

'Which is?' said Gordon, affecting a bravura he did not feel.

'That the lady has not in fact run off alone. That she is not some lonely desperate menopause victim, laddie. She has been sighted in Torquay, disporting herself,' he gave a really rather attractive Scottish roll to the 'r', 'on a ship of sin with a lesbian vice girl in suspenders and a toyboy of twenty-two.'

'He made that up!' blurted Gordon before he could stop himself. The News Editor looked at him with a pitying dislike. 'Know a lot about making it up, do you, laddie?'

'Well,' said Gordon, recovering, 'I'll chase it up, obviously.'

'Obviously not,' said the News Editor, turning to depart. 'Our Miss Douglas is there, on the spot, and will be filing shortly.' Gordon, left alone, crushed his polystyrene cup in his hand.

Eddie McArthur looked out across Torquay harbour and wondered briefly how good an idea his call to the thug had been. In the chilly Northumbrian minor stately home where he grew up, his nurse had been prone to say, 'Temper, temper never won a race; spiteful never won a pretty face.' Temper had stood him in pretty good stead so far in life, and pretty faces could be bought. The temper had been considerable, fuelled not so much by the humiliation of the slap as by the realization that without Guy, he might still be able to command and drive his boat but he had lost command of the rest of his life. He had no idea where anything was, nor how to find the telephone numbers of his other aides, lawyers, and employees; did not know where or when to appear for tonight's West Country business dinner. He had no clue as to where his portable telephone was kept. Guy had been briefed and trained by his last departing secretary who in turn had been instructed by the one before; Eddie did not believe in cluttering his mind with administrative trivia. He did not even know his own home telephone number.

The reappearance on the pontoons of Dinny Douglas, roughly towelled dry on the unabsorbent roller-towel in the Ladies', was a godsend. This woman worked for him; well, let her work.

'Hoy!' he cried 'You! Here!' She had come, babbling apologies for the earlier disturbance.

'Never mind that. You *Chronicle* staff?'

'Yes – staff reporter, six-month contract. Sir.'

'You are seconded. From this minute. To my personal staff.'

'Er, thank you . . . How long, er?'

'While you are needed. You have a mobile? No? There is one in the cabin. Get me your Editor.' It had been as simple as that. Miss Douglas had since then found out the details of his evening appointment, made half a dozen calls as they occurred to him, located his dinner suit, brushed it, unpacked a light lunch of Parma ham and melon left labelled in the vast galley's chill cabinet, and driven Marie to the station after Eddie had treated her to a brief encounter in his cabin. During this latter embarrassingly obvious interlude, Dinny had sat on the flying bridge, thinking that if ever she were to change alliances – say, topple that harpy Maeve Mahoney on the *Globe* – she would have some stirring memoirs to write.

On the way to Paignton station, Marie had bolstered this conviction with some scarifying detail and made Dinny decide that her secondment to Eddie's personal staff should end well before dusk, and certainly before it got too personal. 'I don't know why he's getting shot of me now,' grumbled the call girl. 'He said he'd be too busy tonight. Dunno who with.'

Dinny flinched slightly and pulled up at the station.

The next visitor to *Privateer* was Keith, hot and flustered.

The marina office had directed him vaguely towards the end pontoons, 'outside one of the big boats'. The lack of interest or precision, oddly untypical of the marina Keith vaguely remembered from other visits, was not unconnected with his own quest. For two days, the owners and management of a large chain of marinas had been immured in meetings connected with getting the best deal out of a takeover by McArthur Holdings. For several weeks the staff had been so unsettled that any of them with alternative possibilities of employment had left the chain. The result was a state of uneasy, unhappy chaos, such as almost always presaged a McArthur takeover. (Had the employees but known it, however, this was as nothing to the state of unhappiness which generally occurred after the deal was signed).

The takeover was expected to be given the final nod at tonight's glittering function. It would have been kind of Eddie to have told them he was planning to spend two days in their marina first; but then Eddie was rarely kind. He had sent Guy up to pay the dues, and the student had entered the boat as *Private Ear* and the owner as McMaster. So Keith, not an avid reader of gossip columns, arrived in all innocence at the end of the pontoon where *Privateer*'s great white bulk lay.

There was a blonde woman in leather trousers and a smart but oddly streaked and crumpled green jacket on the stern deck, hammering at a laptop computer. She did not look up until Keith's third tentative 'I say!' and then only to glare at him.

'I say, I'm looking for a boat called *Shearwater*,' he said. The woman looked up properly this time.

'*Shearwater*?'

Her tone made Keith's heart leap. She must have seen the boat, to use such a tone.

'Yes, have you seen her? My wife—'

'Your wife?'

Maybe, Keith thought in brief despair, she was foreign and didn't speak any English. In his defence it must be said that around Bonhurst you didn't get to hear many of the flat, dead cool, up-yours little London voices that Dinny and her friends affected. She did sound faintly as if English was not her first language.

'Yes, my wife – Joanna – we're supposed to meet here.'

Dinny closed her computer, glanced down at Keith's picture in the folded newspaper next to her, and came to the rail.

'Mr Gurney, I have to tell you I am a journalist, *Daily Chronicle*, and we are also trying to trace your wife. If we could work together—'

'But she was here!' said Keith. 'She rang me. She's fine. You printed a lot of irresponsible nonsense—'

'I know. I wasn't involved in that. We'll be printing the facts tomorrow. Meanwhile, do you have any idea of where they might be heading?'

'No! I mean – what do you mean, they?'

'Your wife,' said Dinny, 'and the bisexual London prostitute, and her so-called protector Mr Guy Pastern-Hopkins, aged twenty-two, who has a criminal record for drug offences and has absconded with his employer's credit cards.' She drew breath, slightly puffed. Older reporters in the scandal game had often advised her that if you're going to hit 'em with what you know, you should hit 'em hard and fast. Then shut up, listen, and take down the next thing they say. The drug offence was pushing it a bit, but Eddie had let her ring his contract lawyer who had helpfully come up with Guy's one venture into serious criminality, viz. possession of a half-smoked spliff after the 1991 Varsity match. Every little helped, when you were hitting 'em hard and fast.

Now she waited for Keith to react with a good quote. 'I knew it!' would be nice. Or 'We were so happy – I can't believe that she had a Secret Life.' Dinny cocked an eyebrow enquiringly at the silent, thin, dignified figure below her on the pontoon. Keith looked at this woman, avid and gloating with her sharp little teeth and plucked eyebrows and the moist, red glisten of her lips. With a surge of affection he thought of Joanna's straight intelligent gaze and self-deprecating smile.

'I'm not surprised she sailed away from you lot,' he said. 'I'm going home. If you are planning to print any more libellous material, your Editor will be hearing from me, as my wife's legal adviser. Good afternoon.'

And he walked up the pontoon, without looking back.

20

A filthy, battered, ripped and mended canvas holdall bumped up the Old Vicarage steps, scraping against the worn stones. It lay exhausted, gaping at one seam to reveal a fray of blue denim within, while its owner clinked and fiddled with his keys. At last, the door swung open and the disgraceful bag was borne into the silent hall where motes of dust circled in the autumn sunshine. A rucksack thumped down beside the bag, and – after a sigh and a fumble from above – was joined by a well-worn leather bumbag bearing the initials LKG. The bags lay in the shaft of sunlight from the leaded fanlight over the door, exotically scruffy against the cool dull tiles. They lay untouched while their owner could be heard stamping around the house, opening and shutting doors (including the metallically clunking ones of fridge and freezer), scraping chairs, clattering crockery, and eventually climbing stairs and running taps.

They were still there an hour later, unmoved, when the door opened again and Susan Gurney came in. Her striped, slicked-back hair and beaky little nose gave her the look of a small fierce foreign animal confronting a TV wildlife film crew. She wore the preoccupied and grudging air with which she faced the outer world these days, but at the sight of the bags her eyes widened with pure and spontaneous pleasure and relief. On a rising note, clear and joyful, she cried, 'Lance!'

She could not have borne it, she thought, if he had gone out again. 'Lance!' But a door opened upstairs and a sleepy, tousled figure, hair down to his collar and moustache to his chin, peered over the banisters. He was wearing Joanna's Chinese nylon kimono which made him look like a reluctantly pressed understudy for a budget production of *The Mikado*. To his sister, Lancelot Keith Gurney was, however, an entirely beautiful sight. He yawned.

'Eeuh. Babysis. Sooze. Hi.'

Susan ran up the stairs, and delivered a friendly blow to his dragoned midriff. 'Lance. The hair! The 'tache! Dad'll have a fit. How was Europe?'

'Large and various,' said Lance, his hand on her shoulder. Despite his height and his hairiness, nobody who saw the two together could mistake them for anything but brother and sister. Their small, hawk faces and big intense eyes faced one another, each echoing the other's expressions as he spoke. 'Various and mainly smelly. Beautiful women hurling themselves at me. Hideous men hurling themselves after the beautiful women. Rabid dogs biting the hideous men. Art treasures. Whistling trains. Canals. Spies in trenchcoats coming out of the sewers. Cathedrals. Coffee shops. Great.'

'Why are you back? I thought you had another week.'

'Dunno. There I was in the Galaxy Café in Amsterdam, smelling my own socks and watching various dorks smoking their heads off, including my new friend Rudi the Ludicrous, who is wanted by the police of seven countries, so he says. Only I doubt if any of them would still want him if they had shared a hostel with him for a week.' He took a breath. 'And I suddenly thought: even the chairs are uncomfortable, so why am I here? So I took the train to the Hook and the ferry to Harwich and the coach to Southampton and the thumb to here, dreaming of afternoon tea with cuke sandwiches at the Bun in the Oven.'

Susan turned away and began picking varnish off the banister.

Lance continued, 'So I went to the Bun, and there is Erika Merriam drilling some poor little waitress in hair extensions like it was the Foreign Legion in pink check pinnies. And she looks at me as if I was Jack the Ripper. So I head for home, and on the way I meet Mrs Colefax coming out of Cuisine It All with a wok in brown paper. And she says what a good boy I am, a lovely son to come home and be there for my Poor Father. And I think "What, what?" So I come home, and here's nobody. And I boil a curry in a plastic bag from my baby sister's personal store of disgusting foodstuffs, and I go to bed.'

He paused, and gave her a penetrating glare. His voice dropped to a less theatrical level.

'And I wake up and say, what is going on, Susan? Why am I a Good Son? Why is Frau Obersturmfuehrer Merriam running the Bun?'

During this spirited recital Susan had removed most of the varnish from the ball on top of the newel post and started on the curve of banister, where the flakes proved tougher to dislodge. She abandoned it and kicked the post instead.

'Mum has run off, basically. On the boat. And it's been in the papers.'

'Which papers?' asked Lance, rather stupidly, just to give himself time.

'Heaps of them, the first day, with a little bit each. Now it's big bits in just the *Chronicle*, and a feminist rant in the *Globe*, saying Dad must be like Captain Bligh.'

'You are joking. Sure it didn't say Captain Birdseye?'

'It's not funny.' Susan kicked the post again. 'Yesterday Dad was really worried, in the gale. I couldn't stand it, so I went and slept at Annie's. Now apparently Mum's all right. Gone to Torquay, Alex says, and Dad's gone to find her, and I came back to see that Dad was all right. When he gets back.'

'He's gone to get her?'

'Alex thought that. But I don't know if she'll come with him. She did sail off. And Dad went to the police, and now there's awful things in the paper about how she might be having a, you know, breakdown. And about her having no friends, and being desperate enough to leave her children. Actually, Annie says that bit shows they're talking crap, because they said "innocent children", and she thinks that definitely couldn't mean you.'

'Anneliese is a menace.' Lance considered this information, frowning. 'So, do we worry?' He rubbed his chin, then went back into his bedroom, emerging with a small pocketbook, like a missal, which Susan recognized as an anthology entitled *Scorn* by Matthew Parris. It had been in Lance's Christmas stocking, a habit which Joanna doggedly refused to abandon, and had been an inspired choice. Like many deeply kind and sensitive people, Lance adored literary insults and contumely. He flipped the pages now, frowning.

'Here we are . . . yes . . . Norman Mailer. He should know. He said, "Once a newspaper touches a story, the facts are lost for ever, even to the protagonists." See? Perfect. Thank you, Mr Parris.' He closed the little book with a snap and hurled it through the door and onto his bed. He had been prone to these inconsequential literary gestures all his life; once, made to eat his lettuce at the age of four, he had toddled off to fetch *Peter Rabbit* and produced it as printed proof that 'eating lettuce does kill you, like Peter's Daddy'. Joanna had told that story a lot, until the children stopped her.

'For God's sake,' said Susan, irritated. 'What's the point of that?'

'The point is that you're all going on too much about the newspapers. Bugger what they say. If Mum has gone, the question is why has she gone? We're more likely to know than they are. Reading newspapers will only fog up your mind. What do we actually know? About why.'

'I was on the boat all weekend, with them arguing,' said Susan slowly. 'But it wasn't worse than usual. It was about Mum wanting to pack in the Bun.'

'So? It's her caff, where was the problem? Captain Bligh, don't tell me – he threatened to chain her to the cake rack? Dad?'

'No, course not. I think she sort of wanted him to *agree* that giving up the Bun was a good idea. And he just kept sounding pompous and saying how you shouldn't sell a healthy business in the middle of a recession, and how useful it was to the family finances, and how things were dodgy for him with Alex leaving.'

'Oh, yeah, I forgot. Alex is leaving to be a capitalist bastard, isn't he? So Mandy-pandy can have more holidays. But Dad's got Gus raring to buy in to the partnership, hasn't he?'

'Yeah, but . . . Mum said that. Obviously. Said she couldn't see what all the fuss was about, since Gus was keen to buy in. And Dad stopped being pompous and lawyery and shouted that Gus was a moron and would drive him mad within a year because his clients drive him mad anyway and only Alex makes it bearable. He said if Gus was all he had in the office, he'd be the next one to walk out of work, and then who would keep a roof over our head?'

Susan paused. 'I'll tell you what it was like. It was like, um, that thing Mrs MacEvoy's always going on about in English. A subtext. It was as if *Dad* sort of wanted to give up everything and he was angry Mum thought of it first. And he wanted Mum to have the Bun as security. Only she couldn't see what he had to be angry about, because all she could think about was getting rid of the Bun. And he couldn't see that she really was desperate.'

'You mean they both want to drop out? Change?'

'Well, they can't. They have to keep on working and getting angrier and angrier, because neither of them can bring themselves to let the other one drop out. And they can't drop out themselves without asking. Because the other one would be left with the responsibility.'

It was a long speech for truculent Susan. Two days ago she could not have made such an analysis, nor would she have bothered. A lot had been achieved over two days of mentally replaying those last conversations of her mother's. Lance considered her thesis gravely.

'Do you think they're both burnt out? At work?'

'Well . . . sort of. But they never both said it at the same time. When Mum was talking about getting rid of the Bun, Dad was being all righteous and lawyerish. When he said the stuff about how Gus would drive him mad, Mum went sort of superior and amused as if he was a little boy who didn't like his new teacher.'

'She was never like that!' said Lance warmly. 'When I didn't like Mrs Harris, Mum came in and sorted her out.'

'Well, anyway. I thought she was treating Dad like a silly kid. And he was a bit stuck up, too. And all the time—' She stopped, suddenly struck by the brilliance of her own insight. 'All the time, they actually both want the same thing!'

'Perhaps they should drop out,' said Lance, with all the tranquillity of new-found independence and achievement. 'Be New Age travellers. Old Age travellers. Wrinkly wanderers, on the boat. Sell this heap.' Seeing Susan's appalled look, he added kindly, 'Once you've left school, obviously.'

'Ah. Well,' said Susan, slightly relishing her turn to appal him. 'That's the other thing. I just have.'

*　　*　　*

Keith had not slept more than a few hours since Monday. He had not eaten his Danish pastry, nor drunk his coffee. He had changed a wheel by the roadside in the spray of lorries' wheels and driven a hundred miles only to find his wife gone and in her place a disdainful young woman accusing her of complex and unexpected vice. He had been, for him, rather rude to the young woman. Strangely, that added to the burdens of his troubled mind. Keith did not believe in rudeness and conflict. His clients mainly did, which was why they needed him. Sometimes he felt like a sponge whose only function was to soak up the aggression of others. To be aggressive and unreasonable himself felt alien, as if he had put on someone else's jacket. Or rather, as if he had no jacket at all but stood – as he sometimes did in his nightmares – in front of the magistrates' bench wearing only a string vest. His anger made him feel naked.

Now, just outside Exeter, he was suddenly so weary that none of it mattered next to the pressing need for sleep. He pulled into a lay-by, locked the doors and let his head fall back on the seat. Around him, the Devon darkness gathered.

Erika Merriam was making soup. Not for Ted, who had already supped and was listening to the angling programme on local radio; but in epic quantities, to serve tomorrow at the Bun in the Oven. They ought to do soup. And, later, microwave potatoes with dainty garnishes for a simple hot meal at lunchtime. Mrs Gurney had always vetoed the suggestion, saying, 'Let's do what we do, really well, and not try to be a restaurant.' But Erika was growing daring. Mrs Gurney was off doing God knows what, and Erika was doing her a big favour. And, after prolonged negotiation, she had persuaded Ted that it would be less trouble for him if he popped into the Bun for his lunch. She could look after him with soup and a special bap at the quiet table behind the door while Zoë helped with the real customers.

The thought of Zoë in close conjunction with hot soup made Erika flinch for a moment, but the child was making definite progress. All she needed was training. Mrs Gurney was far too soft on the girls. Erika sliced a carrot, purposefully. Her scheme would work. She knew it.

*   *   *

Mandy Heron shivered on her leather sofa, an empty glass between her hands. Even with the vodka warming the hollow inside her a little, she was cold. She had not spirit enough to turn on the coal-effect fire or to fetch a jumper. On the huge television, the inanities of a quiz show flickered unseen. Alex banged around uncertainly in the kitchen, trying to put together some supper. Anneliese was upstairs, sketching out the furnishings she intended for her tiny Southampton bedsit.

Mandy began, for the third time that day, to cry silently. How dreary, she thought, how drab and pathetic to be crying. She had better think of something to do. The first thing, obviously, was to have another drink.

Sprawled before the fire which Lance, in the first flush of appreciative domesticity, had made in the living room, Susan by nine thirty was finishing her exposition to her brother of the great, the glorious, the daring and outrageous steps she had in secret taken since he left for the summer. She told how, even as her mother was buying her bottle-green sixth-form suit from the second-hand shop at Angela Merici and her father was prosing on about UCAS forms and the importance of working flat out for good grades at A level, she had given up the argument which had poisoned family life for the past year.

'That must have been a relief,' said Lance in superior tones. 'I never heard anybody make such a fuss about staying on for the sixth.'

'*They* never heard me at all. They didn't listen,' said Susan. 'They'd've rather I had a baby or something than not do A levels. So I stopped talking and started arranging.'

'So what did you actually do?'

'Wrote to the FE College, applied for the two-year vocational course in Publishing and Periodical Design – it's like two A levels really – and sent a portfolio. I used Alex's computer to do some desktop publishing. He's got all these amazing programmes he doesn't know how to get into, but Annie and I worked them out. Used the colour printer from the IT room at Angela Merici—'

'How?'

'Nicked it. In a games bag, the last Thursday of term. Brought it back Friday.'

Lance whistled his appreciation.

'Anyway, I sent it off, with all the forms and a letter. I applied for an out-of-area travel grant which they give to particularly promising students whose parents can't afford it.'

'But yours could. If they weren't paying school fees.'

'Yes, well, I sort of used Dad's signature, which is,' she flashed defiance at Lance's shaking head, 'easy peasy. And it's his fault for not listening. I got the grant agreed. It'll cover my half of the rent on Annie's bedsit, then I don't have to travel and I can get on with working. I really, really want to do this, Lance.' She looked at him beseechingly, and this time he nodded. 'It's not a skive. There's art and design history, typography, a really tough Use of English module, and fantastic technical access. There are five student magazines, and you get to work on each of them, from the daily sheet to the monthly glossy. They get people onto national magazines, into big publishers, all the time. One girl did work experience at DK and got taken on that same summer.'

She was flushed and eager, her surliness gone. All summer, with the great plan burning through her days and half her nights, there had been nobody but Anneliese to talk to about it; Anneliese was a mate, a flatmate-to-be, but she had opted for the one-year Fashion Design course, a less arduous business altogether. She rapidly tired of ravings about any form of scholarship. Lance did not. He looked at his sister with affection, then said gently, 'What are you going to live on, Sooze?'

In the ensuing moment of silence, Susan looked bleak. The travel grant manoeuvre had been a bit of bravura. Really, although she never admitted it even to herself, the entire plan would founder if Keith and Joanna stood firm. They could not get her back home by force, but they could starve her out. Back to Angela Merici? Never. Die sooner! But there it was. When you were sixteen, your parents still held all the aces.

Lance broke the silence. 'If it helps,' he said, 'I think you did the right thing.'

'But you're the Grade-A academic Cambridge scholarship wizard. I thought you'd say I ought to do A levels first.'

'I,' said Lance, 'am doing what I want. I want to read Physics as much as you want to learn about typefaces and mastheads and

White Space. My life revolves round the laws of matter which are second only to the power of love.'

'Oh, for God's—' began Susan angrily. He broke in, grinning.

'I may be weird but I am happy. So should you be. If you need money, I shall post you half my scholarship and half my student loan.'

'And what will you do then, dumbo? Starve?'

'Sell my body,' said Lance smugly.

'What, just the once? To the Medical School?'

The two scuffled their feet in battle for a moment like siblings five years younger, then Lance said, 'What about Mum, then?'

'I was dreading telling her,' said Susan. 'I'd have had to this week, 'cos the course starts on Monday and Mrs MacEvoy has been ringing every day from Angela Merici as it is. But now Mum isn't here to have the row with, I feel sort of empty.'

'The house feels empty,' agreed Lance.

'It did even when Dad was here, yesterday.'

'The Bun felt funny, too. Old Erika running it in a different kind of pinny. She's moved the tables round and put Zoë in pink gingham and a hair ribbon.'

'Dad was in a state. He misses her. Alex was all dithery this morning about having to lock up the café. Even Mandy's looking terrible. It's as if,' Susan said judicially, 'as if she'd vanished out of a picture and left a sort of Mum-shaped hole. Like one of those cut-out dolls.'

Lance reached over and threw a knob of coal onto the fire, wiping his hand on the dark part of the hearthrug pattern.

'Well, no wonder she buggered off,' he said.

'What do you mean?'

'Can't be much fun living in a Mum-shaped hole. What would happen if you wanted to move to another bit of the picture? Or wave your arms about? Or grow a bit in one direction and shrink in another?'

'I didn't mean literally.'

'I bet it felt literal, sometimes. Being a Bonhurst mum. Like being a live jellyfish someone's put in a china jellymould. I'll tell you something else, too.'

'What?'

'Bet you that after all this fuss, she couldn't fit back into her exact hole even if she tried.'

It was in the lull following this insightful remark that a white-faced Keith walked into the room and straight to the drinks cupboard. He had gulped down a large tot of whisky before he even noticed, lounging in the firelight and framed in unfamiliar hair, his son.

Shearwater cut through the sunset sea, her bow to glowing west, her outstretched and reddened sails giving her a gentle slant to port. Under the shelter of Prawle Point the water was calmer, and Della roused herself from the sick torpor of the afternoon. She sat, still close to Guy, on the downhill side of the cockpit, looking curiously at the changing coast and firing off streams of observations and questions.

'Doesn't the land look funny from out here. All spiky.'

'That's Bolt Head.'

'What happens if you bang into it when there isn't a proper harbour?'

'You get wrecked,' said Guy, beaming at his pupil.

'That's why you have to have charts.'

'What, like hospital charts?'

'No, it just means maps of the sea.'

'Why not call them maps?'

'Because . . . it's tradition. A lot of things have different names at sea.'

'Yeah, like calling the lounge the cabin. And when you and her were going on before, about sheets, and it turned out to be ropes.'

'There are other ropes with other names. Halyards, reefing lines, the topping lift.'

Della snorted. 'Yeah, and this verandah thing, whassit? Cotpip?'

'Cockpit,' said Guy kindly. 'And the floor isn't the floor, it's the sole. And the walls down there are actually bulkheads, and the ceiling of the cabin is the deckhead.'

'Like dickhead, you mean?'

Joanna, watching them absently from the helm, thought that perhaps the immaculate, classy Guy was not going to find the conquest of this spirited creature quite as smooth and flattering a process as he thought. Something about Della reminded her of Susan, and brought back the vague discomfort and guilt that afflicted her whenever she thought about her daughter.

Why could she appreciate the life and spark in this red-clawed call girl and yet be irritated beyond anything at Susan's defiances? Why was Susan such a thorn? Susan in childhood had been a joy: affectionate and clever, good-natured and energetic. Even two years ago there was still pleasure in family suppers, family holidays. Lance at sixteen and Susan at fourteen had had the normal share of moods but remained true and recognizable inheritors of their wonderful baby selves. Their high spirits energized the household, as they had down all the years from hammer-peg toys to GCSE choices. They fulfilled the ideal of family life that Joanna had chosen. The life that she had *planned*, she thought with sudden, bitter passion. She planned it in that time of silence after Port Meadow.

Keith, Lance, Susan were the family she had dreamt of so fiercely when she turned her back on Oxford, Gabriel, Emily and all the muddled, yearning, suicidally unconfined passion of Leckford Road. She wanted none of it: no more late nights with *Lear* and *Troilus and Criseyde* and Wagner on the record player, no morning bike rides through the misty spires with a breast painfully, gloriously full of unimaginable surging hopes for something she could not even define. All that poetry had led her only to disaster. She had wanted prose. The muck and muddle, the laughter and banality, the relentless small practical demands of family life had been what she wanted. What she needed.

And now they were evaporating. Lance was a joy, but he had been gone two months, faded away leaving only postcards from Inter-Rail Europe to console her. And most of them were as enigmatic as smiles from the Cheshire Cat. Soon he would go to Cambridge and enter his own time of poetry and intensity, perhaps. She would not worry about him overmuch. Lance had sense. He was robust. He had even been proof against the wiles of Anneliese.

Susan? Susan was still home, but distant and sullen. These days, her scorn had a real edge to it, and family life was anathema to her. Joanna had wondered about drugs – the symptoms in the leaflets were all there: change in behaviour, evasiveness, loss of interest in schoolwork – but in her heart she knew this was unlikely. Lance had been caught smoking cannabis in the sixth form but had charmed his headmaster into not sacking him because, he explained, it was the first time and he only did it in order to contemplate Einstein's general theory of relativity when high, just to see if it was even more wonderful.

'But it wasn't,' he had said. 'So that's that, for me, with drugs.' The head had believed him. Susan had called him a dork, and Lance later told his mother that Susan was famous in her circle for scorning drugs, drink, and random snogging. 'She's more serious than any of us,' he said. Joanna could not see it that way, but had held her peace, watching her daughter with loving, anxious, but increasingly joyless attention.

'Do *you* get on with your mother?' she asked Della suddenly, this thought happening to coincide with a lull in the girl's stream of questions. Della considered, pouting slightly.

'Well, I didn't,' she said. 'I def'nitely didn't for a bit. But that was when I was leaving home. Now she's all right. She doesn't like me doing the escort work, obviously, but I do go home. Some weekends, you know.'

'Why did you leave?'

'Just boring. My mum never does anything different. Work, telly, bingo, and off to the library every week for two new Mills and Boons. She really likes her life. She thinks I ought to do a secretarial, then marry a Leicester boy from a nice white family where the Mum's just like her, and do just like she does.'

'And what did you want? Really want? When you decided to go?'

Della wriggled. 'Sounds silly if I say it.'

'No, it doesn't. Go on.'

'We're all a bit silly on this boat today,' said Guy, helpfully. 'I bet you had a jolly good idea what you wanted.'

'Well . . .'

'There's nothing wrong with wanting to be rich and famous,' prompted Guy. 'Like Dick Whittington. I sort of ran away when

I came to work for Mr McArthur. At least, my dad didn't like it.'

Della regarded him with surprised scorn. 'I didn't think of *that*,' she said, with all the grandeur of a duchess to whom someone has mentioned the market value of her ancestral silver tureen. 'I wasn't thinking of being *rich*, not just for the money, anyway. I just wanted to have adventures.'

'Adventures?' said Joanna, trying to keep her voice bland and not too curious.

'Yeah.' Della paused, but something in the hypnotic, swaying, confidential atmosphere of a yacht sailing down the sunset made her go on. 'I had this book, at baby school – I had it a long time 'cos I was a bit slow with the reading. My teacher said I might be dys-leckic but my dad said that was middle-class talk for thick, and he kept threatening to go round and thump the teacher. So she gave up about that. Anyway, the book. It had stuff in it about adventures.'

'What sort?' asked Guy.

'Giants,' said Della firmly. 'And fairies and princes and swords and caves with dragons in.'

Joanna stared at her, entranced. In her flimsy short skirt, strappy sandals and huge Keith sweater, Della looked like a ten-year-old, remembering.

'Do you remember any of the names of the people in the book?'

'Yeah – well, the monsters mainly. Grendel, with long green arms. And Giant Despair.'

'Did everyone get the book?' asked Joanna wonderingly. This child was Lance's age, or a year older. And from his childhood she remembered a dourly multicultural, inner-city, kitchen-sink type of school reader, with not a real adventure in them. Lance's primary teacher had chided her once for reading him *Beowulf* in a modern translation: too violent by far. She was curious that such an outmoded, heroic early reader should have survived into Della's Midlands childhood.

'No,' said Della. 'It was Miss Leckie's own one. She lent it me 'cos I was the only one in slow-reading group that year. I had,' said Della with regret, 'to give it back.'

'Do you mean you ran away to find dragons and things?' said Guy.

'Yeah. S'pose so.' Della huddled into Keith's jumper. 'I s'pose so. Big things, anyway. Adventures. Not just,' she shot an unfathomable look at Guy, 'not just blokes.'

'And you found Eddie McArthur,' said Guy. 'I'd say he was probably the nearest thing to a dragon around, these days.'

'Ahead,' said Joanna, 'is the entrance to Starhole Bay, I think. Guy, could you fetch the chart up?'

Dinny Douglas succeeded, at the fourth try and after reducing a receptionist to tears, in filing her copy by modem from the hotel. This entailed disconnecting the switchboard for five minutes, and was only made possible by the threat that she would bring Mr McArthur up personally. At last, the flickering acknowledgement from the *Chronicle* mainframe computer was on the screen of her laptop. 'Total sent 1500 wds,' it said. Dinny promptly switched off, unplugged her lead from the telephone socket, slid the machine into its flat grey bag, and walked away from the desk without turning her head or thanking the anxious girl behind it. She was unlikely to need any more help from the receptionist, so why waste smiles? The girl had been a pain.

Back on the marina pontoons, she began to phrase her speech to Eddie McArthur. 'Mr McArthur, I think I ought to get myself back to the paper. Perhaps I could call up London and organize you another personal secretary to come straight down, one of your staff there, perhaps, who knows the work . . .' She was not, definitely not, staying the night on that creepy boat with that creepy man.

On the other hand, the creepy man did own the *Chronicle*. And was moving in on other ailing newspapers. There were reporters – and editors – who would give their eye teeth to be where she was now, close and necessary to the Proprietor. Gordon, for one, the oily prat. But then it would be different for Gordon, wouldn't it? He wouldn't feel quite the same threat that she did, would he? She thought of Marie's disgruntled revelations, and shuddered. Bloody men. Nobody preyed on them, did they? They could take their chances without risking – that sort of thing. The laptop computer banged against her hip as she walked faster, more irritably.

Back aboard *Privateer*, Eddie sat smoking a small cigar in the big saloon. He was wearing a purple velvet dinner jacket which made him look like a large, Satanic plum. He raised his terrible peaked black eyebrows and greeted her as expansively as if he had guessed at her reservations.

'My dear. You got your copy filed. Excellent. I am glad your editor has got a few competent people around him. What contract do we have you on?'

'Six monthly, renewable but not rolling.'

The little man's eyebrows shot up, exaggeratedly. 'Six *months*? The man is more careless than I thought. You can't keep really good staff on short contracts. I shall,' he made a note on a silver-backed pad on which he had been scribbling earlier, 'speak to him.' He smiled wolfishly. 'Or, should I say, to his successor.'

Bravely, Dinny struggled on with her speech. 'Mr McArthur, your taxi is arranged for five minutes' time. Perhaps I should be getting back to the paper . . .'

He had stopped listening and was frowning at one of the preceding pages of his silver tablet. Her voice faltered and died. There was a silence.

'Splendid. Taxi back, from the Criterion, at ten thirty sharp. We sail early. You had better make yourself at home in the secretary's quarters. You may choose any clothes you need for sea, and throw the rest of his luggage overboard.' He rose, snapped his silver book shut, threw it onto the varnished table with a clatter, and was gone. He had learned, early in a buccaneering business career, that a good exit was worth five good entrances.

Starhole Bay was not such good cover as Guy had suggested. Anybody steaming across Salcombe Bar could see into it easily and make out any boat silhouetted against the towering cliffs. When *Shearwater*'s anchor was down, Guy fussed for a while over disguising the yacht's silhouette. He laid a dinghy oar out over the bow to look like a bowsprit, took the spinnaker pole and a collection of ropes and rigged the pole upright on the boat's modest after hatch, to mimic a second mast.

'He won't be looking for a yawl,' he said hopefully. The other dinghy oar, with the sail cover bundled round it, did service as a dummy boom. The sun was gone now, and in the dusk against the glimmer of the cliffs and the rising moon his work was moderately convincing. Below decks, Jo had lit the brass paraffin lamps for warmth as much as light, and was rootling under bunks for the emergency stock of food. Della huddled in the corner of the cabin, looking curiously around her at the strange, nautical shapes of things in the flickering lamplight.

'Put the anchor light up,' called Joanna to Guy. 'Side locker.'

'We mustn't.'

'It'll look more suspicious if we don't. Anyway, he won't come.'

'Well . . . all right.' Guy banged around, hunting for the aluminium lantern, filling and lighting it, hauling it up between the forestay and the real mast. Joanna, fumbling under a bunk locker with the lid balanced on her head, pulled out three steak pies designed to be baked in their tins once the top had been taken off, two tins of peas and a tin of carrots. 'That's it, I'm afraid,' she said to Della. Then she remembered something, clawed up a floorboard, and reached down into the boat's damp, cool, bilge. 'Aah! Thought so.' Triumphantly, she hauled out two bottles of white wine.

'I got some chocolate,' said Della unexpectedly. 'And some raisins. Marie said always go on a job with something to eat, you never know when you might feel faint.' She thrust her thin arm into the mock-Gucci bag and hauled out a pound slab of milk chocolate and a plastic bag full of miniature raisin packets, of the kind Joanna used to slip into Susan's lunchbox. Tears sprang unexpectedly to her eyes as she took them.

'Thanks. That's pudding, then.'

Replacing the cushions on the bunk, she straightened up in the small cabin and took one step to the galley. Behind it, stuffed casually upright in a cave locker behind a wooden bar, was an almost full bottle of Scotch, the last of the season.

'Drink?' she asked.

Guy came below. With the pies in the oven and the vegetables ready mixed up in the saucepan, the three sat together in the lamplight, the whisky warming them from within, the cliffs glimmering and swinging lazily across the portholes.

Not everybody is gathered, by nightfall, in the primitive safety of a firelit circle at the hearth. Not everyone is around a lamp with food and friends, or even (like Eddie McArthur at that moment) lapped in the tribal dignity of a banqueting suite, a Rotarian Valhalla.

Some are outsiders, prowling alone, free from the stifling warmth of human kinship. Some prefer it that way. Brief, jagged encounters will do for them, whether of battle or love. They will visit a fire, their wolf eyes gleaming white in the outer shadows. For a moment, maybe for a spell of days or weeks, they will sit, looking almost like the peaceable house-dogs around. But then they will go, without warning or apology, back into their formless darkness at the edge of things. They will be free and alone, available for the next kill or the next mating.

Just such a prowler was picking his way across the network of grimy streets to the north of Oxford Circus, stepping absentmindedly over the outstretched feet of the cardboard-box sleepers who were already settling for the night, propped like November guys in the doorways of wholesale clothing shops under the cold sickle moon. He had come from a lamplit circle, the lone walker; a circle in a cheerful restaurant on the corner of Tichfield Street where diving suits, trombones and stuffed fish hung wittily from the ceiling and every table had a clashing oilskin cloth. He had come from the circle because it bored him.

He had thrown down his share of the bill – or an approximation to it – and said abruptly that he must get back to the office to sort out a couple of things. His companions, all younger than he, had said, 'Oh, shame!' and 'stay for some tiramisu'. But they had been, he could see, secretly relieved at his going. He was prone to rant, these days, at the young. They were so *middle-aged*, with their earnest relationships, their new babies, their footling talk of primary education and play spaces, their bright aseptic clothes and bright boring ideas and their infernal, soul-killing political correctness.

At the moment when he left, they had been discussing a Potrayal Seminar which three of them in the department had been attending. Fascinating, the young ones agreed, to get in touch with the racism and sexism in oneself; even more fascinating to overcome it. They really appreciated the opportunity to learn how fruitful it could be to introduce characters into their work – for these were all, in some degree, peddlers of the Drama – characters which called the stereotypes into question. Jake had a marvellous script sent in, said Ellie, about a deaf-mute Asian storyteller whose pregnancy grew as her tale did, 'so that the childbirth moment and the legend's climax came together, you see, in blood'.

And he, the walker through the streets, had rudely interrupted and asked how the fuck were you going to make a decent radio play out of a bloodstained deaf-mute? And where would the pleasure of it be, anyway? Where the beauty, where the thrill?

They had stared at him uncomfortably. And, leaving, he had known that all the anti-stereotyping seminars in the world would not prevent those colleagues, after he left, from referring to him as an old fart, an ageing hippie, a bit of a throwback. They would say he was losing his edge. Hah!

He padded on through the dark streets in his canvas shoes, his greying hair curling over his collar, the crumpled carrier bag he used as a briefcase completing a trampish appearance. As he negotiated the street sleepers around his feet, he might almost have been about to sit in a doorway himself. Bugger his young colleagues! Bugger the whole lot in charge these days, with their seminars and prissy little workplace sexual harassment guidelines (he had fallen foul of those a good few times, which added greatly to his grievance and his sense of precariousness in employment). He did not belong to this tribe, not any more. The old ones, the good old ones, had gone or died or mutated horribly into supporters of the brisk new regime.

He would get out. Go somewhere clean and new, perhaps to the west of Ireland and the mountain which was his namesake. He would write a magnificent novel and raise two fingers to the Philistine bastards at the BBC.

For it was at Broadcasting House, the great battleship building into which he finally stepped, that he and his convivial colleagues worked. He waved a plastic identity card irritably at the security man and walked a long, wide corridor to the second set of lifts. Inside one of them, alone, he broke deafening wind as he rose six floors: an open, but safe, defiance of his surroundings. Finally he and the carrier bag travelled over a certain carpet – hideously spotted with carpet tiles bearing tragic and comic mask designs, to indicate that this was the Drama Corridor – and turned into his office.

He preferred to keep erratic hours, these days, ever since he had acquired an open-plan office to be shared with Neville and Ellie. Both were immensely talented, he had been told, but to him both were immensely annoying. In the old days, the 1970s even, a man could have his own cell, ten feet by six, in the great honeycombed building and tread his own path. Now the walls were swept down and memos were sent around about creative interpersonal interacting and God knows what, and a man had no privacy to make rather private telephone calls, which were usually to young women in need of a wise mentor. Neville, at the end desk, had a wife and new baby in Greenwich and a penchant for plays by women. No, he thought savagely. Not even women: wimmin, or womyn. Ellie was a total nightmare, dressed all in ragged black, with tight leggings, like a scarecrow witch. She took offence at the slightest thing, especially slight things to do with his fascination with her leggings. She went on and on about the depravity and inadmissibility of any work by dead white males. Which was fine; had he not himself in his day talked down the Shakespeare season, ridiculed the old buffers who wanted to put on Rattigan, and produced a savage parody of Noel Coward?

It was just that these days, even living white males seemed to be out of favour. He had heard Ellie saying Tom Stoppard was a closet fascist, and Samuel Beckett a phallocentricist. He had not argued. A mark of his depression, these days, was that he did not bother. He just drank a little more at lunchtime, and on one memorable occasion vomited, neatly, right onto the nearest fancy carpet tile to his office. The masks of comedy and tragedy looked up at him reproachfully through the pile of sick, and Ellie had refused to clean it up, even though she was the only woman in the office. One mask of tragedy still bore a hideous grey smirk.

Sitting down at his desk now, he listlessly turned over the latest project: a three-part poetic drama about Lilith, first wife of Adam and symbol of the old wild pre-Christian goddesses, dispossessed by demure and obedient Eve and haunting the world in anger down the centuries. He had thought he could sneak it past Ellie and Neville on the feminist ticket and so get some full-blooded politically incorrect poetry onto the air. About thighs, and milky clefts, and breasts. But already the project had run into trouble over the word 'whore'. Ellie felt it was 'being used in a negative way'. Irritably, he pushed it aside.

There was a copy of the *Chronicle* on the desk, left there no doubt by the secretary the three of them shared. He looked at the front – a lot of fuss about some windy night in the Channel – and turned the page listlessly. Then his eye lighted on a woman's face and the years fell away.

MISSING, it said. MISSING. She was missing, all right. She was what he had been missing. The wide eyes, the direct honest gaze, the slight melancholy around the mouth, the cloud of dark hair. Joanna Telford, by God! Joanna Gurney, they called her here, but there was no doubt. She looked hardly different from the girl he had known: still young, open-faced, but perhaps a little more secure, less clinging, than he remembered her. She could not have been more than nineteen then. Ten years his junior.

And women had all been clinging, then. Lord, how women had changed! They seemed to set the pace these days, take their piece of action with one eye still on their career and the safety of their own psyche, and move on with brisk antiseptic firmness of purpose, like nurses. Women in his young days used to yearn and worship and give themselves completely; they used to wash socks and serve meals and be like Ben Bolt's Alice, who wept with delight when he gave her a smile and trembled for fear at his frown. And they used to cling and weep and have to have it gently pointed out to them when it was time to move on. Now, girls seemed to move *him* on, ever more briskly. Women had definitely changed.

Unless it was he who was less clingable-to? He pushed the thought aside. Joanna Telford! Gurney. Who was Gurney? Some chap she had found who let her cling. Kids, it said here. He closed his eyes and imagined her breast-feeding. Nice tits, always had. Like Lilith's in the poetry-drama, 'bird-soft, bird-white, breathing with life's breath'.

Suddenly, he was awake and sober and purposeful. This would kick-start the novel. A great project was swelling within him. Pushing off his canvas shoes, he began pacing the room in his hairy socks. The BBC wanted rid of him, one of the last few staffers in his job. His head of department had hinted heavily at voluntary redundancy with a decent payoff. He would talk the payoff up by a few thousand, take it, and go to the far west of Ireland and rent a cheap cottage. But first he would find this older Joanna and – if her effect on him was anything like her picture's effect – he would rescue her from this blighted Hampshire existence of hers, of which quite clearly she had grown sick and tired. He would appear as the fulfilment of an old dream, change her meaningless life, and permit her, this time, to cling and serve and inspire him while he wrote.

He may not have been quite as sober as he thought. Nonetheless, it did not take him long to pad down to the newsroom where the national telephone directories lived, and find the only Gurney in Bonhurst. From their computer terminals, annoyed-looking young people glanced meaningfully at his socks. Taking no notice, he wrote the number on the back of his broad hand and padded back upstairs, deciding not to call the lift in case the waiting spoilt his purposeful, self-starting mood. On the way out of the long newsroom he saw a pile of early copies of the Thursday morning papers, on their way to the compilers of the morning news bulletins. He glanced around at the young people intent on their terminals, and neatly filched the *Chronicle*. Might be something else about Joanna.

Back in his silent office he spread it out and whistled softly through pursed lips. Even better. The photograph was the same, but to freshen it up the picture desk had cropped it lower down and brushed out the neckline of Joanna's jumper, to give a décolleté impression. Then someone had suggested cropping the hairline at the sides 'to bring out the lesbian theme a bit'. The result was, to the lonely reader in the drama office, even more appealing. As for the text, – headed 'SAILAWAY WIFE IN GAY HOOKER MYSTERY', it could hardly be more stimulating. He pulled down Neville's atlas and looked for a while at the south-west coast of Britain, then picked up the telephone and dialled the number written on the back of his hand. A young man answered.

'Mr Gurney? Sorry to trouble you. I'm an old friend of Joanna's. My name's O'Riordan. Gabriel O'Riordan.'

Lance, who had answered the telephone, had never heard the name before, nor the soft, cultured, faintly Irish tones. He had, however, just spent ten minutes with his father and sister, listening in increasing bafflement and worry to an incoherent answerphone message. More of a short radio drama, really, complete with sound effects: 'Keith . . . *ccrrrr, skcrrrr* . . . leave Torquay – I'll be in – *crrrk* – (cry of "No . . . the Boss!") . . . safe harbour anyway. Don't worry. Tomorrow I'll go in to – *scccrrrk* – *cchhhhh* – ("No . . . not safe – he's a pervert" – *cccrrr* – *thump, eugh* (sounds of vomiting, flapping sails, "Shit!" in a male voice . . . "Are we sinking? Aaaaah" . . . Shut up, you two – *crrrrrk* . . . *thump* – "Owwww . . . are we sinking . . . going to rip!" . . . *shhhrrrrrkkk* . . . too bad, Keith, I will . . . *crrrkkk* . . . Salcombe. 'Bye.'

After this, any coherent voice on the telephone seemed very welcome. Lance was a trusting boy, and was lulled by Gabriel's expressions of concern and the fact that he seemed to be able to put names with some confidence to the background figures on the tape – 'Gather that she's with some friends of ours, Della Jones and Guy Pastern-Hopkins . . . hoping to join them for a drink. Was it Dartmouth they were heading for?' So it was not many moments before Lance shared with Gabriel the one useful word in the answerphone message: Salcombe.

'That could have been the fucking *press*!' howled Susan as he put the receiver down.

'I never thought of that,' said Lance, a little crestfallen. 'I'm not used to all this suspicion, like you lot. Sorry.'

Keith looked up from the sofa where he had been lying with a frequently replenished whisky glass in his fist for the past half-hour.

'Dun't matter,' he said, slurring a little. '"M going to Salcombe in the morning. Sort it out. Sh'can decide if sh's bloody coming or bloody staying away. Sick of it. Whassat doorbell? Inna middle of the night?'

Anneliese stood on the doorstep, apologetic. Behind her trembled an almost unrecognizable Mandy, her hair limp, her eyes red with crying, her puffed-up pink jacket clashing horribly with green Bermudas and a flapping red T-shirt.

'Suzie, Mum can't drive us to college tomorrow,' she said. 'She's going to find your mum, she says.' Lowering her voice, she hissed, '*Vodka*.'

'Got to say sorry, tell her I never said any of it,' said Mandy. 'Going to go to all the harbours, find her. Come to tell Keith it's all my fault. Before bed. Not let the sun go down on it. Wrath.'

'Where's Alex?' asked Susan, practically.

'That's the other thing,' said Anneliese. 'Apparently there's a fire, at the Bun. The fire brigade rang up. It's OK now, but things got a bit wet and muddled. Erika Merriam is there helping, and she rang us, said one of the owners should be represented, so Popsy went.'

'Just as well,' said Lance who was watching Mandy as she knelt by the sofa, clutching the hand of a dazed, complaisant Keith and weeping on it. 'Your ma's breath would probably have started the fire up again.'

The golden glow of *Shearwater*'s paraffin lamp sparkled off the wet cutlery piled up beside the tiny sink, sent gleams along the varnished cabin table and shone, unimpeded, through the clear glass of the empty whisky bottle. It blended prettily with the green of two wine bottles, also empty, which lay propped in the corner of the starboard bunk. Joanna had put them there to make more room for all their elbows.

'Amazing,' Guy said unsteadily, 'how much room elbows take up. Just six elbows.'

'They're ever so handy,' said Della, 'for keeping your head propped up when you go a bit floppy.' She leaned forward, elbows spreading, and was asleep.

Joanna flicked a crump of pie crust from her shoulder, ate her last square of Della's emergency chocolate and rose carefully to her feet, steadying herself on the pillar under the mast.

'I think,' she said, 'we had better have some coffee.'

'We're not *drunk* exactly,' said Guy. 'I've been a lot drunker.'

'Thassright,' said Joanna, ducking expertly under the low deck beam. 'I've had it before on boats. It's the fresh air. And the food. And reaction. Relaxing. It does for you. Not the same as really drunk.'

She leaned on the safety bar in front of the galley, remembering other times. Once, when Lance was a baby, she and Keith had come through a hard Channel crossing, tied up in Cherbourg marina and fallen asleep in their clothes at one o'clock in the morning, their two heads on the cabin table and their hair trailing in spilt cocoa. And that was after just one whisky, the one they had splashed in the cocoa. They had woken at six, miserably uncomfortable, to hear the baby whimpering for his morning feed. While Joanna fed Lance, Keith had fried them both a large breakfast. They ate it, made love while Lance played with his toes and gurgled himself back to sleep in the forecabin, then slept again until nine. It was only then that they had noticed the stiff spikes of dried cocoa in their hair. But they hadn't been drunk, exactly.

Now, her hands flickering around the familiar shapes of the galley, she filled the kettle and reached for the matches. Della was fast asleep on the far corner of the table, her hair spilling over her face, relaxed as a baby. Guy gazed at her.

'Don't you think she's terrific?' he said in a low voice. 'I've never met a girl quite like her.'

Joanna looked across at the sleeping girl. 'Mmm – yes,' she said. 'Guy, if I were you—' She stopped, and concentrated rather too hard on lighting the gas jet.

'What?' said Guy. 'I mean, I really would value your sort of view. There are obvious, sort of, problems—'

'You mean because she's an escort girl?'

'No, no. I mean, things are so different now, aren't they? I mean quite important people, MPs and all that, go out with, um, escort girls. It's not sort of Victorian . . .'

'No,' said Joanna. 'But I think you ought to meet each other in a more ordinary sort of place, perhaps, a few times. Everything might look different.'

'I know,' said Guy. 'I found that before. Round Mr McArthur everything seems kind of different, more sort of brightly coloured, if you know what I mean. You decide things faster. Apparently his last secretary but two went off and joined a sect. Actually,' he added in a burst of confidence, swinging the brass lamp rather irritatingly so that the mugs Joanna was filling with coffee grew long, wavering, menacing shadows, 'if you hadn't been here I think I'd probably have asked Della to marry me by now.'

'I don't think—'

'No, no, of course I won't. Frighten her off, for a start. I'll take her out a bit, back in London. But I'm absolutely sure she's up to it. My parents would love her, honestly.'

Joanna, filling the mugs, decided that Guy would not see her point at all, even if she could bring herself, *in vino veritas*, to be impolite enough to make it. The question was not whether Della was up to Guy's standards, but whether Guy could keep up with Della. Not socially; intellectually.

Good heavens, she thought, passing him his coffee with a guilty smile, is that really what I think? That this nineteen-year-old call girl without an exam pass to her name is more than a match, *intellectually*, for this Cambridge graduate, albeit a scraped one, four years her senior? For this man-of-the-world and aide to one of the most powerful magnates in Britain?

'Yes,' she said inwardly. 'Yes, I do think exactly that. Guy is limited. Always will be.' The Guys, she saw, run along the rails and do as they are told. They are happy inside the system. That is why McArthur chose him as a gopher, she thought. That is why MPs and stuffy institutions take on boys of his type. They run on rails. McArthur's real, cutting-edge workers would surely be more like barrow boys, streetwise kids, the type who turned up in City jobs in the 1980s: student rebels or school dropouts, lads with ideas of their own.

Whereas Della, dyslexic Della, who walked out on home and family to find adventure, who took one look at McArthur and did a pierhead jump, whose spiky little personality provoked Guy into his first ever derailment, Della was different. Joanna looked fondly at Della's tousled blonde head.

Guy had taken his coffee from her during this reverie and climbed unsteadily into the cockpit to drink it on the foredeck. 'Get a bit of air,' he explained, "f that's all right.' At the thumping sound of his progress across the cabin top, Della woke up, looked around wildly, and smiled when she saw Joanna holding out a mug towards her.

'Ta. Where's Guy?'

'On deck.'

'Can he hear us?'

'Nope. Not from the foredeck.'

'Can I ask you something?'

'Yes.'

'What d'you think I oughter do? About him?'

'How do you mean?'

'He's going on about tennis, and meeting in London, and my

staying at his flat while I get another job, and all that. D'you think he's, you know, serious?'

'Yes. I think he is. Are you glad?'

'Well, I was. I really fancied him this morning. But just, you know . . . he's sort of a bit of a bimbo, in't he?'

'Don't you want a bimbo man?'

'Not for always.'

'What do you want? Rhett Butler?'

'Nah. Actually, I'd like . . .'

'What?'

'A rest from blokes. Something else. Some new place. A proper job. *Then* I might fancy going out with Guy.'

'What's brought this on?'

'Well . . . this, actually.' Della gestured, taking in the cabin lamp, the bunks, the varnished lockers, the compact snugness of it all, the chart still lying on the chart table in a businesslike way. 'It's sort of . . . *dignified*.'

'You mean the boat?'

'Yeah, it's like a whole house, with food and everything, only going somewhere, and you steering it.'

'Normally,' said Joanna, 'I sail it with my husband, Keith. Not on my own. This is the first time on my own.'

'Is he the captain, then, when he's here? Not you?' Della looked disappointed.

'No . . . not exactly captain . . . we sort of share the decisions. But it is different when he's here. It's OK, though.'

'Why did you run away with the boat, then?'

'I was upset,' said Jo, slowly. 'I was upset, because Keith wouldn't listen to what I wanted. I wanted to give up my job and try to study again. Or something. I wanted to change my life.'

'And he wouldn't let you?'

'It isn't a matter of letting. I could have done it without asking him. It's my money, my investment. But I wanted him to agree. I wanted him to see why I wanted to change. Once you're married . . .'

She paused. Della hung, interested, on the beginning of that sentence, so immemorially fascinating to women who are not yet married but think they might be. Joanna looked at her and felt a sudden tug of responsibility. She must not mislead this child. She continued, carefully, thinking it out as she spoke.

'Once you're married, all sorts of decisions have to be joint decisions. Else things don't work. If one of you steamrollers the other, it feels bad, even if you're the winner. Feels worse if you're the loser. So you have to work hard at agreeing. You have to put work into thinking the way the other person thinks. Sometimes you feel as if it would be less bother if you each just ran your own life and met for bed, or to discuss the children. But really, that wouldn't work either.'

'You can't agree about everything, though,' said Della, sceptically.

'No. But even if the other person doesn't quite agree, they have to understand what makes you do things. Respect it. Otherwise, it's lonelier than if you weren't married at all.'

Della thought, frowning, her head thrown backwards to rest on the varnished bars of the bookshelf.

'I don't think I want to get married. Not for a long time. It'd really, really slow you down, all that discussing, fitting in with someone else, wouldn't it?'

'Yes,' admitted Joanna. 'It does. But there are compensations.'

'How old were you,' continued Della relentlessly, 'when you got married?'

'Twenty,' said Joanna. 'Too young.'

'So why did you?'

'Because . . . because . . . I don't know,' said Joanna. Again, that strange tug, that insistent voice making her find a truth to tell this girl. 'Yes, I do know.'

'Why then?'

'Because I met a good man. A good, ordinary man. And I wanted a good, ordinary, decent life. Children. Kindness. Ordinary family jokes. Knowing all day who you'd be in bed with at the end of it. I didn't want any more . . . chaos.'

'Did you have chaos before, then?' Della was wide awake now, peering curiously over the mug which she held like a chipmunk in both small paws. What sort of chaos could this grown-up lady, who steered her boat so surely, have ever been involved in?

'Chaos of love,' said Joanna, stretching out on the bunk. 'I was

– had been – terribly in love with a man who wasn't ordinary, and wasn't good either.'

'What'd he do?'

'He used women – girls – for a while and threw them over.'

'Well, lots of them do that. Even at school they did. You don't trust them, ever. It's stupid.'

'I did,' said Joanna. 'I trusted him with my life. But the bad thing, the real point wasn't just that he threw you over. The bad thing he did was that he made it feel as if it was your fault. He made people feel really silly, and small. Sometimes it hurt them so much they – well, very much, anyway.'

'And your ordinary bloke, your husband, he didn't go round hurting people?'

'He asks a lot of himself. He takes blame. He doesn't cause people pain unless he really can't help it, and then he stays awake all night worrying. I told you, he's a good man.'

'So you didn't just marry him to be ordinary and have kids?'

'N-no. I think he was the one,' said Joanna. 'Really, truly, the right one for me. I think he would have been anyway. But when we got married I'm not sure I knew that. I might have been thinking too much about the ordinary secure bit, and not really encouraging him to be anything else.'

'Is he boring?'

'No,' said Joanna, with dignity. 'Certainly not. We have a lot of laughs.'

'So,' said Della. 'Why'd you run away?' She paused, a puzzled frown spreading over her face. 'Oh. Sorry. I asked you that at the start.'

Joanna stared at her for a moment and then began to laugh, and laugh, until tears ran down her face and Guy, tipsily half-asleep on the foredeck, woke and realized that there was a mast cleat sticking into his back and that he would rather be below, cosily in a bunk. Leaving the moon and the cliffs and the cold night air, he came below to find Joanna and Della opposite one another, elbows on the table, heads touching, laughing together like children who have just understood a wicked, adult joke.

Eddie McArthur returned majestically to his boat at midnight, sated with sycophancy. The Rotarian Valhalla had been a fine one; he had kept his taxi waiting for an hour and a quarter while he circulated among the guests for an unprecedented length of time. He had enjoyed the gathering of provincial businessmen, finding that their admiring deference and slight fear, which usually would have rather bored him, on this occasion were balm to wounded pride. Thoughts of revenge on Guy and Della had almost faded from his mind. Life was good. Those who were not with him were against him, but those against him were negligible. Powerless. Barely worth a thought, let alone an undignified pursuit. His small, rotund form almost bounced down the marina pontoon towards the looming bulk of his ship.

The saloon was lighted; beyond its thin curtain he could see the shadowy form of young Miss Douglas, sitting very poised and upright on a chair, reading. In the shadows, he paused to admire her. The blonde hair fell, once again, in a perfectly symmetrical smooth bell; she had found a white shirt somewhere, tucked it in to her leather trousers, and cinched her waist with a broad red belt. She looked cool, elegant and unapproachable. She had put on careful make-up during the evening, a shield against her own uncertainty in this new situation. As he gazed, a memory stirred in Eddie, and a desire. He bent, fiddled with something at his feet, then carrying it he climbed the gangway steps and went along the side deck, moving with the lightness of a cat.

When Dinny looked up, startled, he was standing in the doorway in his dinner jacket, smiling what he no doubt thought was a Clark Gable smile beneath his thin black moustache. She opened her mouth to speak, but he put his finger, unexpectedly, to his lips.

'Ssssh. Don't spoil the picture. My dear, would you do a small thing for me?'

Eddie rarely asked for anything politely. When he did, the shock value was so great that he generally got his way. Dinny nodded and waited.

'Just step out onto the stern deck. It isn't windy. And sit, just as you were sitting. Cool and beautiful.'

Mesmerized, she rose. He stepped aside as she passed through the doorway. She sat down on the white padded chair, folded her hands, and stifled a violent, primitive urge to abandon this passivity and run like hell. She waited. There was a faint sound of running water, distinct from the lapping of the ripples around the harbour boats. Eddie bent down, pulled at a dark shape on the deck, then straightened up and cried 'So!'

The water hit her for the second time that day, icy cold in a thin, violent stream. She put her arms up, crossed, in vain protest, and turned her face away. Still the water came. Behind the hose McArthur watched enraptured as the perfect hairdo disintegrated into wet rat's tails, the crisp shirt shrank clinging round her body, and the mascara ran down her cheeks, which flushed pink beneath the ivory-pale foundation. Even better, she was not hurt or humiliated but comically, gloriously angry. She shrieked, furious as a fishwife. 'Stop it! Bloody stop it! For Christ's sake! You arsehole!'

And Eddie laughed and laughed, a peal of pure unadulterated joy which flickered black-and-white through his innermost heart. He was in his Mack Sennett world, at one with the Stooges, Laurel and Hardy, Keystone Cops and Crazy Gang. He was happy. At last, he let the hose drop and said, through his choking laughter, 'Thank you. That was wonderful.' And, wiping his eyes, he vanished into the interior of the big boat, leaving the hose writhing and pumping vainly across the deck.

The marina was quiet in that late season and middle part of the week, but when Dinny shook the wet hair from her eyes she saw a small, fascinated audience standing silently, in pyjamas and nightshirts, on the pontoons and in the cockpits of neighbouring boats. An elderly couple with white hair and wondering blue eyes; two young men with ragged beards; a child clutching a teddy bear; a naval-looking figure who had put on his reefer jacket and a peaked cap over a striped sarong and bare chest. He was the only one who spoke.

'Torquay,' he clipped, 'is going to the dawgs.'

It was left to Dinny to climb off the boat, turn the tap off, coil the hose, and, squaring her shoulders, march back aboard and into the saloon where Eddie McArthur sat, still giggling, in the bigger of the chairs. Dripping, she confronted him.

'Right' she said. 'I hope you enjoyed yourself.'

'I did,' he replied, shaking a little with remembered mirth. 'Far better than sex. Sex is overrated. You are unique. Wonderful girl. Such dignity.' He erupted again, snorting.

'I didn't exactly do much,' said Dinny.

'It's not what you do, it's what you are. Next time, you can wear pearls and a high lace collar, and I shall . . . I shall throw a custard pie.'

'Why do you think there's going to be a next time?'

'Because you want a very, very good contract with my newspaper.'

'I might not.'

'You do. The Editor is leaving. You want to be the Editor?'

'I'm twenty-three. This is my first reporting job, for God's sake.'

'So it is. So young, yet so regal.' His eyes travelled over her sodden person and a new giggle rose in him, irresistible. 'You will go a very long way. Faster if you stay with me.'

'There was a message,' said Dinny, 'from the London office. On the fax. You told me to check them. Do you want to know what it said?'

'Yes. What?' She pulled a sodden piece of paper from her pocket.

'It's unreadable now. Basically it said that there is a message from the PM's office. About the New Year's Honours. That you will be receiving, very shortly, an invitation. It said congratulations, and asked whether you had decided on what title you want. Lord McArthur of where?'

Eddie was silent. He had not expected this, not yet. A knighthood first, perhaps. But a peerage! Lord McArthur of Melton Mowbray? Of Clapham, where the *Chronicle* was printed? Of Fleet? He would think about it. Meanwhile, he could not bear to let the warmth, the Saturday-matinee childish laughter ebb away in such adult considerations.

'I suppose,' continued Dinny, 'that these things are all very delicate, between the offer and the Honours List. Vulnerable to any breath of scandal.'

He roused himself slightly from his happy euphoria. 'Are you threatening me, young woman?'

'Yes,' said Dinny. 'You've used me as a skivvy all afternoon, and humiliated me in public with a hosepipe in the middle of the night. I can tell this story to the *Globe*, to *The Times*, to the *Telegraph*, to *Private Eye*. I can sue you for harassment and constructive dismissal and assault. People ought to know what you are really like.'

'Or,' said McArthur, closing his eyes as if bored, 'you can pack up all that pompous bloody crap about your rights and look after yourself. You can be a star in your own right, with a direct line up past the Editor to me. And every now and then you can come sailing, and let me throw custard pies at you. And buckets of water. I would like that. I would, of course,' he smiled his worrying smile, 'warm the water first. And you need have no fear for your virtue. Any needs I have in that direction are more easily satisfied. What you can do for me is in another, more celestial, league.'

His eyes remained closed. Dinny, seeing that the audience was at an end, crept wetly into the secretary's cabin, turned the lock on the door, threw off her sodden clothes and slid thankfully into Guy's heavy linen sheets. Some days, she thought as she pulled the duvet over her head, needed a line drawing under them.

The Old Vicarage had been designed in a more spacious, optimistic age. Its builders had meant it to shelter a clerical incumbent, his wife, some half a dozen children, a curate, a visiting bishop, and a couple of exhausted, raw-faced skivvies in the attic.

It had, therefore, no difficulty in accommodating Keith (out cold on the sitting-room sofa), Alex and Mandy (in Lance's double bed), Lance himself (resignedly back in his malodorous trans-European sleeping bag, on his parents' bed), and Erika Merriam (tucked up in Susan's room, rather to Susan's dismay, after insisting that she must stay nearby so as to be in the Bun at crack of dawn, mopping). Susan and Anneliese dossed down in the official guest bedroom in a jutting spur of the house known as the Curate's Annexe, where the radiator had a habit of knocking and gurgling throughout the night. It was, according to family tradition, haunted by a long-gone curate, poisoned by a bad egg he ate to humour the Bishop.

Susan had tried to put Erika there when Alex brought her in. Erika, such was her state, would have gone anywhere. But an ill-timed crack from Lance about the ghost had caused Ted Merriam – up to that moment a silent looming presence, his hands blackened by moving scorched objects around in the wreckage of the Bun – to veto it. 'Erika's nervous of ghosts,' he rumbled. 'If she say she's got to stay here, that's up to her. But I 'ave to get home and feed my old dog, and I won't 'ave my wife shut up in some room with ghosts. She han't deserved that.' Susan rather admired him for it. Protective men appealed to her.

Now, huddled together in the double bed for warmth, with

the curate's radiator groaning and squeaking alongside, the two girls discussed the evening's events.

'Wasn't it amazing,' said Anneliese, 'when Pops was all set to blame the fire on poor little Zoë, going on about how she must have left a hotplate on or boiled something dry, and Erika—'

'Erika went really apeshit, didn't she? I always thought she wouldn't say boo to a goose, let alone a solicitor.'

'Calling him a typical employer, blaming the workers, swearing that Zoë wouldn't possibly have left anything on because she would have done everything she was told.'

'Because for once,' Susan did a creditable imitation of Erika's tremulous fury, 'the poor child had been properly taught her routine and made to take notice, and your wife, pardon my saying it, Mr Heron, does her no favours by letting her get slack.'

'And Pops going all red and furious and gobbling like a turkey, and your dad snoring on the sofa not hearing a word of it . . .' Anneliese paused. Something in Susan's glee had flattened at the last words, and Anneliese felt it. She searched for a tactful conclusion and managed, 'I've never seen Uncle Keef drunk before.'

'Me neither,' said Susan flatly. 'Dad never gets drunk. I suppose he was tired, more than drunk.'

'Yes,' said Anneliese diplomatically. 'Anyway, he was well out of it.'

'So was your mum,' added Susan, to even things up. 'Pretty out of it herself, crying on his arm, saying how she'd let her only real friend down and now Mum might be drowned.'

The momentary rift between the girls healed in mutual enjoyment of the unfolding, unprecedented drama of the evening. Anneliese did not bother to defend Mandy's alcohol levels or plead tiredness for her, but accelerated into the glorious reminiscence.

'Yeah, and Lance telling her your mum was OK—'

'And him trying to get her off Dad, and her clinging on, and your dad gobbling away at Erika, and her standing up for Zoë—'

'And then the fireman arriving!'

The two girls paused again, contemplating the electrical

moment when a knocking on the door had broken into this late-night bedlam, and the assembly had fallen silent as a large fireman stepped inside bearing news that 'the boys reckoned they had found the source of the fire' and that there was no need to worry about arson or vandalism or electrical faults.

'Straightforward careless beggar, sir,' he had said, gleaming in his blue and brass, brushing an invisible speck of ash from his lapel. 'Someone, it appears, threw a cigarette butt into the metal bin in the kitchen. There must have been some cardboard cake boxes in there, possibly bearing traces of fatty materials.' This was not, Susan had dreamily thought, really the most flattering epitaph for a Black Forest gâteau. 'So up went the bin, flames caught the cloths hanging overhead, there you go.'

'Well,' Erika had said into the ensuing deathly silence. 'Zoë doesn't smoke, and nor do I. And customers don't come into the kitchen.' Her eyes were on Alex whose omnipresent, elegantly dangling cigarette was drooping from his fingers at a more than usually perilous angle.

'It was me who locked up,' he said bravely. 'I did go round the kitchen. Stopped and had a look at the big tea urn boiler thing, never really seen one before. I'm not sure if I was smoking. Ummm . . . if that's the case, officer . . . sorry.'

'A very large number of fires and some fatalities,' said the fireman, 'are caused by carelessness with cigarette ends.'

'It was a metal bin,' said Erika, heaping coals of fire on his head. 'And perhaps you thought it'd be safe? Maybe you didn't want to stub it out on the draining board that Zoë left so nice and clean.' There was, Susan thought, a real streak of malice in that nervous-looking woman.

Keith, at this stage, had half woken and found himself being clutched by Mandy, his hand damp from her drunken tears. In a movement of convulsive horror, he threw up his arms and broke her grasp sufficiently for Lance, who was standing nearby shaking with silent mirth, to pick his mother's friend up in his arms and, with a man-to-man apologetic smirk at Alex, carry her upstairs to lay her out in his own room. The amateur dramatic air of the proceedings was heightened by the fact that Lance was still wearing nothing but his mother's Japanese kimono.

Upstairs, after a brief, calming conversation with Mandy,

he left her asleep diagonally across the bed, thumb in her mouth.

'Lance looks terrific with all that hair,' said Anneliese. 'I was quite jealous of Mum, actually. Lance can carry me up to bed anytime.'

'In your dreams,' said Susan rudely. 'God, I suppose we'll have a major breakfast party now. It's funny having everyone here. Bit like a party sleepover when you're all kids.'

'Extra funny having old Erika here,' said Anneliese. 'Didn't know she was allowed to sleep away from home. Who's going to fry Ted's bacon?'

'Well, I thought Ted was very gallant, the way he made her have my room. Hidden depths. He was a lot more gallant than Alex. He was going to push off home if Lance hadn't made him stay with Mandy in case she was sick or anything.'

'Lance,' said Anneliese dreamily, 'is rather taking over the world, isn't he?'

'No chance, Annie,' said Susan. 'He is after higher things. He isn't going to get involved with anyone here. He's off to the big wide world. 'Bye 'bye Bonhurst. 'Bye 'bye little sister's friends.'

'Right, so are we. No more mooning over friends' big brothers. Hoo-ray. I fixed how we can get to college tomorrow, by the way. Taxi. I took fifty quid off Pops while he was in shock over being caught out as King Alfred burning the cake boxes.'

'Serve him right for torching innocent teashops. What a vandal,' said Susan. 'I wouldn't fancy your mum's driving much, after tonight anyway.'

'She's going to Salcombe,' said Anneliese smugly.

'What?' Susan sat upright. 'She's what?'

'She is going to find your mum. Lance said he'd take her. That's how he got her to lie down and go to sleep.'

'What about Alex?'

'He is doing penance with Erika Merriam and a mop.'

'She wouldn't trust him,' said Susan, 'with anything as high tech as a mop. He'll be sent to the office to get on the phone to the insurance company probably. With Gus detailed to stand by with a bucket of sand in case he drops another fag.'

'So Mum and Lance are going to Salcombe. I suppose your dad too? Is Uncle Keef going?'

'Yeah . . . no . . .' Susan frowned. 'Look, I dunno. Nobody's talked to Dad. He's the only one who wasn't going around last night announcing what he wants. He might just be sick of it all.'

'But he'll want to go and meet your mum? On the boat?'

'Well,' Susan said. 'I dunno. He's done his bit. He drove down to Torquay, which is hours – got a flat tyre – got there and she'd buggered off with some woman and a bloke he doesn't even know, no message or anything. Then he's left with some journalist going on about lesbians and conmen. So he drives back. He told us he had a row with the police about falling asleep parked on the hard shoulder, and he obviously hated being told off by some young policeman. I think that's why he started drinking when he did get back. Then all this chaos in the house . . . that Gabriel bloke ringing up seeming to know all about it, and the names of the other people on *Shearwater*, and it is Dad's boat too, and he doesn't know anything.' Susan was sitting up, hugging her knees, talking to the far wall while Anneliese lounged, watching. 'It's all exactly what Dad hates, all muddled and undignified. And if you think about it, it's actually all Mum's fault.'

Anneliese considered. 'You think he might just decide to stay here, ignore her, and let her come back if she wants?'

'Why shouldn't he? He's having an awful time. All they had was an argument, just in the family, and poor old Dad's got landed with all this stuff – newspapers and tragic suicide bids and Captain Bligh and tarts and Alex burning down the teashop and your mum sobbing all over him and Erika Merriam turning up at breakfast tomorrow going on about Zoë when he's got a hangover. He's going to hate it. He's already hating it. He's a *solicitor*, for God's sake. He's about being respectable. I think,' said Susan, warming to her theme, 'I think he ought to stay here, get on with his work, and let her bloody well come back and explain herself. Not go chasing round Devon like a *Carry On* film.'

'My mum,' said Anneliese, 'says that daughters are always hard on their mothers and soft on their dads.'

'Yeah, well. Can see why.'

'So are you going to Salcombe to tell her off? I can take your form and stuff in to college, if you want to go with Lance and Mum.'

'No,' said Susan. 'No. I'm coming to college. I feel like Dad. I want to organize my own life in peace.'

'OK.' Anneliese hauled the duvet round her and curled into her favourite sleeping position. 'I wonder where your mum is now?'

'That Gabriel man who rang up told Lance she was with friends of his – what was it? – someone Jones and Guy Pastern-Hopkins. Whoever the hell they are. Probably having wild parties. I dunno. It's not like Mum. I'm not surprised Dad's out of his depth.'

The first train to Totnes on a weekday morning leaves Paddington station at 5.30 a.m., change at Didcot Parkway, arriving at 9.42 and connecting, God willing, with a bus to Kingsbridge at the head of the spreading Salcombe harbour.

Gabriel, who what with one thing and another was quite accustomed to spending nights without undressing or entering any kind of domicile, let alone his own chaotic flat near Putney Bridge, decided after a brief doze on the floor of his office that he would go to the station and be ready for it. He took a restorative slug from the whisky bottle in his bottom drawer and got up from the floor, unsteady but determined. The idea – nay, project – of finding Joanna, removing her from her pointless life and allowing her to look after him while he wrote his masterpiece in an Irish hovel had seized his imagination. It had haunted his brief sleep under the desk as few things did these days. 'My own Lilith, my primitive, my foreshadowing love,' he said aloud, peering into the cruelly lit mirror in the sixth-floor gents' lavatory. 'I am coming back. "Thy firmness makes my circle just, and makes me end, where I begunne."'

He pocketed the bottle and took the lift down, loudly belching this time in its bland Art Deco privacy, and greeted the disapproving commissionaire with a blast of Johnnie Walker fumes. Walking through the black London darkness to Paddington, he switched from Donne to Yeats. 'Time can but make her beauty over again/Because of that great nobleness of hers/ The fire that stirs about her, when she stirs /Burns but more clearly . . .'

By the corner of Praed Street he had persuaded himself that

Joanna, years ago, had dismissed him and charged him to wander the weary world proving himself worthy of her. A long and noble quest had led him to this place. By the top of the concrete station ramp he was a knight who had served eighteen years, faithful, for a lost mistress whose beauty burned ever brighter as she aged. 'Oh, she had not these ways, when all the wild summer was in her gaze!' The picture in the *Chronicle* was between his fingers as he fell asleep again, contentedly, on an uncompromising yellow plastic Railtrack seating-module on the station concourse.

Over Starhole Bay the moon shone full and golden, throwing long shimmers of light across the still water and whitening the cliffs which rose, absurdly romantic, around the disguised shape of *Shearwater* with her two masts and her counterfeit bowsprit. The anchor light glimmered, sending its own fainter track of light through the blackness of the water. The portholes were darkened; behind them Joanna slept, dreamless and deep, and Guy sprawled on his back, head on his hands, mouth slightly open.

A movement in the companionway, a darker shadow against the pale fibreglass, resolved itself into the silent creeping form of Della. Trying hard not to creak, she climbed on the cabin top dragging her sleeping bag, wrapped herself in it and sat with her back to the mast. Alone with the moon and the cliffs and the water, she stayed for a long, long time, worshipping and thinking. She made decisions: not hard plans, but nebulous, important statements of intent to herself. This night, this moon, the lapping water must not go out of her life entirely. Something of them, something like them, must stay with her and lap around the corners of her life always. While the others slept, Della watched and planned and resolved and shivered through a long, blessed, starry hour on the deck alone.

Then a movement in the hatchway startled her, and the silent figure of Joanna, wrapped in her own sleeping bag, moved into the cockpit.

'Hello,' it whispered. 'Stargazing?'

'Thinking about things,' said Della.

They sat together for a moment, then, shyly, Della said, 'Do you often sit up here, like this?'

'I used to,' said Joanna. 'Not lately.'

'What do you think about?' asked Della.

Joanna half turned to look at the girl who was staring at her with large, candid blue eyes in the moonlight.

'I think about Emily.'

'Who,' asked Della, 'is Emily?'

25

Under the pouring moonlight, under the cliffs and the stars, the two women looked at one another for a moment. Della's 'Who is Emily?' echoed innocently in the silence. Then Joanna hitched her sleeping bag round her shoulders and said quietly, 'All right. I'll tell you. I haven't told anybody, ever.'

Della was alarmed. 'Oh Gawd, I didn't mean to ask something private. Don't tell me secrets, I'm useless.'

'It's not really a secret,' said Joanna. 'Lots of people knew. It was in the papers, eighteen years ago, in Oxford where I lived. It's just that I don't talk about it.'

'You don't have to tell me, then,' said Della, still uneasy.

'I want to. Tonight, I want to. If you'll listen.'

'OK then,' said Della, settling herself down in a corner of the cockpit, out of the wind. 'Who is Emily?'

'Emily,' said Joanna, 'was my best friend. The best friend ever. She was funny, she made me laugh more than anyone else ever has.'

'What was she like?' asked Della, interested. Joanna seemed startled for a moment by the question, but then smiled.

'She was a bit dippy. She once jumped into the river with all her clothes on because she was annoyed with someone who was being pompous. She used to smuggle stray cats into college. Once she threw a rotten tomato at a lecturer who was rude about women students. She could argue down anybody when she got going. But she was very, very kind. She helped people who were down on their luck, even if they had been horrible to her. She never had any money after the middle of term because she'd lent it to all these hopeless people. She had a collection of lame ducks—'

'What?' said Della, startled. 'Like the cats?'

'It's an expression – it means people who can't quite cope on their own. She looked after all the oddballs who didn't have any friends. But if you'd said she was good, she would have made a rude noise at you. Emily was lovely. I loved her. She was,' Joanna repeated, 'my best friend.'

'So,' said Della. 'What happened?'

'Gabriel happened,' said Joanna.

'What, the chaos man? The one who mucked you about?'

'Yes.'

Gradually, in a low, even, emotionless voice, the older woman told the story to the young one. Five and a half months after Joanna was dismissed by Gabriel to the strains of Bob Dylan, Emily succeeded her in Leckford Road. Emily's passion for Gabriel was, if anything, more complete than Joanna's; she had never really noticed men before, other than as friends.

And so very 1970s were they all, so idealistically free-form about 'relationships', that Emily remained Joanna's best friend. Her friend, despite Joanna's long, sleepless, weeping nights and red-eyed days in the library; her friend, although they barely saw one another. Emily's days and nights were too near a copy of Joanna's lost idyll. They could not be close, not when Emily, encountered at lectures, even smelt of Gabriel's joss sticks and Gabriel's self. So, friends though they were, they did not talk any longer of anything below the surfaces of life. The gulf between them was that Joanna was unhappy, Emily happy.

'I almost hated her for being happy,' said Joanna, looking out over the water, along the setting moon's track. 'Isn't that terrible?' Della was silent. It sounded perfectly natural to her.

Emily stayed happy until the night six months on (early summer term, it was, with finals only weeks away) when Gabriel tired of her adoration and told her that, in the words of the invaluable Bob Dylan, 'It ain't me you're looking for, babe.'

Whereon Emily screamed – so the inquest later heard from Gabriel's flatmate, a chemist by the name of Biggis who had always hated him – 'Well, it bloody well ought to be you, because I'm four months gone with your bloody baby!' She then, said Biggis, slammed the front door, kicked over and broke several milk bottles, and ran off.

And there the comedy ended. Gabriel assumed she had run to Joanna's digs down by the canal; or so he said, in evidence given sulkily and without his customary charm. He did not attempt to follow her. But in fact Emily ran to the fifteenth floor of the newest college's newest hall of residence and, breaking more glass, threw herself and Gabriel's unfinished child out into the night sky.

'She died?' said Della's small voice out of the darkness.

'She died,' said Joanna.

College had rung her digs in the morning when Emily was tentatively identified by a shocked undergraduate on an early run. Standing barefoot on the cold cracked linoleum Joanna had heard the news and had shaken all over, cold and ill tuned as she was after months of hard work and heartbroken starvation on coffee and apples.

Over the succeeding eighteen years, the older, better-fed, rational adult Joanna had often, sternly and reasonably, told herself that poor, thin, sad Jo Telford did all she could that day. By noon she had identified the crushed face and matted hair (holding hands, incongruously, with a big fatherly policeman). She had rung Gabriel, waking him well before his accustomed hour, and told him to go to the police and explain whatever had passed before she did it herself. She had been interviewed by the Principal, and volunteered to assemble Emily's possessions and take them to her parents' home twenty miles away in Burford.

The parents were very distraught, warned the don. But, 'I know them. I've had lunch there,' said Joanna. Emily's mother was as blonde and sunnily engaging as Em; she had met her husband when she was working as a waitress, dressed as a lewd rabbit. He, trying to impress an upper-crust fiancée with his sophistication, complained that his salmon was undercooked and the candle not lit. Em's mother the rabbit had lit the candle with a flourish, striking the match on her suspender belt in the club's approved manner, and snapped, 'Hold your bloody salmon over that.' He had, so he said, threatened her with the sack if he reported her; she had retorted, 'It's probably the only sack you're any good in.' Mysteriously, they had been married in Scotland within the fortnight, leaving his enraged fiancée an apologetic note.

Em's parents had told this story, antiphonally, gurgling with laughter twenty years on, a pair of unreformed 1950s ravers. So Joanna had to go to Burford now. 'I'll talk to them,' she said. 'I'll tell them she wasn't unhappy, not until the last minute. That it must have been an awful impulse, and she wouldn't have known what she was doing. Don't they say that attempted suicides say they never remember the half-hour before?'

And so she had gone that afternoon to Burford and told her gauchely merciful tale, and comforted them a little with talk of how well liked Emily was, what a star of her year. She had tried not to think, either in Burford or at the funeral, about the slow fifteen flights up, the lonely sound Em's hard boot heels must have made. Or the determination that it took to smash through reinforced glass with a fire extinguisher. Or the waist-high concrete sill Emily had had to climb. Jo had done her best, put on as good a gloss as it would take and kept the deep horrors to herself. Then she came back, by taxi, to college alone.

'I think you did really well,' said Della, quietened by the bald recitation of all this. 'Going to see her mum and dad. I think that was brave.'

'I had to,' said Joanna. 'I hadn't been to see Em for weeks, had I? Never knew she was pregnant even. I owed her that much.'

Jo Telford, said the Principal to her shaken deputy on the day after these events, was a very thoughtful girl. 'Nice type. Brilliant, in her way. Her tutor spoke most highly of her Chaucer term. Surely a First for the college, if only . . .'

Both women gloomed, in their decorous senior common room, over the unfinished sentence. Student suicides were a tragic waste; unfortunately, their best friends often got wasted too. They abandoned or muffed their degrees, had stupid love affairs, and showed symptoms of shock all round. The college psychiatrist was a disaster, a testy old Freudian bigot who saw no point in anything short of five years' analysis. The counselling industry was barely born. So the dons were grieved, but not unduly surprised, to be called a week later by the City police to a wandering, amnesiac young woman found on Port Meadow barefoot, with a college diary in her pocket.

'And that was the end of Oxford for me,' said Joanna. 'I never took my degree – you know, final exams – at all. I wouldn't go back.'

The dawn was creeping up now, grey and pink over the eastern crags. Della fiddled with a piece of rope, tying and untying a half-knot in its soft white end. She looked up to see whether Joanna had finished telling the story. Jo was looking out to the east with tears in her eyes, but her face was calm. Della ventured to speak at last.

'Why don't you usually talk about it?' she said. 'If it was me, I'd tell everyone, so they knew I'd had something awful to get along with in my life. I would.'

'I suppose,' said Joanna, 'that I have always felt guilty.'

'Why?' asked Della, really astonished this time.

'Because I didn't know Em was pregnant. Because I didn't stay in touch with her for those five months. Because I knew perfectly well that Gabriel was bad trouble, and I knew that Em was too gentle to stand it, so I should have seen it all coming.'

'But you didn't know,' protested Della. 'You were still fancying him, you said. You were only eating apples and stuff, and being miserable. You couldn't have told her he was trouble. She'd have thought you were jealous or something.'

Joanna looked at the girl with affection. 'I don't know,' she said. 'I really don't know. I'm never going to know. It's eighteen years ago. But maybe it doesn't matter.' She stood up abruptly, and reached out a hand to Della. 'Come on. We'll get stiff. No more stars now; look, it's morning. Let's get some sleep.'

'Will you be all right?' asked Della.

'Oh yes,' said Joanna. 'Oh, definitely, yes.'

And one by one, they slipped down the companionway steps and back into the cocooning warmth of the cabin where Guy breathed evenly on, undisturbed. Della curled into the corner of her bunk; Joanna stretched out on hers, relishing the chill of its corners for a moment before hauling the downy layers up round her and closing her eyes.

26

Lance was up first, waking at six from a confused dream in which Rudi and Yelena, companions of his travels, were chasing Erika Merriam along the Amsterdam canals in a speedboat full of firemen dressed in Gouda cheese. Must be, he thought, the smell of his sleeping bag. Wriggling out, he looked at the kimono on the floor and decided against it. Rummaging in the chest of drawers, he found a pair of his father's underpants. On the chair, left over from the disastrous Bank Holiday weekend, was a pair of Keith's sailing trousers, so he annexed those as well and pulled on a blue cotton sweater. He supposed that his shoes were in his own room, but peering in to see Mandy and Alex enwrapped fast asleep on the bed, he shook his head and padded back to adopt a pair of Keith's deck shoes.

With these in his hand, Lance toured the house, checking on its inmates. Erika's door was firmly closed and, he liked to imagine, barricaded against any more terrible Gurney goings-on with a chair wedged under the doorknob. He smiled reassuringly at the blank door. There was no sound from the curate's room, the radiator having spent its force in the small hours. Downstairs, his father lay on the sofa in front of the fire's embers, the blanket Lance had put over him lying sadly crumpled on the floor. Keith looked cold, grey, and older than usual. His son tucked him up with deft gentleness, then went to the kitchen and fetched a tube of Alka-Seltzer, a small bottle of mineral water and a glass, all of which he placed on a low table close to what would presumably be his father's line of sight when he awoke.

The tall young man sat for a while in the kitchen, drinking coffee, lost in thought. Then, with a sudden brisk movement, he jumped up, crossed the hall, took the car keys off the hook on the monstrous Victorian hallstand, and silently let himself out of the front door.

Ted Merriam, answering the door of Tedneric half shaven and in the hope of seeing a ParcelForce deliveryman with his new reel mechanism, glared at the hairy figure before him. 'Yes?' he said austerely. 'What can I do for you?'

'Buy the Bun,' said Lance, without preamble. 'Erika deserves it. Put in a bid. You'll get a good price, I bet you. My mother and Mrs Heron have had it long enough. I would say it brings in £150 a week clear profit after Zoë's wages and what Erika gets for weekends. Could be a lot more if you do lunches. The insurance will pay to have it redecorated and some new equipment. It's a snip.'

Ted stared, open-mouthed, at Lance. The young were, he always said, the last word in cheek. He was deeply grateful to Erika for never having shown any interest in saddling him with young of his own.

''Tain't yours to sell, my boy,' he said, heavily. 'I don't know what you're doing here, trying to sell your mother's things before breakfast—'

'Oh, come on,' said Lance. 'I'm not trying to flog you her jewels for cash. All I'm saying is that I bet if you offered – oh, I dunno – forty thousand for the Bun, you'd have a deal. And Erika would be a brilliant businesswoman. You could give up the ironmongery, after a bit. Take early retirement. Go fishing.'

Ted went on staring. At the word 'fishing' a spasm crossed his face; what sort of spasm, Lance could not divine. He went on, briskly, deciding that to wait for Ted's reactions would only slow and fuddle the issue.

'I think the time is right. I think my mother and Mandy Heron both want to sell it, and an offer would tip them into it. And I think Erika's the girl for the job. A natural. That's it, really. I won't come in, and I'm sorry to have disturbed you. But you're an ironmonger, and you know about striking while iron is hot. I think today is the day for the offer, I really do. It's what tycoons do. They get hunches. I am your hunch. I just have a feeling about today. You know that song, "I can see clearly now"? Look at the way the sunshine is on the leaves. You could see for miles, if it wasn't for the back of Tesco's. It's a day of destiny. Thank you for listening. Have a nice day.'

And he turned, with a little wave, and got back into his father's car – so Ted noted, with acid disapproval – to drive away. In the doorway of Tedneric, the big man stood, lost in thought, hardly noticing the approach of a ParcelForce van bearing his heart's desire.

When Lance got home with a loaf under his arm, a fistful of bacon and a flimsy drooping bag containing a dozen eggs from the corner shop, Keith was stiffly upright on the sofa, cradling his Alka-Seltzer and staring disbelievingly at the empty whisky bottle on the table.

''Lo, Dad.'

'Hello. Did I fall asleep on the sofa?'

'Yes.'

'Must have been the drive. Atrocious road, that. I fell asleep in a lay-by and some twelve-year-old policeman told me off and breathalyzed me.'

'I know. You told us all about it.'

'Did I dream it, or were there a lot of people here later on?'

'Yup,' said Lance, from the kitchen door. 'Come and have a cup of coffee and I'll fill you in.'

Keith rose, groaning, and turned to straighten the cushions. He forgot he was still holding the glass of fizzing water, and as his hand came forward he poured it inadvertently down the back of the sofa. 'Oh, shit. Oh, hell.'

Lance came back, deftly took the glass from him, mixed a new Alka-Seltzer and held it out. He wanted to take his father by the arm and lead him to the warmth of the kitchen, but they did not normally touch, had not for years, not since Lance was twelve or thirteen. Keith stood, not taking the glass, rubbing his eyes on the back of his sleeve. Lance made a decision, and took his father's arm after all. It did not feel too unnatural.

Keith allowed himself to be led to the kitchen and seated with his glass in front of him. He sipped.

'Sorry. To be honest, if it was me who drank all that whisky last night, I may have been a bit blotto.'

'Smashed out of your wits, I would say.' Lance began frying the bacon. 'You were well out of it.'

'Of what?'

'Well, there was a fire at the Bun.' Lance held up his fish-slice commandingly as Keith groaned. 'But it's all right now. Erika Merriam is staying here because she wants to get in there early and find an electrician and all that. She's got a crusading desire to reopen it by the weekend, which is mad. She's in Susan's room. Alex and Mandy are in my room—'

'What the hell are they doing here?'

'Well, Mandy had a bit of a wobbler about Mum. She did have a word with you about it—'

Keith sat upright, staring at his son. 'You mean it wasn't a dream? Her crying on me?'

'It was not. She cried all over you the whole time the fireman was here, and all through the row between Alex and Erika about Zoë. Mandy is not one to bottle her emotions up. She doesn't have a lot of them, but when she does, by God she unbottles them.'

'Do you mind,' said Keith, 'if we don't go into any more of this until I have eaten something?'

'OK. Only I need your car all day, to take Mandy to Salcombe.'

'*What?*' For a wild moment Keith wondered whether his son had contracted a relationship with his mother's friend and signed up as her toyboy. Anything seemed possible, this week.

'Whaddoyou mean, Salcombe?'

'To find Mum. Remember? The phone message? She was going to Salcombe.'

'And what the hell does Mandy Heron want with chasing after her?'

'She wants to say sorry. About the newspaper. She's in a terrible state of remorse.'

'Mandy Heron? Wants to say sorry?'

'That,' said Lance patiently, turning over the bacon, 'is why she was crying on you.'

'Well, I need the car,' said Keith, getting up. 'I need the car to go to Salcombe myself.'

'Are you sure?' asked Lance whose mind had been working

in much the same way as his sister's. 'I can have a chat to her. Wouldn't it be better if you stayed here and got some peace?'

'Certainly not.'

'Well, drive down with us then.'

'No. I am going to see Joanna.'

'Dad, you're not—'

'Not what?'

'Not going to say anything you'll be sorry about. I mean, Mum's caused you a lot of aggro, anyone can see that, but she probably had her reasons—'

'I am going,' said Keith with dignity, 'to meet Joanna. My wife. Alone. She and I have private things to talk about. Without anybody else, especially Mrs Heron. If you insist on coming, you'll have to borrow Alex's car. And keep away from us while we do talk.'

'OK,' said Lance more cheerfully. 'He owes us one, since it was him who burnt down the Bun. Alex,' over Keith's shoulder, 'I can have your car today, can't I? If I promise not to set fire to it?'

Keith turned to see Alex in the doorway wearing Lance's dressing gown from when he was fourteen. It did not quite close over his chest and revealed a pair of Dennis the Menace boxer shorts lower down.

'Is there no lock on your bathroom door?' Alex peevishly enquired. 'I was just decent – only just – when Erika Merriam burst in wearing some sort of striped shroud—'

'Can I borrow your car? Today?'

'The BMW might not be insured—'

'Mandy's car then?'

'You'd have to ask her.'

'It's her I'm driving.'

Keith watched his son as he bargained with Alex. The European tour had changed him; Lance had always been bright and volatile and kind, but now there was an ease about the boy, a new confidence. He seemed no more than amused by the happenings around him. Lance, he thought vaguely, would be a comfort if—

There would be no if. Joanna would come back. If she did not want to come back, then he, Keith, would go with her wherever it was she was off to. He drained his Alka-Seltzer, crossed to the stove, picked up a piece of bread and crushed two rashers of bacon in it. Clutching his improvised sandwich he headed for the bottom of the stairs.

'Is anyone asleep in my bedroom? No? Good. I'm off early. Alex, tell Gus to chase up the Rugely-Smith conveyance this morning. If you would.'

With the same determined, loping stride that had characterized his son as he approached Ted Merriam's front door that morning, Keith climbed the stairs eating his sandwich, swung along the landing peeling off his sweater as he went, and crashed into the bathroom.

A thin, wailing cry made the men downstairs look at one another with eyebrows raised.

'Ze unmistakable alarm call,' said Lance in the voice of a German professor, 'of ze lesser female Erika, disturbed on its nest.'

Moments later, with his last night's sweater back on inside out, Keith flashed through the hall, slamming the door and calling, 'I'll get breakfast on the way – must get going. See Joanna.'

His half-finished bacon sandwich lay on the hallstand where the car keys had been.

The scream had done its work and roused the house. At the top of the stairs, draped in Lance's dark-blue bedspread, pale and tragic as Lady Macbeth with tumbled hair and dark rings under her eyes, stood Mandy. Behind her, Susan and Anneliese, bright-eyed and curious. Erika Merriam emerged from the bathroom in a long striped nightshirt of Susan's and stood in a defensive attitude a little apart from the rest, with a look that suggested she would sell her virtue dearly. The effect, to Alex and Lance as they stood in the hall, was very much that of the climax of Act I of a particularly rowdy opera. Lance, looking at the abandoned bacon sandwich on the hall table, had a momentary, light-headed, happy conviction that his father, in some obscure way, had just sung the principal love aria.

Alex picked up the bacon sandwich and sank his teeth into it. Outside, Keith's car could be heard starting, jerking into gear, easing off the gravel of the drive and fading down the street with a dwindling roar. Susan broke the silence.

'He hasn't got any shoes on,' she said.

27

The train was warm and fusty, empty apart from a dozen grey-faced business travellers and a party of sailors with kitbags and, in their great ham fists, open cans of lager. In the early morning the smell of the beer made Gabriel's stomach churn; he sat as far as he could from their raw adolescent bravado and huddled himself into the corner of a seat with his jacket bunched between his head and the steamy window. After a moment, he kicked off his scruffy plimsolls so that his stockinged feet rested on the empty seat opposite, one toe poking out through the grey wool of his left sock.

He regarded the sock with sorrowful affection. Poor sod. Poor old sod. That really was a classic middle-aged bachelor's foot: uncared for by the ministering hand of a wife, grubby and unappealing. A music hall joke, he was. Poor old bachelor.

It was not, of course, that he minded being a bachelor. Indeed, Gabriel O'Riordan had chosen this high and free destiny with some firmness. He had decided early in life to cast aside clinging women and follow his own star. He had cast aside his homeland, too, fleeing from the cosy Catholic values of the rural west of Ireland by way of Trinity College, Dublin, and then Oxford. He had never gone back, even for a holiday, to the shadow of the mountain in the far south-west which bore his name; never written home to Ballydehob, never turned up at his own mother's funeral.

It had been a considerable shock to him, two years ago, when another boy from his own village appeared at Television Centre where Gabriel, under duress, was sulking his way through a course entitled 'A dramatic matrix for the bi-media age: Edge,

Bottom, and Spin'. This Kieran was a confident young man twenty years his junior and far better paid. The stripling – who, to add insult to injury, was actually one of the lecturers – had casually observed in the BBC Club bar that the far south-west of Ireland was, these days, 'humming with it', and a 'happening place'. He mentioned one-horse towns Gabriel had fled from in 1965 as now being 'amazing', one boasting an award-winning school with its own planetarium, of all things. He reported that the region was now settled by artists, studded with gourmet restaurants, sought after by bohemians. Gore Vidal lived there, for heaven's sake. Hip media rabbis and modish actors claimed it as their secret refuge. There was a fax bureau in Ballydehob.

'But the spirit of the place,' said the young man smugly, 'the ancient magic, has not gone. It's where we draw our strength, we exiles.' And he had laughed a fashionable laugh and Gabriel had had an uneasy sense of having, somehow, thrown away a winning lottery ticket by mistake.

But, he told himself, in his day he had been right. There had been every reason for an artist to throw aside clinging, cloying Ireland at the turn of the 1960s. And clinging women, too, come to that. He was a poet, a creator. He needed freedom, not children and puppydogs. And bloody women never would understand that; so they had had to be detached from his coat tails, as forcibly as need be.

Closing his eyes against the dreary West London suburbs through which the train was listlessly rolling, Gabriel remembered Joanna, eighteen years ago, at the moment when he detached her from his coat tails. He could see her, easily: her half-forgotten face had become vivid to him from the newspaper picture. It haunted him, as faces will when they return from long oblivion. By now he had forgotten the drunken night fantasy of his *belle dame sans merci*, sending him away to work his time for her. He remembered the real Joanna, saw her white face pleading with him, her dark hair in disarray as she knelt by the Leckford Road gas fire in her black faded jeans and filmy Indian cotton shirt.

'Gabriel, Gabe, I love you – doesn't that count?'

'Baby,' he had said, 'it's as difficult for me as it is for you.'

'But what have I done? You loved me, you know you did. We loved each other. Only yesterday—'

'Joanna,' he had deepened and roughened his voice for this line, 'don't make it hard for me. You know the deal. We're both free. I gotta be free. If you want a man to tie up, it ain't me, babe. It never was me. If you've made yourself an imaginary man in my image, I can't help that. I love you, the same way I love life, and light, and everything that is beautiful. But you can't own me, any more than the trees in the wood can own me.'

Joanna had not seemed to appreciate the beauty of his cadences. She had refused the comfort of the joint he offered her and kept on and on at him, hatefully clear-headed in her pursuit.

'Can't I just – stay with you? Look after you? Just be near you? I wouldn't be any – trouble. Oh Gabe . . .' She shed tears, then. Oh, God, yes. Boring tears. Eighteen years later, he suddenly felt irritation as fresh as if it were yesterday. He leaned sideways against the cold window, tugging at his improvised pillow, while the old scene played on behind his eyelids. He was speaking again.

'I'm not the one, babe. I wish I were. You're torturing me. One day you'll find the man you need. When you've had a chance to grow up a bit.'

He hadn't believed it, of course. Hell, no. Women who had been with him were pretty well bound to end up settling for a second best. 'We shall become resigned, and settle sadly/ For gentle husbands in bland suburbs/ And a lifetime of wistful dreams.'

A girl in love had written him that in a poetic letter once, and Gabriel had treasured the idea. All those birds fading into genteel domesticity by their Agas, rearing their pasty-faced, middle-class, cello-playing children, dutifully humping their commuter husbands on Saturday night; all of them remembering the lost paradise of living with him, angelic Gabriel. Amazing. Joanna, though, had shown no sign of being resigned to the end of her idyll.

'I don't want to be grown up,' she said. 'I don't want anybody else, not ever. I just want to be near you. I'll be quiet. I'll help with your typing, cook for you. You can have other girls around, I'm not jealous. Only don't send me away.'

She had looked so small, so pathetic, so embarrassingly eager that he had turned away and put on the Dylan record. Jesus, some girls had no idea of how to go gracefully. It didn't seem to matter how bright they were, they seemed to lose all their self-respect and abase themselves at such moments, so that he, who never lost control except by prior arrangement with himself, looked on appalled.

It never occurred to him that there was in these girls' self-abnegation a generosity worth valuing even if it was misguided. They just seemed pathetic. This one was intelligent; when he first met her she was a bright spark, full of wit and laughter. How did she come to turn into this snivelling, pleading, runny-nosed lump? People who disliked Gabriel thought that he enjoyed bringing women to this pitch of humility. Sometimes they accused him of that. But, he thought indignantly, nothing could be further from the truth. The sniffling bit was quite his least favourite phase of an affair.

That afternoon, he had turned in the doorway where his fine features (as he saw from the Indian mirror opposite) were half in shadow, heartbreaking and mysterious.

'Joanna. It would be better if you were gone before I come back. We'll be friends. When you're ready to be.'

He had not seen her again, except in the distance, a proud, gawky figure in her scholar's gown on her old green bicycle. He never saw her all that winter, never spoke to her until she rang him one morning her voice flat and grim, to tell him that Emily—

He consciously paused, changing a certain mental gear in self-defence at the thought of Emily. Emily was the most intractable part of the stories he told himself. Gabriel had no trouble, as a rule, in shaping his own past life into pleasing romantic twists and patterns, but the matter of Emily required more mental discipline than most. His leaving of other girls, including Joanna, had been for their own sake – they should not be shackled to a burning, demanding creative spirit like his, and it was out of his noble kindness that he let them go before his flame scorched them. Similarly his BBC career, initially brilliant and lately a precarious and ill-tempered liaison, could without much difficulty be fashioned into a story of the artist betrayed, the creator of great drama rejected by a Philistine influx in Armani suits.

His drinking, his personal disasters, his failure to click with any colleague or see any project through for five or six years past could all be reworked into lovable eccentricities in the tradition of Dylan Thomas. But the death of Emily was not so easily dealt with. It would have greatly surprised Joanna, during her years of tormenting Gabriel-dreams, to know how often Gabriel himself thought about Emily. Emily had not pleaded or abased herself; she had shouted angrily at him, and then gone up that damn building and . . .

Well, the girl must have been unbalanced all along. It stood to reason. His college, his housemate, his landlord should have understood that. The junior fellowship should have been his. The following months, during which he had been slowly frozen out of the university city, were an outrageous example of the basic prudishness and hypocrisy of the academic establishment. Women dons, he suspected, had spoken against him, rot their witch-black hearts. He was well out of it; a year after leaving he had attracted the attention of the BBC by his work in the London fringe theatre (thank God he fell in with that actress girl, and thank God she suddenly became the star she did, trailing him upwards in her wake). The rest was history. Nobody he ever met these days knew anything at all about Emily. And Joanna . . . absurd to think that Joanna, seeing him again, would even think of that brief painful episode. He would be her dream returning, lovelier the second time around . . .

His head fell back and his untidy limbs relaxed into baby sleep. When the train stopped with a resigned sigh at Reading, Gabriel was hard asleep. He slept through the green fields of Berkshire and on into the rolling kingdom of Wessex; once he half woke to see the word YEOVIL on a signpost. The sailors at the end of the carriage slept too, waiting for Plymouth to gather greyly round them and return them to duty. A lager can rolled empty from one end of the carriage to another, dribbling, as the train changed speed.

*   *   *

Keith Gurney, too, was heading westward and thinking of past encounters with women. He had no memories of girls weeping and pleading, for he never had been the kind of man women plead with. Various classmates, fellow students and secretaries down the decades had yearned for him, but such was his polite, chivalrous reserve that they would have found it absurdly bad form to throw themselves at his head. By the time you were close enough to Keith to hold any emotional conversation, he was so committed to you as to be equally vulnerable himself.

Before Joanna, only one girl had been that close: Maroussia, his three years' infatuation, who left his bed abruptly to go back to her Russian dissident lover the minute he was freed to the West. Keith's friends had watched, through those years, the impossible chivalry with which the young lawyer worked alongside Maroussia in the campaigns of the 1970s to free her beloved Vladi and other Soviet Jews. His more percipient acquaintances suspected that he had always known that she was only his on loan; Keith himself never spoke of it. If he had a dilemma, it was invisible and never reflected in his actions. Vladi's fare into the West was paid officially by the campaign, but really by Keith out of his own pocket. If he wept as he signed that cheque, nobody ever knew.

A year after Maroussia left to a new life with Vladimir in the USA, Joanna came to work in the office, a pale, sad, reserved figure. It was to her that Keith first told his story. Probably, he realized himself, he was impelled to do it by a need he had to match, and thus coax out of her, whatever the terrible, visible grief was that she carried around. She had told him a little: about a friend who died unexpectedly, and a love affair that didn't work out. They had sat together in the corner of wine bars and pubs, over curries and tacos and Thai meals tasting of peanut butter, and talked endlessly, never of the detail of their lost loves, but of the wounds, the longings, the scars.

'It's being afraid you've lost a bit of yourself. The bit that only came alive with her.'

'I know. Like having something amputated. You think it was the best bit of you. You feel crippled.'

'But then it turns out there are other bits you were suppressing all the time, so one side of you withers and drops off, and the other puts out shoots and you end up a different shape, going somewhere else. Like those things you do in botany.'

'I know. You mean, er, rhizomes?'

'Do I?'

They had begun to laugh; to take long walks over the Dorset cliffs, to steal away for brother-and-sister weekends together. Keith, deeply in love by this time, sensed the danger of hurrying her and carefully made no pass. He held her hand, hugged her, never went further. But on one of these weekends, exhausted by a long wet walk on the cliffs at Beer and a little drunk after a pub supper, they had fallen into one another's arms, jokingly, as if for support; and Joanna had raised her lips to his.

The night that followed was a revelation to them both and, to their surprise, an unspoken, unbreakable guarantee of commitment. For Joanna, lovemaking until now had meant adoring and total submission, rather on the model of St Teresa of Avila being pierced by a divine spear of ecstasy. With Gabriel you did not make demands; you received and applauded. For Keith, the memory of loving Maroussia was a memory of delirious, crazy adoration; to be permitted to touch her was to be admitted to a sacred place. Every encounter was granted as if it were a queen's favour. Maroussia did not like him to stay the night, never wanted him to sleep on her breast afterwards.

So to both Joanna and Keith, stretched on the narrow pub bed with the rain and wind outside, that first night was a miracle.

Love lay suddenly revealed as something equal, no favours being asked or received, no gratitude owed. Love was mutual hunger and shared energy; it was laughter, hugging relaxation, warm satisfied sleep and waking joy. It was reaching out, half drowsy, to feel a fresh longing and know with complete trust that it would be satisfied. For Keith, who had longed for Joanna physically for weeks, the surprise was that the moment should feel so warmly familiar, so little precarious. For Joanna, the amazement was that something she had never considered at all should turn out to be exactly what she needed.

Remembering that first night now, Keith slowed the car, overwhelmed all over again and shaky with desire. Marriage had been inevitable. Indeed, both of them felt married already; walking the next day hand in hand on the clifftop above the

Old Harry rocks, they talked unselfconsciously about the future. Joanna said she had never thought of marrying so young; he said that neither had he. But to both of them it was obvious that married they should be.

In the few weeks before their wedding, the only blemish to their unity would come when he tried to explain that Maroussia had been nothing: a madness, a delusion, at best a pale foreshadowing of this solid love. He had said it, of course, because it was true; but also because he wanted her to say the same about her nameless Oxford lover. She would not. Joanna would never speak of him at all, not even to say his name. Keith was not a man to push such a point, and gave up. Joanna never, in their closest moments, spoke of the old love again.

That one blemish, over the years, had faded into irrelevance. Nothing mattered compared to their unity, their familiarity, their glorious, terrifying sharings of childbirth, their gentle rediscoveries of one another's bodies during the weeks when each new baby lay snuffling alongside the double bed. Only now, during these few days' puzzlement and terror and exasperation and loneliness, did Keith see that the shadow was still there. Something in Joanna was not his, and never had been. A terrible jealousy clawed at him as he drove. At the long roadworks east of Exeter, a woman passenger in the car alongside saw his scowling intensity and shrank, tousled, startled, from the window. She might have shrunk even more if she had seen that he still had no shoes on.

Back at the Old Vicarage, Lance with some difficulty chivvied the ill-assorted houseparty through breakfast and into the proper direction for their day. Erika (strong tea, thin toast) had departed for the Bun with half the contents of Joanna's cleaning cupboard. Alex (bacon sandwich, fried egg, instant coffee, five cigarettes) had trailed behind her, humbly carrying the mop and two buckets. Susan (coffee, two bananas) had departed in a taxi with Anneliese (ginseng tea with a slice of lemon, followed in a moment of weakness by a handful of peanuts and a slice of stale walnut cake). Mandy (three cigarettes, black coffee) now sat watching Lance as he tranquilly finished a fried-egg sandwich. Her hand, with the fourth cigarette dangling from it unsmoked, trembled slightly.

'We ought to go. Lance, we really ought.'

'No hurry. Dad ought to have a chance to see her first. He'll have to find her. Even so, she might not be there.'

'She must! You said that she said Salcombe on the phone.'

'Well, she did. But you don't always end up where you set out for in a boat. Did you know that the Navy never fill in the top of the log page with their destination? You can't say 'Torquay to Salcombe, 3rd September'. You can only say 'Torquay *towards* Salcombe'. Apparently, anyway. Isn't that interesting?'

'No. I want to see Joanna. I have to see Joanna.'

'Indeedy. And so you might. The point is, I'm not really going down to see Mum.' Lance looked across the table at Mandy in her fragile drooping blondeness. 'I'm going down in case Dad doesn't find her.'

'And you're going so you can take me.'

'Yes. And to take you. But if Mum and Dad are there, they'll have a lot to talk about—'

'I know! I know!' Mandy's voice rose shrilly. 'But Lance, you have to understand that I need to see her too. She must be thinking I said terrible things about her. She thinks I betrayed her—'

'*You* think you betrayed her,' said Lance, with the calm confidence of the teenage amateur psychologist. 'You blame yourself for what that reporter wrote. You think you oughtn't to have given him any chance at all.'

'Yes! Yes! I know! I am a show-off cow! I never even *thought* of Joanna, all alone in that gale. I just thought it was fun to have a hunky reporter dangling on my every word.'

'Well, so what?' said Lance, comfortingly. 'Mum will see that. She knows you aren't St Bernadette, doesn't she? She's known you years. There's not much you could do would surprise Mum, is there?'

Mandy bridled slightly. 'And I've known you, young man, since you were shuffling around on a ride-on plastic duck.'

'I remember Ducko. What happened to him?'

'Susan had him. But she liked Anneliese's red tractor better, so they swapped. We had Ducko until the wheels came off.'

Lance dipped the last crust of his sandwich into the remains of Alex's egg yolk, ate it neatly, and clattered the two last plates into the dishwasher.

'Come on then. On the road.'

'Can we go by the office? I ought to say goodbye to Alex.'

But when Lance pulled in to let her enter the tall, crookedly picturesque premises of Heron and Gurney, Mandy was stopped at her husband's office door by a hovering Gus.

'*Terribly* sorry, Mrs H. Thing is, he's in a meeting with Mr Merriam. I don't think I should barge in, he always hates it. If you'd wait twenty minutes or so . . .'

So Mandy had picked up Alex's mobile phone from the secretary's table and come straight out again to the waiting car. Mrs Hopgood, who in her dung-coloured padded jacket had been accompanying Mrs Colefax as she returned her new wok to Cuisine It All with a strong complaint about the quality of the non-stick finish, paused in the shop door to register the hairy, dangerous-looking young man driving Mrs Heron in her own car. Spotting a knot of her friends gathered outside the blackened façade of the Bun in the Oven, she hurried to join them with the news. It really had been a wonderfully interesting week; and it was only Thursday.

Joanna woke at half past eight, with the reflected sunlight rippling the cabin ceiling. No dreams, no fears, no unease had marred the last hours of her night. She felt wonderful. She rolled off the bunk, kicked the sleeping bag from her feet and threw it into the corner. Guy still lay opposite, snoring slightly, twitching like a retriever in a dream. In the quarterbunk she could just see Della's bright, tangled hair with the sun falling on it, betraying darkening roots.

She remembered everything: the gleaming *Privateer*, the terrible newspaper in the rancid-smelling breakfast café, the sleek woman reporter, the hose – here Joanna's hand rose to her cheek, feeling it heat at the very thought. She remembered the fat, black-browed tycoon with his bossy little moustache, the moment when Della had stepped onto her deck, the staggering (in every sense) descent of Guy a moment later.

Joanna Gurney, herself again, remembered it all and marvelled. Yesterday she must have been too tired and overwrought to take in the full import of anything. But she had got here, to Starhole Bay.

She emerged onto the deck and looked around at the cliffs and the green glinting water, and the ridiculous spectacle of *Shearwater*'s disguise, the fake mizzenmast and bowsprit lashed up by Guy in the moonlight. Both were now leaning at drunken and unconvincing angles, one oar threatening to fall into the sea any minute. Smiling, she began to move around the boat, leggy and tousled in her long T-shirt and knickers, and deftly untangled the spars and lines.

Yesterday, my God, yesterday! It ranked with those disjointed college Maydays when, after a night at a party and a dawn on the river, she would wake in some unknown room, among comparative strangers with red eyes, wearing unfamiliar clothing and still clutching an undelivered essay designed for the noon tutorial. On such days you would look at the clock and find that it was eleven, and not know whether it was eleven in the morning or evening, or who it was who had done the Morris dance on the pub table. Emily, probably. This day had the same feeling to it. Light-headed, unregretful, full of hope.

Thursday, was it? Must be. Half-day in Bonhurst. God knows what was going on at the Bun. Mandy running it perhaps? Now there would be a turn-up.

Joanna laughed. On this clear, clean, damp sea-morning there was nothing that could not be faced, cleaned up, sorted out and turned into gold. The first step was to get into Salcombe, ring Keith and Susan, offload the two cuckoos currently nesting below decks, draw an end to this crazy autumn cruise, and take up the reins of real life again.

The prospect no longer disturbed her. Some pressure had lifted itself from Joanna's spirit during the final hours of sleep while the sun came up. Three days ago she had been trapped in a narrowing tunnel, a hostage to her own life, emotionally half-dead but fit to cry at anything. Now, she looked closely and saw that there were no walls to the cell, no boundaries to her future unless she agreed to them. If she had to go home and run the bloody Bun until the economic recovery made it profitably saleable, or until Susan got her A levels from that expensive school, so she would. She would open the damned teashop for shorter hours, give Zoë some responsibility or sack her. She would stop fussing.

She would let standards drop if necessary. Somehow she had come to persuade herself that if she cut any corners at the Bun, permitted Erika to serve nasty microwaved potatoes, use teabags or otherwise compromise her early principles it would be a betrayal of the past. A betrayal of her carefully built family and community life, her wall against chaos; a betrayal of Lance and Susan's babyhood and her early happy years of marriage.

What a load of hogwash! It would just be one more small café which had dropped its standards because its proprietress was sick of it. So what? A teashop was not an intensive-care ward, was it? What had the twittering ladies of Bonhurst done to deserve pampering with real butter croissants? To hell with them.

She, Joanna, would take time for herself, sit down and work out what to do with the second half of her life. Ring Alice. Have a drink, a night in London with Alice and Andy. Talk to them about proper jobs and occupations for an educated woman not yet forty.

Some fog had lifted from her brain after what must have been, she wonderingly thought, years or at least many months. The prospect all around was clear, glittering, an endless vista of amusing choices, The nonsense in the newspaper was unimportant; if it made Mrs Hopgood and Mrs Colefax happy to gossip about her, so much the better for them. Everybody should be happy in their own way. She intended to be, so why not them?

Keith – she paused in her impetuous reverie of freedom. Keith could be free-hearted and happy, too. Of course he could. He must come with her to this exhilarating upland, see this view; it was only a matter of attitude. No longer would Keith have the power to depress her with his doubts and haverings and clingings to the status quo. Not her; no, sir. She would drag him up instead. He would come? Surely?

When she had coiled down the last rope, Joanna stood by the hatch and stretched her arms upward in the rippling sunlight, smiling beatifically at the sky and muttering 'Yes!' rather the way her son Lance used to when, sprawled with his A-level work at the kitchen table (he never would use his own room, preferring the company) he got another of his astonishing calculations right. 'Y-Yess!'

''Scuse me saying,' said a voice down near her groin, 'but you sound chirpy.'

Joanna stepped back, to allow the emergence of a dishevelled Della wearing one of Keith's T-shirts. 'Sorry, I borrowed this. I'll post it back.'

'Keep it,' said Jo. 'You look very fetching with those long brown legs. Do you wax them?'

'Yeah,' said Della. 'You don't, do you?'

'No,' agreed Jo. 'Life is too busy for that. I do have a razor.'

'Can't do the bikini line, though, can you?' said Della, confidentially. 'Wax is the only thing, really.' She looked around at the morning. 'But I can see why you don't bother. Lovely, innit? I was thinking a lot, last night. I'd like to live near the sea.'

'Why not? There's bound to be some way you could. If you want something, just go for it, because you probably deserve it.'

Joanna, even in her moment of morning euphoria, was just able to hear her last sentence hanging on the air, like some disreputable New Age garment in rainbow-striped and draggled velvet. She saluted it with a certain ironic amusement, but the reality of her happiness still glittered around her on the water. 'Yes. That's it. You go and live by the seaside.'

'Proper sea, not seaside. Proper wild bits, like this.'

'Scotland or Ireland then. Or bits of Wales. Nobody ordinary can afford to live in a wild bit down here, in southern England. Wildness is costed, rock by rock, by estate agents.'

'I always fancied Scotland. There was Robert Bruce, in that book, with the spider.'

Guy appeared through the hatch. 'I never fancied Robert Bruce. All that struggling away like a spider. Too much like hard work.' The women looked at his sleepy, unshaven mien with scorn.

'Go get the kettle on, slave,' said Della.

'Tea, toyboy,' said Joanna. 'Then we go into Salcombe, and off you get.'

So Guy made tea while the two women clambered onto the foredeck and Joanna taught Della how to haul up buckets of clean cold seawater and pour them over herself from head to toe with a thrilling fresh shiver. When he came up with three mugs, his blazer already on and his hair combed, Guy saw the back view of two naked women, one with a bucket over its head from the depths of which helpless laughter could be heard.

From the sea, Salcombe is a great harbour, a refuge since Viking days, a narrow-wristed spreading palm of an estuary guarded by Bolt Head and Prawle Point, the Mewstones and Eelstone and Poundstone and Wolf Rock. Once a ship has passed its pouring, swirling sandbar, the harbour lies there deep and safe and welcoming; the town lifeboat bobs reassuringly at its mooring, muddy creeks spread out ahead for exploration; great golden beaches unroll on the right hand side above East Portlemouth;

and the clinging town, pink and blue and grey, climbs the rocks to the west.

Approaching Salcombe from the sea is an occasion. As *Shearwater* crossed the bar and saw these riches before her, the crew's spirits soared even further. Guy sang 'Spanish Ladies' and rang the brass bell in the cabin, presented by Lance for Joanna's thirtieth birthday so that she could call him back from his rowing expeditions around anchorages. Della sat singing little wordless songs on the cabin top, her arms round her bare knees, damp hair streaming, looking at last more like a teenage girl than like Ivana Trump. Joanna steered past the Wolf Rock buoy and turned gladly to starboard, deeply content to be bringing her small ship to such a harbour, on such a morning, with all safe and shipshape aboard. Salcombe spread and glittered, welcoming them.

Keith, as it happens, had never approached any part of Devon from the land. He was tired before he reached Exeter, flattened by the niggling delays of the roadworks, feeling silly without his shoes on, worrying about shortage of petrol and hungry for lack of breakfast. Thankfully he headed south at last, but the road seemed to go on for ever. Christ, this promontory went down a long way! he thought. One never noticed from seaward. Around eleven o'clock he passed Totnes (where, unknown to him, Gabriel, the man whose name he had never known, was engaged in a furious altercation with the driver of the Kingsbridge bus).

From here the road wound interminably onward again until, at last, with signs pointing off to Kingsbridge at the head of the great estuary, he began to feel a sense of sea after his long inland drive. The sea was still invisible beyond the moors, but it reflected in the sky, or gave a smell to the air, or stunted the bushes – anyway, it was there. He put his foot down and traversed the great open fields, expecting a headland any minute. A bend, and to his left he could at last see the upper creeks of the harbour, the same blue water which bore his boat, his wife, his hopes.

The petrol lamp came on, yellow and accusing. At last a filling station appeared on the outskirts of Salcombe. To his relief a stand just inside the door sold beach shoes, translucent red plastic versions of the kind that tiny children wear for scrambling on the rocks. He bought a pair in an incongruous size 11, a chocolate biscuit bar, and a can of fizzy lemon and felt rather like a giant six-year-old out on a day on the beach. On an afterthought, he bought a *Chronicle*, flipped through until he found Joanna's picture, read for a moment and then began to laugh, alone in his car, until he spilt the rest of his lemonade over his trouser leg and ridiculous shoes, which made him laugh some more. Then, a little restored, Keith set off again down the steep descent into the town.

Salcombe was, he thought, far less impressive from landward; a labyrinth of narrow roads and no free parking spaces that he could see except in the forecourts of genteel hotels with spiky palm trees. He drove twice around the steep streets, past craft shops and art galleries and businesses called 'Deck Out' and 'Schooners', wild with impatience to find somewhere to stop and scan the harbour. Once, between houses, he saw a mast moving up the harbour and craned from the driver's window to see it; but a stout middle-aged couple in matching pink canvas fishermen's smocks stood square in the way, laughing and gesticulating and waving their anchor-patterned holdall in front of where the hull would be as it passed the gap in the buildings. A Volvo honked impatiently behind him and, cursing, Keith moved on. Unlike his wife, euphoric out on the demure rippling water, he felt stale and hungover and old. The hope he carried was fragile, and the only shaft of light in his cell was Joanna. Somewhere, on that harbour, she must be there. Close by, the only woman . . . Where?

In the great snakes-and-ladders race to reach the West Country, conducted year in year out between public transport and the motor car, you can never quite tell who will win. Gabriel, rocking rapidly along on the Inter City express, had beaten Keith hands down as far as Exeter, quite neutralizing the advantage his rival had in starting from Hampshire. But, due to his own ineptness at Exeter, Gabriel had missed the Totnes connection and been forced to get a bus, then change at Totnes for Kingsbridge. This second bus had lagged behind Keith a little, but arrived in Kingsbridge at the very moment when the car driver was waiting for his change and his red jelly sandals at the petrol station. Gabriel had been told, not without impolitely protesting at the news, that there was no bus to take him on to Salcombe. That was a snake. But by chance, arriving in the little town at the head of the estuary, he found a ladder.

There was a small excursion boat, *River Darling*, half full of late holidaymakers and clearly about to leave the quay at Kingsbridge as the bus swished past it. Gabriel, properly awake by now, saw the word SALCOMBE on its stern and opened the bus's electric doors (using a trick he had learnt from a left-wing Hampstead novelist who kept losing his driving licence but did not believe in the fascist rigidities of the bus stop system). Having done this, and set off a loud alarm in the cab in the process, he leapt from the moving bus, followed by the driver's loud reproofs. Yelling an oath in return, Gabriel ran towards the little boat at something between a sprint and a lumber, his grey locks flapping, and threw himself aboard just as its red-faced skipper was untying his stern line.

'Bit of a 'urry, moi lover?' said the man. 'Salcombe excursion, this be. Two pound sixty pee single.'

'Good. Yes. Here.' Gabriel sat down, fishing awkwardly for change, and moments later was chugging between green banks and mudflats towards the Salcombe anchorage, on the water already while Keith was only just beginning his search for a parking space.

Shearwater, meanwhile, was nicely anchored off the Marine Hotel, with Guy on the foredeck, his leg pumping up and down as he inflated the rubber dinghy with the boat's slightly leaky footpump. But it was neither Keith nor Gabriel who found Joanna first. It was the harbourmaster's launch which left its quay even as they were laying the anchor, and swished alongside minutes later with two grim-faced policemen standing in the well.

Joanna, who had been below turning off the engine, emerged to find herself face to face with a warrant card, listening in astonishment to a poker-faced request that she allow them to search the vessel for one Guy Amadeus Pastern-Hopkins who was being sought to help the police in their enquiries concerning a number of stolen credit cards.

Eddie McArthur, to do him justice, had entirely forgotten his quarrel with the private secretary. When he had seen to it that the police were told that Guy had gone off with his credit cards (not, of course, mentioning that Guy always carried them as part of his duties) he instantly forgot having done so. It had only been one of the half-dozen rapid orders he had, in yesterday's brief irritation, barked at Dinny Douglas. Dinny had complied with his wishes, described Guy and *Shearwater* with considerable journalistic accuracy to the police on the telephone, stopped the cards, and herself in turn forgotten the whole matter.

So, at the moment when the police fingered – metaphorically speaking – the collar of Guy's blue blazer in Salcombe harbour, Eddie McArthur had virtually blotted the secretary's existence from his memory. He was gliding up-Channel at twenty-five knots on *Privateer*, making for Southampton Water where, his fax machine informed him, time was running out for a struggling boatbuilder with several acres of prime undeveloped waterfront among his assets. His agents could pounce, haggle and buy quite adequately without him, but he always enjoyed making personal swoops from the sea in these cases. He hummed, contentedly, a nameless little tune.

Below decks, Dinny had woken at ten to find the engines throbbing discreetly behind the wall of what she defiantly persisted in calling her bedroom. She had pulled on a pair of Guy's white trousers and a heavy blue sweater from the locker under his bunk, and come out onto what she preferred to call the verandah (although its rise and fall and feline sway betrayed it to be, horribly, a deck). She leaned on the rail to find herself staring out, blankly appalled, at open water. Unsteadily she climbed the white-painted steps to the flying bridge overhead, and with a reckless lack of tact or prudence rudely addressed the broad back of the figure at the helm.

'Where the fuck are we?'

'Lyme Bay, thirty miles off Portland. You slept well, my dear.'

'No, I didn't – look, for God's sake! Where – I mean I ought to be at the office—'

'The new Editor, appointed this morning, knows that you are on special research duties. The features editor is drawing up some dummies for your new by-lined page. It begins either next Wednesday or the one after, as you wish. The new Editor feels that Wednesday is a very good day, as it puts you right up against,' he glanced down at the pad next to his mobile telephone, 'Maeve Mahoney of the *Globe*. Two researchers will be available to assist you. You will be in the office tomorrow to look at the dummies. A studio session has been booked with Kurt Anhart for the photographs.'

An Anhart picture? For a by-line? Hers? Up against Maeve Mahoney? Dinny, three years into her newspaper career, felt faint. Was it Jesus who was taken to a high, dizzy place by Satan and shown things he could have if he wanted? Did Jesus, at that moment, feel as sick as she did right now? She held onto the rail, and protested automatically.

'Yes, but—'

'Tonight,' continued Eddie, tiring of the wheel and punching in the self-steering course so he could turn to face her, 'you will accompany me to dinner in Kingsbois Lodge, the home of my good friend Edmund Weissbraun, in the New Forest. He has a very remarkable Art Deco private cinema and a large collection of early Hollywood comedy.' He gave a sly, unfathomable look at the rigid little figure in the blue sweater and seemed to shake with an inward laughter which Dinny found peculiarly sinister. 'He and I share many interests.'

'I am not a hook—' began Dinny, but found a pudgy finger, smelling faintly of lavender hand cream, laid disconcertingly across her lips. It was the first time McArthur had touched her, and accordingly it froze her into shocked silence.

'Not a hooker. Understood,' he purred. 'A nasty word. Not a word for a lady's lips. Never use it again. And I would prefer it,' this rather coldly, 'if you were to go below and pay some attention to your grooming. I prefer to see you . . . immaculate. The eventual contrast is then more stimulating. So I find.'

And Dinny had slunk below, washed her hair and set it on some efficient heated rollers she found in the enormous bathroom; she had shaved her legs, been seasick twice in the process, and finally dressed in a cream linen shift and strappy gold sandals from the wardrobe in the cabin, presumably the property of some bygone mistress. Grooming, which normally soothed and uplifted her spirits, was in that heaving environment a peculiarly hateful occupation. When she returned to the bridge Eddie, by then smoothly rounding Portland Bill, promptly sent her below again to replace the strappy sandals with 'something more ladylike'.

Equipped at last with chaste medium-heeled leather sling-backs, her mouth sour, her head spinning, Dinny accepted defeat. She sat through the afternoon on the stern deck, pretending to read and breathing deeply in the hope of averting nausea, while her tormentor spun and bounced the powerful boat towards the Solent and the calm of Southampton Water.

The Devon and Cornwall Constabulary, of course, were not to know how little the robbed citizen cared about his deprivation. All they knew was that an important personage, with contacts at the highest level, who had actually dined the night before in the same room as the Deputy Chief Constable, had been robbed of his credit cards by a fraudulent employee known to be aboard the yacht *Shearwater*, last seen proceeding westward round the Devon coast. On Thursday morning, one Sergeant Renfrew of Totnes remembered the previous day's alert as he ate his breakfast and studied the newspaper, and remarked to his wife that the case had even made the morning papers. She, taking the *Chronicle* from him, had been more interested in Dinny's florid account of the lesbian prostitute and the toyboy, and observed that she did not know what things were coming to, and hoped he would catch them and teach them a lesson.

Fortified by this evidence of the case's moral importance, the sergeant repeated his observation about the newspaper story when he arrived at the station and dropped some hints about the importance of the police force being seen, by the public, to clear up prominent cases. It was a quiet day; his remarks inspired one ambitious younger spirit to ring round his contacts among harbourmasters and other likely sea-watchers along the coast. No joy from Brixham, or Dartmouth, or Plymouth or Newton Ferrers; but shortly after 10 a.m. PC Dingwall hit the jackpot. Salcombe harbour rang back to say that if it was a sloop called *Shearwater* they really wanted, the boy had spotted one when he came home from fishing this morning, just off the bar and heading in, with a lot of people singing and acting a bit daft. Though the dear Lord knew there were enough yachties called their boats *Shearwater*, since they didn't have a lot of imagination, in the speaker's opinion; so it could all be a damn waste of time.

The sergeant, however, decided to give PC Dingwall's information a chance. Within minutes his nearest patrol car crew were at the harbourmaster's office on the front at Salcombe, and two policemen reached *Shearwater* within moments of her anchoring, before the dinghy was even half inflated. Joanna, speechless, merely pointed at Guy. The officers spoke impersonally, officially, of their need to question him regarding the theft of credit cards.

There was a moment's silence, then, 'No, well, I say, gosh,' replied Guy, feeling that some response was expected of him. He was still a little out of breath from pumping. 'I mean, you can – he can – have them back – look – they always live here – in my wallet – Mr McArthur won't carry a wallet, it's a thing he's got, like the, you know, the Queen. Not carrying money. I was going to send them back.'

'We'll see about that, sir,' said the older policeman. 'For the moment it's best you come along with us.'

Joanna, the lawyer's wife, thought rapidly. 'Officer, it seems clear there was no intent, um, permanently to deprive the owner of these cards. Any charge of theft would hardly apply—'

'Be that as it may, madam,' said the officer heavily. 'We must ask this gentleman to accompany us to the station. Er,' he corrected himself, 'to the harbourmaster's office, perhaps, in the first instance, so that he can give us a statement.'

Guy was white. He turned to Joanna and spoke under his

breath. 'Mr McArthur – is ever so – I mean, he just knows everybody – I think – he'll have me in prison.'

Joanna looked at him. 'I,' she said with sudden firmness, 'am coming too.' She turned to the officers. 'I will help him to make a telephone call to his solicitor.'

'I haven't got a solicitor,' said Guy, hopelessly.

'You have now. My husband or his partner will deal with it.'

A part of Joanna was irritated to find herself acting like Guy's mother, but she was unable to stop. Something about the way his mouth fell open as he stared at the policeman, the way his eyes widened and his shoulders hunched reminded her too forcibly of Lance, aged ten, too bright for his own good and a year too young for his secondary school. She had arrived late to pick him up one afternoon and happened on an unforgettable scene: her small boy facing three much larger ones who were waving his treasured new leather briefcase in the air. She had waded in then, and she waded in now. Joanna had not liked what she had seen of Eddie McArthur, still less what she had heard. God knew what mischief he could make for this nice dim boy unless someone stood up to him. Once a mummy, always a mummy, she reflected, and turned to the girl.

'Della, if I go ashore, you'll be OK? The anchor's fine. I'll be back. You can come if you like, but there's not much point you being involved.'

'Can I stay here?' The answer came fast. Della had wondered whether she ought to go with Guy out of politeness, since after all he had only made his pierhead jump because of her. But going off with policemen went against the grain. She had not been, so far, in trouble; but Marie had lectured her on the train in the ways of the world and the inadvisability of getting tangled up with police, ever.

Besides, she was entranced by this boat, this rippling water, by the gulls and the harbour smells and the pride of having come in from the open sea. She did not want to be ashore again and on the way back to the bedsit in London. Any delay was welcome.

So Joanna and Guy climbed into the launch with the amused harbourmaster and the two policemen, and Della stayed.

Which is how it came about that when Gabriel landed from the Kingsbridge ferry and stood staring out at the boat he had spotted bearing the label *Shearwater*, he was in fact only yards from Joanna on the shore and never knew it. Instead of walking towards her he walked away, down the hard, and offered a bored small boy in an outboard dinghy fifty pence to take him out to the yacht. The boy jerked his head to indicate that Gabriel should sit in the bow, pulled his oily Seagull engine into coughing life, and shot off across the harbour, describing a couple of fancy arabesques across the tide-rip which succeeded in soaking the seat of Gabriel's trousers. When they eventually came alongside *Shearwater*, Gabriel grasped the guardwires and climbed determinedly aboard, the damp weight of his trouser seat making itself unpleasantly known. Peering into the cabin he found only Della, alone and startled, looking through a book about the Western Isles of Scotland. They stared at one another in complete bafflement.

Leaning on the wall of the harbourmaster's little waterfront cabin, the telephone pressed to her ear, Joanna was doing her best to interpret to her husband's depleted office the position of a still gabbling, dumbstruck Guy. 'Look, Gus, listen. Mr Pastern-Hopkins resigned his position, in effect, yesterday afternoon. There was no opportunity to return the credit cards which he routinely carried as part of his duties— What? No, in his own wallet. It was a genuine mistake.'

She shifted the telephone to the other hand and wiped a damp palm down her canvas trousers. 'No, it isn't the same as if he drove off in a company car. It's completely different. Think about it. Oh God, can't you ask Alex to break off his other call? I think someone should tell these policemen that Mr McArthur is a violent and vindictive man. In the moments following Mr Pastern-Hopkins' resignation, he couldn't have given the cards back because Mr McArthur was trying to shoot a Verey pistol in our direction – that's V-E-R-E-Y, not a regular firearm but a signalling device, registered under the firearms legislation. Oh, for God's sake, Gus, look it up. The police surely must have discretion over whether they just caution our client. He really can do without any more problems, McArthur is a maniac— Oh my God, Keith!'

Pressed to the window, pale and determined, Joanna saw the face of her husband. Keith looked oddly bloodless behind the misty glass, his face unreadable. The telephone in her hand buzzed with Gus's earnest voice.

She snapped into it, 'No, I know Keith isn't in the office, he's bloody well here. Outside the window. Look, I'll get him to deal with this. Simpler. Alex? No, I really don't want to talk to Alex – I don't see how it can be urgent. Look, Gus, you have no *idea* – oh, all right, put him on.'

In the moments that followed Joanna stood motionless, listening to the telephone in her hand, looking into the eyes of her husband through the harbourmaster's damp window, oblivious of the fascinated harbourmaster's assistant, the two stony-faced policemen, and Guy, who was edging, shrinking, shimmying imperceptibly towards the door. Finally she said into the telephone, 'Yes. Yes, I see. Call back on the car phone and tell Mandy yes, I think it's the best thing too. If Keith agrees. OK, Alex. Say thanks to Gus for being such a – help – with this business here. Storm in a teacup. Keith will cope.'

Putting down the telephone, she turned to the policemen. 'Mr Pastern-Hopkins' solicitor is in fact here. I think you'll find he can explain everything. If you'd wait one moment, I will fetch him.'

She walked out onto the tarmac square outside the office where Keith was now pacing up and down, fiddling with the wing mirrors of parked cars. Seeing him there, with his odd socks, his scarlet jelly sandals, his dishevelled thinning hair and huge, troubled green eyes, her heart turned over.

'Sweetheart. I'm sorry.'

'No, I am. It was my fault.'

They stood, close, not touching, searching one another's faces. Each seemed at once to find the assurance they most wanted; Joanna ducked her head, embarrassed by the intensity of her feeling in that public place. Gently, Keith spoke again.

'Can we go into that café over there and have a cup of coffee and talk?'

'Oh God, yes. Yes. Very soon. Only there's something else first. There's someone – one of my stowaways – who's in trouble. Lawyer sort of trouble. I'm really sorry, but might you—'

'Would this,' enquired Keith, 'be the gay teenage prostitute or the upper-class dope fiend on the run with the boss's wallet? Just so I know.'

A commotion behind her made Joanna swing round. Guy, deprived of her steadying presence, seeing only the terror of McArthur lying behind and before him, had panicked. She should have known that he would. Before their horrified eyes he erupted through the door of the harbour office, leaving one policeman spinning off balance and the other sprawled hatless on the floor. Joanna started towards him with some inarticulate protest on her lips, but Keith, who had spent half a lifetime trying to prevent his clients from making their situation worse at moments like this, was faster. Before she could see what happened, both men were afloat in a small green dinghy which had been tied to a ring on the hard. Keith was standing in the stern, reaching out to remonstrate with Guy; Guy, still visibly trembling, was threatening Keith with an oar. The flood tide took the little boat in its grip and moved it inexorably up the harbour and into midstream, silent and smooth as a revolving stage in a musical. At first it travelled upright; then a moment later, when Guy's lunge and Keith's neat duck had worked their mischief on the equilibrium of the dinghy, upside down.

Joanna held her breath until she had seen two heads, one sandy, one glossy brown, bob wetly up from underneath the boat and two pairs of hands take a firm grip of it. Then she ran down the pontoon behind the harbourmaster's assistant and the two policemen to parlay her way onto the launch for the second time that morning.

Fifty miles away, Mandy Heron was fiddling with the aerial of the mobile phone she had borrowed from her husband's office and looking sideways at the imperturbable face of Lance as he drove across the border into Devon.

'That was a funny thing,' she said. 'I rang Alex, and he actually had Ted Merriam in his office, making an offer on the Bun.'

'Good,' said Lance. 'Erika deserves the Bun. And Ted deserves to take early retirement from snarling at customers about soldering irons and pan scrubs.'

'It just seems odd that he should suddenly offer now,' said Mandy. 'I suppose it must be the fire. Made Erika realize how much she wanted the café, and Ted realize how serious she was.'

'Probably.' agreed Lance. 'So, did you say yes?'

'You heard what I said.' Mandy's spirit was returning as the car forged westwards. 'I said yes, but only if it was what Joanna wanted. And I said that I shouldn't get the full half, because I haven't kept the goodwill going as much as she has, not for years.'

'And Alex said?'

'He said it was possible to make an apportionment of the value into goodwill, and that could go to Joanna.'

'Well,' said Lance. 'That was very generous of you.'

'Shut up,' said Mandy. 'I've got embarrassing stories about when you were a baby. I've never used them yet, but I might. I might tell all your new Cambridge friends about you peeing through the letterbox when you were three.'

Lance smiled, and patted her knee in a fatherly way, and kept on driving.

Della had originally gone below to fetch the last squares of chocolate from her scuffed mock-Gucci holdall, planning to eat them on deck in quiet felicity and watch the water and the squabbling gulls. The book on the Western Isles, sticking awkwardly from the shelf, had caught her eye in passing, leading her idly to pull it out and turn its pages. By the time Gabriel clambered on board, however, she was lost in it. The photographs, harsh black-and-white studies by a notable war photographer who had retired to Skye after a breakdown, showed her a world she had never considered before. This was not the chocolate-box Mediterranean 'scenery' of holiday brochures and travelogues, not the illustrations from a CSE geography book. This was what she had seen by moonlight in Starhole Bay, only larger and grander, wilder and more uncompromising. This was . . . wilderness.

She said the word aloud, looking at a study of Loch Hourn, the Mouth of Hell, with mist pouring down from the mountaintops and curling over the sea. 'Wilderness.' She said it again, this time pronouncing the 'wild' as if it were the adjective. Della wanted wildness, wilderness. Nothing in her family life behind the Leicester curtains, nothing in her education – except perhaps the Grendel book – certainly nothing in her London life had made it likely that she should want any such thing. Marie and the others, she thought fleetingly, would not see much point in it. You could get cold out there in wilderness, cold and bored and wet. Seasick, if you were on a boat, like she was yesterday. She could see that. But still, there it was: Della wanted cliffs and gulls, the drama of spiked rocks with the moon behind, of crashing breakers, gales and rain and great swollen clouds and apocalyptic shafts of sunlight. One of the photographs – she turned the pages impatiently – had a beam of sun coming through dark clouds, over something called Ard-na – Ard-na-something. She bent her bright head, searching for it.

This was how Gabriel, landing in the cockpit and peering through the companionway into the dim cabin, first saw her. He was irritated at the sight of her blonde hair: this was not Joanna. His rehearsed overture was useless. He had planned to say, 'I have come back. It's our time now, it has come.' No point now. He glared for a moment. Della raised her head and glared back.

Neither of them was particularly prone to social embarrassment; Gabriel had caused too much, in his time, even to notice awkwardness. Della was too young, and had too much of the insolent kitten about her, to be bothered. She spoke first.

'Whaddyou want? Joanna's not here. She's ashore.'

'So this is Joanna's boat? I wasn't sure.'

'Yeah. How did you get on here?'

'I thumbed a lift. What are you doing here?'

'I,' said Della with dignity, 'sailed here. I was a crew. Now I'm minding the boat, for Joanna. I dunno what you think you're doing.'

'Searching,' said Gabriel grandly. 'I am searching for a woman I once knew, to make amends and take her to the Kingdom of the Blest.' That really sounded rather good. Since Joanna was not here for the moment, he might as well impress this one. 'The Kingdom,' he went on, 'of my ancestors, in the far, far west, under the mountain called by my name, where the sea of faith meets the land of saints and heroes.'

That, perhaps, was a bit over the top. He had spent too much time with that poet who wrote the Lilith plays. Certainly the line did not seem to be working on the little blonde; she was staring at him like someone about to pull the communication cord. She could make a lot of trouble if she yelled and screamed, and create quite the wrong atmosphere (he saw with a sinking heart) for his lyrical reunion with Joanna. She had better be soothed. He noticed the book on her lap, and took his line from that.

'Nice pictures, those. I know the man who took them. We used to drink together, when he first came back from Vietnam. He lives on Skye now. I told him he ought to go to Ireland. The Hebrides aren't a patch on south-west Ireland. Not to my way of thinking.'

'Whassat like, then?' asked Della. 'Ireland?' She too felt that perhaps she should humour this shaggy, craggy, grey old man. Another loony, she thought parenthetically; funny, how many you met around these yachts. Poor old Joanna seemed to know a lot of loonies. 'You from there?'

'Long ago,' said Gabriel. 'Long, long ago, I came from Ireland, from the holy western islands.'

'Did you live on an island, then?'

'No. I lived in a village on the mainland. But if you looked out to sea you could see Cape Clear and Sherkin, Castle Island and Horse Island and Illaunbeg. The sea is blue there, and the land is green and rocky, and the gulls cry over the peat moors and the grey seals dive among the rocks—'

'Real seals? Like, swimming, furry ones?' Della squeaked excitedly. 'Did you get close?'

Gabriel was not accustomed to being interrupted in his Yeatsian flow of ideas, polemic, and somewhat inaccurate descriptions. For years girls had listened to it entranced, sometimes daring to rest their heads on his knee as they sat literally at his feet. Lately, colleagues had merely ignored it, tuning it out as they did the builders' radios on the scaffolding outside the windows of Broadcasting House. He glared, now, at Della. He had, in fact, never actually seen a seal, being notoriously the least observant boy in West Cork and terrified of the water. Abruptly, he changed tack, plumping himself down in the corner of the seat opposite her.

'Never mind that. Where's Joanna? I need to see her.'

'She went ashore with the police, 'cos they got Guy, for stolen credit cards. She was going to ring her husband, the solicitor bloke, and get it sorted out for him. She's ever so kind to Guy.'

'Is he . . .' For once, Della caught Gabriel's meaning instantly.

'Nah. He's too young for her. He's a berk, really, but ever so sweet. He came because of me.'

'He's your lover?'

'Do you mind!' said Della indignantly. 'I only said he fancied me. I quite fancy him, too, but like I said, he's a berk. If he was an escort customer, like, you'd think you was really, really lucky. He's a gentleman, and ever so good-looking, like Hugh Grant, sort of. But if you were *choosing* – no. Not my cup of Horlicks.'

She giggled, with a certain unnerving coarseness, and appeared to be looking Gabriel over in much the same critical spirit. Suddenly, unusually, he was aware of his grubby plimsolls, his wrinkled, slept-in flannel trousers and stained jacket. This girl might well not recognize an intellectual bohemian when she saw one. He pushed back his dishevelled, greying mop of hair, felt how it was receding from his forehead, and hastily pulled it forward again. The seat of his trousers was still uncomfortably damp from the dinghy.

'Did Joanna say how long she'd be?'

'Don't think she knew,' said Della. 'Shall I give her a message?'

'I'll stay. I can't get ashore anyway. I came out in some child's dinghy, and he's gone.'

'Where'd you come from?'

'I came from London. When I saw the newspaper. I used to know Joanna. Years ago.'

A look of terrible comprehension came over Della's sweet little kitten-face, sharpening it, widening her eyes, bringing an incredulous smile to the pretty pink lips. Gabriel wished he had not spoken.

'I know who you are! I *bet* I know! You're the bad man, aren't you? You're the chaos man!'

She watched him, still as a cat. Gabriel could have denied it. There was no way she could be sure. He could have said, 'Don't be ridiculous, I'm a family friend.' Somehow, under the headlamp gaze of those big eyes, he failed and blustered.

'I – did – once, long ago. We were close friends, er, lovers, yes – before she was married—'

'And you're the one that chucked her?'

'Er, we broke up. She was very young at the time . . .' Oh Christ, why was he saying all this? On this damn claustrophobic boat, in this chilly harbour, to this little cow?

'Yeah,' said Della. 'You made it look like her fault. That's what she said. You screwed up her poor friend Emily, too, didn't you?'

Gabriel was silent.

Della paused and continued, 'What you come for, anyway?'

Still he did not speak. Instead, he pulled his quarter-bottle of Scotch from his jacket pocket and drank from it, wiping his mouth on his hand with a panache which took much of the sordidness from the gesture. Della peered at him, at the handsome ruin of a face, the still-dark brows, the high unhealthy colour on his cheeks where the drink had broken the veins, and the not entirely clean mane of greying hair. Bit of an old hippy. Nothing to be afraid of, this one. She ventured a guess.

'You haven't,' she said, 'come to get her back, have you?'

Gabriel was never short of a swashbuckling plot for long. He decided to make the most of this uncomfortable situation.

'Yes,' he said. 'She has run away from a pointless life. I have come to take her to the west, to the islands. We are going to start again, together, and make beautiful things, poems and pictures, in Ireland.' He was quite pleased with that. It had a certain simple grandeur.

Della gave him a long, penetrating, faintly satirical look. 'She won't come, you know. She really, really doesn't like you.'

'She will. She will understand that things have changed between us. Our moment has come, really, this time.'

'Yeah, but she likes her husband. Keith. You can tell.'

Gabriel, more incautious by the moment, the whisky burning in his gut, took issue. 'No, she doesn't. She ran away from him. He is just a shadow. I am the real thing.'

Della's laughter was a glad, young sound in the dim cabin. 'Ooh,' she said. 'You're just like the telly, aren't you?' And before he could bridle at this, she added, 'But go on, tell me more things about Ireland. Is it really *wild* where you're going to live? Rocks and caves and stuff?'

'Yes,' said Gabriel sulkily. 'I shall rent a small, ruinous cottage on the side of Mount Gabriel and draw water from a stream. I shall gather wood and cut peat to keep me warm, and walk miles for food and human company by a pub fire. I will write poetry by candlelight, and hear the sea crashing on the rocks below all winter. I shall live alone, a hermit above Dunmanus harbour, and die alone by the western shore. It will be better than laying waste my powers, getting and spending, in the shallow meretricious charade that is the BBC.'

He was quite pleased with that, too. So was Della, for different reasons. After a long, considering look she said, 'Tell you what. She's not going to come, is she? Be reasonable. But I will. I'd like to see seals and mountains and things. I could cook.'

Gabriel had never thought that anything could startle a conventional reaction out of him, and was horrified to hear himself say, 'But we hardly know each other.'

Della, who did not mind conventional reactions at all, merely nodded. 'Yeah, but I want to do somethin' different, and so do you, and you're a bloke, and I bet you can't look after yourself. And I'm a girl, and I'm not fussy. I just know what I want, right? And I want to live somewhere wild, with seals and cliffs. For a bit, anyway.'

Gabriel opened his mouth, and shut it again. Della, perhaps misunderstanding his hesitation, blithely continued, 'I won't be like that silly tart in that *Castaway* film, you know, that Lucy one who went off to a tropical island and then wouldn't do it with Oliver Reed. I'm not stupid, I know blokes all want a shag now and then. You prob'ly couldn't live with a girl without that. Well, that's all right. It's all the same to me. So is that a deal, then? 'Cos I can tell you, Joanna won't go anywhere near your Irish ruins. Bet you anything. She likes her husband really.'

Gabriel, for the first time ever, had nothing to say to a girl. All his life he had seduced, he had persuaded, he had elevated the sexual act into realms of symbolism and spiritual union, into a token of intellectual freedom; into anything at all that would get a hesitant, idealistic female undergraduate into his bed. Women had, of course, sometimes offered first. But they too had always dressed it up in a similar glittering gown of fine words. Nobody had ever classified him with whistling builders and randy bikers before, nor included him in the cheerful phrase 'blokes all want a shag now and then'. He did not know what he felt. When he examined it closely, though, he discovered that it was, in fact, relief. But he still had no words.

It was just as well for Gabriel that in that instant a commotion from just uptide of the anchored *Shearwater* brought this astonishing negotiation to a close. There was too much shouting and splashing to ignore. Both of them made for the companionway, colliding momentarily in the narrow entrance, and climbed out into the cockpit. Looking down at the upturned dinghy swirling past, Gabriel unknowingly saw for the first time the man who had succeeded him in Joanna's life, a dank, flailing figure clinging to an upturned dinghy which bumped its way along the yacht's side. Keith shot out an arm to grip the folded stern ladder, let the dinghy float away lopsidedly with Guy holding on to the other side, and began to struggle to reach the catch on the folding ladder so he could climb aboard.

Meanwhile, as the harbourmaster's launch drew alongside, Gabriel found himself, after eighteen years of forgetfulness and a night of tropic fantasy, looking straight at Joanna herself. Flushed, tousled and pretty, anxious and solicitous, there she was, jumping over the rail and hurrying to the help of another man. She was saying, 'Sweetheart! Hang on! Careful – OK, love. Oh Keith, oh God – there!' and then standing on the stern deck, laughing and crying as she embraced a thin, streaming wet man.

Gabriel stood stupidly, his hand raised towards her. She had not even recognized him.

Guy was picked up by the launch and returned, after some hesitation on the part of the policemen, to *Shearwater* since, as the elder of them put it, 'That's where his solicitor is.' After a confused conversation, it was, however, not Keith but Della who solved the problem. She suggested that the harbourmaster's assistant, on his portable phone, should ring up Eddie McArthur and let Keith ask him directly whether he wanted to pursue the case. "Cos I bet he's forgotten it by now.'

The call reached Eddie on the gleaming, leaping, eastbound *Privateer* just as Dinny Douglas emerged for the second time, wearing the ladylike shoes he had demanded. Keith, to his surprise, found himself met with a bonhomous, expansive assurance that it had all been a misunderstanding, that the cards were cancelled, and that Mr Pastern-Hopkins would be hearing from his contracts people about the formal termination of his employment. Keith, still dripping, asked McArthur to repeat these assurances to the senior of the two policemen, which, with some impatience, the tycoon did.

So that was that, and the police departed in the harbour launch after the formality of taking Guy's address and Keith's. Guy, his teeth chattering, sat wrapped in Joanna's sleeping bag thanking everybody over and over again. Della, with a kind of annoyed pity, helped him off with his soaking socks and trousers.

Gabriel, during these exchanges, remained on the foredeck, his back to the company. He was severely shaken by the sight of Joanna, not only by her demonstrated affection for the bloody Keith man, but by a certain air of competence, a swiftness of movement, a lack of tremulousness and a womanly determination which did not match his memories and which dismayed him greatly. The whole thing had been, he saw, a silly idea. He must have been more drunk than he thought. This was not his woman. Not what his mate the photographer used to call a 'Ben Bolt woman'. The old song curled mockingly again through his mind, satirizing his own now visibly futile and contemptible desire:

> Oh don't you remember sweet Alice, Ben Bolt?
> Sweet Alice whose hair was so brown
> Who wept with delight when you gave her a smile
> And trembled with fear at your frown . . .

This damn woman had brought this cramped little boat halfway along the English Channel, alone, in a gale, on the sort of horrible sea which used to make him sick when he went out on his cousin's fishing boat from Dunmanus. She had even taken passengers. She had been the captain. She would not come with him to his dreaming new life; even if she did, she would wreck the dream. It wasn't her. *It ain't me, babe*. Jo Telford no longer existed. Probably hadn't for years.

Della, on the other hand, was no Ben Bolt girl either. Her offer, made so coolly, both fascinated and appalled him. No trembling submission, no seduction, just a business arrangement? Board and lodging in return for cooking, company and sex if and when required – was that what the great dream had come to? It was with blustering reluctance, but still that sense of relief, that Gabriel admitted to himself that the idea struck him, above all, as restful.

He wished he could get off the boat, but the launch had gone without him and the dinghy on which he was sitting was only half inflated. When the police had left, with enormous reluctance he turned to face Keith and Joanna where they stood together in the cockpit. Joanna was rubbing Keith's hair dry with a towel and laughing a little. She glanced sideways at the movement from the foredeck, and at last realized who the other presence on the deck had been for all this time. She stopped rubbing. Keith, without thinking, took over, his head covered, seeing nothing.

'What are you doing here?' asked Joanna, levelly. She barely knew what she felt except for an absurd anger that moments like this, in plays and novels, never occur in front of a ludicrous audience of husbands with towels on their head and shivering idiots in sleeping bags having their wet trousers pulled off, with difficulty, by strange blondes. Reunions of old, angry lovers after eighteen years ought to happen on mountaintops and moorland, in parked cars, on quiet trains or in the corners of restaurants where mournful gypsy violinists drown confidences with their wailing. The scene was badly set, and she herself miscast. She could feel nothing for Gabriel, nothing at all. He was a scruffy middle-aged man who was in the way.

'I came to see if you were all right,' he replied now, meek and lame. 'I got talking to your friend there, and the time just passed. I am,' he added hastily, 'actually on the way to Ireland. To find somewhere to live. I'm leaving the BBC.'

'Didn't know you were in the BBC,' said Joanna. It was a lie; she had heard his name more than once on the credits of plays and readings, and each time had seen the Chinese letters, smelt the joss sticks, felt her self-esteem plummet and the old rejection throb. None of this, however, was happening now. The real Gabriel was less impressive than the dream had ever been. Experimentally, she allowed herself to think of Emily in his presence; only a faint ghostly sorrow touched her, gently, without rancour. Alas, poor Emily.

'Well,' she said. 'We'd better get you and these two ashore.'

Keith emerged from his towel, hair sticking up in ginger tufts. He seemed to Joanna twice as vital as Gabriel, a solid active presence rather than a wispy grey ghost. Gabriel shrank further into himself as Keith said, 'I'm wet anyway – I'll finish off that dinghy and run you all to the quay.'

This, however, was not necessary. A buzzing heralded the fresh approach of the pasty-faced child and his outboard dinghy, this time bearing Lance and Mandy.

'Hello! Hi! Mum! Jo! You OK? Oh, Jo, I am so sorry,' shrieked the dinghy.

Joanna sat down suddenly. 'Keith. I've had it. Get them all ashore, for God's sake.'

'Mum,' said Lance, bobbing alongside at knee level, holding the wire. 'Mandy just needs to know that you aren't furious with her.'

'About what?'

'Talking to the newspaper. She never said it. The thing is,' he hissed, *sotto voce*, 'she's been very upset.'

'Mandy,' said Joanna, 'I am not remotely annoyed about anything. I'm fine. And I told Alex, yes, we'll sell the Bun, if Keith agrees.'

Mandy looked up at her from the dinghy and smiled stiffly.

'Sure? Really sure?'

'Yup. Only do one thing for me: just go back ashore. I'll see you there. This boat is too crowded. You can take this gentleman.' She gestured at the cockpit, abruptly.

'The gentleman with the trousers,' enquired Mandy, much revived, 'or the one without?' Guy had now emerged, leggy in his neat white designer-label jockey pants, to stand blinking behind Gabriel.

'Both,' said Jo firmly. Standing up, she reached into the cockpit locker, extracted a faded towelling bag with snorkels and the straps from rubber flippers sticking out of it, and rummaged. Finding a pair of garish beach shorts belonging to Lance, with ALOHA OHE! down the side, she held them out to Guy. 'These are decent enough to go uptown and buy something dry. I gather,' she added nastily, 'you have a lot of credit cards.'

Lance, Gabriel, Mandy and Guy were ferried back to the shore in the first load by the pasty child. Keith, freed from his towel, looked surprisedly at the shaggy grey figure climbing down into the dinghy.

'Who was that?' he said as they puttered away.

'That was Gabriel O'Riordan,' said Joanna. 'Someone I used to know. I want to tell you all about Gabriel, later.'

Keith nodded, smiled at her, and vanished forward to search for some dry clothes. Joanna and Della were left looking at one another.

'I'm sorry you got invaded by Gabriel,' began Joanna.

'It's all right,' said Della. 'He's a sad old bugger, isn't he? I'm going to try living in Ireland with him. On a mountain.'

Joanna sat down again. 'Della, you can't!'

'I can. Give it a whirl, anyway. I might get a job out there. He'll do, meanwhile.'

'Della, you're nineteen. He has to be – oh, forty-three, more. He's evil. He wrecks women's lives—'

'Only,' said Della, 'if he gets a chance. If they let him. I've got a big advantage. I'm not in love, am I?'

'But you might be. You might get pregnant.'

Della looked at her in amazement, as if at a creature from another age. Joanna gave up that tack.

'Well,' she said, 'stay in touch. Keith and I might sail out and see you. Take you away.'

'Yeah, maybe,' said Della.

EPILOGUE

Ray Brewer hitched his trousers, scratched his ample stomach and thought about lunch. Knock off in ten minutes, maybe. First, he took a deep breath of warm spring air and stood back from the job he had all but finished. For an hour he had been slapping brown anti-fouling paint on the belly of the blue yacht and thinking about the day, six months earlier, when he watched *Shearwater* butting angrily out of the harbour, with the Fury – he remembered thinking about Furies, and land girls too – at the helm. Six months since the woman threw the keys at his chest.

There had been newspaper nonsense about it, which had upset the wife and annoyed him. *Roy Brewster*, indeed, and the yard not named right either. He had wondered, more than he told his wife, about the Gurney girl. But she had come back, mild as you like, with her husband, sailing into Brewmarine in the middle of September just as he was wondering about re-letting the berth and the lay-up space ashore. They had asked for an early launching, on the first of April, because they were taking a long cruise.

'Bit of extra holiday?' he had asked, and they had both laughed. 'Between jobs, really,' the husband said, and the wife giggled, said something about spending the school fees and seeing what happened next. So Ray Brewer probed no further. Redundant, probably. A lot of his clients had taken extra long holidays in extra scruffy clothes during this recession. Probably did some of them good.

Emerging from Cuisine It All, Mrs Hopgood met Mrs Colefax,

which was fortunate because together they could stand for as long as they liked, pretending to talk idly but watching all the time the door of the solicitors' office across the road. The new brass plaque had caused a small, pleasurable stir: Terson and Terson. Terson One they knew, of course – the stammering young man who had been clerk to Mr Gurney. Terson Two was his wife, newly arrived, without even a honeymoon, and rumour had it that the lady solicitor – fancy! – was actually *Chinese* as well. Fancy!

The watchers were rewarded. Tall, bespectacled Mr Terson appeared, hand in hand with tiny, dark-headed, white-skinned Mrs Terson. Together they turned to gaze raptly at their brass plate, then crossed the road – waving at Mrs Hopgood, hardly like lawyers at all, really, *very* informal – and vanished into the Snappy Snack.

At least it was supposed to be called the Snappy Snack, but to Mrs Hopgood and Mrs Colefax and the older generation of Bonhurst women it would, for many years yet, be the Bun in the Oven. Nor could they, without some pursing of lips, contemplate the changes wrought by Mrs Merriam: the microwave, the filled (but stony-hearted) baked potatoes, the tomato soup, the burgers, the catering-size fruit loaf. Thinking about the fruit loaf, Mrs Colefax shuddered. Still, the Tersons seemed more than happy to eat their lunch there. Young love!

In the kitchen of the Old Vicarage, a scratch lunch of bread and cheese and rather better soup was being washed down with convivial draughts of beer from a box balanced on the sideboard. Lance had bought it from a traditional brewery some distance east of Cambridge, a place of pilgrimage for the physicists of his year. He had insisted that it stand undisturbed for twelve hours before tasting.

Susan, clad in what looked to her mother like loose black curtains but which was in fact a set of separates designed as Anneliese's first-term project ('You can wear them inside out and upside down, it's a *Comme des Garçons* revival'), was drinking the beer and screwing up her face. 'Total horse piss, Lance, it's foul.' Keith liked it and was engaged in debate with his son over whether or not a couple of boxes would work on the boat, provided they were only broached after twelve hours stillness in a totally calm harbour.

'There'll be a lot of times when we stay a few days in harbours in Ireland and Scotland. We could wait until the second day to have the beer.' Lance was wondering aloud whether the preceding rough sea might not damage the molecular structure of the real ale.

Joanna said she would prefer wine boxes and had to that end ordered two dozen from the off-licence, because apparently wine costs a lot in Ireland and they would be two or three months sailing round its more remote coasts while Susan grafted away at college and stayed with Annie, and Lance drank his disgusting beer in Cambridge. She added that having her share of the Bun money in the bank was causing her to do some unconscionably extravagant things and that she would regret it. But at least there were no school fees, thanks to Mandy's daughter so sneakily corrupting her daughter out of doing A levels and into the dubious new GNVQ system.

At this point, she looked across at her daughter with love. Her capitulation to the college scheme had been as complete as it was sudden. Returning from Salcombe on the day of their reunion, Joanna and Keith had been confronted by a defiant, determined Susan prepared to make her last stand for sixth-form freedom. Joanna, thinking of Della's bold striking out into the far west, of her own casting-off of the Bun and the discussion she had just had with Keith about the chances of him wriggling free from Heron and Gurney in time for the spring, had surprised her daughter considerably by hugging her and saying it was a good idea, well thought out, and that she was proud of her.

Lance said she was out of date about GNVQ, that Susan would end up richer than any of them because early vocational training was the thing now; and that besides, there was no need to load the boat to its waterline with cheap booze because he and Susan could always bring some out, in the car, to West Cork in the summer vacation. Provided Dad sent them some money.

Mandy, who was five months pregnant, said it would be a miracle if Lance's terrible car made it to Fishguard, let alone West Cork. Alex, eating soup, said he didn't know, it wasn't a bad little car. Might buy Annie one of the new ones, to tootle around in. If and when she passed her first-year exams by designing some even more fetching black shrouds. The only mystery to him was that Anneliese, the fashion designer, only ever wore jeans and T-shirts these days, while Susan went around in Annie's bad-dream outfits. Susan could be very pretty, said Alex gallantly, if she allowed her mother to choose her clothes instead of letting Anneliese dress her like a doll. A voodoo doll, actually.

Susan, looking at her mother with tolerant affection, said that Joanna's clothes wouldn't suit her, and that hers wouldn't suit Joanna because every woman was different. Even mothers and daughters. There had been a really good piece about that in the *Chronicle*, by what's-her-name, Dinny Douglas. It was really good, that column; not nearly as spiteful as all the others. A girl at college had cut it out and stuck it on the board; something about how women shouldn't judge each other harshly for how they led their lives, because everyone had to find her own route to success, however odd it might look to other people. It was true, that, wasn't it?

Joanna said yes, it was. She leaned back, drinking her wine, while Lance took each plate away in a motherly fashion, and ladled out more soup.